# The
# ASH
# MUSEUM

## REBECCA SMITH

Legend Press Ltd, 51 Gower Street, London, WC1E 6HJ
info@legendpress.co.uk | www.legendpress.co.uk

Contents © Rebecca Smith 2021
The right of the above author to be identified as the author of this work has
been asserted in accordance with the Copyright, Designs and Patents Act
1988. British Library Cataloguing in Publication Data available.

Print ISBN 978-1-78955-9-019
Ebook ISBN 978-1-78955-9-026
Set in Times. Printing managed by Jellyfish Solutions Ltd
Cover design by Sarah Whittaker | www.whittakerbookdesign.com

**Rebecca Smith** was born in London and grew up in rural Surrey. She has Indian, English and Scottish heritage. She studied History at the University of Southampton and is now a principal teaching fellow in English and Creative Writing there.

Rebecca is the author of three previous novels for adults (*The Bluebird Café, Happy Birthday and All That,* and *A Bit of Earth*), a novel for children, two works of nonfiction (*Jane Austen's Guide to Modern Life's Dilemmas* and *The Jane Austen Writers' Club: Inspiration and Advice from The World's Best-Loved Novelist*) and the text for a picture book, *Where's Jane?*. From 2009 to 2010 she was the writer in residence at Jane Austen's House in Chawton, Hampshire. *The Ash Museum* was inspired by her time there and by being left hundreds of old family photographs and letters.

Follow Rebecca
@RMSmithAuthor

*For my beloved dad, Robin Francis Brown*

*"In the Block Universe, the past is also out there. My idyllic summer's day in 1972, with Mum and Dad and sister, doesn't exist only in my memory. It hasn't gone, although I can never revisit it. It is still there; all those people, all those moments, always and forever, somewhere in spacetime. I love that."*

– Professor Brian Cox in *Forces of Nature*
(William Collins, 2017)

# MAKING THE MOST OF YOUR VISIT

Welcome to the Ash Museum.

On display are objects and letters telling the story of one hundred years of the Ash family. The museum's collection is arranged across many floors and through multiple rooms. You may not be able to see everything on one visit. Our guide offers a path through the museum that we hope visitors will find enjoyable and enlightening. If you wish to view the displays chronologically (i.e. in the order in which the objects on display were made or discovered), you will have to start elsewhere.

# 1940s

## Wooden Tennis Racket – some
## strings broken (c. 1930s)

Some stupid words from a poem were going round in James's head when he woke, still sitting and clutching his rifle in the trench. *Miss Joan Hunter Dunn, Miss Joan Hunter Dunn, something and something the dance has begun.* The moon and stars were bright. He hadn't meant to drop off, but they had to snatch sleep when they could. Lewis was dozing to his right, Daas to his left. They should have been more alert – he should have been more alert. His back had seized up but he hardly dared move in case he made a noise.

For days they'd been dug in on Garrison Hill, above Imphal on the Kohima Ridge. They were pretty much surrounded, and the Japanese wore soft shoes – some sort of plimsolls instead of boots – so you never knew when they were going to come padding across the broken earth. There were a couple dead a few feet away. Just boys really. The stench was bad. James could see the district commissioner's bungalow, what was left of it, silhouetted up ahead. Some of their chaps were probably still in there, holding out. He'd envied them at first – lucky buggers with a roof over their heads – but judging by the mess and word coming down the line, they'd been some of the first to go.

And here he was on what had been a tennis court. The plateau of it was useful. The grass was long gone but the remains of a tennis racket lay in the mud between him and the dead boys. *Miss Joan Hunter Dunn, Miss Joan Hunter Dunn, the dum de dum racket is back in its press*. He couldn't remember enough of the poem to get it out of his head. Margaret had sent it to him a while ago – his sister was always sending things snipped out of newspapers and magazines. He often had to read both sides of the cutting to work out which bit was meant to be significant. He wondered what she might be doing now, and his parents, and most of all, Josmi and the children. Asleep probably, all of them. Asleep in beds with clean sheets. Still the stupid words were beating time in his head – something about a summerhouse and a veranda and gin. He'd seen straight away why Margaret had sent it – it was about a girl like Lucinda. He hoped he wouldn't still be thinking about it when he copped it, as he probably would. They all probably would.

It wasn't yet dawn and the birds were silent. Any creature with any sense would have fled long ago. A few sounds came from the forest, occasional shots, and sometimes a vehicle noise somewhere far away. They'd been told other regiments were coming, reinforcements. God, they needed them. They couldn't hold out forever. They'd be picked off one by one, line by line, and the Japanese would stream over their corpses into India. There was a line about *ominous dancing ahead* – he had no idea what that meant. Mist was forming, dangerous stuff, ominous stuff. He heard something like a shuffling – shots and cries closer now. He nudged Lewis and Daas to wake up.

# 1970s

## Child's Fancy Dress Outfit – Native American (c. 1974)

'This cause must be especially close to your heart, Mr. Ash,' said the vicar's wife, offering him a Rich Tea.

'Jay,' he said, 'please.' He wondered why the plight of children in Africa should be closer to his heart than hers. Perhaps she thought that India and Africa were interchangeable. Aspects of Otterham reminded him of his early days in England when people had said in slow, loud voices, 'It Must Seem Very Cold To You.' After the first few times he'd just agreed with them. Why bother explaining that actually he had grown up in the shadow of the Himalayas where people often needed warm clothes just as much as they did here? He'd spent most of his childhood in a home for orphans and the discarded children of the Empire. He'd been constantly reminded that he was one of the lucky ones, as an aunt on the English side of his family was sponsoring him and he would be going to live with her when he'd finished school. Having met very few of his relations, Jay had pictured the two sides of his family as opposing hockey teams. He had been picked for one side, though he looked much more like a member of the other.

All Jay had left of his mother now were a few fragments of memories: a flash of silver and blue bangles; an image of pieces of broken crockery that they'd pressed into a flowerbed at the front of their bungalow after he'd driven his toy truck into a rattan table and sent cups and saucers crashing to the ground; a feeling of her gripping his hand when his father had returned from shooting a leopard that had been menacing the company lines; and a few words of an Assamese song that she'd sung about the moon.

Now, here he was in an English vicar's dining room, wondering if there was any way he could make his excuses and leave, not just the meeting, but the committee, everything. It had all been Pammy's idea, but when she'd talked about signing up for the committee and getting more involved in village life he'd thought that she meant both of them, not just him.

They were planning the annual village fête. Otterham Overseas Aid would have a stall and a float in the parade. He found himself offering to drive the float; he had a licence for the right size of truck from his apprentice days. The committee had decided on the theme of 'Peoples of the World'. They all seemed very keen to have Emmie among the local children in the tableau. They would wave collecting tins as they went. Somebody asked if Pammy would dress up too. The vicar's wife said that she could imagine Pammy as a Dutch girl with two long blonde plaits and a pair of clogs. Jay knew that Pammy's cooperation was extremely unlikely; she took three quarters of an hour to do her make-up before putting out the milk bottles, she would never appear in fancy dress unless it was something glamorous.

'Do you have some traditional dress that Emmie could wear?' Audrey Pheasant asked. She was a huge woman, taller than Jay. When he'd been introduced to her he'd thought 'Pheasant' must be a nickname. She had the beakiest profile he'd ever seen and little bright eyes that were alert for challenges to her running of village affairs, but then, as she was so tall, 'Audrey Cassowary' might have been a better moniker. There was a picture of one in Emmie's *Atlas of Animals*. They could disembowel a man with one kick.

'Traditional dress?' Jay asked.

'Oh, a sari or some of those pyjama things that your people wear.'

He took a sip of his coffee. It was disgustingly weak and smelt as though the milk was on the turn.

'Not really, Emmie's always worn what the other children wear.' He might have added that Emmie's traditional dress was shorts and a t-shirt, and that she had only joined the Brownies when she'd accepted that she couldn't be a Cub. She considered the Cubs' uniform superior and had a Cub's cap from a jumble sale. She wore it at home for meetings of the Cub pack of which she and her collection of toy animals were the only members.

'Pity,' said Audrey Pheasant. 'Perhaps your wife could run something up from an old tablecloth or some sheets...?'

The other committee members smiled and nodded.

'I'll see what Pammy thinks,' said Jay in a way that he hoped was non-committal. He could imagine how Pammy would react to this suggestion. His sister, Molly, wouldn't have minded doing it, or Aunt Lucinda, but Pammy? Not bloody likely.

Matters moved on to the forthcoming Christian Aid week. They were all to be allocated streets and asked to go door to door with little envelopes, and then return a week later to collect them. The idea filled Jay with horror – knocking on the doors of strangers to ask for money? He knew the assumptions some people would make. Perhaps Emmie and Pammy could go.

The vicar's wife had a map and a list of streets. He prepared himself to say no, he got back from London too late each evening.

'Jay,' she said, turning to him, 'your road has always been done by Mrs. Greenfield. She used to be on the committee but her knees aren't up to it now. I think she'd be very sad not be asked, though. Would you mind awfully if we asked her first, and then had you in reserve if she can't do it?'

'That's quite alright. I do get back from work very late some days. I expect the neighbours would prefer a familiar face anyway.'

'Well, just between these walls, and this really isn't for the minutes, but I'm not sure if we have always had *all* of the envelopes back from Rhododendron Gardens, so perhaps you could offer to go with her?'

'Perhaps,' said Jay. He knew Mrs. Greenfield. She lived on the corner and had never once acknowledged his 'good mornings'. She had several dogs with limps and her garden had no lawn, just compacted earth and collapsing sheds that appeared to be held together with a horrible sort of orange nylon string. Her washing line was made of the same string and hosted a permanent collection of greying nighties and huge pairs of knickers and Y-fronts. He had never seen Mr. Greenfield, but there was usually a gang of other Greenfields fixing cars and growling at the dogs. 'I don't know her at all well. The offer would probably be better coming from one of the ladies on the committee.' He hoped that they would minute that.


The next morning, Jay told Emmie about the float.

'Can I ask my friends? Can we choose what to wear?'

'The theme is "Peoples of the World". I think they'd like you to dress up as an Indian girl.'

'Great!' said Emmie. She had all the stuff: the headdress, a waistcoat, some brown trousers with a red pattern on that were cut at the bottom so that they looked all raggedy. It wasn't an Indian girl's outfit, it was a chief's, but she could be an Indian girl chief if they wanted to say that she was a girl. 'Dad, do we all have to be from the same country?'

'Any country is fine. Peoples of the World.'

'The twins will want to do it. I hope Sue Namey won't be on the float.'

'There's no one called Namey on the committee,' he said.

'Does that mean she won't be allowed on the float? And why's it called a float?' She pictured a giant glass with a big blob of vanilla ice cream melting to a glorious foamy slick on top of some cream soda.

'Maybe they used to have parades of boats on wheels,' said her mum. 'Mrs. Namey's always trying to make people join her stoolball team. If they're on any float it'll probably be something like that.'

'What's stoolball?'

'Like rounders,' said her mum as she forked cat food into Freddy's bowl, 'but meaner.'

'Hmm,' said Emmie. She would have preferred to be on a float with other people dressed up as animals, or maybe as robots or pirates.

# Otterham Village Fête

**June 22nd 1974**
**Programme of Stalls and Events**
**5p**
**Noon - Arrival of the Carnival Procession
and Official Opening of the Fête by Our
Special Guest Mr. Roy Castle**

**Stalls: Raffle, Tombola, White Elephant,
Treasure Map, Stocks and Pillories – Sponge
the Vicar! Plate-Smashing, Cakes and
Preserves, Smash the Rat, Flowers and
Produce, Books and Toys, Teas, Cream
Cracker Eating Contest and Many,
Many More.**

**Events in the Arena**
**1pm - Performance by the Scouts Brass Band**
**1.30pm - Police Dog Performance Team**
**2pm - Children's Fancy Dress Judging**
**2.30pm - More from the Scouts Brass Band**
**3pm - Drawing of the Raffle and Other Prizes**
**Your Lucky Number is** 283

Jay hardly thought about the Overseas Aid committee and village fête for the next few weeks. He was busy at work, and when he got home in the evenings Pammy was distant, plonking his dinner down on the table, saying that she'd already eaten with Emmie and was very tired. Village life didn't seem to be suiting her at the moment. At least Emmie was happy. She played with a group of children outside and always had stories to tell him about school: who'd won which race, how Sue Namey had been in trouble for wearing see-through nail polish, what Mr. Long had said about the trip to Arundel Castle. The details of her days delighted his heart.

She would sit next to him while he ate his dinner, soothing him with her chatter and smiles. His dinner was often some reheated thing, and now that the village shop sold Findus Crispy Pancakes, they seemed to feature quite often on the menu. He thought of Aunt Lucinda returning home from her work at the centre for blind veterans that she managed and cooking them meat and two veg. She'd soon taught him and Molly her own style of cooking. But Pammy was a vegetarian and Emmie, consequently, was one too. He decided that he would try to do more of the cooking, at least when he was on holiday. They usually all did the shopping together on Saturday mornings, but today was different. It was the day of the fête. Emmie was excited out of all proportion.

He was to meet Audrey Pheasant in the car park behind the rugby club. The truck would be there, decorated by Audrey and the poor souls she referred to as her Band of Willing Helpers. At least he had escaped that. Perhaps he could resign after this event. There would never be any question of him having to collect envelopes with Mrs. Greenfield if he did. Aunt Lucinda had probably never resigned from a committee in her life. She'd see things through, and if they weren't running properly, she'd change them. He sighed.

Emmie was downstairs. He heard the clatter of her breakfast things. Golden Nuggets were her current favourite. He'd tried them. They exploded in the mouth like lumps of honeycomb toffee, a bit like the Space Dust that was her favourite sweet. Each Thursday night he'd ask what she would like and bring it home from work with him on Friday. When he asked Pammy she always said: 'The usual, please, love,' which meant a bar of Old Jamaica rum and raisin chocolate. She'd eat the whole bar on Friday night, occasionally offering him a piece. He always declined. Emmie would be given one square. Pammy said that the alcohol content might be bad for her. Sometimes he brought home Indian sweets from a shop near where he worked. Emmie wanted to know what the different ones were called but he had no idea. He'd not had them often when he was growing up.

Jay went downstairs and buttered himself a piece of cold toast. He heard the doorbell and Emmie's excited voice. The twins from two doors down were coming with them. Pammy said she'd watch the procession go by and meet them at the fête. The girls came clattering through the hall and into the kitchen. Samantha and Deborah were dressed as Chinamen, wearing embroidered blue tunics over matching trousers. Their mother must be good at running things up from old tablecloths, Jay thought, or perhaps from specially bought blue material, sequins and embroidery thread. Their red hair was scraped back into single tight plaits that hung down their backs. They wore straw coolie hats and when they took them off, he saw that their faces had been painted bright yellow and black lines had been drawn to extend their eyes upwards.

'Can I have make-up?' Emmie asked, standing on her toes and leaning over the breakfast bar. 'Please?'

'Our mum does the make-up for the All Village Show,' said Samantha (or possibly Deborah; Jay was never sure which one was which). 'She could make Emmie all red.'

Jay shook his head. 'I don't think there's time. We'd better go now. Emmie, go and get your costume on.'

Emmie ran upstairs, and a few minutes later reappeared in her Indian chief's outfit: a feathered headdress, a printed waistcoat over a plain yellow T-shirt, and brown trousers which had zigzags and stencilled buffalo running down the sides. The girls all wore their black school plimsolls – the accepted neutral footwear for any child in fancy dress.

'Can we take the wigwam and put it up on the float?' she asked. Jay laughed.

'I think it might blow over, and it probably isn't quite what Mrs. Pheasant had in mind.' But if they wanted an Indian, he thought, let them have whatever type of Indian Emmie wanted to be.


Emmie was ready to go when her mum appeared, hairbrush in hand.

'You can't ride on the back of a lorry for all the village to see without brushing your hair!'

'Red Indians didn't have hairbrushes,' said Emmie.

'Of course they did, teasels or combs made out of horses' hooves or something,' said Pammy. She grabbed Emmie's unruly mane and began to drag the brush through it. Emmie squealed.

'Just stand still,' Pammy said. 'It won't hurt if you stop pulling away.' She raised the brush threateningly at Emmie in the mirror, but she was smiling. Emmie stood to attention and submitted to the brushing.

'Can I have two plaits?'

'Ok.'

Emmie tried not to move as her mum used a biro to get the parting straight. Her dad and the Chinamen watched in silence. She hoped her mum wasn't drawing a blue line down the back of her neck.

'Come on, girls, time to go,' said her dad.

They walked up the road and across the big field where Emmie and her best friend, Karen, often flew homemade kites. In winter it would have been churned up by rugby boots and speckled with peel from half-time orange quarters. Giant puffballs grew there too. Emmie had seen the vicar's wife collecting them. She'd said that you could slice them and fry them like steaks. Samantha and Deborah kept stopping because they thought they saw four-leaved clovers.

Soon they saw the decorated truck and the other Peoples of the World waiting for them. There were some extras from *The Black and White Minstrels Show*, a few self-declared Eskimos already sweating in parkas with the hoods up, various Mexicans, a flamenco dancer and a bullfighter. The vicar's wife was wearing an orange-and-red African dress with big puffy sleeves. There were some little Dutch girls with plaits made from yellow wool that had been wired so that they curved upwards, and a man in lederhosen that was much too tight for him.

Audrey Pheasant marched towards them, clipboard poised. As she came closer Emmie saw her face fall. 'Oh,' she said, 'this wasn't what I wanted at all!'

Emmie looked at her dad and he gave her a smile, then turned to Mrs. Pheasant, raising both eyebrows and tilting his head as if he was confused.

'I wanted Emmie as our centrepiece – look!' She gestured towards the truck which was festooned with sheets painted with slogans like 'Overseas Aid – Please Give Generously!', 'Help the World's Poor!', 'Hunger Kills!' and 'Help the Needy'. In the centre of the float was a dais, just big enough for a child to sit on, with a wooden bowl positioned next to it.

'Don't worry!' barked Mrs. Pheasant. 'I've got some blankets in the car we can use to get her dressed up properly!' She marched off to her blue Range Rover, opened the boot and grabbed an armful of itchy-looking tartan travel rugs and a patchwork blanket made from knitted squares.

'What's she talking about, Dad?' Emmie whispered. But Mrs. Pheasant was already back beside them. She dumped the blankets on the ground. A miasma of dog fur and dust rose into the air.

'That's the blanket we made at Brownies!' said Samantha. 'That's the blue square I made!'

'That's my purple one!' said Deborah. 'I wonder why Mrs. Pheasant's got it for her dog. It was meant to go to the earthquake children!'

Emmie couldn't tell which square of the many in the grey school-cardigan wool that Brown Owl had supplied was hers. Mrs. Pheasant appeared not to have heard them.

'Now, Emmie,' she said, 'you can carry on wearing that T-shirt and the trousers will be hidden, so they don't really matter. You were expected to come as your *own* sort of Indian, because we need a pretty little beggar-girl to go at the centre of the float.'

'I don't want to be a beggar-girl,' said Emmie. If only she'd worn war paint and brought her bow and arrows and the scalping knife – though that was plastic and not very sharp, and the arrows had orange rubber tips, though you could take those off.

'If we have a pretty little beggar-girl, don't you think we'll raise much more money for children around the world, children who wish that they lived in a nice village and went to a nice school, with nice friends like yours; children who wish that they were as lucky as you?' Mrs. Pheasant said.

Samantha and Deborah smiled and nodded from beneath their hats.

Mrs. Pheasant made a lunge for Emmie's headdress, grabbing and crumpling some of the feathers. 'You won't be needing these!'

'You're damaging it!' Emmie cried. 'You can never fix a feather once the little hooks have been undone!'

'Now, don't be silly,' said Mrs. Pheasant. 'It can ride in the truck with your dad. You can put it back on for the fancy dress parade. Now don't you want to raise as much money as possible for the starving children?'

'I really don't think that she wants to be a beggar,' said Emmie's dad, stepping forward. 'Why can't some of these other children do it? The Eskimos could just take off their anoraks.'

'Emmie's perfect – anybody can see that. She'll look just right. The dais is just the right size for her.'

The vicar's wife appeared with a concerned smile. 'Is there a problem?'

'Emmie's come as the wrong sort of Indian. I was led to expect an *Indian* Indian. They are reluctant to cooperate.'

Emmie felt her dad clutch her hand and give it a squeeze.

'I don't mind being a beggar,' said the vicar's wife. 'After all, "Blessed are the poor…"'

'Anybody else willing to be a beggar with Emmie?' cried Mrs. Pheasant.

Samantha and Deborah shook their heads so vigorously that their plaits swished from side to side.

'I don't mind,' said one of the so-called Eskimos. 'I'm dying to get out of this coat already. Even a dog blanket would be preferable…' She shed the parka, revealing herself to be Carol, one of the ladies from the nursery school. Emmie remembered that she'd spent most of the sessions hanging people's paintings on a sort of indoor washing line and taking them down again to see if they were dry; they never were.

'What do you think then, Emmie?' said Mrs. Pheasant. 'It isn't as though anybody's gone to much trouble with your costume. You can wear this nice patchwork blanket and the big beggars can wear the tartan ones.'

'You really don't have to, Emmie, if you don't want to,' said Jay, still holding her hand firmly.

'Mr. Ash, would you like to familiarise yourself with the truck's controls while we get everybody into position?'

'Only when Emmie's made up her mind,' said Jay.

Mrs. Pheasant squatted down in front of Emmie. 'Come along now, Emmie, it will make all the difference,' she said. 'Afterwards I'll buy you and the other girls some ice cream or candy floss.'

'Go on, Emmie!' chorused the Chinamen.

'Well, OK,' said Emmie.

'Good girl!' said Mrs. Pheasant. 'Come on, everybody! Let's get you all into position!'

Mrs. Pheasant lifted Emmie up onto the truck and struggled up after her to construct her tableau. Emmie was led to the dais and instructed to sit down.

'If you can squat on your haunches like a real beggar, all the better,' said Mrs. Pheasant.

'I can't,' said Emmie, 'my legs don't like doing that.'

'Just do your best.' Mrs. Pheasant draped the Brownies' blanket over her. The vicar's wife and Carol from the nursery school sat down either side of her. The dais was so high that, even sitting, she towered above them.

'At least we get to sit down,' said the vicar's wife. 'I've been on my feet since six thirty this morning setting up the teas and building the stocks and pillories.'

'What's stocks and pillories?' asked Emmie.

'A medieval punishment device. The person who'd done something wrong was put in them, trapped, so that all of the villagers could laugh at them and throw rotten tomatoes and fish.'

'A bit like this?' Emmie asked.

'Of course not! Nobody will throw anything apart from money into our buckets. People will be throwing wet sponges at my husband and the akela. And it's for fun.'

'Not like this then,' said Emmie grimly.

'No, not like this at all.'

'I'm going to tell Brown Owl that Mrs. Pheasant has stolen the blanket we made for Africa,' said Emmie. The grown-ups pretended not to have heard, but Emmie saw Carol give a little smile.

The Peoples of the World were in position now. The so-called Eskimos had begun catching tin foil fish from a pink washing-up bowl using rods made from bamboo canes.

'Everybody ready? Mr. Ash, time to go!' shouted Mrs. Pheasant.

Emmie's dad gave her a reassuring wave and plodded towards the cab.

Mrs. Pheasant loomed up at his window. 'Ready to go? Just give me a minute to climb back onboard, and then we can be off. Take it nice and steady, please, no more than ten miles an hour. The procession is forming on the road to the green.' She climbed up onto the truck and gave two sharp bangs on the roof of the cab. They fell into position behind the village cricket team's not very imaginative effort on the theme of cricket teams through the ages.

'They always do that. No imagination, men,' said Carol, craning round to look at the float in front of them. Behind them was the St John's Ambulance float which was on the theme of the St John's Ambulance because, the vicar's wife pointed out, its members were also on duty.

'What if one of them gets hurt?' asked Emmie.

'Well, I suppose the others can easily look after them,' said Carol.

'But what if they all get hurt?'

'That's very unlikely,' said the vicar's wife, 'but I suppose somebody would just call a proper ambulance.'

Emmie couldn't think of anything worse than being one of the members of the St John's Ambulance on that float. Imagine having to wear a grey dress that was even more boring than a Brownie's dress! Imagine having to just watch everything, waiting, probably just *hoping* that somebody would get hurt by falling into the hook-the-duck paddling pool. As the truck's fumes began to envelop them, she realised that there was something worse than being in uniform on the St John's Ambulance float, and that was being made to dress up as a beggar and wear a blanket that was meant to be sent to starving children in Africa and was now covered in dog fur. Everybody would see her. They might think she was really a beggar. She pulled the blanket up over her head and threw one end of it over her shoulder so that it was wrapped around her. She could only just see out. Up ahead was a brass band playing tunes that she recognised but didn't know the names of. A few floats behind them were some majorettes with their own music. She hoped they'd all drop their stupid pompoms. And why did they have to wear those stupid long white boots?

'Excellent, Emmie! That's the spirit! You look just the little Indian beggar-girl!' shouted Mrs. Pheasant from her position at the back of the float. 'But keep those big brown eyes on show!'

Emmie shrank down even lower. Perhaps if she made herself small enough people might not realise there was anybody there. They might think that there were just two grown-up beggars sitting beside an old blanket.

'Don't forget your begging bowl! Let's see that little brown hand reaching out for alms!' called Mrs. Pheasant.

Emmie could feel the tears welling up. They might start falling into Mrs. Pheasant's stupid wooden fruit bowl. She'd probably love that. She felt the vicar's wife patting her leg.

'I'll hold the bowl. You've been really nice, Emmie, doing what Mrs. Pheasant wants. Just sit tight there, and everybody will be clapping and giving money as we go by.'

Emmie nodded, unable to speak. She thought of her class on Monday morning. Would everybody be laughing and pointing at her? Through the tiny gap she'd left for her eyes she could see that people had come out of their houses and were standing outside their front gates, clapping and shouting hello to people they knew as the procession passed. There was a gang of boys from the class above her on bikes. She pulled the blanket tighter and hoped and hoped that nobody could tell it was her. There were bits of dried mud and grass and fur caught in the wool. Mrs. Pheasant had three big spaniels. Until now Emmie had liked them because they were so bouncy and their ears were so silky; she'd often seen them on walks or tied up outside the shop or the village hall. Now she knew how awful the smell of them was. They were probably secretly mean dogs who snarled and bit.

Samantha and Deborah were blowing kisses to people and waving as though they were royal. The boys on bikes were riding alongside them now. Emmie saw one of them throw something. It landed near her feet. Debbie scrambled for it, so it couldn't be something disgusting, the sort of yucky thing that boys usually threw. It was the end of a packet of strawberry Spangles. Debbie pushed one through a gap in the blanket at her.

'Who's that under the blanket?' the boy yelled.

'It's Emmie Ash!' Samantha yelled back.

'Why's she hiding? Is she in the nuddy?' He cackled and rode back to his friends.

'Get off and milk it!' yelled Debbie, but the boy was already out of earshot. *Get off and milk it.* Emmie had always found that phrase completely baffling, and if someone shouted it at you when you rode by, there didn't seem to be anything to reply. But then, her own bike was decorated with red-and-white Humphrey stickers from the milkman, so perhaps in a way it did make sense.

They were getting near the river and the procession was slowing now. As they went over the bridge she could jump up, throw off the blanket (or keep it as evidence to take to the police) and dive into the water and swim away. She would miss the worst bit – circling the village green. But then she remembered, the water would be at its summer lowness. It wouldn't even cover her ankles. She'd have to climb down from the truck and run away, or else just stay there and hope she was invisible until it was all over. Now it was their turn to go over the bridge. She saw the sign *No Heavy Goods Vehicles*. What was a heavy goods vehicle? No idea. She imagined the bridge crumbling and collapsing, the truck landing in the gravel. She would just paddle to the riverbank and go home. She crossed her fingers and hoped. With the brass band ahead of them, the noise of all the trucks, and the majorettes somewhere behind them, she couldn't even hear the water as they passed over to the other side. The truck picked up speed. She was trapped.

Jay was growing hotter inside the cab. The seats were made from a pale brown leatherette, the exact colour of Caramac, the sort of chocolate that Emmie hated because it wasn't actually chocolate. They felt sticky beneath him, as though they had begun melting already. An ancient copy of the *Daily Express* lay crackling into dust on the floor, alongside what was probably the remains of somebody's meat paste sandwich. He nudged them aside with his foot. He thought of the beloved cargo balanced on that dais behind him. He could see a Viking ship and a Noah's Ark up ahead. He had not only sold his precious daughter down the river but was driving the boat himself.

He glanced over at the crumpled feathers on the seat beside him. That woman! How dare she do that to Emmie and her headdress! He thought he might send her a bill for it. A dark blue and a green feather were badly bent, and those either side of them looked ruffled and greasy where they'd been grabbed. Bloody bully. Emmie loved that costume.

He couldn't wait for this stupid morning to be over. He'd buy Emmie as many ice creams as she wanted at the fête, and then they'd go home. Well, he'd have to drive the truck back to the rugby club, but that shouldn't take long. Emmie could ride back in the cab with him if she wanted. She'd like that. It would be a good antidote to this whole sorry morning. And then he'd resign from the committee. He wasn't going to put up with any more of this, and neither was Emmie. He tried to go a little faster, but the crucial gap he was meant to be keeping between his lot and the load ahead disappeared, and he had to slow down again. They were approaching the green now for the final laps. Pammy should be here somewhere. He hoped Emmie would spot her and that it would cheer her up. Past The Royal Oak. They'd only been there once. The landlord had stood there polishing glasses and talking to everybody but him until he'd been forced to return empty-handed to the table in the garden, where Pammy and Emmie were waiting, and say that they had to leave. They crawled past the Spar. He didn't often go in there either, but that was because it was hardly ever open when he wasn't at work.

Maybe one day he could slip in and ask them to stop stocking Findus Crispy Pancakes, or at least see if they had anything preferable and mention it to Pammy. Tonight he would make it up to Emmie. They'd have one of their special Saturday nights. Emmie loved it when they got their old records out. They had a great big basket of singles – the Everly Brothers, Elvis, Ricky Nelson (who Pammy said he looked like when they met), The Beatles, The Crystals, The Ronettes. Emmie loved the songs with stories – 'Leader of the Pack', 'Take a Message to Mary', 'Twenty-Four Hours from Tulsa'.

They passed the church and had to circle the green once more. He spotted Pammy with some other mothers, all dressed in identical outfits of white cheesecloth shirts and jeans.

At last they reached their final position. He parked and climbed out of the cab. Emmie was sitting at the back with the blanket rolled up and cradled in her arms like a newborn. He smiled and lifted her down.

'Let's steal the blanket back, Dad, and send it to the poor.'

'Ok.' He stashed it in the cab and gave Emmie her headdress. She let it dangle from her wrist rather than putting it on. They found Pammy looking at the plant stall.

'Did it look like me on the lorry, Mum?' Emmie said.

Jay, standing behind Emmie, shook his head vigorously.

'I could hardly tell which one was you!'

'Mrs. Pheasant made me be a beggar!'

'Well, you don't look anything like a beggar now. Let's go and look at the other stalls.' She took Emmie's hand. Jay wondered if he could go home for the next two hours.

'I think I'll just go and wait on that bench,' he said. 'Come and find me when you're done.'

After a very long time, Pammy brought him a cheese scone with margarine wrapped in a paper napkin. It was time for the fancy dress parade. They watched as Emmie, now wearing her headdress, walked in a huge circle with a few dozen other children. She was behind her best friend, Karen Martin, who was wearing a baffling ensemble – a blue nylon zip-up tracksuit with bright green crêpe paper stems and leaves coiling around her legs and body, and a green crêpe paper hat like the one the Disney Robin Hood wore. There was a gang of princesses in party dresses teamed with conical hats made from old wallpaper with chiffon scarves sellotaped to the top, cowboys, knights, kings and queens, a penguin, several cats and dogs, and someone who had come as the red double-decker bus that was kept in the vicarage drive and used for Sunday school outings.

'That girl's jolly good,' said Jay, indicating an elaborate Elizabeth I.

'Don't say that to Emmie, that's Sue Namey, the girl she doesn't like.'

There wasn't really a contest. Elizabeth I won. The bus came second and a toddler cat third. Roy Castle played the *Record Breakers* tune on his trumpet and presented the prizes.

'Is it going to be a world record of something?' asked Emmie.

World's Longest Day, thought Jay, Slowest Moving Queue for the Candy Floss.

'Most Unwanted Bath Salts Donated to a Village Fête?' said Pammy. They bought Emmie and Karen ice creams, Audrey Pheasant's offer having melted away.

'I'm really tired,' said Pammy, as she took Jay's hand, and they found a table outside the tea tent. 'Get us a cup of tea, love.' She smiled up at him. 'Is every fête so exhausting?'


Karen had to go home. She hadn't minded that her runner bean costume hadn't won a prize. Karen never minded much about anything. Emmie had minded on her behalf, and had hoped to win herself too, of course. They were calling the raffle numbers, but she and Mum hadn't bought any tickets so it didn't matter.

Emmie couldn't see her mum and dad. She took off her headdress and hung it around one of her wrists again. She decided to walk around the edge of everything to try to find them. Lots of the stalls had been abandoned while the grown-ups gathered to see if they had won raffle prizes. It was lucky, she thought, that nobody was stealing the leftover things on the tombola or having free goes on the coconut shy or hook-the-duck. She came to the plate-smashing stall. There were a few plates left on the shelves and a big cardboard box with a few saucers that had escaped. How awful, Emmie thought, to deliberately break such pretty things. The ground was littered with pieces of broken china. She squatted to get a better look. Lots had flowers or ivy leaves on, some were a bright blue with big white dots, and the most beautiful piece had a yellow bird. She started to look for other yellow birds or pieces of the beautiful blue. There was a screwed-up paper bag in the cardboard box. She checked nobody was looking and then took that to put her pieces in. Perhaps she could glue all the bits back together or make a mosaic. She started to pick up pieces with tiny pink roses on as well. She cut her finger a bit, but it wasn't too bad.

'What are you doing? Picking up rubbish like a gypsy? You think you can sell it?' Emmie looked up. Sue loomed above her in her Elizabeth I costume. She was eating candy floss and bits of it were stuck around her mouth.

'I'm going to make something,' said Emmie, standing up.

'No one would want to buy anything you made. It would be too dirty.'

'I wouldn't *sell* it. And there's a wasp on your hair,' said Emmie. 'You'd better stand still until it goes away.' Now she could see her parents walking towards her. Emmie took her bag of fragments and set off to meet them. After a while she glanced back. Sue had dropped her candy floss and was standing there as still as a statue with her arms stretched out. There would probably be a wasp by now anyway.

Her dad had to deliver the truck back to the rugby club, so they squashed into the cab together. She sat in the middle, leaning her head first on her mum's shoulder and then on her dad's.

'Let's go for a little drive,' said her dad. They drove away from the village and on to the main road. Her dad said that if they kept going they would hit the south coast. They could take the truck and run away. They could get the ferry from Newhaven and be in France in a few hours. They would just keep driving. He sped up.

'Let's just go,' he said. 'We can go to Italy and all the places we've always wanted to see, drive across Europe, follow the hippy trail, the Silk Road...' Emmie's mum laughed and reached behind Emmie to put her cool hand on the back of his neck, the way she did. At the next roundabout there were signs for Brighton. He took that exit. Her mother laughed some more.

'But who will feed Freddy?' cried Emmie.

'Ah,' he said, 'that's a good point.' At the next roundabout they turned back.

At home, Emmie realised that there was no way she could rebuild any of the plates. She took the fragments out to the little flowerbed that was hers. The marigolds she had grown were strong and bright. She fetched some buckets of sand from her old sandpit to make a background then pressed the china pieces into patterns around her flowers. She was going to call her mum and dad to come and have a look but decided to keep it a secret. They'd get a lovely surprise when they saw it. They might think it was a real one like at Fishbourne Roman Palace. When she went back indoors her parents were in the kitchen making potato and cauliflower curry for tea and listening to the Everly Brothers.

'Can we have poppadoms?'

'Of course!' said her mum.

After dinner they closed the curtains in the front room even though it wasn't dark, and her mum lit some candles. Emmie chose a stack of records and piled them up ready to play. Then the three of them danced, twisting and shouting as though they were the only people in the world.

Emmie's dad always put on 'Elizabethan Serenade' when it was time for Emmie to go to bed, and he always said the same thing:

'Your Aunty Molly and I stood on deck when the ship was leaving Bombay and they played this tune. We were so excited. I arrived in England richer already because I was so good at working out how many miles the ship had travelled each day. Every time I bought a ticket I won. Other people guessed, but I worked it out.'

When Emmie was in bed her mum came in to kiss her goodnight. She sat on the bed trying to smooth out the feathers of the headdress.

'Happy? Nice day?' Emmie sat up.

'Mum, was Daddy a beggar in India?'

'Of course he wasn't! His parents died, it was the war, and then his English family looked after him.'

'What about his Indian family?'

'We don't know much about them. He didn't see them again after he went away to boarding school.'

'Not even his mum?'

'Not even his mum, Josmi. He doesn't even have a photo of her.' She rubbed the end of one of Emmie's plaits against her cheek.

'Are the Indian family all dead then?'

'We don't really know.'

'He could go and look for them.'

'He doesn't want to go back. Everything has changed.'

'I would want to go back. I would want to find out.'

'You know he doesn't like talking about the sad things.' She kissed Emmie on the forehead and gently pushed her back down. 'Sleep well, sweetheart.'

'I'll have to wash my hair tomorrow or Sue Namey will say that it smells of curry.'

'OK, honey. Sleep well. Don't think about Sue Namey.'

Emmie tried not to think about Sue Namey. Instead she thought about the grandmother whose photo they didn't have. She knew that her name had been Josmi Tantiani, and that was really pretty. She said it out loud: *Josmi Tantiani, Josmi Tantiani.* But what had she looked like? Perhaps like the soppy girl with huge eyes at the end of *The Jungle Book*. Emmie would have stayed with Baloo. She knew what her dead grandpa had looked like – they had a picture of him on the mantelpiece. He was riding a horse. You couldn't see his face very well. Imagine, thought Emmie, if you suddenly never saw your own mum ever again.

Press the button to hear the Everly Brothers sing
'Take A Message to Mary'.

### Ladybird Book *Flight Four: India* – School Library Copy (First Published 1960)

Emmie's dad might not want to talk about India, but he wasn't in charge of choosing her library books. She lay on her bed with her latest acquisition. The cover showed the Taj Mahal; it looked like Brighton Pavilion which she'd visited before, only bigger and with rectangular ponds. Her favourite thing at Brighton Pavilion was the rats stealing food in the kitchen – they looked so real that she thought they might be actual stuffed dead ones.

In *Flight Four: India* there were no stuffed rats, instead there was an English family with a boy called John, who liked writing facts in a notebook, and a girl called Alison who did sketches. The mother seemed to have stayed at home. Alison and John got to travel around the whole of India with their dad who was a businessman. It didn't say what his business was. Emmie thought the book should have shown Alison's sketches, but perhaps they hadn't been much good. After a flight on a modern, luxurious airliner belonging to Air India, the three English people arrived at Bombay airport. They were met by a Mr. Ram Chand, one of the father's business friends, and his children, Gopal and Shanti, who put garlands of flowers around John and Alison's necks. Everywhere John and Alison went, kind, smiling people looked after them. Emmie studied an illustration of women picking tea in Darjeeling. They all wore white dresses and necklaces of orange beads and had huge baskets on their backs held on by straps that went across their foreheads. That must give you a headache.

The best picture was of a tiger, but there were lots more: a huge dam that was being built by Canadians as a present to India to show friendship; a village where people lived quietly and simply and the women carried jars of water on their heads (perhaps everyone *was* like the soppy girl in *The Jungle Book*); and temples and temple paintings that showed, John pointed out (he was always pointing things out), how there was civilisation in India two thousand years before Britain stopped being a savage land. There were pictures of people playing polo – she knew her grandpa had done that, it was one of the things her dad *had* told her – and a market, lemurs, rhinos, elephants, monkeys and parrots, rickshaws being pulled by men, and an ugly factory. Beggars were only mentioned at the end.

*'It's such a kind country,' Alison said thoughtfully, 'and peaceful, too. It's horrid to see so many beggars and very poor people, of course. But so many people are gracious and good-looking.'*

*'I like the great mountains,' said John, 'and the valley of the Ganges, full of people and colour, excitement, and all the old temples. And I like to think of the British people who lived here and helped to make India a great nation. And I like the animals – especially that tiger!'*

It was good, Emmie thought, that her grandpa had been one of the people who'd helped make India a great nation, although if it had already been one when England was full of savages, there must have been a time when things went wrong.

## Breast Feather from a White Goose (c. mid-1970s)

'You think you're so posh,' said Sue Namey. 'Everyone has ponchos of *old* towels, but you just have to copy us with one made of a *brand-new* towel.' She had got meaner since the fête.

Emmie didn't know what to say, so she looked away and quietly got changed.

'You're really weird,' said Sue. 'When you turn your hand sideways you've got a line where it's brown and then pink. My dad says you can tell coloured people because the palms of their hands are a different colour from the backs of their hands, so you must be coloured. But then your dad is coloured.'

Emmie looked down at her feet which seemed more greyish than anything else at the moment. It was freezing in the changing rooms. They had been built by a team of dads (including hers) and were made from fence panels. The girls stuffed loo paper into the holes left by knots in the wood; the boys poked it out and kept trying to peep through. The only thing that made the changing rooms bearable was the smell of creosote. If she was ready early Emmie would lean her face against the walls (carefully so as not to get a splinter) and breathe deeply, even though it was the sort of thing that Sue Namey would think was weird. Emmie had helped her parents creosote the fence at home. She and her mum had worn old shirts of her dad's, but she had still managed to get the stuff on her shorts and plimsolls. Now she remembered how the creosote had got under her nails and made them look dirty for ages, and how tiny flies had landed on the wet fence and been impossible to rescue.

'Nignogs have those hands,' said Sue. 'Is your dad a nignog?'

'He's half Indian,' said Emmie, turning to face her.

'Then he's a half-caste,' said Sue. 'Half a nignog.'

'His dad owned a tea plantation and helped make India a great nation and he was killed in the war. His mum was an Indian princess. And they had horses for playing water polo.' She hung her school clothes on the peg below her towel so that everything was ready for when they got out.

'Which side was he on? I bet he was on the Germans'?'

'Our side.' Emmie gulped and walked out of the changing room, trying not to cry. She headed for the pool. Once she was in the water her eyes would go red from the chlorine anyway.

Behind her she heard Karen, springing to her defence: 'Leave her alone, Sue, she can't help being a choccy biccy.'

It was best to be one of the first through the footbath before it became even more of a soup of plasters, dead wasps and bits of grass. She was the first girl in line for the steps. It meant that she would have to swim next to a boy, but she didn't care. The boys were always much quicker at getting changed. She got in quickly. The water was freezing but she dunked herself under and then stayed down, keeping as much of herself as she could below the surface, waiting for the lesson to start. Actually, her skin looked a really nice colour under the water. She knew that Sue Namey's legs would be turning to a hideous jigsaw puzzle of pink and blue and that she'd end up looking like she was made of the horrible smelly white cheese with blue veins that her parents bought at Christmas when Aunt Lucinda and Aunt Margaret were coming to visit.

Emmie could beat all the girls and all but two of the boys at front crawl. She was nearly as good at backstroke and breaststroke. Her mum did a gentle form of breaststroke, trying to keep her hair dry, but her dad was something else. His butterfly was so fast and splashy that he only did it in the fast lane if nobody else was there. He and Emmie liked diving for their locker keys when they went to the new pool in Dorking. She could go really deep and do somersaults and handstands underwater. Today, when it came to swimming underwater, she broke her own record and did a whole length, banging her head on the wall at the other side and coming up gasping. The teacher blew the whistle.

'Well done, Emmie! Three house points!'

Sue Namey could hardly swim underwater at all. Emmie pictured what would happen if they both fell off a boat and had to swim to land or got stuck in a cave that suddenly started filling with water. If she saved Sue's life, Sue would have to stop being so mean, though she would probably say it had been Emmie's fault that she'd nearly drowned. She could leave her to drown, but what if Sue survived and told everyone what she'd done?

Back in the changing room Emmie found her clothes screwed up and trodden into a puddle on the floor, but she told herself that it didn't matter; she was going to tea at Karen's that afternoon and she always got muddy there anyway.

Karen's mum collected them in their Land Rover. Emmie loved how she slid about on the metal bench seats in the back. There were blankets to sit on, covered in dog fur and feathers and bits of muddy straw. Karen had two Border Collies and a Jack Russell. The Collies were friendly, though a bit jumpy, but Emmie was secretly scared of Beth, the Jack Russell, who would sit outside the bathroom door and growl if anyone tried to get in or out. Emmie avoided using the bathroom at Karen's. She worried that one day Beth might really go for her and that she would accidentally kick Beth away in self-defence and be caught being Cruel To Dogs. When they were in reception class Karen had told Emmie that she couldn't be her best friend because Beth was her best friend and always would be. This loyalty wasn't returned. When Beth wasn't guarding the bathroom, she was patrolling with *her* best friend, a cockerel called Feathers. Karen said that the hens didn't have names because there were about thirty of them, and anyway, they were only going to get eaten, so it wasn't worth the bother. Emmie had tried counting them but they wouldn't keep still. Mrs. Martin sold the eggs to local shops and from a table by the front gate where passing motorists were asked to 'Please Leave Right Change' in a Quality Street tin. Today, as they reached the gate, Emmie saw that there were also tomatoes, marrows and bunches of big pink earwiggy dahlias on sale.

Another sign invited customers to 'Please Call At House For Fresh Frozen Poultry'. Whenever she visited, Emmie thought about Fresh Frozen. She guessed it must mean frozen soon after death. But how long would something be frozen for before it was no longer called Fresh Frozen and became Old Frozen or Old Fresh Frozen? She had seen an article in a magazine at the doctors' about a mammoth that had been found frozen in Siberia. It still had fur, and the contents of its poor sad stomach. The people who had found it had cooked and eaten some of it before any scientists or archaeologists arrived. Emmie had worried that the mammoth might not have been dead. Maybe it had been so suddenly, so freshly frozen, that it had just been in a deep sleep. How awful to sleep for thousands of years and then wake up to be killed and eaten. She wondered what it had been dreaming about – probably other mammoths and new grass in spring. She hoped that it hadn't been dreaming about hunters, fierce Neanderthals saying 'Ug!' and throwing spears – if it was Neanderthals in those days and in Siberia.

The dogs were waiting, barking and leaping with joy at their owners' return. Karen got out of the van and slammed the door shut behind her. Emmie watched as she opened the heavy wooden gate and stood by, saluting as they drove through. Karen did that every time and then ran along beside the van with the three dogs at her heels, all the way up the long drive. She was a good runner, not so great at sprinting, but she could keep going forever and always won at cross-country. Emmie semi-dreaded getting out of the van, but she did her best to hide it, carrying hers and Karen's school bags in front of her for protection, pretending to enjoy patting the dogs and not to mind when they jumped up and licked her face.

Karen fetched orange squash in pink Tupperware beakers and Lincoln biscuits. Emmie ate hers quickly as she knew the dogs would be onto her. They sniffed around their ankles, licking crumbs from the floor. Karen wore lacy white socks up to her knees, the sort with a pattern of big holes so that patches of leg peeped through. She had strong pink legs and when she took her socks off the lace pattern would be imprinted on her skin. Emmie had asked her mum to get her some of the same socks, but they didn't look as good on her, and after they had been washed, they seemed to go crunchy. She wondered which washing powder Karen's mum used but thought it might be rude to ask. It must be something good because Karen's socks always looked really white, even though her life was full of mud and dogs.

'What do you wanna do?' Karen asked, taking a fourth (contraband) Lincoln. She put it in the palm of one hand and then brought her other elbow down on it. 'Aw, four bits!' You had to get either three or seven bits for a wish. They both knew that only gingernuts were lucky. Karen tossed the pieces one by one high into the air so that the dogs would leap for them.

'We could make a dog circus,' said Emmie, 'or a dog obstacle course.' The dogs outside were much better.

'OK. If only we had some sheep, we could do sheepdog trials.'

'I'd like that,' said Emmie, 'but I can't whistle. You have to do a special whistle. And you're the one they would obey.'

Emmie couldn't roll her 'r's either. Sue Namey would stand behind her in the queue for lunch going 'rrrrrrrrrr'. Sue Namey could touch her nose with her sharp pink tongue too. Emmie blinked thoughts of Sue away.

They went out the back through the lean-to where the

washing machine was underneath a fake marble counter laden with sacks of dog biscuits, wormer for hens, geese and dogs, flea treatments, baskets of washing and ironing, and slug pellets. Emmie took note of the washing powder brand – Ariel.

The Martins' field had been taken up with their strawberry crop but that was all over now and what remained was a deeply rutted landscape strewn with muddy straw. Karen and Emmie liked digging at the edges of it (or in the middle when nothing was growing). They often found crumbling oyster shells, mysteriously washed up in the middle of Surrey. When the girls looked up from their digging, they saw the chalk escarpments of the North Downs where Roman snails grazed and bee orchids bloomed unseen. Walkers around the chalk pits could hack out fossils to take home. The Ash family had been there many times, climbing on the abandoned quarry trains or riding on the ones that a group of enthusiasts still ran on special Sundays. Emmie had thought that the Martins' oysters must be from when the land was sea, but the name of the single-track road that ran behind the field told a different story: Hangman's Lane. The good folk of Otterham had once enjoyed fine days out, eating oysters and watching the executions.

Karen led Emmie into one of the outbuildings where there was an old white Mini Traveller with no doors. There were sacks of hen and goose food and a dustbin filled with shiny mixed grain. Emmie loved to lift the lid and let it run through her fingers.

'Can I give some to the hens and geese later?'

'Course.'

Emmie stood for a few moments playing with the grain, enjoying the warmth and dustiness of it. How strange that something made of such hard, little nubs could be so silky and almost soft when you had a whole heap of it.

'It's like the seven fat years,' she said. They had been doing the story of Joseph at school.

'Fat ears!' Karen said and bopped her on the arm. After a

quick fight with bamboo canes, they gathered things for the dog obstacle course – empty plastic drums, lots of canes, a load of netting that Karen said was for putting on fruit bushes not catching fish, and some bigger planks of wood.

Soon the dogs became leaping crescents of black, brown and white, clearing every hurdle. The girls ran alongside them shouting 'Hup! Hup!'

'Faster than witches!' Emmie shouted.

'Faster than… dogs!' Karen replied. Beth was the best at going under the net. Straw clung to the girls' hair and school jumpers and the Border Collies' coats. Mrs. Martin appeared at the edge of the field.

'Just going to pick up Crystal!'

'OK, Mum!'

They collapsed onto the ground with the dogs panting beside them.

'I know,' said Karen, 'follow me.' Emmie followed. Back in the outhouse Karen jerked her head towards the Mini.

'Get in.'

Emmie climbed into the passenger side and Karen got into the driver's seat. The keys were in the ignition. The dogs jumped into the back. The red leatherette seats were already coated with dried mud. The floor had rusted through in places but the engine started first time.

'Karen! Are you allowed? Can you drive?'

'My dad taught me. It's easy. I do it all the time at the weekend.' The car jolted backwards and then forwards. 'Oops,' said Karen, wrenching at the gear stick.

They vroomed out into the yard. Emmie tried to position her feet away from the holes. Wires dangled from the dashboard onto their knees. Beth yapped in the back. Emmie squealed as Karen steered towards the strawberry field.

Karen laughed. 'You aren't scared, are you?'

'Um, no…'

'I'll show you how fast I can go!' Karen wrestled with the gear stick again. There was no doorhandle to grip, no seatbelt.

Emmie grabbed the edges of her seat. She tried staring at the floor but saw only mud, straw and stones beneath her. She looked up, screamed with laughter, and they were off, bumping over the rutted field.

'I'm drawing a flag!' Karen yelled, finishing a diagonal sweep across the middle and heading around the perimeter. 'The handbrake can help you turn. I'm a better driver than Crystal. She stalls.'

Brambles and branches of hawthorn from the perilously close hedge scratched at the car as they passed.

'Mind the hedge! Mind the ditch!' Emmie screamed.

'There is no ditch!'

Back across the diagonal. The car left the ground over some of the biggest ridges and furrows. They zoomed along the fence by the road. They ploughed through a mess of white feathers where a fox must have got something.

'Sue cried and told her mum when we did this,' Karen scoffed, taking a hand off the wheel to brush a mangled quill away. The big dogs started barking. A huge bird flew up from somewhere.

'Just the cross down the middle. Do you want a go?'

Emmie was laughing too much to reply. The jagged ends of the springs in the seat dug into her legs with every bump. 'I might be sick!' she hiccupped, then, 'Don't stop!'

Karen sped up and did one more circuit then slowed down back across the yard and rolled back into the barn. The car stopped. Emmie expected to see smoke come out of the bonnet like in a cartoon. The dogs jumped out of the back and ran towards the field.

Emmie climbed out of the car, still laughing and hiccupping, her legs shaking, as Karen turned off the engine and got out too.

'Oh, the handbrake.' She got back in to yank it up.

'It's facing a different way now,' Emmie said. Karen looked at the car and pulled a face.

'They probably won't notice. Do you want some more squash?'

They had finished their squash and were colouring pages from Karen's pattern pad when Mrs. Martin and Crystal got back.

'You're a neat colourer, Emmie,' Crystal said, leaning over to look at what they were doing. She smelt of PE mats. Emmie knew that she wasn't a good colourer and that Crystal was only saying that to annoy her little sister.

'That's because she goes around the edges first,' said Karen evenly. Emmie nodded, unable to think of a suitable reply. 'I do that sometimes too but I can't always be bothered. If you go around the edges of whatever you want to colour it stops you going over the lines, but it's really boring. Can I have the turquoise, and the flesh?'

Emmie passed her the pens. They were the ones she'd got Karen for her birthday. They were Caran D'Ache, in a metal box with a picture of mountains on the front. Her mum had chosen them without asking Emmie's opinion. She would have said that they should get Karen something to do with dogs or horses, but it looked like she liked them.

'Those are really nice, posh pens you got Karen,' said Mrs. Martin. 'Put the lids back on straight away, Karen, I know what you're like.'

Karen smiled at Emmie. 'I will, and I won't put them back the wrong way round.'

'Do you want baked beans or spaghetti hoops with your dinner? It's Welsh rarebit for you, Emmie, the rest of us are having gammon.'

Emmie was pleased that Mrs. Martin had remembered that she was the sort of vegetarian who didn't eat fish. She hadn't seen a gammon before. It must be something big and pink and smelly. She knew now that Welsh rarebit was toasted cheese. On her first visit she had had to pluck up courage to say that she couldn't eat rabbit. She hated being different. People always thought it was because she was a Hindu or something; it was too complicated to explain that it was her mum who didn't eat meat.

Mr. Martin appeared in his usual garb of brown cords and wellies and a khaki jumper with patches on the shoulders and elbows, the sort a soldier would wear.

'Boots!' shouted Mrs. Martin without even looking round.

'How are all my girls then? And little Hiawatha?' Crystal dodged out of his way but he ruffled Karen's hair and then Emmie's.

'Dad!' laughed Karen.

'What's for dinner then, love, apart from a bowl of grass for our guest?' Emmie was used to this and knew that she didn't have to respond, but just smiled up at him.

He sat down on one of the pine chairs. He pulled off his boots and little mouldings of mud from the soles fell to the floor. Mrs. Martin tsked and put a big mug of tea in front of him, a Frosties mug with Tony the Tiger saying *They're GRRRREAT!'* The trouble with being an only child, Emmie thought, was that you could never get enough packet tops or tokens to send off for things. By the time you got through one box, the offer would have changed. They did collect Green Shield Stamps but never seemed to have enough for anything any of them might want. Everybody had Humphrey stickers. They were so common that they didn't count. Emmie now regretted putting them on her bike, a light blue Raleigh, because it made it look scruffy, but it would look even worse if she tried to peel them off. She might have to wait until she grew out of the bike to get away from them.

Emmie felt herself about to sneeze and reached into her pocket where she found the handful of hen feed, along with a screwed-up bit of loo paper. The sneeze subsided.

'We didn't feed the hens,' she said.

'Pack up your crayons first,' said Mrs. Martin. 'And give them some of that spinach.'

'Pens, Mum. Only babies have crayons.'

Emmie put the pens back in the box in the correct rainbow order.

Karen got an enamel mugful of scratch feed on the way out and grabbed a handful of perpetual spinach leaves from a bed that in another garden might have contained flowers. The hens were in a fenced-off bit of field behind the barn. Emmie was glad that the geese were kept separately as they could be a bit fierce, but today she saw that none were there and their beige fibreglass pond (which had been there forever but had never been sunk into the ground) was half-empty and covered with yellowish green algae that looked as though you could walk on it.

'Oh. Your geese are gone.'

'Lots of orders,' said Karen. Emmie hoped that the geese would have nicer ponds in their new homes. There was a soft white feather as long as the palm of her hand on the ground. She picked it up and put it in the pocket that didn't contain scratch feed.

They unlatched the wire mesh door and the chickens ran towards them, some leaping up to get the leaves. The hens were all shades of russet and apricot. Karen threw down the spinach and then launched the scratch feed in an arc across the pen. Emmie emptied her pocket. Some of the feed fell on her shoe and a few of the hens started pecking at it.

'Lucky you aren't wearing sandals. They think toes are worms.'

'Which one's your favourite?'

'That one with the blackest tail – she's really cheeky. That one with the pale back is the leader. She always comes out first in the morning and gets the best of everything. Pecking order.' Emmie immediately liked Pale Back the least.

'I'd give them names,' she said. Her mum had a little book called *Naming Baby* which for some reason lived in her round wicker sewing basket instead of on the shelves. The book couldn't have been that useful as Emmie had just been named after her dad's grandmother and then been given Margaret as a middle name, which was conveniently the name of her mum's mum as well as one of her great-aunts. You would need a book like that if you had thirty hens. Emmie always borrowed it if she had a new toy to name.

'Girls! Tea!' The dogs started barking excitedly from across the big field.

'Probably think it's *their* tea,' said Karen.

They ran back inside. It turned out that gammon was some sort of thick meaty thing and perhaps not a fish at all. The Martins always had pudding. Today it was a rhubarb cobbler that Crystal had made in her home economics class. The scone part went from black around the edges to soggy, pink dumpling underneath.

'Are they meant to be like that?' Karen asked, lifting a dollop of uncooked scone up to examine it. 'It looks like the inside of something.' Wet strings of the dough stretched back towards the bowl like the tentacles of a jellyfish.

Emmie started to plough through hers.

She heard her father's car pull up outside. She thought of how he must have had to get out to open the gate, and then drive through, and then get out again to shut it. At least she hoped he had known to shut it or the dogs might get out and be run over and Karen and her family would be so sad and would hate them forever. She went with Karen to open the door, hoping it would mean that she could now abandon what was left of her cobbler.

Her dad stood on the step in his navy-blue Crombie and shiny shoes. Beth ran past him into the house, dragging something long and white with an orange beak, and then the two Collies barrelled past, each with one of the same thing in their jaws. It took Emmie a moment to realise what they were: the heads and necks of geese.

She screamed and her dad pulled her towards him.

'What the…?!'

'Mum!' Karen yelled. 'They've dug up the geese heads again!'

The dogs made it down the hall before Mr. Martin bellowed 'Out!' and came stomping towards them. 'Out!' The Collies dropped their prizes and fled. Beth stayed where she was and snarled.

Emmie shrank between her father and the wall, not sure whether it was better to look or not look. Mr. Martin picked up the goose neck with Beth still clinging to it, carried it to the front door and flung it outside, dog and all. He picked up the other necks, looked at them, and chucked them back down where they landed on a couple of carrier bags that were lurking in the corner; he managed to do this and extend his hand to Emmie's dad in one smooth movement.

'Bloody dogs!'

'Ha, ha, yes,' her dad said, nodding as though three hounds charging in with the heads of geese dangling from their jaws was nothing remarkable. 'Say "thank you", Emmie.'

'Thank you for having me,' said Emmie. She wondered if she should say something about her cobbler. If she did, would they insist that she went back into the kitchen to finish it? 'Thank you for my nice tea, I'm really full.'

'You ate like a bird!' said Mrs. Martin. 'Karen always gobbles hers down.'

'Bye, Emmie,' said Karen.

Emmie smiled and nodded. 'Bye.'

'That your school bag, Emmie?' her dad asked. The goose necks lay perilously close to her satchel. He reached to pick it up but Emmie dived for it. No goose remains from people's hands would touch her stuff.

Beth ran beside their car down the drive, Karen running along behind her and saluting as they went through the gate.

Emmie managed not to cry until they had pulled out onto the road.

'He shook your hand, Dad, with his dead goose hands!' she wailed, looking at her dad's gentle hands on the steering wheel.

Back at home she made her dad wash his hands before he

did anything else, and then she got the J-cloth and cleaned the steering wheel and the handles inside and out on his side of the car. And the front door knob. She put the cloth in the bin even though it was a newish one.

Up in her room she found the white feather in her pocket, inspected it for blood, then put it in the treasure chest her great-aunt Margaret had given her. She wondered if it was from one of the dead geese. She wasn't sure if she hoped that it was or that it wasn't.

'Where are your swimming things, Em?' her mum called up the stairs. Emmie thought for a moment and then remembered: they were in one of the carrier bags on the Martins' hall floor, with two goose necks on top of them.

## Lists Made by a Nine-year-old Girl (c. 1976)

'Emmie! Why aren't you in bed? It's midnight!'

'I couldn't sleep, Mum. I keep thinking that something bad is going to happen.'

'Don't be silly. Nothing bad is going to happen. Nothing bad could happen here.'

'The moon's too bright.'

'Well, you have got the curtains open. Come on, get back into bed.'

'I thought I saw something in the garden like a lost dog or a leopard or a wolf. It might be the Surrey Puma.'

'There's no such thing as the Surrey Puma.'

But Emmie knew that there was. There was even a terrifying chapter about it in *Olga da Polga*.

Pammy tucked Emmie in and drew the curtains, but slivers of moonlight kept slithering in. 'When I can't sleep, I make lists in my head, not of things that I have to do, but of nice things. You try it. An A to Z of names you like or places you'd like to go or foods you like.'

'No foods begin with X.'

'You'll be asleep before X.'


Angel Delight

Butterscotch Angel Delight

Chocolate – Flakes – and Flakes in 99s

Dream Topping on trifle with hundreds and thousands with the colours running

Eggy bread

Freddos

Green jelly. Could you get green jelly? Greengages – not always nice.

Hula Hoops. Sue Namey made one of the little ones at school cry. She said, 'Do you want a Hula Hoop? You can have a hoop or a pillow.' The little girl said, 'Pillow!' because she thought it would be bigger and Sue broke a hoop, gave the girl the much smaller bit and said, 'There's your pillow.'

Ice cream – Neapolitan – and Cornish at Kelly's on holiday.

Japanese rice crackers – best food in the world – at Dad's work friend's house – real seaweed on them.

KitKats, but Karen got an electric shock when she bit the foil.

Lemonade – cream soda better – a magic trick at the twin's party – the lemonade turned blue. Their mum secretly put drops of food colouring in the paper cups.

Mashed potato, but not school mash, mash that Mum made with cheese on top.

Nuts. Dad roasting peanuts in the big pan.

Orange Space Dust

Pancakes with lemon and sugar

Q… Q… Q… Quick Jel. No other Qs. Not with mandarin oranges in – like bits of dead goldfish.

Radishes – the Japanese-rice-cracker-friends cut them in half and put butter and salt and pepper on them – Dad said in India there were white radishes as long as a school ruler.

S... S... Salt and vinegar crisps, never cheese and onion – too smelly – boys liked cheese and onion – they didn't care.

Sandwiches – jam or Marmite and lettuce.

T... Tomato sandwiches at the beach – but not with sand in but on a picnic – warm in the sun – salt and pepper and the bread gone soggy...

U... U... U or...

# Middle School Report for a Ten-year-old Girl, England (4 July 1977)

Everybody knew that Sue Namey would be the next head girl. She was already vice-captain of the netball team and played centre, a position that allowed her to move freely around the court though not to shoot. She offered encouragement to team members when they had the ball and were taking aim, shouting 'Shoot, shoot!' as if the idea hadn't occurred to them. Her long hair was the yellow of Spry cooking oil. It had taken her mother half an hour to do her Elizabeth I hairdo back when she'd won first prize at the fête; but even on school days she had it in an elaborate style – plaits pinned up on her head with multiple kirby grips or bunches with two sets of bobbles, one at the top and one halfway down or with a bit pinned back to make her big shiny forehead look even bigger and shinier.

Everybody else liked her. Sue's birthday was in September and she was the oldest girl in the year. She often told people that if she'd been born two days earlier, she'd be in the year above. If only, thought Emmie. Sue gave her invitations out on the second to last day of the summer term. She went around the class just before afternoon register and gave them out one by one to all the popular boys and to every girl in the class, except Emmie.

Emmie's desk was in the back row. 'Oh, I must have forgotten yours,' said Sue when she reached it. But she didn't mention bringing it in the next day and Emmie didn't ask. She tried to look busy with the contents of her pencil case, but she couldn't help but see Karen's invitation on its Holly Hobbie paper. Emmie would have been embarrassed to use Holly Hobbie paper, especially for the boys, but Sue seemed to have no such qualms. Emmie hated the way that Holly Hobbie didn't have a face, but maybe the artist just wasn't very good at drawing faces. Emmie was rubbish at men's faces. She always had to give them beards or moustaches to stop them from looking like women.

There was no invitation the next day either and that was the end of term. Lots of people were giving Sue back the reply slips and she collected them into a big peach-coloured envelope, the sort that you would have with an enormous birthday card. Emmie hated the colour peach and she hated those stupid big birthday cards too. She imagined Sue getting those giant cards from her family. They would all say things like 'Best Niece' and 'Happy Birthday to Our Special Daughter' and be padded with hideous roses on, roses in colours that roses didn't even exist in. They might as well make something out of Andrex wrappers.

She tried not to think about Sue's party as the last day unfolded. They had to clear out their desks, putting all their exercise books into the carrier bags they'd brought in specially so that they could take them home to show their parents. There was a special assembly to say goodbye to the top form. Next year Emmie's would be the top form going up one by one to be given a Bible and shake hands with Mr. Pikestaff, standing on the stage while everyone clapped. Lots of the big girls cried. The boys all grinned. Emmie remembered how huge they'd seemed when she'd started school – the boys so scary and the girls like fully-grown women, with bras showing through their school shirts. She didn't think she could possibly look like that in just a year's time. She certainly hoped she wouldn't.

*End of Year Report*
*Emmeline Margaret Ash*
*Form 4 July 1977*
*Class Teacher's Comments*

*Emmie is a well-behaved pupil and a pleasure to have in the class. She follows instructions quickly and quietly and is never late or disruptive. She always carries out her duties as a library monitor with a smile and has kept the library shelves nicely organised. I am also grateful for her help in washing up the glue and paint pots after art lessons. A good year's work. Well done!*

### English    A-
*Emmie has a flair for reading and writing. She should try to make her writing neater. She does sometimes get carried away with her stories and forget to stay on the lines. She is reading well above her age.*

### Maths    B
*Emmeline has made sound progress this year and copes well with fractions and trigonometry. She should practise long division over the summer as she often seems intimidated by some of the more challenging calculations.*

### Geography    B+
*Emmeline draws very good maps though she has a tendency to add unnecessary illustrations. Her work on cocoa bean farming after our trip to the Commonwealth Institute was very good.*

### History    A-
*Emmeline's project on Norman castles was very good. She has a good understanding of the feudal system and of farming after the Norman Conquest. Her contribution to Form 4's Bayeux Tapestry was good though she should learn to accept other pupils' offers to contribute to her artwork with better grace.*

### Science    A

*Emmeline has been a reliable weather monitor this year. She is methodical and tidy in her experiments and is able to suggest reasons for unexpected results. She was particularly enthusiastic when it came to trying paper chromatography and stayed behind during breaks to experiment with other colours. She correctly labelled the parts of an earthworm, the water cycle, and a skeleton in the end of year test.*

### Music    B+

*Emmie is a proficient recorder player. She should try to open her mouth wider when singing. She sometimes hides her musical light under a bushel. She played the chime bars nicely at the concert for the pensioners' tea party.*

### Art and Craft    A-

*Emmeline has made more excellent progress this year. She prefers working by herself to taking part in group projects. She is easily upset when what she produces doesn't meet her own high standards. She is particularly good at needlework and craft projects and made a very neat patchwork cushion cover. Her stitches on this were the neatest I have ever seen in many years of teaching at Otterham First and Middle School.*

### PE    B

*Emmeline has been a reliable first reserve for the netball team and didn't allow her disappointment to show when she had few opportunities to take part in interschool matches. She is as agile as a monkey and performs well on the apparatus. She should extend her arms more when finishing a movement.*

### RE    B

*Emmeline's team raised over £6 for Christian Aid during Christian Aid Week with their cake sales and sponsored silence. She has done some very good work on Jesus Healing the Sick and The Sermon on The Mount. A lively mind is a*

*good thing but questioning the story of Noah in a whole school*
*assembly is not.*

### Headmaster's Comments
*Another good report for Emmeline. I note Mrs. Anderson's*
*comment about the appropriateness of making critical*
*comments and trust that Emmeline will have learnt her lesson*
*and will endeavour to be one of the best-behaved pupils in the*
*school next year.*

**Signed:** Richard Pikestaff


That night Emmie's dad brought home Indian sweets as well
as Old Jamaica chocolate and some Revels.

'Emmie, good report. Well done! What's this about
Noah's Ark, though?' Emmie put the flat chocolate Revel
she'd been about to eat back in the bag.

'They were so mean,' she said. 'Mrs. Anderson asked
what we should learn from the story and I know she wanted
someone to say about the rainbow and God keeps his promises
but I think it's horrible. All those people drowned. Why didn't
Noah's family try to save them? There must have been loads
of children and they just sailed off and left them, and worse,
if they took two of every animal, what about all those other
animals? Not many animals could keep swimming for forty
days and forty nights with *no* food, so all the other animals
must have drowned or got eaten by sharks and crocodiles.
They must have taken mothers from baby animals and left
nearly everyone to die.'

'Oh, Emmie…'

'But she didn't have an answer. She just said not to be
facetious which sounds really dirty and horrible and Sue
Namey kept calling me Faeces Emmie. And Mrs. Anderson
only wrote about it because it was last week. I bet it wouldn't
have gone in my report if I'd said it in autumn term. She

would have just forgotten.' Tears sprang to her eyes at the injustice of it all.

'Try to forget about it now, school's finished. You've got six weeks off! And we're going to Cornwall.'

'I do one thing that they think is wrong all year and it goes on my report forever! My next school will see it!'

'Ignore them, Emmie, forget about it,' said her dad. 'It has to be water off a duck's back, you know.'

'Emmie, Emmie!' her mum said and pulled her into her soft arms. Emmie felt too hot to be there. Her mum's skin was always cool and smelt of Bronley lemon soap. Her hair was the colour of butterscotch. If Emmie had hair like that, Sue would have invited her to the party. Her mum's T-shirt was striped like Neapolitan ice cream. Emmie loved the way the pink looked next to the soft brown and how the vanilla colour made it look even softer. Mrs. Anderson would never wear a T-shirt like this. She wore hideous blouses with collars and bust darts. They were always horrible colours that were pretending to be nice. Pale blue that was too bright for a proper pale blue, like the shirts she would have to wear at secondary school, or dark blue with white stripes like a butcher's apron, or pale green that was the same colour as the school corridors.

## Postcard of Prussia Cove
## (Postmarked 7 August 1977)


*Having a lovely time. Wish you were here,* Emmie wrote to Aunt Lucinda. *We might go on a boat to the Silly Isles next week. Thank you for the pocket money. I have bought a little torch and two denim purses that look like some shorts. One is for me and one is for my friend Karen. I hope you and Aunt Margaret are well.*
   *Love from Emmie xxx*


There was a car park on top of the cliffs. They walked down the track carrying their swimming things, the blow-up dinghy and the picnic. Emmie always carried the oars. She could use them as walking sticks or put them over her shoulder as though she was setting out to seek her fortune. Some gift shops sold red-and-white or blue-and-white spotted handkerchiefs along with Guernsey jumpers and hats for people who were going sailing. She'd have liked one of the red and white ones to put her lunch in. Emmie knew that if an old woman was sitting by the side of the road you should stop and share your hunk of dried bread, lump of cheese and half-bottle of sour wine with them. There were no fairies or witches in disguise by the side of the path, but there were hedgerows of hazel and blackthorn, red and white campion, cuckoo pint and Jack by the hedge. Soon there was only pineapple-scented gorse and the scene expanded to reveal the clifftops and Prussia Cove beneath them.

The beach they went to was the next one along, called Kenneggy Cove, but they called it Prussia Cove too because the name was so much nicer. Her dad had come on holiday here with Aunt Lucinda and his sister Molly when they'd been teenagers and just arrived in England. He always pointed out the house where they'd stayed or looked at it and nodded as they passed. And every year he told the story about one of Aunt Lucinda's dogs, Bramble, who had been chasing rabbits and had run into a gorse bush and right over the cliff, and how he had found a way down to where Bramble had landed on a ledge and brought him back very shaken but perfectly alright.

There was a choice of going down the first path to the beach and then walking over the rocks or carrying on along the cliffs and then going down a steep path where a piece of rope had been fixed to help people scramble down. If it was low tide, they'd go over the rocks, though Emmie preferred the other way. She wasn't very quick at walking across rocks, her plimsolls were so old that their soles were worn smooth. The rocks were often littered with dead legs – brown appendages that looked like parts of the unwrapped mummy she'd seen in the British Museum – though her parents claimed that they were long stalks of seaweed that had been broken off in storms and washed up. She also had to keep stopping to look in the pools where purple and yellow periwinkles shone beneath the water, anemones waved their tiny arms, transparent shrimps darted away from her shadow. If she was really lucky, she might see a crab disappearing sideways into a crevasse. She wondered if the creatures knew how big the world really was; that there was a huge ocean out there, to say nothing of the land and the infinite sky. After looking down for a long time she would rock back on her heels and look up and wonder if there was another land or ocean or sky beyond the sky that she could see. She loved the grey-blue of the mussels; the same colour as the roof slates when it rained in Porthleven where they stayed.

Today the tide was in so they were going along the clifftop. They could see other families ahead of them on the path, like the figures in Monet's *Poppies* which they had up in their front room. Emmie stopped to watch a pair of yellow butterflies dancing above the bushes. She hoped that they knew about the thorns and that they'd be careful if they landed. She thought about the whales and dolphins that must be out there somewhere in the sea. Perhaps if she stood still long enough and watched she might see one, but the light was too bright to stare for more than a few minutes. Emmie's head swirled with the heat and the smell of the gorse, the azure of the sea meeting the sky, and the cries of gulls, and she wondered if the groups of people up ahead might be them, just a few minutes forward in time. There was a lady with grey hair up in a bun with a little black Scottie dog trotting along beside her, and ahead of her some teenagers, a boy and a girl, in jumpers and shorts whose skinny legs were as brown and polished as old broom handles. Her parents seemed to have disappeared. She knew they must be somewhere up ahead. Then the lady with the dog disappeared around a bend in the path and she saw her parents, waiting for her on the bench at the top of the path down to the beach. Her dad had his arm around her mum but something was wrong – Mum was staring down at her knees, not out at the view. Emmie hurried towards them, the oars dragging behind her as she ran.

'Your mummy's not feeling very well,' her dad said. Emmie sat down on the bench next to them, hoping that nobody would come up from the beach as the bench was meant for people who had just made the long climb and they would have to move or explain that her mum needed to sit down.

'Shall I get you a cup of tea out of the flask, Mum?'

No reply.

Then her mum looked up.

'I'll be fine. It's going away now. I just had a sudden bad pain, but it's probably just a stitch.' But they hadn't been walking that fast. Bees buzzed around them. Or maybe wasps.

'Shall we go back, dear?' said Jay.

'Um…' Pammy grimaced and put a hand onto her stomach. 'No, I'll be OK.'

'You know there's no loos down there.'

'It's not that sort of pain. There, I'm OK now.' She stood up and smiled. 'Maybe it's just because I skipped breakfast.'

The path down seemed steeper and slipperier than usual. Dry sand and tiny stones followed them in a cloud of dust. There were a few groups dotted around on the beach. Emmie looked for the lady with the dog but couldn't see her. She loved watching dogs playing on the beach. Her mum went more slowly than usual and Emmie's dad took the picnic bag and everything else so that she didn't have to carry anything at all. Normally they would all change into their costumes the moment they arrived on the sand, but today her mum just sank down on a rock while Emmie and her dad spread out the rug. Then she lay down on the rug, resting her head on a rolled-up towel. Emmie put her own costume on using the towelling poncho Aunt Lucinda had made her from a lovely new yellow towel, as fluffy as a duckling. She blinked away thoughts of Sue Namey being mean about it. She would never tell her mum and dad about the things Sue said.

Emmie started picking her way down towards the sea. The sun was warm but the sand beneath her feet was cool. In the distance she spotted the little black dog from earlier playing in the sea with the teenagers. They were too old to want to talk to her. She stopped every so often to examine a stone or a shell. She sometimes found what her mum said were carnelians, though they didn't look that different to other pebbles. Back when she was little, she'd liked licking stones on the beach for the salt. She didn't do that now, too dirty. It was a good beach for shells – mussels, razor shells, winkles and periwinkles in violet, slate, brimstone and orange. She tried to avoid stepping on the worm casts even though she knew that they didn't really have worms in but were just the shapes of sand that had been through the creatures' insides. A jellyfish lay not far from the shallows. She wondered if it could be rescued but she couldn't see anything to lift it with to get it back in the sea. She turned and went back up the beach.

Her dad normally went swimming straight away with her before lunch. He was in his trunks now but still had his jumper on and was sitting on a towel next to her mum who was lying on her side on their brown towel with another one, their dark green one, over her legs so that she looked like a washed-up mermaid. Her hair was trailing across the brown towel and onto the sand. Mum hated getting sand in her hair. Emmie walked carefully around her so that she didn't kick up any more (Mum hated that too) and gently lifted and folded her hair onto the towel.

'I just came to get an oar,' said Emmie. 'There's a jellyfish. I'm seeing if I can rescue it.'

'OK, sweetheart,' said her dad. Her mum had her eyes closed and didn't say anything. Emmie took the oar and dragged it down the beach, leaving a trail in the sand behind her. The jellyfish was hard to manoeuvre. She used the oar as a shovel and picked it up on its bed of sand. Now there were some little children playing in the sea. What if it stung them? She carried the oar in front of her as though she were in a giants' egg and spoon race with an egg that had already broken. Surely a jellyfish should wobble, but it didn't, it just lay there, a strange alien thing, transparent with a purple ring, seeming to grow as she walked. Now a brown dog was running towards her, wanting whatever precious thing she was carrying. She walked faster and headed for the rocks and gently slid the jellyfish into the first deep pool. If it was alive it would be able to rest there and then leave at the next high tide. It floated in the water but did not move. She hoped she would be able to see what happened. They usually stayed all day. If it was dead then surely it was better for it to be carried out to sea. No creature would want to end up in the wrong world. She left it there and moved on to another pool so that she wouldn't have to look at it anymore.

Here were sea anemones above the water line like overblown red wine gums and below it with their tentacles extended and tiny shrimps that darted away as her shadow moved over the water. Something glinted, half-obscured by a pebble. Was it pirate silver, a piece of eight, or perhaps a doubloon, whatever they were? No, it was the ring from a coke can. She remembered when she had thought that Puff the Magic Dragon lived in a cave at the end of the cove. She and two girls she'd met on the beach had gone looking for him but he hadn't been there. Emmie would never have stopped visiting him. She still hoped that she might meet those girls again. They had been on holiday too. She remembered that they had worn scratchy-looking navy-blue jumpers over their swimming costumes and that one had had red curly hair and one yellow plaits, but she couldn't remember their names. She wondered if they remembered her. If you had a sister you would always have someone to play with; you wouldn't be bothered about meeting other children at the beach. She remembered that their dad had been really tall with a beard, and that he had said hello to her dad and that they had shaken hands even though they had both been up to their thighs in the sea. She had laughed out loud at that; luckily, they must have thought she had just been laughing at the waves.

Now she stood up and picked her way back across the rocks, using the oar to steady herself. She saw that her dad was beckoning her back. It couldn't be lunchtime already. Emmie could see that her mum was still lying down and realised she'd forgotten that she hadn't been feeling well. It seemed to take ages to walk all the way back to them. When she got there her dad gave her a Penguin from the picnic and said that he was sorry but that they were going to go home.

Her mum couldn't decide if she wanted to go back across the rocks which meant that the path up to the car park was less steep or back up all along the cliffs. Emmie suggested using an oar as a walking stick and her mum did that, leaning on her father too. There were dead legs galore and places where the rocks were slippery with bladderwrack, and there were other washed-up purple ring jellyfish along the beach, a whole plague of them.

## Tammy, Jinty and Judy Comics
### (Dated Mid- to Late 1970s)

Karen and Emmie lay on Emmie's bed surrounded by comics. They had piles and piles more waiting to be read on the floor. Emmie's mum bought her loads of comics – almost every single one she wanted – and bought herself lots of magazines too – *Woman* and *Woman's Own* and *She* – and Lesley who lived down the road always gave her copies of *Honey*, which Emmie's mum said was a bit common, but she liked reading it anyway. Emmie's favourite way of spending an afternoon with her mum was to lie on a rug in the garden and read. Her mum said that they would get sun loungers one day. In winter, Emmie's mum lay on the sofa and Emmie lay on the floor with her elbows on a cushion.

'Next birthday,' said Emmie, 'I don't want a normal party with games, I want a comics party where everyone just brings lots of comics and you all just swap them and read and eat party food.' Sue had boasted that they were going to play spin the bottle at her party. You had to kiss the person the bottle pointed to, as long as it wasn't another girl, though Emmie thought she would rather kiss most of the girls than any of the boys. Almost all of the boys smelled like their ham sandwiches and had dirty nails or warts on their hands or knees. But she could never play spin the bottle. Nobody would want to kiss her.

Her mum had taken a long time to answer, but Emmie didn't mind. It was like that when you were reading.

'That wouldn't really be a party, Ems, would it?' she said after a while.

'But it would be nicer.' A long pause.

'Mmm.'

But today she *was* having a comics party. Dad had the day off to take Mum to a hospital appointment. Emmie was allowed to stay at home with Karen for company. She had hardly ever stayed at home by herself before – only when she was ill and off school and her mum had to go to the shop. Karen had brought round a huge box of comics that Crystal had given her. Some were quite old and a bit funny-smelling, but that didn't really matter. Those were mostly *Jinty*s. Emmie liked *Tammy* and *Judy* better because they had real-life stories, mostly about orphans. She liked *The Dand*y as well, and sometimes *The Beano*, but she was a bit grown up for that now.

'What's wrong with your mum, then?' Karen asked. She had been eating Black Jacks and her lips and tongue were stained.

'Your tongue's gone black. Do any of your dogs have black tongues? I saw a Chow Chow once and it had a purple tongue and lips,' Emmie said. 'She keeps feeling sick and too full to eat. And having tummy aches.' Emmie had been eating Fruit Salads and was now feeling a bit sick too. Just saying 'tummy ache' gave her one. She slipped off the bed and started sorting through the comics. 'I'm going to put them in order and then we can read our favourite stories in the right order.'

'OK,' said Karen. 'I don't care what order they're in, though.'

'How can there have been thousands of issues of *Judy*? It must be so old.' Emmie soon had the comics sorted into their own piles. Her tummy ache had disappeared and she could read *Blind Ballerina* from the beginning. It was funny how so many people in the comics had really old-fashioned names like Carol. Nobody at school was called Carol. Carol was a mum's name. Would Karen be the sort of friend to help her to achieve her dream of being a dancer if she went blind? Emmie wondered. She hoped they would be able to find an empty hall where she could learn to dance again. Sue Namey would definitely move the scenery around to trick her.

'Why doesn't she just tell everyone she's blind?' said Karen, reading over her shoulder. But Emmie knew the rules. If you wanted to succeed in life you had to smile through tears. You had to conquer your worst qualities, like Darrell did her temper in *Malory Towers*. You had to be plucky and to treat your enemies well, even if they were as mean as Freda Winters and Gladys Payne in the comic. She put down the magazine and turned to the pile of *Tammy*s instead.

'When we get another dog, I might call it *Tammy*,' said Karen. 'It would suit a dog.' Emmie thought Karen would probably be too busy with her dogs to help anyone become a prima ballerina. And Karen was going to a different secondary school. Emmie was dreading that already.

*Bella at the Bar* was a bit more cheerful. They read on for a while and there were no sounds apart from pages turning and Karen chewing more Black Jacks and then a Curly Wurly.

'The only trouble with reading,' said Karen, 'is that it makes your elbows ache.' She sat up and flipped over onto her back.

'What I don't understand,' said Emmie, 'is how Bella keeps such short hair in bunches. Nobody with hair that short would have bunches, and if they did it would keep slipping out and there'd be a funny bit at the back that wouldn't reach to their bobbles. Maybe if she had three bunches. But that would look stupid.'

'Maybe gymnasts have some special tricks for hair as well,' said Karen. 'I mean, look at Olga Korbut. She has really short bunches and they stay in. Let's see who can stand on their head for the longest.'

They held the record for their class. They had once stood

on their heads at lunchtime in the school field for twenty-five minutes. They could have kept going until the bell rang but Mrs. Colley, the dinner lady, told them they had to stop because their faces were going too red. Emmie could still remember the feelings of victory and dizziness that had followed. They'd laid on the grass with the clouds and blue sky spinning around them.

They went out into the back garden and stood on their heads until Emmie's parents came back from the hospital.

# 1910s

## Fragment of Bone – Probably Herbivore. Origin Uncertain (Found Saskatchewan, Canada 1911)

The sky was too big. The land stretched away too far. Emmeline Ash watched Margaret march down the hill and away from her. If Margaret kept going (and Emmeline thought it quite likely that she would) she would reach the tip of Patagonia. Emmeline pictured the sturdy little figure of her daughter moving determinedly south down the map. There was only the flimsiest of fences at the edge of their land, and Edward was likely to have left their gate unsecured.

'Margaret!' she called. 'Stop!'

Nothing in the movement of the little fair head indicated that Margaret might have heard her mother.

'Stop!'

Margaret did stop to examine something, a stone or a leaf or an insect. For a minute Emmeline stayed where she was too, rocking in the chair on the veranda and watching her daughter. Between here and the tip of Patagonia was a lake, then a forest where there were bears and wolves, then the town, then more wilderness, lakes, the rest of Canada and the whole of the United States, Mexico... the rest of the Americas; she couldn't recall the order or placing of the countries now. Emmeline stood up. The baby was kicking or punching her. She felt too heavy to run. She brushed the dust from her skirts. When Edward got back, she would insist, really insist, that he fenced in an area around the house. Things were only going to get more difficult when the baby arrived. None of it was how she had imagined; but is anything ever how we imagine? It had been too big to imagine – Canada – an exciting new way in the world.

She set off after Margaret, at first willing her not to abandon whatever it was that she had found and start her determined march towards the southern hemisphere, but then checked herself. If Margaret sensed that she was being willed to do one thing, she would do the opposite. Emmeline hurried on, trying to keep her mind as white and clear as a sheet of ice so that her daughter could not detect what she wanted.

By some miracle, Margaret sat down in the dust. Emmeline felt like joining her. As she approached, she saw what it was that had halted Margaret's progress. It was a bone, or possibly, she hoped, a piece of antler. Margaret offered it up to her mother.

'Goodness, darling. What a lucky find…' Emmeline said. Her voice emerged as cracked and dry as the Canadian dust. 'Let's bring it back to the house and then you can show Father when he gets back…'

Margaret jumped up and started marching back up the hill. Emmeline could hardly keep up with her. She knew that later Margaret and Edward's fair heads would be bent over one of Edward's many books of natural history, as they tried to identify the thing. When they had decided what it was, Edward would write a label for it on a piece of card and they would put it into the little chest of drawers where Margaret kept her treasures. Emmeline would be alone in her own circle of lamplight, sewing clothes for the baby. Margaret was only four, but Edward talked to her as though she were his intellectual equal. Emmeline couldn't help but feel slightly annoyed, even jealous of this. The sickness that came with the baby had solidified, it seemed, and turned into something else, a sickness and longing that was hard to name. She had felt it before, on the boat, but never for so long, or with such intensity, and when she felt it, she sometimes thought she caught the dying notes of the ship's orchestra floating across the plains to her.

Years later, her great-granddaughter would find the postcard she had sent home. The breathlessness of the newlyweds was evident in the few lines Emmeline had written, and disguised the nausea she had felt even then:

*Today – our first iceberg – colossal and blue-white – unfathomable in its brightness.*

The sunlight had caught the iceberg in strange ways and seemed to be reflected back, as though the iceberg was illuminated from the inside, as though somebody had put a lantern inside it. Emmeline imagined a child somewhere like Finland or Greenland seeing the iceberg from the shore and carefully placing their lantern inside it, then watching as it was carried away. Emmeline had stood and watched as the ship was carried further and further away from the iceberg. Her gloved hands had seemed frozen to the rail, her booted feet frozen to the deck. She heard the orchestra begin to play.

'Come inside, Emmeline,' Edward had said. He had put one of his hands in their more substantial gloves over hers. 'Come inside, Emmeline, your tiny hands will be frozen.' She smiled but did not move. They were being carried ever onwards and the iceberg was floating away from them. She longed for it to come with them. Perhaps it could be captured and towed along behind them, perhaps all one had to do was ask.

'I have become rather fond of this iceberg,' she would tell one of the crew. 'Perhaps...' And the man would smile and say, 'But, of course...' and make immediate arrangements for the iceberg to be tethered and brought with them to Canada. It would tower behind the ship like a captured castle.

And then she realised why she could hardly bear to leave it behind. It wasn't just the crystalline beauty and mystery of it, the many planes of light; it was the illumination and the shape. It looked like Selfridges floating there, and it was getting further and further away from them. If they couldn't take the iceberg, then she'd ask for the ship to turn back. She knew it now, she couldn't go. She would long for Selfridges and home too much. She was twenty-three, newly married. She loved Edward, but... already there were buts. She loved Edward, but already she wished that their life together could be different. He was the fourth of five brothers and he must make his own way in the world. His family were importers of wheat and corn from around the world. Edward wanted to see what life was like at the other end of the line. They were going to make a new life as homesteaders. If only he were the eldest brother, or even the second or third one, they could have stayed at home. There was no imaginable calamity in 1911 that could elevate him into the position of eldest son (not that she would ever wish for such a thing) and allow their return. Emmeline tried to put the thoughts aside.

'Come inside,' Edward said again. 'There will be dancing...'

She smiled at him. She must be happy. She loved that they were going somewhere. The orchestra began another waltz.

Press the button to hear 'Che Gelida Manina (Your Tiny Hand Is Frozen)' from *La Bohème* sung by Enrico Caruso, a version enjoyed by Emmeline and Edward Ash.

## A Cabinet Used by a Child for 'Treasures' and 'Things Lost and Found' - Victorian Apprentice Piece

Edward returned just before dusk and Margaret ran down the track to meet him. He had supplies from the store eight miles away and news of the latest families to settle nearby, and what Emmeline longed for most: letters from home, even though she had no brothers or sisters of her own, and her mother's letters often had a querulous tone, as though the whole Canadian enterprise was some selfish folly. Emmeline would spend the evening reading and rereading the letters, trying to discern things that were not there between the bland lines about church and village matters and the health of people whom she sometimes struggled to picture. The letters took so long in transit that asking questions about small matters was pointless. Emmeline paid far more attention to the letters from Edward's family. She realised that she was reading them hoping for news of some miracle that would mean that their fortunes in England were assured, and that they could return home. But no such news ever came. With all those brothers, how could he possibly be needed for the business in England?

Margaret rode back up the track with Edward. Emmeline went out onto the veranda to meet them. Margaret was perched precariously on top of a large package. Emmeline saw how she was holding onto the string that bound it. The brown paper looked new and slippery. It couldn't be a parcel from home.

Edward jumped down from the trap and swung Margaret down too. Emmeline envied the lightness of their movements.

'My love, I have a present for you.'

'Letters?'

'Not just letters, something better.' He patted the package.

'And a present for me?' Margaret demanded.

'Of course, a present for you!' The package was soft and heavy in Emmeline's arms.

'Blankets?' she asked. 'We always need more blankets.'

'Warmer than blankets!' Emmeline sat down in a kitchen chair and waited for Edward to carry the supplies indoors. It looked as though he had a good haul. They had to buy what they could, when they could. They could never be sure that the store would have what they wanted when they wanted it. 'Open it!' said Edward. His pale green eyes were bright with excitement, almost as they had been on the night that they became engaged or when she had told him about each baby.

She untied the string and slipped her hand under the paper. She screamed and drew it back. The startled baby kicked.

'Dear Lord, what is it?' She could feel tears gathering.

'Darling, it's a coat, a fur coat for you and jacket for Margaret.' She peeled the paper back. The pelts were shiny and silvery, the fur deep. Emmeline stretched her hand out again and let it rest lightly on top of them.

'Fur coats! Fur coats!' Margaret sang, hopping from foot to foot.

'I thought it was something still alive, or something dead,' she said, then realised that it was. 'Thank you, but weren't they terribly expensive?'

'They would have been, but a trader left them with Ivor. They were samples, left as collateral, and he hasn't returned. Try them on! They don't have linings, but I thought you could do something about that.'

Emmeline nodded. She could imagine how hard it would be to sew through a pelt; there must be special needles, perhaps like the ones that upholsterers or sailmakers used.

Her fingers were so hot and tired and swollen at the moment. She couldn't attempt it until after the baby, and then she'd have to find something suitable for linings.

'Try them on!'

'Oh, Edward, it's so hot!' She knew how feeble she must sound, and how ungrateful. Edward unfolded the coats. Margaret had hers on in an instant.

'Darling, you look lovely, like a little Russian,' said Emmeline. 'Edward, it's perfect for her.'

'It's as soft as a puppy,' said Margaret. She stroked the sleeves. 'Mummy, put yours on.'

'Didn't they have one for you, Edward?' Emmeline asked, stalling, putting off the moment when she must stand up and put the heavy thing on.

'Just these,' said Edward. He looked away and Emmeline knew that there must have been others but that he wouldn't have wanted to spend the money on himself. Then he took her hand and helped her to her feet. He slipped the coat around her shoulders.

'Oh!' It wasn't nearly as heavy as it looked. She rubbed a sleeve against her face – so soft. The fur was dense, an upper layer of longer white strands overlaying the dark grey beneath. Without a lining, it was exactly like putting on the skin of an animal.

'What are they, Edward? Did he say?'

'Grey wolf,' he said. '*Canis lupus*.'

'I hope they don't come back for them.' They had heard the pack howling in the distance often enough.

Margaret took her jacket off, curled it round on itself, and placed it on the hearthrug. 'Look, a wolf cub asleep!' she laughed.

Edward laughed. Emmeline shuddered and shed the pelt that was now hers. She hung it on one of the rather stumpy pegs that Edward had made for the back of the door. The wolf at the door, the wolf inside the door.

'And Daddy, I've got something for you!' Margaret drew

the piece of antler or bone from her pocket. Edward opened his hand to take it.

'Thank you. This was probably a wolf's dinner. Or perhaps an Indian's or a settler's.'

The whole history of mankind, Emmeline thought, is a story of conquering and stealing and taking and selling, of finding ways to dominate, to enclose, and to slaughter. And the stew would be cooked by now. She could hardly bear to eat anything, but Edward and Margaret would be hungry. They all must eat.

After dinner, Edward and Margaret sat in a circle of lamplight, just as Emmeline had imagined. But she was too tired to read the letters more than once, or to attempt any sewing. She watched as Edward wrote a label for the bone: *Fragment of Bone (Probably Herbivore). Origin Uncertain* and Margaret laid it to rest in her cabinet. It shared a drawer with some dried moss, some buttons, and a piece of charcoal that they had found on the prairie.

A few days later, just before dawn, it started. She woke Edward straight away. He must go immediately to fetch help; the doctor, if possible, but most of all Louisa Lucas, who was kind and capable. Edward pulled his trousers on and rode off immediately; she watched from the veranda, his nightshirt billowed out behind him, making his back look huge. She wished he had taken Margaret with him, but she was still asleep. Emmeline willed her daughter to stay asleep, then tried to banish her from her mind lest the thoughts themselves woke her. The pains were still quite a way apart, but she knew that second babies often came quickly. She sat down in the rocking chair. At least it was still cool on the veranda. Rocking helped. She tried to drift back to sleep, knowing that it would be impossible. The sun was creeping towards her. She closed her eyes.

Fur swept across her clasped hands. She opened her

eyes. Margaret was there beside her, wearing the wolf jacket over her nightdress. Emmeline couldn't speak, another pain washed over her. When it had passed, she opened her eyes again and Margaret was still beside her but eating a piece of bread thickly spread with raspberry jam.

'Margaret,' she started, but another pain was coming, 'don't... get... it... on... your... coat.' When she opened her eyes again, she saw it was too late. Gobs of red had fallen into the fur.

'Mummy, is the baby coming? When will it be able to play with me?'

Emmeline groaned. 'Go inside. Please. Go inside. Daddy will be back soon. Please. Go and play inside.'

The next time she opened her eyes Margaret had disappeared. A sticky crust of bread lay on the floor beside the chair. Ants were swarming it already. Perhaps the ants would take the wolf skins. Perhaps the ants would take them all. When she opened her eyes again Edward was there with Louisa. They led her inside.


A baby boy. They called him James.

## 1913 Pocket Diary with Notes Written in Pencil, Approx. 3 ½ inches x 2 ½ inches

**January**

M told a story to J that began – 'Once there was a little boy called James who was very hardhearted, not to his family, but to bears…'

M hurt her knee. E offered to kiss it better. 'Oh no, that would only add to my sorrow. I do so hate getting wet.'

Edward's birthday. Margaret helped make and ice the cake. J enjoyed a slice.

**February**

Daffodils came out. M – 'I do seem to have seen these before.'

J using sentences – 'More egg for James' – 'James outside now.'

J drawing with chalks on paper.

M said 'All the goodness got together and that made God.'

M, after being read fairy tales – 'Mummy, how would you feel if you left J in a forest and then couldn't find him?'

## March
J walked right to the fence and back.

Telling M about the seaside – 'It's great fun in the sea. You would get wet through and then have to be changed.' 'Oh, Mother, what into?'

M, on the swing – 'Daddy! Keep your solid eyes on me!'

M – 'However fast you run you cannot get ahead or behind of Mr. Wind.'

## April
*Peter and Wendy* arrived for M, also Peter Rabbit Painting Book. Louisa observed that M has 'many natural affectations'. Could only laugh and agree.

## May
Remarked to M after bathing J 'What could be nicer than a clean little boy in a clean smock?' M replied 'Oh, Mother, anything. Any kind of dog or any book at all.'

M's birthday. A magnifying glass of her own. *Heidi* by Johanna Spyri, *The Tale of Timmy Tiptoes* and *The Tale of Mr. Tod.*

## June
Wheat in ear.
M retelling stories of Peter and Wendy and inventing her own.

J able to count to twenty.
J able to hold his own cup.

M brought him a cricket in a box 'for a present'.
I wish they could have an English education.

## July

M's song – Little blue flax buds under the moon
Open wide in the morning
Softly they sleep under the moon
Then open wide every day in the blue morning.

## August

21st – wheat cut.
M – 'I do love wearing white because then I seem to believe in fairies quite easily.'

J able to kick a ball to the fence and back. Sings 'Hey Diddle Diddle' with M.
*The Duck and The Kangaroo* arrived for his birthday from grandmother.

## September

New puppy. M named him Ben. M – 'I do think that when I look into his eyes, he is cleverer than we think.'
Picnic by the river, so so lovely. M said 'I can't eat my lunch because of all the beauty.'
J recognises 'J' and 'A'. M says he will soon be able to read, though never as well as she can.

## October

M: 'If we fly away to Neverland we will come back and talk to you through the window, but only sometimes.'
M writing her own book *The Story of a Very Brave Girl and Her Family*. We made a book for J to draw in, filled with swirls of orange. M said it is the story of a tiger.

## November

1st November. First snow. Children built a snowman 'to scare away wolves'.

**December**

*Alice's Adventures in Wonderland* for M.
*The Owl and The Pussy Cat* for J.
*Howards End* for me from E.
*The Lost World* for E.

# LATE 1970s

### Secondary School Class Photo (c. 1978)

Emmie loved 'When a Knight Won His Spurs', along with old-fashioned hymns like 'Praise, My Soul, the King of Heaven', 'Jerusalem' (even though it was completely nonsensical) and 'Dear Lord and Father of Mankind'. Everybody else liked 'Lord of the Dance', but she thought it was stupid. Jesus had never, as far as she knew, said that he was the Lord of the Dance or told everybody to dance. Some other songs seemed written specifically to embarrass her. When they sang 'The Ink is Black, The Page is White' in Assembly the whole school looked upon her, apart from the people who were looking upon Arun Choudhury who was in the year above her; but as his family had just moved to the area he was new and had no friends. He had the only Not English name in the school. Arun Choudhury. People called him a Paki. People asked Emmie if Arun Choudhury was her brother or her cousin. He was brown and she was brownish so they must be related.

Press the button to see 'Black and White' performed by Greyhound in 1971. The band and this performance are brilliant, but you can imagine why, when sung in Assembly, the song would make Emmie shrink.

He was on her bus home. Emmie had people to sit with, even though Karen had gone to the other school, along with, thank goodness, Sue Namey. Arun Choudhury did not.

He would sit on the lower deck, near the front. His hair was deep black, truly black, unlike Emmie's which was dark brown but looked reddish if the sun caught it. His hair was thick and straight. Emmie's had stubborn waves and would go frizzy in the rain. His did not go frizzy. Sometimes she sat behind him on the bus (by chance not by design) and studied the back of his head. He never had flakes of dandruff on his collar. He did not have spots on the back of his neck. So many of the boys Emmie knew had hideous spots, real pustules, particularly on their foreheads and emerging from the collars of their shirts, and yet people did not despise them or spit at them. The back of Arun Choudhury's neck was a very deep brown. Emmie knew that hers went as dark in the summer.

'The back of your neck is practically black!' people would tell her. She didn't like to think of people studying the blackness of her neck if they were standing behind her in Assembly, or sitting behind her on the bus, though she sat behind Arun Choudhury on the bus and looked at the back of his neck, which she did really like to do as his skin was so smooth and clean-looking. As he was a year above her, she had never spoken to him. Not once. He got off a few stops before her, and she watched out of the corner of her eye as the bus pulled away and he scurried off, quickly putting as much distance as he could between himself and the bus, knowing that he must avoid missiles and the jeers of the kids who were on the top deck, yelling and gobbing out of the windows.

She didn't get that treatment. She would always fear it, but she had yet to get it. She didn't know why. Was it because she was a paler shade of brown? Was it because she was a girl, and so people treated her more kindly or saw her as less of a threat? Could it have been because people had seen her mum, back when her mum had been well enough to do all the normal things?

'Do I look different?' Emmie asked after school one day. That afternoon she had watched as a can had sailed through the air and landed just in front of Arun Choudhury, splattering him in what she hoped was only coke. He had pretended not to notice and had hurried on, head down. If I have a son, Emmie thought, he will not wear a stupid mac with a belt and epaulettes. He will not carry a brown leather music case for a school bag. He will have something trendy. He will have what everybody else has or wants. I will help him to look ordinary, like everybody else.

'We all look different,' her mum said. 'You just look like you.'

But it was easy for her to say that. And Emmie felt different. She was more different than other people.

'Look!' her mum had said, holding up Emmie's class photo. 'Everybody's different!'

But when Emmie looked at the photo only a few people stood out. There was George Rutter who was fat, Debbie Dooley who had ginger hair (the sort of red that went with green eyes and that Emmie would have loved because it was like Anne of Green Gables' hair), Darren Toon who stood out because he was very small, and Benedict Kent who was really lanky; but she was the only one who stood out because of the colour of her skin. Emmie glanced down at her wrists which were sticking bonily out of the acrylic cuffs of her school cardigan. Her skin was sort of dark beige, like the colour of old ladies' coats. It was the colour people called 'camel'. She walked over to the mirror above the fireplace and looked into her own dark brown eyes. Perhaps she looked like a camel. The thought made her laugh out loud. They had been doing the story of Jacob and Rachel and Leah in RE. Mr. Ormond said that Leah was cow-eyed, meaning that she must have had big brown kind eyes. Emmie thought it was awful to be called cow-eyed, even if it was meant as a compliment. She worried that her eyebrows were going to join up in the middle. People said that that was a sign of schizophrenia or being mad, like Heathcliff in *Wuthering Heights*. Mrs. Millet said that Heathcliff was a gypsy or a foreigner, that his shadowy origins were used by Emily Brontë to emphasise the darkness of his character. Did people think that she had a dark character? She had felt like putting her hand up and asking if Mrs. Millet thought that everybody dark had a dark character, if everybody in Africa and India and all of those places had dark natures because their skin was dark, but of course she didn't want to draw attention to herself. She'd learnt her lesson after the Noah's Ark incident.

She picked up the hairbrush and pulled it through her thick brown curls. She used the blunt end of a pencil to get her parting straight. Her hair parted naturally to the left of the centre. She pulled it back as tightly as she could, as neatly as possible, and fastened it into a ponytail. Her mum appeared in the mirror behind her looking even paler and thinner than usual.

'Emmie,' she sighed, 'do you want to look beautiful and exotic, or plain and ordinary?'

'Plain and ordinary!' Emmie cried, and ran upstairs.

When the next school year started, Arun was no longer on the bus. She sometimes saw him cycling with some sort of musical instrument strapped to his back. She was pleased he didn't have people throwing things at him anymore. And, when she saw him at break or in the corridor, he seemed to have made some friends – as much as boys seemed to have friends anyway. He still had lovely skin that never got spots.

# 1980s

## Brown Leather Lace-up School Shoes (c. 1980)

Mum was in hospital again, so Emmie and her dad set out with the list for school. They had the blouses and the skirt and the hockey boots, the PE skirt and the Aertex blouses. Last year's cardigans would still do. Only the shoes remained.

'We're getting quality,' Dad said. 'I don't want them breaking after a few weeks.'

They went to K Shoes. She had been hoping for Dolcis or Freeman Hardy Willis. A man as skinny and shiny as a shoehorn knelt and measured her feet.

'She's a 6, but we'll see if we can get away with a 6 ½ or a 7 to last longer,' he said.

'Dad…' pleaded Emmie, the moment the man had disappeared again. 'I don't like any of the shoes here.'

'Let's just be quick and then we can go and visit your mum.'

The shoehorn man was back with three boxes.

'Buckles or laces?' he asked.

'Um,' said Emmie.

The first pair had straps and looked like the sort of shoes her Geography teacher would wear.

'Not those,' said Emmie.

Out came the next pair. They were black and flat and very long.

'These are a 7 ½ but they come up small.'

'I think they're for boys,' said Emmie. 'Or clowns.' Her

dad looked at his watch. The next pair were brown and bulbous with laces and hideous big chunky heels.

'Dad,' said Emmie, 'they look like giant conkers.'

'Just right for the autumn term,' said the man.

'Um, are there any others?' Emmie asked, feeling desperate.

'Emmie, please try some on.' She put on the clown shoes. There was no way they would fit.

'Hmm, take a little walk,' said the man. Emmie eyed the shop door. Flap, flap, flap.

'We could try them with an insole.'

'No, no,' said her dad. 'We want a proper fit. Try some others, Em.'

It was impossible to say which of the other pairs was the least bad. Perhaps neither would fit. But the bulbous conkers did.

'Take a walk,' said the man. She clomped across the room and back.

'I feel too tall,' said Emmie.

'We'll take them,' said her dad.

# Pifco Princess Box (Manufactured Early 1970s)

The ward was in a prefab hut with an asbestos roof, like one of the oldest classrooms at school, but it went on for much longer and the windows didn't open. It stretched on and on like a building in a dream. The curtains around each bed were patterned with grey-leaved tulips and daffodils. The flowers were yellow. Emmie suddenly couldn't remember if you could get yellow tulips. It seemed likely that the curtains would have flowers in an unnatural colour.

They had brought some real flowers from the stall outside. Emmie was carrying them; water from their stems was leaving a trail of drips like the crumbs in *Hansel and Gretel*. They kept walking and walking. Emmie worried that one day she might not recognise her mum and accidentally go straight past, but then there she was. She looked very asleep, but not how she looked when she was asleep on one of the loungers in the garden. Her honey-coloured hair was spread over the pillow but it didn't look like Sleeping Beauty's hair, the way it should. It was darker and thinner now. Emmie wondered if her mum would have been able to wash it. She didn't have her hairdryer here because it was still at home. Its Pifco Princess box was on the shelf in her parents' bedroom, although the hairdryer lived on the dressing table. Emmie was fascinated to the point of repulsion by the picture on the box. A woman in the palest pink smiled out from behind a branch of blossom. Her hair was the same colour as Emmie's mum's but had been dried and styled, presumably with the Pifco Princess, so that it was smooth and shiny and the ends flicked upwards all the way round. The curls looked firm enough to hang things on – mugs or kitchen implements or pairs of scissors. Emmie knew that when she was grown up, however skilled she got with a Pifco Princess, she would never look that perfect, smooth and neat. Her hair would never be straight or curl in places that it was meant to. The box was full of things that her mum kept but didn't use, things that Emmie had liked to look at when she was little. Everything had a thin coating of powder because there was a compact in there that had belonged to Emmie's granny before she died and the powder in it had cracked and spilled. And there were lipsticks that her mum said had been a mistake, buttons, gift tags, a card that had come with some flowers, though the writing had faded away so you couldn't see who they had been from – her dad, Emmie supposed – and a pair of tiny white leather shoes that had once been her own. 'Pram shoes,' her mum always said. 'And when I took you on the bus everyone smiled and said, "Just like a little doll."' Emmie's reins from when she was a toddler were there too. These were made of pale blue leather and had very many buckles so that the fit would be perfect. On the bit that went over the child's chest was a picture of a puppy with a big head next to a teddy and three bricks – A, B, C. The box also held bits of broken jewellery that Emmie had once thought might be really valuable – a paste diamond necklace with a broken clasp, huge clip-on earrings with clusters of pearls as big as grapes, a purse that had been her granny's, brown silk with a gold clasp and a neat little oblong mirror inside. Emmie wished that she was at home and little again and playing with the things in the box while her mum talked about them all.

Her mum's mouth was slightly open but her eyes were closed. She was wearing the nightdress they'd bought her at C&A. It had a collar like the frill around the legs of dead things that you saw in butchers' windows. Emmie tried not to look at those but sometimes she couldn't help it. She hated those weird bright green plastic leaves too. And this nightdress had sprigs on as well; little pink flowers with greyish-blue leaves. Why hadn't they done the leaves green? They were nearly as bad as the curtains. She liked pink and green together. She had wanted them to get a silky green nightdress. It was much nicer – a sort of pale jade like some beads that Aunt Lucinda had once given her mum. It was the sort of nightdress that her mum usually wore, but Dad had said that they had been told to get sensible ones, ones with sleeves. They had bought two the same.

There was a chair with a red plastic seat next to her mum's bed. Each bed had just one chair. Emmie wondered what they were meant to do. A nurse had once tutted at her for sitting on the bed. It wasn't as though she could sit on her dad's lap. She was much too old for that now. They stood together next to the bed.

'Mum,' Emmie whispered. There was no answer. Emmie checked and she could just see her mum's chest moving up and slowly down under the sheets.

'Pammy,' her dad whispered. Neither of them touched her. 'Pammy…'

'Mum,' said Emmie and reached out and touched her hand.

Other visitors were arriving for the other patients. Visiting hours were from 3pm until 6pm which meant that they couldn't come very often because of work and school.

Emmie felt the water from the flowers dripping onto her hideous new shoes. She glanced back and saw the trail of drips on the grey linoleum going around the bed and reaching back the way they had come. People might think she had wet herself. Or what if a nurse carrying a load of needles and medicines slipped, or one of the patients got out of bed and then fell over and died. There was nowhere to put the flowers and no way to stop them dripping, apart from by using her own clothes. She pulled the cuff of her school cardigan down over her right hand. It was extra baggy because without Mum at home it had missed out on being washed. She was able to grab and ball up enough sleeve to catch the water and stop the flowers dripping onto the floor. She wondered about taking the cardigan off and using it to mop the floor. It already looked like the string mops they used at school and would soon turn into one. She expected that the hospital had those mops too. It was surprising that they made anything clean. Mr. Gunnersby, the school caretaker, had a huge broom too, much wider than people's brooms at home, so that he could sweep up the school hall in double-quick time. Emmie had once accidentally stepped in his sweepings and he'd yelled 'Oi! Mind my dust!' at her. He was always shouting at people but she still worried that he bore a grudge against her and she avoided him whenever she could.

Her mum opened her eyes.

'Emmie... Jay...'

They both leant over and kissed her.

'Come on the bed, honey,' she whispered to Emmie. Emmie perched. 'Lie down next to me.'

'I don't want to squash you, Mum.'

'I'm very tough,' her mum said and then laughed, but the laugh turned into a cough.

Emmie's dad passed her a glass of water from the plastic jug. When the coughing had stopped, Emmie lay down on the bed. She dangled her feet off the side so that her shoes didn't go on the white sheets.

'School shoes?' asked Mum.

'Don't worry. We got the whole list,' said Dad. Mum nodded.

'Show me,' she said.

Emmie got back up and stepped away from the bed so that her mum could see her shoes. Her mum pulled a face, and suddenly she looked like herself again.

'Jay,' she said, 'you have to let Emmie choose her own shoes.' Emmie unlaced the hideous conkers and put them under the bed. She lay down again and cried into her mum's pillow.

# LATE 1920s –
# EARLY 1930s

**Three Postcards Sent from a Young Man
to His Mother**


(postmarked 15 August 1929)

*Climbing "The Nose" Pillar Rock (Abrahams' Series)*

*We climbed on Gable on Thursday. Yesterday Scafell.
Having a very nice time.
Love,
James*


(postmarked 8 August 1930)

*Snowdon from Carned Llewelyn. – Snowdon 3,560 feet. Highest
mountain in Wales, seen from above the paths of men, where the
clouds gather.*

*We did the Great Gully on Friday. It is fine today. I will
make the list. We seem short of large plates. Will be on the
later bus Sunday. Harry has terrible blisters.
Love,
James*

*Llyn Boclywd and Llyn Idwal from Tryfan – Llyn Boclywd is 1,806 feet above sea level, the summit of Tryfan, a picturesque mountain commanding the Nant Ffrancon, is 2,780 feet high.*

*We have a lovely day for our first climb. If possible, could you send a few nails from the right top drawer in the passage room chest – Harry needs them for his boots. Thank you.*
*Love,*
*James*

## Letter Sent by a Newly Arrived Tea Garden Manager to His Family (1933)

*The Bungalow*
*Garden 1*
*Sonajuli*
*Assam*
*India*

*May 17th*

*Dear Mother and Father,*
*Arrived safely three days ago. I hope you received mine sent en route. By miracle my things have made it here too. I lost count of the number of trains. At each change bearers appeared and seemed to know whose luggage was whose and where it should go. I haven't been ill yet but McKenzie says it's only a matter of time. I had thought that he lived here but he's at the neighbouring garden where most of the packing is done. There are a couple of other fellows, Anders and Woods, who look after the machinery. We meet in the evenings sometimes. They share a bungalow and seem to keep to themselves. McKenzie is staying for a couple of weeks to show me the ropes. The bungalow is not bad at all. Quite large, good bathrooms and many servants long established. One is employed just to sweep. Mosquito nets a must. Tell Margaret I have managed not to step on a snake yet – or seen any. McKenzie says there*

*are plenty right here – pythons (rock and reticulated) and king cobra the biggest, also vipers, various kraits, and many smaller but equally deadly. The bungalow is raised because of them but I check my shoes before I put them on etc. as vicious spiders too. On a cheerier note, elephants are used in the garden. Perhaps they will soon seem as ordinary as horses. Wild ones are a nuisance. Plucking is from March to November so things are at full pelt.*

*I thought I'd made good progress with Hindi on the way over but find that Bengali and Assamese might be more useful and workers speak a combination as they come from different places and tribes. I can see the company lines where most live from the bungalow, and beyond that, jungle. It's summer now. Monsoon in a couple of months. Winter (after monsoon) said to be most pleasant. Five years feels like a long time, but don't worry about me. It's all going pretty well. There's a club where chaps can meet up, but at some distance, and a local part-time outfit that sounds like OTC but with more games, hunting, etc. Will join that too so it's not all work and no play.*

*I'll write more soon. Hope you are all well.*

*Love from,*

*James*

# 1930s

## Photograph of Some Indian Dancers
## (Mid- to Late 1930s)

The first time Josmi saw him she was just a girl. He had sat proudly on his horse, acting the rajah already, as her brother put it. And they all noticed his thick moustache that looked like a broom or as though it had been made from clippings of the horse's tail. He had thick dark hair, and he was brown from the sun already. He might soon look like one of them, except of course he was taller and heavier. He swung himself down from the horse and smiled at them all. Mr. Woods and Mr. Anders were there too. He said a few words in Hindi and they all smiled and managed not to laugh.

'I'm very pleased to meet you all. My name is Mr. Ash. I am the new manager.'

Her uncle, who was quite senior in the garden, had stepped forward and replied in English that they would all do all they could to make him welcome and assist him. Mr. Ash had looked very relieved. What had he expected, that none of them would be able to speak the language of the company? She had watched as his boxes were unloaded and carried into his bungalow. That night he had looked so happy and content, sitting on his veranda smoking his pipe and drinking a glass of something golden.

They all hoped that he wasn't going to be a drinker like the last one, Mr. Campbell, who had pickled himself. He'd had horrible orange hair and skin that had turned bright red. They'd heard that the company had sent him back to Britain or somewhere because he'd been too ill to carry on, or perhaps he'd fallen down drunk too many times, even for a Britisher. This Mr. Ash couldn't be much worse or more useless than him.

Mr. Ash didn't notice her until she was older. She had been just another one of the pickers' children, destined to be a picker herself. If she hadn't been one of the dancers when some important British lady was visiting, he might never have noticed her at all.

James sat at the table on the veranda and began to write:

*The Bungalow*
*Garden 1*
*Sonajuli*
*Assam*
*India*

*May 28th 1936*

*Dear Mother,*
*I thought that you might like these photographs of Lady Huntsford's visit to the garden. It all went off very well. All v. pleased with the way the garden was looking, workers content, dancing display, tea at club, etc. We had the children spell out 'welcome' when she arrived, though you may not be able to tell that from the picture. That's the Bishop of Assam on the right of her. Woods and Anders standing behind. Also enclosed is one of the dancers – they were jolly good and went down well with all.*

James wondered if perhaps the visit might result in promotion. Everything in the garden had been running perfectly, the workers were looking happy, he had talked about how production was up by a third since he'd taken over (he didn't mention that this was inevitable as it was so appalling under Campbell's management). Lady Huntsford had pronounced the dancers delightful. He stopped writing. There were, as usual, many things that he wouldn't mention to his mother.

One dancer had stood out, a girl of around eighteen, he supposed, whose limbs seemed more sinuous, whose fingers in the dance seemed so long and delicate, like the fingers of a harpist or some seventeenth-century lady in a portrait. He imagined those fingers drumming on his back, those limbs entwined around him. He thought of the statues he'd seen in temples. This was what men in his position did. He'd been here three years and had held out long enough. The day after the visit he had asked for the dancers to be sent to him so that he could thank them for their performance.

They waited a few feet back from the veranda. He spotted her at once. Yes, she was different. There was something that seemed luminous about her, her skin was more golden than that of her companions, her cheekbones were higher. Her eyes were downcast. How old was she? Not too young, he hoped. He made a little speech about how well the visit had gone, thanked them all and gave them some money, asked them all their names and how old they were. But he only listened to her reply.

Her name was Josmi. She was seventeen years old. He thanked them all again and dismissed them, but as they turned to go, he called her back.

'Josmi, would you remain here a moment? You others can go back to your work.' They left. He knew that there would be nudging and giggling from her companions. He spoke to her in Assamese. 'Do you speak English?'

'A little, sir.'

He continued in Assamese.

'Are you happy in your work as a picker?'

'Yes, sir, we are all happy.'

'Are you married?'

'No, sir. Not yet.' He saw her give a little smile. There was quite likely some arrangement made or in progress. He hoped it wasn't with anybody she cared for.

'I am looking for a housekeeper. I have my people who cook and clean, but there is a room here and work for a housekeeper. You would earn more than as a picker and live here in comfort with me. You'd have your own room and the duties would not be too onerous. Would you like to come and see? Shall I talk to your parents about it?'

'My parents are dead, sir. You could talk to my uncle or my brothers. My uncle is the letter writer. He taught me some English.'

'Very good. Come inside.'


Josmi followed him up the steps and across the veranda. She had never been inside the bungalow before. Her family's house would have fitted inside the first room. There was a large soft rug on the floor, and so many chairs and sofas for just one man, all alone. There were cases of books and a clock that was taller than she was. Why would anybody need such a tall clock? There were some dusty vases and a desk with its top open, papers and envelopes sticking out of little drawers and boxes. There were photographs of British people: a woman, quite pretty in an old-fashioned dress, like something a queen would have worn, and a stern-looking man with a beard. She guessed they must be his parents. In another photo Mr. Ash and another British man and two British girls (one very plain) were standing in some hilly place, drinking out of small glasses. Another showed the plain British girl with her hair in two plaits coiled around her ears. In another they were sitting on a rug with a big basket of food. The prettier one was smiling up at the photographer. She had light-coloured hair cut straight and short.

'My sister and her friend in Cambridge,' said Mr. Ash.

Josmi smiled politely and wondered what to say. He led her into a room with a big table and uncomfortable-looking chairs. No wonder Mr. Ash was lonely if he had to eat in here all by himself every night. Pictures of places in Britain hung around the room. She would have liked to look at each one, but he led her on. The kitchen was also large and with more pans and things than anybody could need.

'You cook well?' he asked.

'My uncle and aunt think so.'

'My cook is getting old, I think he could do with some help. His rooms are out there,' he said, indicating across the yard with a jerk of his head.

'Yes, sir.' Only men worked in the manager's house. Didn't he know that?

He showed her more rooms; a little one for storing food, another with sofas and rugs.

'I don't often come in here,' he said. She nodded. Imagine having rooms that you didn't need, that you didn't bother to come into! Beyond that was a small room with nothing in it at all, just a low bed. A window with a blue curtain looked out towards the tea garden where she would normally be hard at work. There was a mirror on the wall with a dark wooden frame carved into a pattern of leaves; the glass was spotted with age. She caught a glimpse of herself in it. He was behind her. Their eyes met in the mirror. It was hard to judge his expression because his moustache hid much of his mouth, but then he smiled.

'This could be your room,' he said. 'We could have other furniture moved in here if you wanted it, a dressing table perhaps…'

She found herself nodding. Did that mean she had agreed? Did she have a choice anyway?

'Let me show you the rest of the house.'

She followed him and saw four more rooms, three of them bedrooms. He had space for many visitors. The ceilings sloped, and because he was so tall, there were places where he wasn't able to stand upright. In a bathroom there was a huge white bath. It looked so cool, and she stared longingly at it. His shaving things had been left out on the sink. She averted her gaze from them, but only after she'd seen the brush which was stiff and bristly in shades of grey and white and must be made from the fur of some animal. She wondered if his moustache would look like that when he was older.

She realised the last room was his bedroom. There was a quilt on his bed, and she couldn't help but walk over and look at it. It was made from many different shades and patterns of greens and browns, some looked as though they had been cut from the sort of dresses British ladies wore, or from tablecloths or curtains, but all together they looked beautiful.

'My mother and sister and her friend made it for me,' he said.

'It's very pretty, sir.'

Around the room were shelves of books and more books piled up on the floor in every corner. He certainly needed somebody to dust and to try to put all of these books away. More photos lined the walls; in some, teams of men were lined up in rows wearing different sporting uniforms, in others there were the people from the other photos. In one, the lady who looked like his sister and the bigger lady were sitting on a bench that curved around a tree trunk. She realised that she was staring and backed away towards the door. None of the girls she knew had been inside Mr. Ash's house. She didn't know what she would tell them when they asked her about it. Going inside with him meant that she was different and that people would talk and treat her differently. She supposed that it was all very ordinary for a British man. It would make no difference to him.

James wondered how to continue his letter. He couldn't possibly tell them. How would he put it? *And by the way, I have arranged for a pretty seventeen-year-old Indian girl to move in as my housekeeper. I have yet to inform her of the full range of her duties.* Josmi wouldn't be his first; there had been girls from the town in Oxford, others during spells on leave in Calcutta. It was pretty much inevitable for a man in his position. Managers were expected not to marry until after five years of service. By that time, most of them had a woman in the house and children stashed away somewhere. He put thoughts of Lucinda Theodore away and signed and sealed the letter.

There wasn't much for Josmi to do in the day at first. It quickly became clear that she wasn't expected to do much work, and that she was allowed to do as she pleased. She liked to take long baths, filling it more and more each day. Mr. Ash said that she should call him James, and after a while she did. She ate with him, but only if there were no visitors. When Mr. Woods and Mr. Anders came over, she disappeared. She liked sewing and he loved to watch in the evenings. He talked, she listened. As she got to know him better, she said more. He was always polite to her. She soon realised what her position at the house was going to be. She wondered what would have happened if she had tried to tell him to stop. But she didn't. He was a very kind and gentle man. She didn't want to.

Nobody came to visit her, not her brothers or their wives. They must have known what Mr. Ash was intending, and yet they had seemed quite happy for her to be taken like that. If her parents had been alive, would they have said no? Or would they have thought it a good position for her – she had been given a home and a wage higher than a picker's. Would they have worried about what might happen to her or just been pleased that she wasn't their responsibility anymore? But people respected Mr. Ash. It wasn't as though her brothers had given her away to Mr. Falling Over Drunk All The Time Campbell. Josmi thought of that man's peeling pink skin, the way that his head looked as though it had been boiled, the smell of his breath, and his fat red fingers pinching the pickers' arms and cheeks on the rare occasions he had anything to do with the tea. They had all been pleased when Mr. Campbell finally went.

Nobody really thought that Mr. Ash would turn out like that. He was much busier and more in control. They hadn't seen him lose his temper over nothing. He wasn't found dead drunk on his veranda. He didn't sleep in his clothes and have whisky for breakfast. Even his skin seemed better suited to India. But Mr. Ash didn't always seem happy. He seemed like an actor who had wandered onto the wrong stage and was looking for a way to leave without anybody noticing. Josmi thought he seemed most content when he had something particular to do; preparations for a visit by his bosses or some grand person from England. He seemed to love it when a tiger or a leopard took the goats from the village and he had to organise parties to go after them. It had taken three days to find the last tiger. But when he and the men had come back with the tiger hanging upside down from a great branch with its huge pink tongue lolling out, he'd just looked sad, even though all the villagers were cheering. He hadn't wanted anything to do with the skin, so the men on the hunt had been able to sell it and share the money. Her eldest brother had laughed and said, 'What kind of British man shoots something, and then doesn't want it?' Perhaps, Josmi thought, the kind of British man who takes someone and then throws her away.

They said that James had been a dead shot. That he'd potted the tiger the moment that he'd caught a glimpse of it, and that he'd been holding the rifle awkwardly, the left-handed way, even though he was right-handed, almost as though he had wanted to give it a chance to get away.

*August 9th 1936*

*Dear Mother,*
*I hope you're all well and had a good time at the cottage. Wish I could join you for a dose of the Welsh mountains and a swim in a cold lake. All going well here. I'm enclosing a picture of the new horse I've taken on for rough polo. She's turning out very well. I rode her down to watch them bathing the working elephants in the river yesterday but didn't think to take my camera – you would enjoy seeing that. Lucky I was there – a little boy got swept away – the father plunged after him but the river was too fast and both were swept downstream. I was able to ride along the bank and pull them both out – scared but no harm done. You wanted to know who the dancers in the photograph were – those dancers are nobody.*
   *Please tell Father thanks for the book. I'll write more soon.*
   *All love,*
   *James*

## Fragments of Broken China, Various Origins
## (Mostly 19<sup>th</sup> and Early 20<sup>th</sup> Century)

Sometimes James would be gone for several days, away to the town to meet with people and to see about the tea or with other British men to their camps. When he came back, even if he said that things had gone well, he would seem sad, restless. She wondered what he had been doing. He would bring her nice things; often the sorts of things that a British lady would want. Her favourites were a brush and comb set with a mirror, a blue glass bowl with a lid that he'd said was for powder (she might ask him to get her some powder next time), and a set of silver and blue bangles.

She had the feeling that when he bought them, he was pretending that they were for a British lady; his mother or his sister – the one in the photograph with the peculiar plaits – or for some other wife, a British wife.

They called the baby James, Jay for short. Once he'd arrived, James brought back more presents for him than he did for her. James would buy useful things – the things she had asked for. But she wished that she could go with him to choose them. She knew that she would make better bargains. James had plenty of money – some he kept in the house, and much more that he kept in a bank, though she didn't know where. She had asked him to take her with him once, in the early days, but he had just given a short bark, a bitter laugh, and said that he would like nothing better than for her to go with him, but that it was completely impossible, there was nowhere for her to stay.

'Nowhere in that whole big town?'

'You could not stay at the Club, and that is where I have to stay. It wouldn't be right for you to stay somewhere else and you can't stay there, so it's impossible. Maybe one day it will be possible, but I can't see things ever changing, not in our lifetimes, anyway. It would take a revolution. It's a crazy world.'

'I hate it when you go away. I think people are laughing at me.'

'Of course, they're not. Why would anybody laugh at you?'

She didn't answer, but they both knew why. He had put her in an impossible position. And what if he went away forever? He might go away and never come back. She had heard of it happening to other girls, people's cousins who were taken on as housekeepers to be given the role of invisible wife. And then the manager was moved to another garden or went back to England and left his Indian family behind. Sometimes an English lady would arrive and take over being the wife. But it was better than picking tea all day long, the sun beating down on her, her fingers and neck aching. And now she had little Jay.

Jay had far more toys than she or her brothers had ever had, toys that he was mostly far too young to play with. James brought back painted puppets – a horse and a prince – but a baby would only break them, so she hung them up where Jay could see but not reach them. There were balls and a cricket bat that was nearly as tall as Jay was, and he saw to it that although Jay had the cheap cotton clothes that the pickers' children wore to play in, he also had some smarter clothes made, little versions of the clothes that he wore himself. Jay soon had more possessions than she had owned in her whole life.

'I'll get him a bicycle,' James told her. 'Every boy must have one.'

Her brothers had never had bicycles. Her nephews didn't have bicycles. Jay would be a child apart. She wondered where there might be other children like him, children for him to play with.

Josmi felt tired and different now – not like the girl James had chosen – and she worried that he might send her away, that he might keep Jay and get rid of her or send them both away. She remembered other pickers pointing out a girl who had been working nearby; her name had been Lakshmi, but they didn't call her that. They said that she had been taken on by a British man but that he had died suddenly and she'd been turned out of the house the very next day. This Lakshmi had been pregnant, but none of the Britishers had cared. The baby had died before it was born and she had ended up back with her parents, who didn't want her, and with nothing. Josmi had seen how hard this girl had worked. People barely spoke to her, and she just kept picking, picking. People said that it was lucky that she had lost the baby.

When James was out on the estate and Jay was asleep, Josmi slept too or she sewed. She embroidered and mended and made things they didn't need and garments that wouldn't fit Jay for years. She made clothes for her brother's family. She would wrap them up and ask Ravi, the cook, to see that they got them. No message of thanks ever came back, but she was pleased when she saw them being used. The cloth she used was nicer, finer but stronger, than the sort that other people could afford.

She loved it when people called at the house selling things; she would keep them for as long as possible, giving them cold drinks and asking to see everything, dithering over fabrics in two very similar shades of pale yellow or almost identical sets of buttons. They were happy for her to take her time – they knew that she would buy plenty.

Josmi loved to sit rocking in the wicker chair on the veranda, staring out across the garden. She could see the lines moving up and down, up and down, and beyond them the village. Sometimes, although she hadn't forgotten how the work made every part of her ache, she thought of joining the pickers again so that she could listen to the chatter and maybe join in a little, but nobody would trust her now. Even though people thought James was a good manager, nobody would ever talk freely in front of her again.

From her position on the veranda, Josmi tried to make out which house had been her parents'. It had been on the edge of the village, and behind it a path led up into the forest. All the children liked to follow that path to a clearing where there was a view out over the valley. There were loose rocks and boulders and the big boys had pushed them into a semi-circle and built a fort. It looked out over the tea gardens and they could see for miles. They played soldiers, firing sticks and stones onto the ever-present enemies below. Josmi would slip away by herself. A little further up the path was another smaller clearing. This was hers. She had found treasures to decorate it – smooth stones, flowers, pieces of things that people had thrown away. Her best treasures had been the pieces of china that she'd found at the end of the path near where the old managers' houses had been. It seemed that whenever something had broken, the servants had thrown it out into the undergrowth. Now Josmi wondered whether those servants had been hiding the evidence of broken dishes and teacups. It must have been going on for as long as there had been a house and nice things to get broken, because there were pieces of blue, green and brown glass and china with several different patterns. She could never spend too long looking in case someone spotted her and asked what she was doing, but each time she passed she picked up any piece that she could find. Neither her brothers nor her friends were interested in old broken things, so she did it by herself, and carried the fragments up to the little clearing where she arranged them in patterns, pressing them into the ground in circles and spirals, always leaving a pattern unfinished so that there was space to carry on when she returned with more pieces. She liked the blue and green glass much better than the brown, though she washed each piece with equal care in the stream. The china fragments were the real treasures. She liked to mix the pieces up and see how they looked next to each other. Her favourite had a pair of blue birds on it and there were others that seemed to have come from the same plate with sections of a garden and a bridge. Perhaps, she thought, she could recreate that garden in the clearing and some blue birds would come and live there with her. Other pieces had flowers and leaves, but she loved the blue birds most of all.

Now, she sat on the veranda and looked up to where the clearing must be and wondered whether her garden was still there. Other children might have taken it over or destroyed it, or the rain might have washed it away. She thought that she might take Jay with her one day to look.

James's family was coming to visit soon. She wondered what they would be like.

She got up from her chair and went back inside. Jay would be asleep for a little while yet. Ravi was nowhere to be seen. She went into the kitchen. Flies were circling. She opened the window and shoed them out, flapping at them with one end of her dupatta because she couldn't see anything else to use. She opened a cupboard and stared at the teacups and saucers, the dishes, bowls and plates. There were plenty that they never used. She took a plate from near the bottom of a pile. It was white with green and gold lines around the edge. They never used this plate. She turned it over. There was some English writing on the bottom. She carried it outside and dropped it on the hard earth. It broke in two – not enough pieces to be pretty. It was border bits she really wanted with the green and gold. She tried again and this time there were plenty of fragments. She gathered them all up and folded them into a corner of her dupatta. She could hear Jay calling for her. His naps were getting shorter but she didn't mind. She hid the broken china under some cloth in her sewing box and hurried upstairs. If some more things got broken, they could make their own little treasure garden.

You might as well now turn to Emmeline's letter to her daughter:

**Letter from a Mother to Her Daughter.**
**Posted from India to England (1938)**

*Sonajuli*
*Assam*
*India*

*Dear Margaret,*
*We arrived safely and were met, just as James had promised, by a boy from the company. He helped us locate our luggage before driving us here – a drive which was very long and dusty. I'll spare you the details, but your father was unwell, doubtless due to the climate, which is, of course, oppressive, and the food, which is somehow exactly as we expected and yet nothing like. The dishes we had thought of as Indian now seem anything but.*

*I trust that you are well and not too exhausted by your extra hours at the library. You were quite right that the climate wouldn't suit you here, but we all miss you and James had got it into his head that you would come.*

*James eats curry at most meals – there is very little choice here. I'm sure that one would get used to it and even quite enjoy it after a while. He says that he used to long for something plain. I keep thinking of Becky Sharp biting into that chilli, thinking it was named for being chilly. James's days are long and often hard. The workers look to him to settle disputes, and often queue up to petition him about the most trivial things, but he deals with it all very well. He says sometimes the days seem all the same and that he rides out in the evening for some more English company. He is rather isolated here. The other men are friendly but not really his type.*

*James came out to meet us, having got word that we were not far off – some sort of bush telegraph, I suppose. The bungalow is just as we imagined from the pictures but different too. One feels that things here could never be very permanent, that wood would be eaten by ants or termites or some such, and that things would crumble away. There are good rugs and he has the china we sent from home, plus various things that seem to belong to the house. The bed linen was bought locally, as were the chairs (all rattan), but they are good, nonetheless. Most servants are male apart from a local woman who keeps house for him. She seems rather young, but then it is hard to tell with Indians. She has a very beautiful child with a mop of dark curls.*

*I can imagine Lucinda here, though not perhaps in this bungalow – perhaps once James is promoted, which he says cannot be long. The director seems to think very highly of him. Things are changing, but James says that the younger men are still expected to remain unmarried.*

*Well, I must finish now if I am to be in time for the boy who is taking our letters. James says that his housekeeper's brother writes letters for the pickers and other staff when they need them. Imagine not being able to write and read one's own! There is a school, but it seems rather ramshackle in a tin-roofed building, which must be very hot and also very noisy when it rains. They don't seem to have any books. We will send some from home, though how long they would last here I don't know.*

*Your father and James send their love, as do I.*

*Mother*

*P.S. I thought that the boy had come to collect our letters but it was a man about a leopard! One that took someone's goat has been spotted again. It will be up to James to do something. He says that he will be perfectly safe on one of his horses, and of course he has rifles.*

# 1940s

## Green-and-Yellow Patterned Cotton Dupatta of Inexpensive Fabric (c. 1940s)

James said that the fighting was nowhere nearby which was good, because she and Jay wouldn't be in any danger. But also bad, she thought, because it meant that he would be going so far away. He would have to travel for several days before he even reached his unit. He said that the Assam Regiment was unlikely to see much action. They would be part of the line of defence against the Japanese, but she wouldn't have to worry about that. He was a captain. They hadn't wanted him at first as he'd broken his arm and collarbone when he was a boy and so had to fire his gun left-handed, but he'd proved that he could do that, he was proud to tell her. He told her that the regiment was very pleased to have him; he could speak Hindi and a bit of Bengali and Assamese and was used to giving directions and making sure that they were followed. He said that they knew he would be able to command the respect of his men. His own father, he said, had missed the last war because he'd been a farmer in Canada, but all of his uncles had been killed in it. It was his duty to go, he said. She mustn't worry, he said. He'd be back to visit when he could and after the war everything would be better.

There was a full moon on the night before he left. After supper they sat in the lamplight as they always did, with the blinds up because James liked it that way, even though the moths banged against the glass. She was sewing as usual, making some shorts for Jay. James came and knelt in front of her.

'Josmi, I need you to listen to me. This is important.'

She was always listening to him. Listening for him when he was out, and then when he was there, listening to him. She and Jay, it was what they did. She put down her sewing and smiled up at him, as always.

'You know I am coming back to you. I love you and I love Jay and I think of you as my wife. I should have married you, but that will have to wait now. I will come back.'

She looked down, not wanting to admit the possibility that he wouldn't.

'I've talked to Freddie,' he went on, 'and he said that you can stay here until I'm back. He gave me his word. He'll be looking after everything here while I'm away, overseeing the garden, everything. You can always ask Anders and Woods if you need help with anything.'

He put one finger under her chin and pushed upwards so that she was forced to look at him.

'I've got some money for you.' He got up and went to the bureau and then came back to her but stayed standing. 'You must keep this safe somewhere that no one will look.' He glanced around the room, slightly wildly. 'Your sewing basket – that will do. Don't tell anybody about it. It's for you and Jay in case anything happens to me. You understand?'

Of course, she did. Behind her the moths were hammering on the windowpane like so many yellow ghosts. She would shut the blinds when he was gone. He passed her the envelope.

'Look inside,' he said. 'You should know how much is there. It's a lot. Don't tell anybody. Be careful who you trust.'

She nodded and opened the envelope. She had never seen so much money in her life. It felt smooth and dirty in her hands. She didn't like touching it.

'I…' she started. She didn't know what to say, but he held up his hand and stopped her anyway.

'Go on then, find something old that needs mending, something nobody would want, and hide it underneath that.'

She always mended things so quickly, there was never much waiting. She fetched a dupatta. It was a yellow-and-green-patterned one that she had never liked much. She put the envelope in the bottom of her basket and folded the dupatta on top.

'Come to bed, now,' he said. 'It's my last night.'


The sickness started the next morning. She didn't want to bother him with it, at least until she was sure. She spent a long time in the bathroom – she thought he probably wouldn't notice anyway. He was so busy polishing his rifle and then riding Jay around on the horse that he was going to have sent after him. He was being collected by some other soldier.

Josmi heard the jeep pulling into the yard, rinsed her mouth out again, and hurried outside. Jay was clambering to get into the jeep too. James let him climb in for a minute, hold the steering wheel and beep the horn. Then he lifted him back out and swung him around and put him back down. Josmi stood and watched with the workers who had come to see him leave. She saw him bend down, ruffle Jay's hair, and then with a jaunty wave he was off. She guessed that he hadn't told his fellow officers who Jay was, let alone who she was. That hair-ruffling looked designed to say, 'servant's child, bit of a nuisance but endearing with it'. Jay stood on the veranda and waved until the cloud of dust following the jeep disappeared. Josmi watched until she had to hurry back to the bathroom.

She wished that she had told him.

Later on, when the sickness had passed, she felt so weak that all she could do was collapse on the seat on the veranda. Jay was playing with the cook's children, marching up and down with sticks over their shoulders for guns.

'I am an officer,' she heard Jay say. 'That means that you have to do what I say and go where I say. If I say "attack", you must attack. If I say "retreat" that means you must run away, but I will never say retreat. Only cowards retreat.'

Sometimes, Josmi thought, retreating might be the best idea, but she felt too exhausted to speak. She hoped that James would tell his men to retreat when he needed to. She had no idea what would happen to her and Jay – and now this new baby – if he didn't come back.

But James did come back. The war went on and on. The baby arrived. He visited. They named her Margaret after his sister, but Molly for every day. He went away again. He came back. He went away again.

## Wooden Toy Truck of Simple Design
### (c. Early 1940s)

The heat was sliding out of the day. They were sitting on the veranda, Jay playing with his truck, Molly lying with her hot heavy head in Josmi's lap, when they saw the cloud of dust in the distance. Josmi stood up, hoisting Molly onto her hip and straightening her clothes before whoever it could be arrived.

It could be him.

Through the dust she saw that it was a car, but Freddie McKenzie's.

He hardly looked at her as he got out of it. He nodded at her and then came up the steps slowly, not with the usual brisk step that she'd seen so many times. She noticed, yet again, how heavy British men's shoes were.

'Josmi,' he said.

'Mr. McKenzie, please come inside. I will get you some tea.'

'Thank you.'

He sat down on the sofa. He looked too big and heavy, and very red and sweaty. He smelt of gin. Josmi left him there. Jay stayed in the room with him, quietly watching. She carried Molly, who was falling asleep, and gently put her down in her cot.

When Josmi came back in, Jay was rolling his truck back and forth under the table. It looked as though Mr. McKenzie had fallen asleep. He had done so on their sofa enough times before. His head was tilted back, his eyes were closed, but when she put the tray down, he slowly opened his eyes.

'Josmi,' he said again, 'I...'

She poured him some tea and offered him one of the biscuits that James liked. He took the tea but shook his head at the biscuits. She stood in front of him, not knowing what was expected.

'I... Please sit down, I'm afraid I have something to tell you, something very bad.'

She sat down.

'I had a telegram today. I'm afraid that James is missing. There was a terrible battle and he hasn't been found. I'm so sorry.' He stood up and went towards her but didn't dare to touch her.

'No!' she cried. 'No!'

'He was very brave. The company asked me to contact his family. They meant his family in England...'

He stopped and looked at her, as if unsure what to say next. She sat there, her shoulders shaking, her face buried in her hands.

'I'm so sorry,' he said.

Jay began to roll his truck backwards and forwards again.

'Is there anybody I can have fetched? Somebody who could come and sit with you?'

She didn't answer.


Freddie sat there while she rocked backwards and forwards. The little boy left his truck and climbed onto the sofa next to his mother. Freddie watched as the child started to pat his mother's arm and try to burrow into her.

'What's wrong, Mummy? What's wrong? Are you crying? Why are you crying?'

And then he heard another voice calling 'Mumma, Mumma!' The little girl must have woken up already. Josmi wiped her face with her scarf and hurried out of the room.

Freddie McKenzie packed his pipe and went out on the veranda. He had yet to tell her his other reason for coming. She couldn't stay in the house. Not on the same terms, anyway. He could leave, he thought, and come back another day. He walked around to the back of the house where the other servants lived. There might well be a room where Josmi and her offspring could be accommodated. An insolent-looking old fellow was there, poking half-heartedly at a patch of some native vegetables, some sort of spinachy thing, perhaps actual spinach. He went over to the man who stopped his hoeing.

'We have very bad news,' he told him. 'Captain Ash is missing in action, presumed dead.'

The man bowed his head for a long time. Why did these people have to take so long over everything?

'I am very, very sorry, sir,' he said at last. He saw tears running down the old fellow's face. Felt one running down his own.

'A battle with the Japanese,' he went on. 'Do you have a wife? A daughter? Somebody who could come here to be with Josmi and her children?'

'I will fetch my son's wife.' He hobbled away towards one of the huts and Freddie went back to the veranda and relit his pipe. After what seemed an unnecessarily long time, the old man appeared with a pretty young woman. This one didn't seem to be crying or even the slightest bit upset. They made to go towards the back door, but Josmi appeared. The little boy was holding her hand and the little girl was sitting on her hip. Josmi looked composed now, though still rather dishevelled. Lucky, he thought, that they don't feel things as we do.

'Mr. McKenzie,' she said, 'you said that James was missing, but that you do not know anything else. All that means is that you do not know where he is, which must be very common in wars. He promised us he would come back. He has been away and come home before. Until we know anything else, I must hope, for me and for our children. Now, can I bring you something to eat?'

She looked so determined. There was nothing for it. He would have to return in a few days' time.

'Josmi,' he said, 'you must prepare yourself for the worst. The worst has probably already happened.' He patted her on the upper arm and went off to break the news to Anders and Woods.


That night, Josmi let the children sleep with her. The moon was full and so bright. She lay in the middle and prayed that James would come back. Molly's soft curls spread across the pillow. Jay, like a little bundle of sticks, was all elbows and knees. She stared hard at the moon, determined not to cry, or at least to cry soundlessly. Her cheeks were soon stinging with hot tears.

'Mummy, the sheet is getting wet,' Jay whispered. 'Are you crying because Daddy is lost?'

She nodded but was unable to speak.

'Don't cry,' Jay said. 'They will find him. He'll come back. He can ride a horse or drive a car. He can look at a map.'

She nodded again and managed to say 'yes'. Then she leant over and stroked Jay's face.

'Go to sleep.'

'I am sad now too.'

'Don't be sad. I'm not sad anymore.' She gulped. 'He promised he'd come back. He's been away before lots of times and he always comes back.'

'But when? Tell me when?'

After a while she answered. 'One beautiful day, you'll be outside playing, and you'll see the cloud of dust that comes with a car or a horse, and we'll guess that it's him. Then we'll see that it *is* him coming towards us and he'll call out our names. But we won't answer. We'll be too happy to answer. Instead we'll hide. And he'll call out our names, he'll sound a little bit worried that we are not here. He'll shout "Where is my beautiful boy and my beautiful girl? And where is my beautiful wife, Josmi, that I love so much?" And then we'll appear. And we'll all hug and dance because we'll all be so happy that he is home. That's what will happen.'

'Yes,' said Jay. And Molly snuggled in towards them.


They heard nothing the next day, or the next. Josmi tried to put it all out of her mind. After all, they had gone weeks and weeks without hearing anything from James before. But then Mr. McKenzie was back. There was another man with him, somebody Josmi hadn't seen before. She watched from the window as they got out of their car and walked up to the front door in their heavy shoes. They weren't smiling. The man with Mr. McKenzie was peering at everything. They rapped on the door. Slowly, slowly she went to the door, and slowly, slowly, she let them in.

But they had no more news, they had only come to ask her to start packing James's things.

## A Black Leather Trunk, Measuring 6' by 2'6' by 2'6' (c. Late 1920s)

Ravi helped her pull James's trunk out. Perhaps they would send the things to a hospital or the army camp when James was found. The furniture, Mr. McKenzie said, was being kept for the next manager. She thought that it would be alright if she kept a few things, the quilt from the bed where they had slept, some teacups that she thought they wouldn't need in England, where they must have so much of everything. She packed up the clothes that James hadn't taken with him, his books, his pens. Things that were to do with the tea garden she had been told to leave. She carried everything that she was keeping into the little room at the back of the house where she had first slept. With a mat on the floor there would be room for the children too. She made sure that her sewing box was tucked safely behind the door where no one would notice it. Molly didn't understand that they had to stay in this room and the kitchen now, and Jay protested. There was nowhere to play with his truck in that tiny room. She told him he would have to play with it outside.

But a few days later, when nobody had arrived, they began to drift back into the other rooms, only sleeping in the little room. Perhaps, she thought, if we quietly wait, he will return, or else we will be able to stay here forever. They had sacks of rice and flour and much else. She could work with Ravi. She had the money in her sewing basket.

* * *

Ravi was kind to her. She started to work beside him while the children played nearby. The other servants soon stopped doing anything in the house, but she didn't mind. It was better not to have to put up with the looks that had been pitying at first but soon turned scornful. And she hated venturing beyond the compound where the pickers would stop speaking if she approached. As always, she would sit and watch the lines of them moving up and down and half-wish that she was still one of them – but then no little James, no Molly. She could have carried on as one of the dancers. She wished she had the picture that James had taken that day. It had been on the mantelpiece soon after she'd arrived along with a picture of him with his sister and his friend and his sister's friend. She looked at that picture now. They were on top of a mountain. James and his friend were grinning, his sister, who looked like an angry cat, was squinting. She wore little glasses. The sun must have been in her eyes. Josmi knew that James was younger than his sister, but he looked like a man and she just a girl – a cross girl. Josmi hoped that Molly wouldn't grow up to be that cross-looking. The other girl had a big British face like a dish of yoghurt. They were sitting down, but you could see that she was very tall, even for a British lady. They were all wearing heavy woollen clothes. She wondered what colours they had been. They looked similar to the colours of the British mountain on which they sat, all grey probably. The yoghurt-faced girl looked friendly though. She was smiling, but not at the camera. You could see that she was looking at James and laughing at something he said. She looked as though she were in love with him. Josmi could tell – the way she was leaning towards him. She and James were both holding metal cups, but he was raising his to the camera, toasting the day, she was raising hers to him. This photo was in a silver frame. The photo of her with the other dancers had never had a frame. Perhaps he had just thrown it away.

She was standing there, holding the mountain picture, thinking that she had never been up a mountain and would probably never go up a mountain, or want to go up a mountain, when she heard the car. Her hand was shaking as she put the photo back in its place. She listened, hoping to hear James calling her name. There was only a loud, abrupt knock at the door. She smoothed her hair and went to answer it.

Freddie McKenzie was standing there again and she saw, on the back seat of his car, another huge black trunk.

'Josmi,' he said, 'I need to talk to you.'

She stepped aside and he went past her into the bungalow. He didn't sit down, though, but stood just where she had been standing before. She followed him in.

'Please sit down, Josmi. I'm afraid I have some more news for you.'

'No, oh no!' she cried.

'It is the worst possible news. Captain Ash – that is, James – has been killed. He was wounded in a battle and died that same day. He was very brave, repelling the Japanese advance in a battle that probably saved India. He was taken to a field hospital, but it was too late. I'm so sorry.'

'No,' she said. 'No.'

He came and sat down next to her, putting one of his heavy hands on her shoulder.

'We knew this was the most likely outcome after the news that he was missing. It was only a matter of time before we found out.'

She couldn't speak. Jay and Molly came in as his meaty hand was patting her shoulder as though she were a horse.

'I'll give you a moment to tell them, while I bring in the extra trunk.'

But she still couldn't tell them. They ran to her and buried their heads in the folds of her clothes. Her tears fell into their hair.

Ravi came backing into the room, dragging the big black trunk.

'Is Daddy in there?' asked Jay.

'No!' said Ravi. 'Of course not. This is for his things.'

'As I said before,' said Mr McKenzie, 'we need you and the other staff to pack up all his belongings. The carriers will be back in a couple of days. They are to be shipped home. Not the furniture. That's all to stay. Just the personal effects. It must all go back to his family. It's all arranged. A new manager will be moving in. You can stay on as one of the staff for the time being.'

'But what happens to soldiers who die?' asked Jay. 'Where do they go?'

Nobody answered him.

After a while Josmi looked up.

'Daddy was very brave,' she told the children. 'But he isn't going to be able to come home.'

The trunk now lay on the rug in front of them. Normally Jay and Molly would have wanted to climb on it and into it, but they just stared.

'But I want him to come home! He said he would come home!'

'I do too.'

She held tight to the children. When she looked up a while later, Mr. McKenzie was gone but the black leather trunk was still there.

A few days later, Freddie returned to collect the trunk. The little boy was sitting on the veranda in what had been his father's chair. He was staring at the floor, and as Freddie got closer, he saw that the boy was watching a line of ants who were marching into the house. The constant sweeping that was necessary in these places must have ceased.

'Hullo, little fellow, is your mother about?'

'She's ill. And Molly's ill too.'

Freddie knocked, but nobody came to the door. He found Josmi in the sitting room, lying on the sofa. She looked terrible – pale and yellowish. Who would want her now, and with two children? At first, he didn't notice the little girl, she was so small, curled into a corner of the sofa; she could have been a bag of rags or a broken doll. And she was an even worse shade of yellow. He didn't want to get too close.

He went back into the hall and called for the servant. No answer. Freddie had never been into the kitchen before, but he found it at the back of the house. He fetched two glasses of water and took them to Josmi.

'Here. You must all try to drink lots of water. Or tea would be better. Weak tea for you all. Where's that cook?'

Josmi sat up. 'Sorry, Mr. McKenzie, we have all been ill, but I'm getting better now.'

The cook appeared.

'Please make some tea,' Freddie told him. 'For everybody, and the children. And some food.'

'We cannot eat,' Josmi said. 'Jay can eat, but Molly and I cannot.'

Was this some Indian widow custom, he wondered. Perhaps she was mourning and this was what she had to do. But she and the little girl looked bloody awful.

He dragged the trunk out to the car and then sat on the veranda. The little boy had always seemed such a bright little thing. He would write to James's family about him. They might want to make provision. It wasn't worth mentioning the girl. She clearly wasn't going to last long. There was a school, a home, he could suggest, run by Scots in the shadow of the Himalayas. A much better climate. The little boy could be sent there and might end up with a half-decent life. Before he left he thought he'd better take one last look around – check that nothing important of James's had been forgotten and ask the cook to take care of them all. He glanced into the sitting room. Josmi and the little girl were asleep now. The little boy was playing with his truck again, slowly pushing it backwards and forwards across the rug but without looking at it. The cook had disappeared from the kitchen again. Freddie checked in a little room next to the kitchen. He wasn't there either, but there was one of James's shirts folded on top of a wicker basket. Perhaps he should send that back to the family along with everything else. Under the shirt was some old yellow Indian scarf thing, very neatly arranged. Something made him pull it out, and there, at the bottom of the basket, was a wad of cash. Well, some crafty servant clearly thought they could pull one over on James's grieving family. Freddie McKenzie tucked the money into his jacket pocket. He would send it back to James's parents, after he'd taken his own not inconsiderable expenses.

## WWII Telegram Giving News of a Captain in the Assam Regiment (April 1944)

It was an April morning. The last of the daffodils and the first of the tulips were flowering. Emmeline put her mac on over her dressing gown and went out into the front garden to cut a few tulips for the table. Margaret was home for a few days – they would have a late breakfast. Emmeline was crouching over the cold spring earth, scissors poised, when she heard the gate clang.

'Mrs. Ash?'

She rose – knees stiff, hands damp from the grass and the green blades of the tulip leaves – and turned. A young man – a young man with a telegram.

'No!' she cried. 'No, oh no!' She swayed, looked down, saw red flowers and the scissors.


The man had his hand on her arm, was leading her to the front door, calling for help. Edward was there on the step, leading her inside.


Edward opened the telegram, couldn't speak; his arms were around her, then, gruffly, he said, 'Killed in action.' They wept. Margaret appeared, read the telegram and sobbed into her mother's lap.

Emmeline awoke in the dark. It must have been a dream, a terrible fever dream – her head was so heavy and her eyes so sore. Edward was beside her but sleeping on top of the covers in his clothes. She must be ill.

She swung her leaden legs, her freezing feet, towards the floor, switched on the lamp. Her mac was there, lying across a chair. She remembered the tulips, the scissors, the telegram, and her boy, her little boy, her beautiful boy.


Days passed. The doctor kept coming. Margaret stayed.

'They are worried about your heart,' Edward said.

'My heart, our hearts…'

'You have to try to get strong again. My darling, you have to eat.' He took her hand.

'Why eat, why sleep – our boy—'

'I know, my darling, but for me, for Margaret. Doctor Brown says your heart's rhythm is disturbed, that it's much weakened.'

What did they expect? Of course, it was. How could it not be? But later that day she got up and went downstairs. It was early evening and Margaret was sitting reading, just as she had when she was a girl, by the window to catch the last of the light, too engrossed in her book to stop to turn a lamp on. There was dust everywhere and petals and pollen from flowers that people must have brought.

She smelt Edward's pipe smoke, wondered where he was.

Margaret looked up. 'Oh, Mother, you're up. I'll make some tea. Lucinda's coming later. She's been every day with flowers and casseroles and things, but you've been asleep.'

'Casseroles…' said Emmeline. 'Cass-er-oles.' She couldn't remember what they were. And Lucinda. She hadn't even thought about Lucinda. Lucinda who was waiting for James to come back too. 'Casseroles.' Something that a vicar wore, or that women embroidered for people to kneel on in church? 'Why would a person bring us a casserole?'

Now Edward was sitting beside her, holding her hand. 'Darling,' he said, 'you're up.'

She nodded, or thought she nodded, or planned to nod. She closed her eyes.

When she opened them Margaret and Lucinda were there. Her own face was wet. Tears must have been falling while she slept. Lucinda came and sat beside her, gave her a handkerchief.

'Oh, Lucinda, all your hopes and dreams.'

They sat holding hands while Edward smoked his pipe and Margaret listened to the rain splattering against the windows.

'Why did I bother?' Emmeline said after a while. 'Months in Canada, loving him before he was even born, nights when he was ill, measles, chicken pox, mumps that Christmas, holding his hands when he was learning to walk, teaching him to read, and shoelaces, all those trips for school shoes and uniforms, flu when all he would eat for days were mandarins, the endless knitting and mending and getting kits ready and buying cricket bats, the name tapes I sewed in, and wiping of grazes, when he broke his collarbone, all the days out and friends to stay, and worrying about him on mountains and swimming in cold lakes – only for him to be taken so far away – and just be one of the fallen – so far away – and we will never, ever—'

## Yellow Velvet Chair-backs Embroidered with a Design of Trees and Tropical Fauna (Mid-1940s)

More news. Margaret let the letter fall from her fingers. But even in this moment of shock and revulsion, she found herself thinking that it was like something in a novel. She sank heavily into a chair. The letter remained beneath the dining room table. She glanced down at it. There were a few strands of embroidery thread enmeshed in the carpet beside it. They had been there for months. A lifetime ago she and Lucinda had given themselves the task of replacing the chair-backs before James returned. They had chosen a design of a tree and had been vying to outdo each other with their additions to it – tropical birds, snakes, lizards, tigers and leopards twining their tails around the trunks, a bear like Baloo in the branches, animals of India, or animals that might possibly be Indian. They had got rather carried away with *The Just So Stories* and strayed into other continents. Lucinda particularly liked the work; she had always been the more practical one. Margaret would have preferred to spend the evenings reading or listening to the wireless if her eyes grew too tired. But it didn't matter now. Work on the chair-backs had stopped after the telegram arrived and no one cared that the floors weren't swept so often.

And now, months later, this. She watched as her mother picked the letter up and read it again and then found a handkerchief in her mac pocket. Her mother wore her mac indoors much of the time now. Margaret didn't know why.

'A little boy,' her mother said. 'There is a little boy.'

Margaret realised that her mother was pleased.

'Oh, what can we do? What if he isn't safe? Who can the mother be? We must make provision for them. Make sure that she is detained before she disappears with him. Oh, why didn't James tell us? I know that it happens, people say that it happens…'

Margaret said nothing for a while and then she realised that she ought to get up and pat her mother's arm. She did so.

'How can we be sure that this child is really James's?' she said.

'I think we can be sure – Freddie McKenzie says that there are papers – and his name – James Edward Ash. He must be James's.'

'We must make enquiries. This might be some clever native woman trying to take advantage,' said Margaret.

'It seems likely to me that the mother may not have been the one who was taking advantage.'

Margaret pursed her lips in distaste and turned away.

'Oh, what will your father say? How can he not be pleased – a grandson! Perhaps I should telephone him.'

'Mother, don't. It would be so terrible to find out surrounded by other people. So terrible to find out anyway.'

'Margaret – we have a grandson – a nephew for you!'

'I would rather have been given a nephew the proper way.' Margaret wondered how soon she could leave the room. Now she would have to spend the whole day with her mother, agreeing to things and having her suggestions ignored. 'I think I'll make some more tea,' she said.

'Yes, tea. Tea. Always tea.' Her mother was crying and laughing now. 'Tea, tea, tea.' Margaret patted her mother's arm again and gathered up the tea things.

'There is someone we have forgotten about, who James must have forgotten about. Lucinda. We shall have to tell Lucinda,' Margaret said and left the room.

'We must make arrangements!' her mother called after her. 'We must do everything that we can!'

'I am so tired of doing everything we can,' Margaret muttered to the teapot. 'And now this.' The letter had said that the boy was seven. If he was seven then he had existed for seven years – more than seven years – without James telling them about him. He must have been there when her parents went to visit. Had James loved him as a father loves a son? What did this child look like? Perhaps he looked exactly as James had looked at seven. There was a photograph on the piano of James at about that age. Of course, this boy would be several shades darker. And was he clever? Could he speak English? Had James taught him how to read? Presumably he spoke English to him. James had learnt various Indian languages, but presumably his son would be spoken to in English. He probably looked like a little maharajah. She imagined him spoilt and silent, in an azure turban and shoes from *One Thousand and One Nights* that turned up at the ends – a boy who would make pronouncements and ride on elephants. An unreformed male version of Mary in *The Secret Garden*.

Everybody always said that Lucinda was a splendid person. James had always said that she was a good sport. And what sport he had made of her, Margaret thought, knowing that Lucinda would visit later that day, knowing that it was going to be up to her, as Lucinda's friend and supposed future sister-in-law, to tell her about the child. She had the letter ready in her embroidery bag, the embroidery bag that Lucinda had made for her with a design of golden and orange chrysanthemums on a background of blackout material. She felt that proof might be needed, that the news she had to impart was so shocking and distasteful that Lucinda might need to see it in writing to believe it.

She took Lucinda out into the garden. They sat on the

bench that circled the yew tree. Lucinda smiled as she always did, and Margaret remembered seeing James and Lucinda kissing there once. She put her embroidery bag down on the seat beside her. Yew berries studded the grass and the path – many had been trodden underfoot, so that it looked as though there had been some sort of unpleasant accident.

'Shall we go back inside?' Margaret asked.

'Oh, no, it's nice here. I love it here. I often feel that James is still with us when I'm here.'

'Oh,' said Margaret. 'I don't.'

Lucinda laughed. 'Margaret, always so blunt.'

Perhaps, thought Margaret, I should just be blunt. If I am to break my friend's heart – a heart which has already been broken – perhaps I should just be blunt.

'I'm afraid we have had some news…'

'Oh?'

'We've had a letter. From the tea company. I have something rather dreadful to tell you.'

'I have enough details. I know the details,' said Lucinda. Margaret knew what she was referring to. The details were etched on her brain too. That there had been hand-to-hand combat on some tennis courts. Fighting with bayonets. That James had been carried on some sort of wooden cart but that he had reached the hospital too late. Too many times had she thought about that last ride, James lying prone, wounded, bleeding on some dreadful wooden cart being pulled along rutted roads while his last blood seeped into the dust.

'I know enough,' Lucinda said.

'There is more and I'm afraid that I must tell you because it is something that my parents have to deal with.'

'Oh?'

'He, James, had a child – with an Indian woman. A boy. They have written to tell us. He has survived and he is seven years old.'

'Seven? A boy of seven and he never told us? He left me thinking… A son of seven!'

'Would you like to see the letter?' Margaret reached into her bag. The letter looked old already, like some sort of artefact or exhibit or evidence in a court case. It had taken months to reach them – even longer than had become normal – and her parents had read it so many times. Margaret had only read it twice. She passed it folded to Lucinda, as though opening it might imply that she approved of what her brother had done.

Lucinda read it and began to cry. Margaret leant over and began the familiar process of arm-patting and kind words. There were wasps crawling among the yew berries in the grass, late wasps, drowsy and slow. She hoped that they wouldn't crawl into her shoes or up her legs. If she kept her legs very still, would they ignore her, or think that she was part of the furniture and something to be crawled up?

'I'm so terribly sorry. I'm sure that it didn't mean that he loved you any the less, thought any the less of you...' Margaret wasn't sure of this at all. 'I think it must be just one of these things that happens out there...'

Lucinda carried on crying.

'I'm so sorry,' said Margaret, feeling that she must be held partially responsible for her brother's appalling indiscretion.

'I knew these things happened,' said Lucinda. 'I knew that sometimes men leave whole families of children behind when they come home, but I never thought that James... I wonder if he ever intended to come home...'

'Of course, he did,' said Margaret. 'He sounded so pleased about the chair-backs!'

'Oh, the chair-backs! Here I was embroidering chair-backs, and there he was with a son – a son of seven! Seven is older than the war! Oh, what a fool I've been!'

Margaret didn't know what to say. 'I feel as though he's made fools of us all,' she said.

'Oh, Margaret!'

'Well, he has. And now we are left to do something about this boy.'

'But your parents must be pleased in a way. They have a grandson – a part of him has lived on.'

'They'll have to make provision for him. He'll have to be looked after somehow.'

'Your mother must be so happy. I'll never forget what she said – "Why did I go to all that trouble, all the sleepless nights, the fevers, the broken collarbone, all that worry, all the thousands of little things one has to do, loving him so much, just for him to be killed in a foreign land?"'

'Mmm,' said Margaret, not wanting to think of it.

'I'll look after him,' said Lucinda.

'Don't be ridiculous. And besides, he is probably still with his mother.'

'Oh, yes, of course. The mother.'

'But we will intervene for his education,' said Margaret, 'oversee it.'

'I mean it, though,' said Lucinda. She had stopped crying now. She was a splendid person.

## Obituary from a Prep School Magazine (1944)

*The Draconian, Summer 1944*
*Ash. – Killed in Action in April, 1944, Captain James Edward*
*Ash (d. o. leaving school 1926), Assam Regt., dearly loved*
*and only son of Mr. and Mrs. Edward Ash and brother of*
*Margaret.*

## MEMORIALS
## JAMES ASH (1926)

*James became a Dragon in September 1921 and celebrated*
*his first term by being top of his form in Maths and Geography*
*and second in Classics and French. This foreshadowed an*
*all-round ability which was to win him a scholarship to*
*Winchester College. James made many appearances in*
*Dragon plays, playing the Second Gravedigger in* Hamlet *as*
*well as speaking the 'Prologue' in his final year.*

*At games he was a good all-rounder. He won his tie for*
*Cricket, the game he liked best, in 1924, and also represented*
*the school in Rugger where he was Captain of the Second XI,*
*also playing in the First XI on many occasions.*

*James continued to excel on and off the field at Winchester*
*College. From there he came to Hertford College, Oxford, in*
*1930 as an Exhibitioner reading Geology. Here he continued*
*with Rugger and Cricket, Beagled, became an expert in*

Ju-jitsu, acted in College Dramatic Society productions, and even, on one occasion, rowed in a humorous College Third Boat. He also joined the OU Artillery; this led to a love of horses which he never lost. His interest in Geology likely stemmed from his favourite pastimes: fell-walking and rock-climbing. Childhood holidays were spent at his family's cottage in Wales, or in Cumberland or Skye where, often joined by other Dragons or Wickhamists, he conquered many of the most challenging peaks. His cousin, fellow Dragon Harry Stolly (now a POW), was a frequent companion on these trips. When not climbing, James liked to read books about rock-climbing. His extensive library of these accompanied him on his next move: to India.

After Oxford, James tried for the Colonial Service but although he came in the first 50 out of 1000, only 20 were taken that year due to the slump which was at its height. And so, when an offer came of a post on a tea estate in Assam, he accepted it and left for India almost at once. As things turned out, he never came home again.

In India, James was happy and successful. He was universally popular and continued with a number of sports, adding 'Rough Polo' to the many he enjoyed. But after six years he was ready for a spell at home. He was actually packing for his overdue leave when war broke out and all leave was stopped.

At first, owing to a shortage of staff due to men on furlough, James could not be released for service; but in August 1940 he got his wish. Characteristically, he declined an offer to become Military A.D.C. to the Governor of Bengal, preferring the ordinary services. A badly set collarbone might have barred him from active deployment, but he had taught himself to shoot left-handed and was commissioned to the Assam Regiment. He was a popular officer and leader of his men, renowned for his fairness, bravery and determination. His quiet depth of character inspired confidence as well as affection. He was killed on the Burma front in April 1944.

From friends:

*I associate him so much with wind and mist and the crags of Tryfan that I find it hard to imagine James as a soldier in the tropics; but he had so much determination, doggedness and endless good nature that I know that he would have tackled any obstacle in any situation.*

*He was a true friend, always good-natured and ready to think the best of others. He will be lamented more than ordinarily by his fellow officers and men. He must have left scores of friends behind and not a single enemy.*

## White China Bowl of Low Quality – Broken
## (Manufactured c. 1930s)

Jay could hardly remember how they had got there. There had been an arm – a lady's arm, but not their mother's – and it was clad in shades of yellow. This arm had restrained him, its fingers had prodded him in the back and pushed him into different trains. He had been given food. Molly had cried a lot. He saw all of this through some sort of haze, as if he had been looking at things through steam and mist, so maybe he had been crying too.

He remembered the sound of the trains chuffing him to sleep, and the sharp fingers poking him and shaking him awake.

Wherever it was they were going, they had arrived.

There was a long walk up a hill to the place that was called The Homes but that looked nothing like home.

'Here they are, James and Molly Ash.'

The woman in charge had looked them up and down. They had been weighed, measured and tutted at. Molly had cried some more. She was taken away to another place. Jay didn't know where.

'You are a very lucky child,' the woman told him. 'Your grandparents in England have arranged for you to be kept here.'

'What about Molly?' he asked. 'Where have you taken Molly? When is Mummy coming to collect us?'

'You are both quite filthy and must have baths. We'll

decide what to do about Molly presently. Now stop asking questions and sit down there.'

He had sat on a chair that was so high that his feet couldn't reach the ground. The back of his knees ached. The seat was made of some sort of straw that dug into him and scratched him. Someone brought him a bowl of food. The bowl was thick and white. The food was heavy and tasted of nothing, but he ate it anyway. They carried on talking about him as he ate. They seemed to be especially cross about Molly. The lady who had brought them talked to some of the new people. More people came into the room. He didn't look up from his food in case they got cross with him again. There were several voices.

'Why did you bring this girl?'

'We didn't know there was a girl too.'

'Is there provision for her?'

'I shall have to write to the grandparents, we only have provision for a boy.'

'Well, he clearly meant to keep them both and acknowledge them as his own. There are birth certificates for them both. They have his name.'

'Are you sure they are from the same mother? This isn't a case of some woman trying to pass off a child as Anglo-Indian, to take advantage of us? The girl is rather dark.'

'We really cannot keep her without being certain and without provision.'

At 'cannot keep her', Jay's spoon halted mid-air, and warm milk dripped back into his bowl. He gave a sob, a choking gulp. The bowl fell to the floor and cracked. The food slopped out of it into a shameful puddle.

'Please,' he said, 'don't send my sister away. She has to stay with me until Mummy collects us.'

'James! Look at that terrible mess! A broken bowl! You must not interrupt while we are talking. Your sister has been taken to the girls' house. When you've finished your supper, you will be taken to the infirmary – it's too late for you to join your dorm. Now, no more questions.'

Jay looked down at the congealing mess and the fragments of china on the floor. His eyes and throat and stomach ached. He realised that he was still holding the spoon and that it made his hand hurt.

Jay woke up on a bed far higher than he'd known was possible. Everything was painted white. There was a picture of a man with long hair wearing a long dress and holding a lantern. The full moon was glowing spookily behind the man's head.

Jay swung his legs over the side of the bed and slid down. His clothes had disappeared. He was wearing a pair of blue and white stripy trousers and a blue and white stripy shirt. They were very soft and smelt clean, but they weren't his. He went to look at the picture. The man had a beard and a sad, kind face. He was in a forest. The plants at the front of the picture were dead. Perhaps that was why he was sad, or perhaps it was because he was all alone in a forest. There weren't any animals in the picture. It would have been better with some animals. Jay heard a cockerel crowing somewhere and crept to the door. There was nobody about. He guessed that it was still early in the morning. He walked along a corridor, hardly making a sound. There were other rooms with high beds, but he didn't find Molly. He came to a door to the outside. It wasn't locked.

He was somewhere high up a hill. There were mountains with snow on the top that had been turned pink and the colour of mangos by the sunrise. It was a bit like his daddy's pictures of mountains in England. But he didn't think it could be England. There was a grey stone building with a pointy tower and lots of other big houses, even bigger than their own house and much, much bigger than the tea workers' houses. There were paths and lots of grass. Far away, down in a valley, was a town. The smells were different here. It was colder. There were trees but there wasn't any tea growing. He sat down outside the building where he'd slept and looked at all the things that were different and wrong.

## Letter Sent from a Children's Home in Northwest India to a Sponsor Family in England (c. 1945)

*Dear Mr. and Mrs. Ash,*

*James has arrived safely. I must tell you first of all that there is another child, a girl. She has your son's name and he is named on the papers which came with her. Her name is Margaret Emmeline Ash, though her brother calls her Molly and that is what she answers to. The mother is named as the same. James seems very attached to and protective of his sister. She calls him Jay and we have adopted that habit too. We have little doubt that she is who the papers claim her to be and that they are siblings. Molly is a pretty little thing, though rather dark for an Anglo-Indian child.*

*I know you will understand that it will be difficult for us to keep her without provision. I would trouble you to make the necessary arrangements if that is your wish.*

*The children were very thin when they arrived and full of worms. We have treated them for this and will send you regular reports as to their health, growth and progress. On arrival, James's weight was 3 stone 7. He is under height and weight for his age. Molly weighed 2 stone 4 and is similarly well below expectations for her age.*

*We shall encourage such communication with the mother as you deem desirable. All of our children are encouraged to write letters home to their families or sponsors in England as soon as they are able to. James seems to be an intelligent child who already reads and is quick with figures.*

*I remain*
*Yours sincerely,*
*Mrs. S. Cameron*
*House Matron*

# Wicker Sewing Basket – Empty (Mid-20th Century)

She was back on the lines now, but hardly anyone spoke to her. She worked all day in the sun and then went back to her brother's house and made the evening meal. She cooked, swept, mended and cleaned and, because nobody said anything apart from 'fetch this' or 'do that' to her, lay down to sleep before the others. Her sister-in-law let her do everything because, as she kept pointing out, she had children to look after and Josmi did not.

One day they will come and visit, Josmi thought. She had stopped saying it aloud. When Molly and Jay had been taken away to school, the manager had read her a letter from James's parents that said they would send money so that visits could be arranged. When she asked the manager about it he said that nothing had come, and then the next time, that she should ask her brother about it as it had been given to him for safekeeping. When she asked her brother he said that it was not enough for a train ticket, and anyway, how could she leave the garden and travel across India all by herself? It was too dangerous.

She went back to her uncle, the letter writer.

'Keep quiet. Nobody respects a woman who went with a British man. Forget about those children. You can remarry and have more children. You have an offer already.'

She couldn't speak. She hid her face and her tears in her dupatta.

'Please,' she said after a while, 'they are my children. They will think I have forgotten them. Please write to the children and the school for me. And to James's family.'

'I haven't time now, perhaps next week.'

She walked slowly back to her brother's house. There were more people than usual outside. Her brother wasn't there, but her sister-in-law, her brother's mother-in-law and her sister-in-law's three brothers were.

'Where have you been? You shouldn't wander about by yourself,' her sister-in-law said.

'She has no reputation to keep up. Everyone knows what she was. If she married again it might be different,' one of the brothers said.

'Hey!' shouted another one. 'You still refusing?'

She put her head down and moved towards the house. She would pretend to sleep. She felt a shove, then another from a different direction, a push towards the fire. She fell. The flames caught her sari. She was surrounded by men and flames.

## Hand-knitted Grey Pullover for a Young Boy
## (c. Mid-1940s)

Once they had finished the chair-backs, Lucinda and Margaret didn't know what to do. The chairs were repositioned in the dining room and everybody used them without comment; this rather annoyed Margaret who didn't often devote so much time to sewing and that sort of thing. Lucinda still called in several times a week. It was as though they were still waiting for James's return. The conversation lagged in the evenings. Margaret didn't mind, but the air was full of unspoken Ifs: If James hadn't been killed... If James was coming back... If James and Lucinda had been engaged and married...

Emmeline had carried on knitting for the war effort, but those things were no longer required. Margaret suspected that no soldier would want the misshapen socks that she was producing. They looked like the work of a demented spider, though Margaret knew better than to point this out. The library where she was employed had been temporarily closed after a bomb fell next door, so she had no work to return to. Her only escape was reading, but she couldn't read when Lucinda was visiting. Perhaps more knitting was the answer.

Emmeline had saved the patterns for everything she had ever made; they were kept in a drawer of the dresser. Margaret had never liked that drawer – it seemed so chaotic – like a drawer of randomly kept packets of onion skins. She pulled a handful out and examined them but soon lost interest and shoved them all back in, making a mess that she never would have tolerated at the library.

That morning another letter had arrived updating them on the health and educational progress of the children. They were said to be gaining weight (did that mean they were greedy?) and were doing well in their classes.

'Those dear little things,' said Emmeline, looking down at the cardigan she had been making for Margaret. Margaret had been under-enthusiastic about it, saying that she had plenty of perfectly serviceable cardigans. And here was the answer; Margaret wondered aloud whether they could all knit for the children.

'What a good idea,' said Emmeline. They could start straight away. She had some leftovers of grey wool already; Edward liked grey. James had always had grey pullovers. Grey was such a good colour for boys. In fact, there was a pullover of Edward's that she had been going to darn and which could be unravelled. She had always loved the way that wool kinked into pretty squiggles, almost like astrakhan. Did astrakhan come from the region where the home was? In the foothills of the Himalayas, children would definitely need warm clothes.

Lucinda helped her wind the wool.

Margaret seized her opportunity and picked up *Green for Danger*.

# WINCHESTER COLLEGE

## WAR MEMORIAL CLOISTER REDEDICATED

### FROM OUR CORRESPONDENT

#### WINCHESTER, Nov. 14

To-day the beautiful Winchester College War Memorial cloister—" This noblest memorial of all," as Field-Marshal Lord Wavell described it in his oration—was rededicated in the presence of the Warden, Fellows, the school and staff, and a large number of relatives and friends of those Wykehamists who fell during the war. The names of the fallen have been added to the cloister without upsetting in any way the balance of Sir Herbert Baker's original design. They are inscribed on 13 panels which have been added to the insides of the inner pillars of the cloister, so that they face, across the paving stones of the ambulatory, the panels that bear the names of their fellow Wykehamists who fell in the 1914-18 war.

A prefatory panel at the entrance of the cloister reads: " Here in equal honour facing the names of the fallen in the first world war are inscribed those of the 270 Wykehamists who died serving in the same faith 1939-1945."

The rededication was carried out by the Bishop of Winchester (Dr. Mervyn Haigh). In an address Lord Wavell referred to the ideals of faith and service to Church, King, and people of their founder William of Wykeham. " So long as we maintain these traditions," he said, " and are prepared, if needs be, to give our lives in their defence, as these our brethren have done, so long will this great country of ours endure the trials and storms such as even now gather to threaten us."

## Walkers Shortbread Biscuit Tin – Tartan Design
## (c. Late 1940s to Early 1950s)

'But how can you be scared of the moon?' Gina asked her.

'I didn't say I was scared, I just said I didn't like it at night.'

'Well, it's not there in the day, is it? So nobody likes or doesn't like it in the day.'

'Sometimes it's there in the day,' said Molly.

Now Molly wished she had never told her. They were walking down to breakfast, which was always porridge, so there was no point in wondering what it might be. Sometimes she wondered why she was friends with Gina, though she knew the answer – it was because their beds had been next to each other from the very start.

They collected their porridge and waited for grace.

'I wish it was something different,' said Molly. She might as well have wished for the moon, though of course she wouldn't have wanted that, unless it was dish-sized and could have been bounced like a ball. She didn't understand how it was that the others always seemed able to sleep, and then to wake up when they were meant to. She so often lay there, and however hard she pulled the curtains and however evenly she tried to make them hang, the moon could still peer in through the spaces between the rings at the top and then, as the night wore on, through the skylight.

She hated that skylight too. Why did they need a skylight?

They had plenty of sky and plenty of light, but the moon would be there, sending scary, greenish beams onto her bed. And if the moon could be up there, and able to get in, what else might follow? A snake could easily get in. A snake could slip the catch open and come slithering down. Her bed would be the one it landed on, and then why would it bother to eat anybody else? She wondered how long it would take her to die. It might bite her and then she'd turn black and have a long agonising death, or else it might swallow her whole and she would die slowly inside it, trapped with a dead goat. Nobody would wake up and hear her muffled screams from inside its stomach. Nothing woke the other girls. They lay there like bricks. If it was a boa constrictor, she wouldn't be able to scream at all, not once she was in its coils. But a snake might not even be the worst thing. If she were awake when the snake started coming through, she might be able to get away (and warn the others, of course). But what if a leopard came? A leopard could easily jump onto the dormitory roof. She had looked at this from outside. There were easy paths for leopards over the garden wall and up onto the kitchen roof and then along to the dormitories. Molly's would be the first one it came to. The skylight would be the obvious way in. It might smash through the glass with its mighty paws or, more likely, hook the window open with one claw and silently pour itself down into the room. It would land on her bed.

She knew that one of the gardeners had been attacked by a leopard. He had big scars down the back of his head and neck. It had happened when he was a boy, but the scars were still there. They must have grown with him. He had got away, but his friend had been taken. And there might even be a tiger. She didn't think a tiger would fit so easily through the skylight, but you never knew. She could imagine one just wandering in, following the path of moonlight to her bed. It was one of the rules that nobody ever swapped beds. This would be hers now until she left.

'You have to eat your porridge,' Gina said.

Molly peered down into her bowl. A skin was forming. It looked as strange as the moon, but greyer. She began to spoon it into her mouth, knowing that it was better just to get it over with, that she would face dosing and interrogation if she was thought to have Lost Her Appetite. She managed to make it look as though enough of it was gone. Then they had to go up to the bathrooms where they had to be done within five minutes and then be at Assembly ten minutes later. Assembly was one of the few times each week when she could see Jay; not to talk to, but she would always smile and wave and he would smile back and sometimes wave, depending where they were and who he was with. She always had so many things that she wanted to ask him and tell him about. She wished that she could ask him to help her with her Maths. He was really good at Maths. And at Hindi, probably because he could remember talking it when they had lived at home. She couldn't remember that and it was just as hard as trying to learn French. She was good at English Composition though, and at Geography.

She saw Jay on her way into Assembly. He was sitting on the end of his row and was looking round, and he grinned when he spotted her.

'Hey! We've got a box!' he whispered as she passed. 'I won't open it until Sunday!' Molly grinned. This was more than most big brothers would do. Today was Wednesday. Now she would have the painful, delightful anticipation of what might be inside.

On Sunday afternoon they opened it. There were new jumpers for both of them – dark grey (again) for Jay and yellow for Molly. And a book each: *What Katy Did at School* for her and *The Fauna of Northern India* for Jay. They knew who each one was for as Aunt Lucinda had written inside them. There were two sets of coloured pencils, two tennis balls and two yoyos. There was a ragdoll with brown woollen plaits, black buttons for eyes and a smiley red mouth embroidered on her creamy white face. She was dressed in a blue-checked dress like the ones they wore in summer.

'Her name is Lucinda,' said Molly, making her dance across the table.

'I think she's made out of a pillowcase,' said Jay. There was a cricket ball for him. The last thing they opened was a biscuit tin. It didn't have biscuits inside, but cubes of a brown sweet that had raisins in. It dissolved on their tongues in a blissful, slightly grainy, creamy mess. They shared it out. Jay wrapped his up in the paper and let Molly have the box, which had come all the way from Scotland.

# 1980s

## Cut-out Doll - 'Indra', a Girl from India
## (Kit Produced Mid-1970s)

*Dear Emmie,*
*I know you will probably consider yourself too grown up for*
*dolls, but I hope you will enjoy making this one. Your Aunt*
*Margaret and I thought it looked fun and rather an ingenious*
*idea.*
*With love,*
*Aunt Lucinda*

Indra, a girl from India, came printed on one piece of cloth
inside a clear plastic bag. She would have a purply-blue sari
decorated with orange smiling elephants and birds and stripy
cats who looked more moggy than tiger. The instructions were
said to be *inside this header card*, a piece of folded card (also
orange – so much orange) with two staples to keep the whole
package closed. By the state of the holes punched in the top,
Emmie guessed it had hung in a shop for a long time. The
colours were so early '70s.

She thought she had better make Indra, who, despite the
orange circles on her cheeks and her smile, looked sad in her
unmade form – just like a tea towel, or like somebody who
had been sliced in two and run over by a cartoon steamroller.
Emmie *was* too old for dolls, but she had never had an Indian
doll before, and she'd always wanted a ragdoll. Plus her aunt

might ask how she had got on with the sewing. Emmie had learnt sewing at school and with Aunt Lucinda who was in the Hampshire Guild of Embroiderers. Her mum had hated it – she was nothing like the other mums who all had sewing machines – but Emmie loved it. She was good at stitching things by hand and sewed in her name tapes now much faster than her mum had ever done.

The instructions told her to *stuff firmly with kapok or old tights*. She didn't have any kapok or any old tights. She considered stealing some kapok from school, but she wanted to make the doll right now. Plus she might get caught and be forever The Girl Who Stole Kapok. She went into her parents' bedroom. Her mum had had a whole drawer full of tights. They still hadn't sorted out all her clothes. Some of her mum's best dresses and a few of her favourite tops still hung in the wardrobe. Emmie buried her face in one, but the lovely smell was long gone. And they looked so out of date now. She wished she could keep buying clothes for her mum; she would have hated that her things were now like stuff in an Oxfam shop that nobody would buy. She opened the drawer where her mum's tights had been kept. It was empty. They were all gone. Her dad must have thrown them away without saying. Her mum had hated the sort of light brown tights that other people's mums wore. She hadn't owned a single pair of those. Her mum had liked Christian Dior tights and stockings and had them in all sorts of colours plus black.

Emmie went back to the wardrobe and chose a white cheesecloth blouse. She put it on and stood in front of the mirror. She looked like someone dressing up as an angel. One of her mum's bags was hanging in the wardrobe too, a cream-coloured one that looked as though it had been crocheted from string. It had smooth wooden handles. She didn't remember her mum using it much. There was something inside it – a packet of Christian Dior 15 denier stockings in French Navy. She pictured her mum going somewhere with the bag, somewhere nice, and taking spare stockings in case of ladders. Emmie carefully shut the wardrobe door and took the stockings back to her room where the doll was waiting to be filled. She hung the cheesecloth blouse in her own wardrobe.

Emmie knew that you were meant to cut up old tights if you were going to stuff something with them, but she couldn't possibly do that. Instead she found some T-shirts she'd grown out of and cut them into strips. She put the stockings, still in their packet, in first and then filled the space around them with bits of T-shirt. She worked quickly and soon had the doll finished. It wasn't the sort of doll you could cuddle. Emmie stood her on her desk.

'Wait there,' she said. Emmie could smell that her dad was making omelettes for supper. She turned off the light and went downstairs to join him. She didn't mention the empty drawer or the stockings or the blouse or the doll.

**School Library Copy of *Pride and Prejudice*
with Bookplate Listing Pupils' Names
Dating Back to 1963**

Emmie had a seat that was not only next to a radiator, but by a window. English was her favourite subject, but she couldn't help but gaze out across the churned-up pitches towards Box Hill. She liked Leith Hill better because she'd been there so many times with her mum and dad and because it had a tower.

It was February, and the kind of light and weather when you struggled to remember what time of year it was. The new decade, the 1980s, still felt the same as the old one. Had they ever had a *really* new year? Had they just had summer or was it on the way? She had the feeling that Box Hill was actually much bigger than it pretended to be, and that it was somehow crouching down and would one day start to push upwards and outwards like a mushroom or an island appearing out of the ocean.

They were reading *Pride and Prejudice* in class, but she had finished it already and was reading *Emma* at home. She had meant to bring that to school so that she could read it when they were supposed to be doing Silent Reading. Why couldn't these dummies read the book at home so that they didn't have to carry on ploughing through it in class? The lessons were like trudging across a rugby pitch that stretched to infinity. They'd been doing the book for two weeks and they hadn't even met Mr. Collins yet. They'd all have died of old age before Lizzy even saw Pemberley. She could smell that somebody behind her was eating Skips. How could you read *Pride and Prejudice* and eat Skips at the same time? Did they have prawns in Jane Austen's day? She had no idea, though she was pretty sure that they wouldn't have had prawn cocktail flavouring or crisps. They should be drinking tea from pretty cups and eating little cakes or fruit from a stately home's glasshouse.

Now she could detect Beef Monster Munch too. It was exactly like in comics – the way that smelly things had lines of waftiness. She guessed that it would be Gary and Martin. They were always eating smelly things. She reached over and tried to open the window, but it had been painted shut. She pulled the V neckline of her jumper up and until it covered half of her face and breathed through that.

Box Hill was now obscured by grey clouds and drizzle. She wished that it was summer and that she was Emma and that she was going to marry Mr. Knightley. She would never have been rude to Miss Bates and got into a position where he felt that he had to tell her off, but then…

Mrs. Cooper was now reading a bit aloud to them. Emmie tuned out her voice and continued gazing out. The caretaker was walking across the playing field. She hoped he was going to start painting the white lines on it, or was it somebody else who did that?

'The girls stared at their father,' Mrs. Cooper read. 'Mrs. Bennet said only, "Nonsense, nonsense!"

'"What can be the meaning of that emphatic exclamation?" cried he. "Do you consider the forms of introduction, and the stress that is laid on them, as nonsense? I cannot quite agree with you *there*. What say you, Mary? for you are a young lady of deep reflection, I know, and read great books and make extracts."

'Mary wished to say something very sensible, but knew not how.

'"While Mary is adjusting her ideas," he continued, "let us return to Mr. Bingley."

'"I am sick of Mr. Bingley," cried his wife…'

The caretaker was doing something to the football goalposts. Perhaps he was taking the nets down because they were going mouldy.

A hand slammed a book down right in front of her – bang! Emmie cried out, really startled. Everybody laughed.

'Miss Ash,' said Mrs. Cooper, 'pay attention! It's about time that *you* adjusted your ideas. What is the answer to my question?'

Emmie had no idea. 'Um…'

'I thought that you were a young lady of deep reflection who reads great books and makes extracts,' said Mrs. Cooper.

'Um,' said Emmie, wishing to say something very sensible, but knowing not how.

'I will repeat my question: What do you think of Mr. Bennet in this scene?'

'Well,' Emmie began, but Mrs. Cooper interrupted her.

'You have no idea, do you? Perhaps somebody better suited to the study of Jane Austen would like to tell us. Isabella?'

'He was much cleverer than his wife and most of his daughters,' said Isabella.

'Good, Isabella!' said Mrs. Cooper. 'I'm glad somebody's been paying attention.'

The bell went before anybody could say anything else, but Mrs. Cooper kept them there.

'Class! I want two sides on the characters of Mr. and Mrs. Bennet in these opening scenes for your homework.'


*Mr. Bennet was lazy and a bully*, Emmie wrote later. *He liked to make his wife and daughters, particularly Mary, look stupid. He might have encouraged Mary's reading and talked to her about books but instead he showed favouritism…* She went on in some detail with quotations, etc.

*C +*, wrote Mrs. Cooper. *Don't waste time in my lessons.* C+ was the worst mark Emmie had ever had.

## School Disco Ticket (Summer 1981)

'Oh, you have to come, Emmie, everybody is going,' Sam Watson said. 'What will you wear?'

Emmie had really no idea. Probably jeans. Hers weren't as tight as Sam's. Sam had to lie down to zip hers up. Emmie's were drainpipes, but they weren't as sprayed on as everybody else's. She wondered if she should try taking them in a bit. There was a good few inches around the ankle that could go. She hoped that they didn't look like the kind of jeans that you bought at C&A. She had a yellow skirt that *was* actually from C&A but she liked it. She had cut the label out, not that anybody ever saw it. She thought that she might wear that or the jeans with a white top that looked like the sort of camisole somebody in a Thomas Hardy novel would wear. Or should she try to look discoey, like a dancer on *Top of the Pops*? Maybe she should have her hair in a ponytail on the side of her head and wear something sparkly. God. Maybe she should just not go.

But then it seemed that actually everybody *was* going and she found herself queueing to buy a ticket. *No Tickets on the Door* the posters had announced. The ticket had a silhouette of two dancers from the '50s jiving. *No Alcohol* it said. The 50p admission included a plastic cup of cola and there would be crisps to buy. But she wouldn't want to risk smelling of prawn cocktail or cheese and onion (bound to be the only flavours on offer) in the unlikely event that anybody asked her to dance, or – even more unlikely – wanted to kiss her.

The brother of somebody in the sixth form was doing the disco. 'Native New Yorker', 'Dancing Queen' and the livelier songs from *Grease* had everybody on the dance floor. Well, all the girls. The boys, of course, just stood around and watched them or shoulder-barged into each other, sometimes knocking into groups of dancers who were at the edges. Emmie's group was in the middle, and invisible, she hoped. The air was hot and heavy with the scent of Impulse and Quavers. Actually, she loved dancing, and was glad that she had worn the yellow skirt. She would say it was from Miss Selfridge if anybody asked. She had worn her latest pair of dollies. They were the perfect shoes for everything, only £1.99 a pair, and she loved how they were sold from wire baskets outside every shoe shop. You didn't even have to do that taking-one-shoe-up-to-the-counter-and-asking thing. A few teachers sat on the stage, most of them wearing the clothes they'd worn all day at school. None of Emmie's favourites were there. Staffing the disco was more something for the PE teachers, it seemed.

'Echo Beach'. 'Call Me'. 'You're the One That I Want'. 'Going Underground'. 'Turning Japanese'.

A group of boys from her class came and danced near them. She tried to stick close to Sam, but realised that Gary O'Reilly and Sam were now dancing together. And then the first slow dance started. She wasn't going to be left there like a lemon in her yellow C&A skirt when Gary and Sam started snogging. She practically ran out of the hall.

There was still twenty minutes before her dad was coming. She walked towards the loos, but it was full of girls shrieking with laughter so she couldn't hide in there. The door to the back playground was open. She stepped outside.

The summer heat had gone out of the day and it had been raining. The air smelt deliciously of rain on hot pavements.

She could still hear the music. Now they were playing 'Three Times a Lady' which she'd always thought silly – it made no sense. Around the corner was a bench where she could wait until her dad arrived. The song came to an end. The bench was at the other end of the playground where it sloped upwards towards the school fields. She was halfway there before she realised that there was already somebody else heading towards it from the Music block. She could just keep on walking and go out of the school by the side gate then go along the road to wait there. She and the other person reached the bench at the same moment.

It was a boy, a boy in a plain black T-shirt and jeans. Arun Choudhury. He looked so different out of school uniform.

'Hello, it's Emmeline Ash, isn't it?'

How did he know her name? She nodded.

'I'm Arun.'

'I know,' she said. 'You're a fifth year, aren't you?'

'Yes. Leaving, thank God.'

'Where are you going?'

'A college in Guildford. For Music.'

'Much nicer than here, I expect.'

He sat down on the bench.

'Where were you going just now?'

'Nowhere, really. I just had to get out of the hall. I don't know why I came.'

'I came because my mum would have been sad if I hadn't,' he said.

Emmie didn't say that she didn't have a mum anymore.

'I didn't see you in there,' she said. 'Not that you can really see much, just bodies and lights.'

'I wasn't in there for long,' he said. 'Some of us were in the Music block.'

He had lots of friends now, she knew.

He sat down on the bench. 'Why don't you sit down? The stars are coming out,' he said.

How different and strange, and almost beautiful, the

school buildings looked. Coloured lights flashed across the hall windows. She could pretend that they were outside a grand house, in the gardens of Pemberley or Hartfield. Planes heading for Gatwick glittered above them. She sat down.

'I have one more year to go,' she sighed.

The disco music stopped, and she wondered if it was over. She suddenly hoped not. Another song started.

'Would you like to dance?' Arun stood up and semi-bowed and extended a hand towards her. She smiled and stood up too.

It was Dire Straits' 'Romeo and Juliet'. She couldn't make out all the words, but they could hear the melody and she knew the lyrics off by heart anyway. Emmie didn't like Dire Straits because of Mark Knopfler's headband, but she loved this song.

'Here's a convenient streetlight,' he said, smiling.

She didn't know how to dance to this sort of music, but Arun reached out and took her hand and they danced a twirling slow jive. His hand was warm but dry in hers. Her yellow skirt tuliped out when he spun her round. The whole world spun – the concrete of the playground, the pools of light from the hall, the music, the stars.

When the music stopped, they stood there, still holding hands. The lights from the hall went out. Everything was indigo. Still he held her hand. She didn't move, wondering, hoping that he might pull her close and kiss her like in a film. But parents' cars were starting to pull into the car park next to the playground. Her dad would be there – always one of the first to arrive anywhere.

'I'd better go,' she said, and her hand slipped out of his. 'Um…' She didn't want to appear too keen, or as though she thought the dance might have meant something and she was expecting anything else. 'Good luck at sixth form.'

'Um, bye, Emmeline,' he said.

She turned and walked towards the gate, feeling his eyes upon her back. She hoped she wouldn't stumble. One of her shoes felt as though it was going to fall off – the buckles on dollies always came loose. At the exit she turned. He was still there in a square of light. He lifted one hand and waved, took a step towards her, but then three other boys came up behind him, shouting 'Oi, Choudhury!' and he turned and walked away.

Press the button to see Dire Straits performing 'Romeo and Juliet'. Pay no attention to the headband.

**O Level Physics Homework, Fifth Year –
duplicated sheet, some fading (1981)**

*Tasks for the Summer Holidays (Mr. Newt's Groups)*

1. *Revise work on Electricity and Electromagnets for a test in the first week of term.*

2. *Devise three questions or problems on any area of Physics to challenge the class next term.*

The first one was boring. Emmie would do that at the end of the holidays. Number 2 was better and helpful when she was trying to get to sleep. She had a lot more than three questions.

*2a) Why when you take a photo of a headlight won't it come out as bright as that headlight?*

*2b) Do flames have shadows that we cannot see?*

*2c) If you put something big and metal on the moon, could you pull it back to Earth if you had a strong enough magnet?*

*2d) If you had a really strong telescope and went far into space and then looked back at Earth, could you see what had happened in the past? Could you see your own relatives who had died?*

# VHS Player (c. 1982)

'What are you doing at Christmas, Jay?' Sheila asked. She was pinning up foil decorations around the reception desk. Granby Engineering, where they'd both worked for years, was a pretty dull place most of the year – nothing but draughtsmen's desks at sloping angles, grey carpet, banks of filing cabinets, grey Venetian blinds and views across Croydon. Sheila tried to cheer things up, not just for Jay, but for everybody.

She still remembered Pammy's first day. It had been her first job out of secretarial college. Jay Ash, always so polite and reserved, had been completely smitten from the moment he saw her. She remembered how she had taken Pammy around the office and introduced her to everyone. Jay had got up from his desk and shaken Pammy's hand. She was so pretty, of course, her long dark blonde hair up in a bun, and she always wore such neat little shoes. She'd had on her winklepickers on the first day and a hound's tooth check skirt with a white blouse and a black cardigan with little black beads for buttons. She always wore black and white for work. And unlike the other women at Granby, Pammy didn't wear tan nylons all year round.

When Pammy had looked around the office that first day she'd reminded Sheila of a child dressed up, pretending to be an adult. Sheila gave her lots of letters to type and then disappeared to take the minutes of a meeting. They all had to be done by the end of the day. Pammy had set to work, but then her ribbon had run out and it had taken her ages to find where the replacements were kept. She'd told Sheila that first day nerves had got the better of her; she'd got the new ribbon twisted and ended up with smudges all over her hands and on the letter for the director that had to be done by 11 o'clock. She'd been on the point of tears when suddenly Jay had been there beside her desk, asking if she needed help and sorting out the ribbon in a few moments.

'That Jayash is a real gentleman,' Pammy said over sandwiches in the park with Sheila the next day.

'Oh, Jay,' Shelia said. 'Yes, he's nice. Watch out for Martin, you don't want to get stuck in the stationery cupboard with him.' She gave Pammy a run-down of everyone in the office, the directors' likes and dislikes, and who else she should watch out for. Sheila was about to say something else about Jay when a mother duck came towards them leading four little yellow ducklings, and then they noticed that Jay himself was walking around the edge of the lake with his own lunch in a paper bag, and then they realised the time and rushed back to the office.

'I thought his name was Jayash,' said Pammy, over coffee a few days later. 'I was typing that report and thought, who's this James Ash? I can't have met him yet. And then I realised that he wasn't called Jayash, you know, like some foreign name.' She laughed. 'Jay suits him. His hair is that shiny black that's almost blue. There's a pair of jays in my parents' garden. They always look a bit magical – not like all the usual birds – and so pretty when they're in the cherry tree with the pink blossom, you should see them.'

A few weeks later, Pammy told Sheila in the ladies' that Jay had asked her to the cinema. A year later they'd got engaged. Pammy had confided that her parents hadn't been keen at first, but after a while they'd warmed to Jay, seen that he was reliable and earning a good wage, even if he wouldn't have been their first choice for a son-in-law. Pammy's own mum had died of the Big C, as they all called it, soon after she married Jay. Pammy had given up work when she was expecting Emmie, but she and Sheila stayed in touch. Sheila just couldn't believe it when Jay told her that Pammy had got it too. And now Jay was alone, bringing up a daughter by himself. He had a sister (but she'd emigrated to New Zealand with her husband) and two aunts, but really it was just him and Emmie. Sheila wished she could help more, but Jay declined any offers, even around Christmas. She would have been happy to help him pick out presents, or anything at all. She didn't like to think of them all alone on Christmas Day.

'We're just doing the usual, at home, then going to see my aunts in Winchester for Boxing Day. We'll go and see Pammy's dad too at some point.' Jay said that Pammy's dad always spent Christmas at his sister's near Eastbourne, and they would usually visit on one of the dead days between Christmas and New Year. They always took him out to the local Indian restaurant, which would be the only thing open. He said that Emmie loved the lychees they served in a shiny steel bowl – she'd thought it was real silver for a long time – and always had them for pudding.

'You and Emmie are welcome to come to us,' Sheila said, as she had every year since Pammy had died.

'Thanks, but I think Emmie likes to be at home. You know what teenagers are like.'

Sheila certainly did. She had three boys of her own, the youngest a couple of years older than Emmie. Their Christmas was a raucous affair.

'You should get a video machine,' Sheila said. 'We're getting one. It would be great for you and Emmie. You can buy the Disney films each time they put out a new one. You can build up a real collection.'


It was pouring. Emmie's desert boots (despite the expensive waterproofing spray the lady in the shop had made her buy) were soaked. She had stuffed them with loo paper and put them in front of the gas fire in the hope of getting them dry before the morning. The PE kit she'd forgotten to wash at the weekend was steaming on the radiators too. Emmie had made baked potatoes for supper again using the metal prongs that speeded up cooking time but were horrible to clean.

Her dad was late, and she was worrying, as usual. And then there he was, coming through the door with his black woollen coat studded with raindrops, and he was carrying a great big Allders of Croydon bag. Inside it was a big flat box in another bag to stop it from getting wet.

'I've got us a present,' he said, 'but we'll have it now.' He put it down on the kitchen table at the end where they didn't eat. 'Unwrap that, Em. I'll just get the rest.' The second bag was smaller and contained five blank VHS tapes.

'We can watch our favourite programmes whenever we like now,' he said.

We already do, thought Emmie, we know when they are on and watch them; but she didn't say it as he was so excited. Instead she said, 'And you'll be able to tape your favourite films when they're on TV and then watch them whenever you like.'

Jay's favourite films were James Bond ones, but he liked old black-and-white ones too. Emmie remembered the way that her parents used to watch films together. They'd shout, 'It's him, it's him!' or 'It's her, it's her!' at so many obscure actors and then vie with each other to remember the names of all the movies they'd ever been in. How could anyone remember so many old films? *High Society* had been her mum's favourite.


On Christmas morning, sitting in her pyjamas and the black suede ankle boots from her dad that she'd chosen, and the pink scarf he'd got her that she would have to wear, at least sometimes, she unwrapped her present from Sheila. *Dumbo*.

'Oh!'

'The video machine was Sheila's idea,' said Jay.

Emmie peered at it. She knew Sheila knew how old she was as she always sent her a birthday card with her age on it. Sheila always got her presents too. When she'd been little it had been dolls in elaborate clothes. Sheila didn't know that she would have preferred a toy animal or something that she could do something with. One of her favourite presents ever had been a Got A Minute game from her dad. She loved how neat and contained it was. It consisted of a Perspex cube with an egg timer and dice with letters on inside it – you shook it and then had to make as many words as you could before the sand ran out. She was better with words than her dad and beat him every time. They liked playing board games together, but she knew that they'd never be like the people in ads on TV who always seemed to be having so much more fun than they did, falling about with laughter while they played Buckaroo or Hungry Hippos. They played chess too (he still beat her at that) and Racing Demon with Aunt Lucinda. Emmie had taken Got A Minute on the Christmas visit when it had been new. Aunt Margaret had loved it too and she and Emmie had played for hours. It had been one of the easiest visits ever. Now Emmie stared at the *Dumbo* box.

'We can watch it later,' she said and set it aside.


On the 29th of December they watched it. They'd just got back from visiting Emmie's grandpa and, after a John Denver concert, there was nothing else on the telly. Jay was in his armchair with his long skinny feet in the new socks she'd got him up on the footstool. He was soon asleep. He always fell asleep early after they visited Grandpa. He said it was the long drive.

Emmie half-remembered going to see *Dumbo* when she was little. She remembered that it had been quite scary. Now she sat alone on the green Draylon sofa watching in horror and then crying while Dumbo's mum rocked him in her trunk to 'Baby Mine'.

* * *

The next day she wrote her thank-you letters.

*Dear Sheila,*
*I hope you are well and had a good Christmas. Thank you very much for giving me* Dumbo. *Dad and I watched it and really enjoyed it. I expect we will watch it again soon.*
*Love from,*
*Emmie x*

Press the button to watch the 'Baby Mine' scene from *Dumbo*
(Not suitable for under 18s).

*Dear Aunt Lucinda,*
*Thank you very much for my Christmas present. I am going to buy a new bag for school and some clothes. Thank you for having us on Boxing Day. We had a lovely time and enjoyed seeing you and Aunt Margaret and taking Agnes to the water meadows.*
*I hope to see you again soon,*
*Lots of love,*
*Emmie x*

Emmie considered the fact that her mother's father and Aunt Lucinda would be very unlikely to meet unless she got married or something, and she certainly didn't have any plans for that. And if they did meet, they probably wouldn't compare the thank-you letters they'd received over the years. She copied the letter to Aunt Lucinda, making just a few changes.

*Dear Grandpa,*
*Thank you very much for my Christmas present. I am going to buy a new bag for school and some clothes. Thank you for having us. We had a lovely time and enjoyed seeing you again.*
*I hope you have a happy new year.*
*Love from*
*Emmie x*

The letter to Aunt Margaret would be a different matter.

*Dear Aunt Margaret,*
*Thank you very much for the book token. I am really looking forward to spending it. I am going to buy* Howards End *as I will be studying it next term and always like to have my own copy of books, not just the school one.*

No, that wouldn't do. Aunt Margaret had been a librarian and always thought people were wasting money if they bought anything at all. She tore it up.

*Dear Aunt Margaret,*
*Thank you very much for the book token. I am really looking forward to spending it. I am going to buy* A Room with a View *and* A Passage to India. *We have started doing* Howard's End *at college and I want to read E.M. Forster's other books too.*
*I hope you have a happy new year.*
*With love from*
*Emmie x*

She still had Aunty Molly to do. She could have copied last year's letter – each Christmas Molly sent a scarf and mittens that she'd crocheted and something with some sort of New Zealand emblem on. Emmie would wear the crocheted things as long as the colour wasn't embarrassing, but she couldn't possibly have used a New Zealand pencil case in public.

*Dear Aunty Molly, Uncle Bill, Will and Edward,*
*Thank you very much for the scarf and mittens. I will wear them*
*all the time. I really like blue-and-white stripes. It's very cold*
*here at the moment. Thank you for the New Zealand pencil case*
*too. It's really cute. I wish England had flightless parrots. Dad*
*says thank you for the wallet. It will be really useful.*

*I hope you had a happy Christmas and will have a happy*
*new year.*

*Lots of love,*
*Emmie x*

Emmie checked the letters over. It would be awful to send a letter with a spelling or punctuation mistake. She also had a fear that she might accidentally write *fuck off!* even though she wasn't thinking it. She realised that she sounded like the most boring teenager in the history of the world. Perhaps she should write saying that she was going to spend all her Christmas money on drugs, or a one-way ticket to Berlin, or at least records. She had been with Sam and Lucy to see *Christiane F.* They had all put on loads of make-up and nobody had even asked if they were eighteen.

She looked out at the damp Surrey countryside and wished that she could swim, like dolphins could swim. She wanted to stand with guns shooting over her head and to kiss and be kissed as though nothing could fall. She put on her coat and went out in the rain. Lucy had gone skiing and Sam had gone to stay with her granny in the Lake District. Why didn't she have a granny in the Lake District? She bought some cigarettes and stood on the bridge over the railway line, smoking one after another and wishing something would happen. What was she meant to do? Go home and watch *Dumbo* again?

She was going to get out of Surrey and they wouldn't see her for dust; or, she supposed, for grass cuttings and fragments of moss.

# 1960s

## Blue-and-White-Striped Polyester Tie
## (c. Mid-1960s)

Molly spotted Bill's Morris Minor Traveller outside the hospital. She loved it when he picked her up from work. The bus conductors usually gave nurses a free ride but being picked up by Bill in his car beat everything. He was coming to supper with Aunt Lucinda that night. Aunt Margaret would doubtless be there too. Molly's cape billowed out as she hurried towards where he had parked.

'My blue angel,' he said as he closed the passenger door for her. Inside the car he kissed her. 'I missed you.'

'I missed you too. New tie,' she said, 'it's nice.'

'I want to impress your Aunt Lucinda tonight.'

'Aunty likes you already,' said Molly. 'She's always liked you.' It was true that Aunt Lucinda had liked Bill when they'd first met, but he had been Mr. Elderkin then and Molly's science teacher. 'Aunt Margaret is the harder one to impress.'

Bill's tie was the new style and wider than he usually wore. Molly was pleased he'd made the effort, but she was fond of the thin knitted ties he'd always worn and suspected that her aunts would like those better too. There was a light dusting of chalk on his cuffs, as usual, and on his trousers; he had a habit of dusting off his hands on the sides of his thighs when he was teaching. His hair always smelt a bit chalky and his hands often smelt of the chemicals used in lessons. Molly sniffed at her own hands. They smelt of hospitals.

It was pouring when they arrived. The laurel hedge was sparkling with raindrops in the streetlight and the puddles contained drops of amber and citrine. Molly hung up her cape and Bill's jacket. She hurried upstairs to change and to swap her headache-inducing bun for a looser ponytail. Where was Jay? His bedroom door was ajar, but the room was empty and in darkness. He'd said he'd be in tonight. He had probably gone out with Pammy from his office, again.

When she came back downstairs in her dark blue jeans with the turn-ups and the Guernsey sweater Aunty had bought her in Cornwall, Bill was sipping sherry with Aunt Margaret. How brave he was. He was leaning on the mantelpiece, his elbow perilously close to one of her aunt's glass vases. The fire had just been lit. Molly hoped that Aunt Margaret wouldn't think that Bill was taking up all the heat. She was always in charge of tending the fire; nobody, she said, did it as well as she. Molly and Jay had soon learnt not to start doing what she called 'podging it' when she was there. It was a different matter when she wasn't visiting. Lucinda had taught them how to build and tend the fire and put them in charge of sweeping out the clinker and ashes in the morning. She had been happy for them to lie on the hearthrug and gaze at the flames with Bramble all evening, and never minded if they flicked bits of paper or tossed walnut shells in, or – best of all – threw on screwed-up Christmas wrapping paper which burnt with pretty colours.

'Do sit down, Bill,' Molly said. He did, joining her on the sofa. Molly hoped he wouldn't crack his knuckles. It was a terrible habit – one she was hoping he would lose. She knew that when he stood up the backs of his trousers would be covered with Bramble's fur.

'Supper's ready!' Lucinda called from kitchen. Molly hurried to help her and wheeled the trolley with the fish pie and boiled potatoes and the dishes of carrots and cabbage into the dining room. Lucinda and Bramble followed; Bramble hoping for scraps but ready to spend the meal sitting on Lucinda's feet as usual. Margaret was already sitting in her favourite place, which was lucky as it meant that Bill couldn't accidentally take it. This evening Bramble didn't sit on Lucinda's feet; he sat on Bill's instead.

'Perhaps I smell of the Lake District,' said Bill. 'I was there in half-term. It's a pity Molly couldn't have time off – we teachers are much luckier than nurses.'

'I don't know if I'd be very good at going up mountains,' said Molly. 'I've seen mountains but I've never climbed one.'

'Of course, you would,' said Margaret. 'There's nothing to it. You just need a good pair of boots and to keep going.' She turned to Bill, 'Which ones did you climb?'

'Scafell, Great Gable, Skiddaw. Molly could start with Cat Bells.'

'Cat bells?' asked Molly, picturing herself with tinkling silver anklets. 'Is that in case you get lost?'

'Cat Bells! I'm sure Molly could do a lot better than that,' barked Margaret.

'Cat Bells is a big hill, Molly,' said Lucinda. 'You could easily climb it. Mustard, Bill?'

'Thank you.' He took a tiny amount. Molly had warned him that Margaret always said 'Mr. Colman made his fortune from the mustard left on the sides of people's plates' if she or Jay took more than a dot.

'Your aunt and your father were great fell walkers,' Lucinda went on. 'James loved rock-climbing too – our hearts were always in our mouths – he and his cousin Harry Stolly. We had lots of holidays in the Lakes and North Wales when we were younger.'

'Desperate walkers,' said Margaret, smiling and helping herself to more carrots. Molly looked across to Bill. Was now a good moment? But he waited until they had finished their apple pie and he and Molly had done the washing up.

Molly passed around the coffee. Lucinda offered them all butterscotch and fudge.

'Miss Theodore, Miss Ash,' said Bill (even though he now

called Lucinda by her first name), 'there is something I would like to ask you.' Margaret put down her cup with a louder than normal clink. 'I would like Molly to marry me.'

'Oh, my dears,' said Lucinda, her eyes filling with tears.

'And would Molly like to marry you?' asked Margaret, turning to Molly.

'Yes,' said Molly, 'I would.'

'I will take the greatest care of her,' said Bill. 'I've loved her for a long time.'

'Hmm,' said Margaret, and Molly knew she was thinking of the fact that he'd been a teacher in love with one of his pupils.

'You don't need our permission to marry,' said Lucinda. 'But of course, you have my—' she glanced at Margaret – 'our blessing.'

'Thank you, Aunty,' said Molly. 'Thank you both.'

'Where will you live?' asked Margaret.

'Well,' Bill began, 'when Molly's finished her training, we'll both be able to get jobs anywhere.' Molly caught his eye, gave a tiny shake of the head. She hadn't agreed to that yet. Why did they have to go somewhere so far away? 'We don't always want to live in London,' he said. 'It would be nice to be somewhere with better air, and mountains, and the sea.'


He drove home grinning. Molly had walked him to the door and kissed him in the porch. She was so tiny in his arms. He *had* loved her from the moment he'd seen her. She'd been crying in a corridor, lost on one of her first days at school. Somehow, she'd got separated from her classmates. She didn't understand the timetable. Didn't know where anything was. He'd put a reassuring arm around her shoulders and shown her the way to her next lesson, and then offered to help her at any time.

'Your parents must be very proud of you, Molly,' he'd said. 'It's hard starting at a new school, in a new place.'

'My parents are dead, sir,' she'd said, very quietly and calmly, as though she was used to saying it. He'd wanted to hold her then but managed not to. It was his first job – he wasn't that much older than her – less than ten years anyway. He'd hoped that she wouldn't think of him as an old man. He'd waited until she left school and started her training, then happened to be passing the hospital every night on his way home from work until he happened to bump into her and was able to ask her out. And she had said yes.

'I am pleased,' Lucinda told Margaret the next day when they were walking Bramble on the heath. 'But it has all gone so quickly. I knew she was never mine to keep. I wish they'd come to England when they were smaller. I can't remember why it didn't seem like the best idea at the time.'

'I know you're putting a brave face on, dear,' said Margaret, 'but they probably won't move very far away.'

# 1980s

## Penguin Classics Copy of *Wuthering Heights* (c. 1984)

There were cold cooked carrots and slices of avocado dotted with peanuts for high tea because Aunt Lucinda had read that those were rich in protein and she worried that Emmie wouldn't get enough protein to eat when she visited. Lucinda and Margaret were having theirs without the peanuts; peanuts, like Coca-Cola, were something for The Young.

'All vegetarian,' Aunt Lucinda said, smiling at Emmie, who was visiting for a weekend.

'Well,' Aunt Margaret said, addressing Lucinda, 'I suppose Emmeline is being true to her Hindu ancestry.'

'Oh, it's not because I want to be a Hindu,' said Emmie, blushing. But Aunt Margaret either didn't hear her or ignored her. Emmie looked beyond the tea table to the flowerbed that ran along the back wall of Aunt Lucinda's garden. It was all pinks and blues – peonies, delphiniums, pink roses, cornflowers and just a few stars of white – white cornflowers and ox-eye daisies.

'And what's this?' Aunt Margaret asked.

'Avocado, dear,' said Aunt Lucinda.

Margaret jabbed her fork into one of the slices. They were all turning brown.

'Huh.' She took a bite. 'Another one of those things that tastes of nothing.'

'It is nice,' said Emmie, knowing that Aunt Lucinda would

have got it especially for her. 'Some people have vinaigrette on it, or just lemon juice.'

'More unnecessary expense,' said Margaret.

Emmie wondered if she was the first unnecessary expense, whether Aunt Margaret considered her visit, perhaps her whole existence, to be an unnecessary expense.


Later that afternoon Margaret stood in the window and watched her great-niece's retreating back. For a moment she thought that Emmie had taken her mac. From behind, the girl did look rather like her. Same taste in macs, and she'd noticed that Emmie had also been wearing flat brown shoes, rather like her own. Another sensible choice. She did hope that Emmie would make something of herself. She seemed a clever girl, though rather simpering, and too eager to please, though she was quite right to want to please Lucinda. Everybody should want to please Lucinda. Margaret hoped that Emmie realised how much Lucinda had done for the family. She had noticed a copy of *Wuthering Heights* in Emmie's bag. Well, everybody had to go through that Brontë phase. She wondered whether Emmie had read *Persuasion*. Now that was a far better novel, though perhaps not to teenage tastes. Emmie had said that she was going to do English at university. Well, that was good anyway. Not everybody could go to Cambridge and read Greats.


Emmie sat on a bench at Winchester station. Her train wasn't due for another twenty minutes. She took *Wuthering Heights* out of her bag. Everybody in it was so unpleasant. But she still wished that somebody would love her the way that Heathcliff loved Cathy. '*I cannot live without my soul*' – would anybody ever say that about her, or feel that about her? It didn't seem likely. Although hopefully she wouldn't be dead if they did.

*Mansfield Park* had been the equivalent book on the

syllabus last year; she wished that they had got that instead. She liked Fanny Price. At least Fanny Price tried to be nice to people. Fanny Price was even polite to her Aunt Norris. And imagine how horrible it would be to live with Aunt Norris, or Great-aunt Margaret, come to that. Emmie wondered if Aunt Margaret hated her, the way that Aunt Norris hated Fanny Price, but it wasn't as though she, Emmie, was living with Aunt Lucinda, or in a position to usurp anybody's position. Perhaps Aunt Margaret just didn't like anybody, apart from Aunt Lucinda. Emmie had gone into the garden with Aunt Lucinda to cut some cornflowers before she left. They were poking out of her bag now, wrapped in some pages of last week's *Hampshire Chronicle*.

## Blue-Striped Indian Cotton Bedspread (c. 1980s)

The parcel arrived a week after her results. Inside was a thin Indian cotton bedspread, a £20 book token and this letter:

*My Dear Emmeline,*
*Many congratulations on your excellent exam results and your place at university. Your Aunt Lucinda and I were delighted to hear the news, and also to learn that you were going to be just a few miles away from us in Southampton. Your aunt says to tell you that we hope you will come to tea once you have settled in.*

*We also hope you will find the enclosed useful. We thought that it might be your sort of thing and know that you will have very many books to buy.*

*Your affectionate aunt,*
*Margaret*

It was the nicest thing Aunt Margaret had ever said to her. Emmie knew to send a thank-you letter by return of post.

## InterRail Pass (Summer 1986)

Emmie was home for the Easter vacation, back to the boredom of Surrey and the quiet politeness of life with her dad. She had an essay to finish on *Wide Sargasso Sea* and exams to revise for, but she'd been spending the day lost in *Heat and Dust*. She was going to India that summer with her friends Jo and Ian (who she secretly had a thing for), but her dad didn't know this yet. She'd always wanted to go and now, at last, she was. She kept her *Rough Guide to India* hidden in her room. She put aside *Heat and Dust* and made cannelloni stuffed with spinach and cheese sauce for dinner. Her dad liked that.

'Dad,' she said, once they'd started eating, 'this summer, I thought I might go away with some friends for a few weeks.'

'That's fine. I knew you wouldn't always want to go on holiday with your boring old dad.'

'Dad, it's not that, but I want to go somewhere further away, somewhere new. Ian, he's not my boyfriend, and he's really sensible, and so's Jo. A girl Jo. You met her. You liked her. We've been planning it and we're booking flights and trains soon. It will all be very safe and organised.'

'Flights *and* trains?'

'To India, I—'

'No!' He slammed the flat of his hand down on the table. 'You are not going to India!'

'But, Dad…'

'No! Absolutely not. I won't have you going there. It's too dangerous. Diseases. It's not safe for a girl like you.'

'We'll stay safe. Loads of my friends have been. I feel silly that I haven't.'

'I said no. I don't want you to go. I don't want you doing something so risky. I don't want you exposed to that poverty. What if something happened to you? Emmeline, no.'

'But, Dad!'

'No buts.' He pushed his plate away and left the room.

Emmie went out into the garden and smoked one of her secret cigarettes, not caring if he saw. She sat there as it grew dark. When she came back in, her dad wasn't watching TV. He was in his bedroom with the door shut.

I will go, she thought, he can't stop me. She scraped the uneaten food into the bin and did the washing up. If she acted like his good girl, maybe tomorrow he would have changed his mind.

He left for work before she was up the next day. She finished *Heat and Dust* and started the essay. When he came home, he hugged her. Maybe he had relented.

'Emmie,' he said, 'I just don't want you to go there.'

'But, Dad—'

'No buts. You're too precious. What if something happens to you. Emmie, you're all I have.'

And she found herself acquiescing.

Later she cried on the phone to Jo.

'It must be hard for your dad,' said Jo.

'It's hard for me!'

'Eleanor and Anna want to go InterRailing. You could go with them.'

'Maybe. If they want me.'

'Course they will.'


When Jo and Ian got back from India, they had become an item. Emmie forced herself to smile at their endless photos and anecdotes about the places they'd stayed and the brilliant bargains they'd got everywhere they went, never paying as much as people asked, eating out for almost no money. She was pleased when they split up in the second week of term, though she had gone off Ian; he looked so pink and peeling in the photos.

## Replica WWII Flying Jacket - Brown
## Leather (c. 1986)

He was known as Seb Soviet Worker. This was a time when regular young men didn't work out and gyms barely existed, but Seb had a set of weights in his room and got up early to go rowing. And when he wasn't rowing, he was running or caving or rock-climbing.

Apart from the rowing, he wasn't that into team sport; individual attainment of perfection was his aim. He had the profile and big arms of a man on a Soviet tractor poster. Despite his nickname, Seb wasn't left wing. He described himself as apolitical; it was the '80s and CND badges were becoming rarer on campus. Stock Soc. was the fastest growing student society, and pearls and braying were widespread.

Emmie had felt as though she was the only person not to be excitedly trying to buy shares in BT. Seb had a growing portfolio, but it wasn't something he discussed. He had a slick of fair hair that he pushed upwards and backwards, while the short back and sides were always neatly clipped. He wore a brown leather flying jacket. Emmie longed for a jacket like that. She could imagine the weight of it around her shoulders, the silky lining, how cool it would look with a pretty little skirt; but he never lent it to anybody. She had never spotted a girl (or a boy) wearing it, or indeed any of his jumpers, the way girls wore the big jumpers as trophies of whoever they were entangled with. ('Look at me, I'm wearing his jumper!

And don't my wrists and collar bones look thin, the way they are jutting out of it?') Seb was friendly and charming with the easy confidence of the expensively educated, but it was his perfect profile, chiselled cheekbones and huge arms that earned him his nickname. He was in most of her lectures, and some of her tutorial groups, but there was no point in hoping – there must be dozens of girls in love with him.

And now here he was in a crisp creamy-white shirt, a silky white pilot's scarf (or was it the sort people wore with a tuxedo?), black jeans, and that jacket. He didn't look uncomfortable in the jacket, even though it was boiling at the party, and the room was thick with Christian Dior *Poison* and smoke. Talking Heads were playing. Seb wasn't dancing, he was standing there, not like Mr. Darcy, but smiling, and holding a bottle of Pils. In pubs, they all drank Pils or Grolsch (until they all drank Sol with pieces of lime stuck in the top), but at this party other people were drinking cheap wine bought by the hosts on a daytrip to France or cans of horrible cheap lager. So how come he had a pristine bottle of Pils in his hand? Emmie hated those bottles of Pils. It was impossible to hold one, or to have one on the table in front of you without starting to pick at the label. The result was always an ugly mess. They looked nice when they were studded with diamonds of condensation, but the moment someone started picking that label…

A girl with long pale brown hair was dancing a crazy dance in a corner with her eyes closed. She was wearing a pale blue Laura Ashley blouse with a big pie-crust collar and jeans. Emmie suspected that she had been a born-again sixth-former, and now at university she was becoming unborn again and was busy losing her religion. Emmie pretended not to be watching her. There must be a crucial time for first years from Christian families, she thought, a point at which they had to decide whether to enrol at the Christian Union and get up early for church on Sundays, or to leave their Good News Bible in a suitcase under the bed, to not put up any posters with sunsets and messages, and to try to just blend in. Emmie's paper cup of wine was empty. She moved away towards the kitchen. The corridor, like the corridor of every student house she had been in, was dark because the bulb had gone and nobody would buy a new one. There were couples snogging already. Emmie looked away, and glanced up, noticing the pretty plaster coving, the ceiling rose that would be yellow with filth and smoke, and felt a hand on her shoulder. She turned. Seb Soviet Worker was smiling down at her.

'You aren't going already?'

'Just looking for some wine…'

'I'll come with you.'

The light in the kitchen was bright. The floor was sticky with spilt lager. Somebody had made some food, but as there were no plates or forks, nobody was eating it, or perhaps they wouldn't have anyway. Some loaves of French bread had been cut into circles and spread with something brownish. Wafts of garlicy steam were coming from the oven. Emmie suspected that there was forgotten garlic bread in there, but a couple were so engrossed in each other in front of it, that she didn't want to interrupt to intervene. Their clothes and hair would stink the next day. There was a wheel of camembert with a cigarette stubbed out in it.

'Plebs,' said Seb. Emmie agreed, although she wouldn't ever have said 'plebs'. The centrepiece was a huge glass bowl of wholemeal pasta salad. It was coloured green with what Emmie suspected was mint sauce and decorated with peas and leaves of mint. Nobody would eat it. How sad to think of some girl going to the effort of making it only for it to sit there in its ridiculous greenness. Emmie felt like chucking the whole lot into the open bin bag in the corner now, just to save the poor girl having to do it later. She had come with Ian and Anna; Ian was in a class with one of the boys in the house. Emmie didn't know them but judging from the names on the unfunny quotes board, there were people who lived here called Katie, Sophie, Phil and Si.

'Wine,' Seb announced. 'Hmm.' It was Liebfraumilch.

'I don't think you should drink that. Let's see if there's anything better.'

'What about you?'

He patted his jacket, and Emmie heard a gentle clink. 'Brought my own.'

She disapproved of people who did that, who brought a bottle and then hogged it, though it did make perfect sense, when other people brought such appalling things – perry or lager that was only 1.5%. She had once seen a guy put Top Deck Limeade and Lager down on the table and then help himself to the Carlsberg that somebody else had brought.

'This looks better.' He poured her a paper cupful of Soave. 'So, Annie,' he said, 'why don't you ever talk to me after tutorials, why do you always hurry away?'

'It's Emmie,' said Emmie. 'Do I?'

He put his finger under her chin and tilted her face up towards him. 'Emmie. Emmie is pretty. Prettier than Annie, much more unusual.'

'Boys don't usually use the word "pretty",' said Emmie. And no boy had ever used it about her name before.

'Emmie is sweet, Emmie is cute, Emmie is graceful.'

Was he laughing at her? 'It's Emmeline, really, after my great-grandmother.'

He had a strand of her hair curled around his finger now.

'Not *the* Emmeline Pankhurst?'

'Oh no, but same generation,' said Emmie, thinking of the portrait of Emmeline in red above her aunts' fireplace and the photographs of Emmeline in her wedding dress with the velvet ribbon choker. Who would want to wear something that tight around her throat for her wedding? His finger was running along her clavicle now. Emmie was secretly vain about her clavicles. His finger slipped under the necklace of black jet beads she was wearing. Aunt Lucinda had given them to her. Emmie smiled. It was as though her great-aunts and great-grandmother were with her at the party, hovering somewhere behind her. What would they be saying? They must have been to parties, though probably not ones like this. She couldn't imagine Aunt Margaret gulping wine from a paper cup while being seduced. Emmie shifted her feet. She felt she had to move them every so often to stop them from sticking permanently to the floor. The jet beads were coiled around his finger now; she hoped he wouldn't twist them any tighter and risk breaking the string or choking her.

'They're Victorian,' she said. 'My great-aunt gave them to me.'

'You aren't in mourning?' he asked. Last week's tutorial had been on Masha's role in *The Three Sisters*.

'Only for my life,' said Emmie. 'Actually, I'm not. Not at all.' She smiled. Life was taking off.

The suspected Christian renegade came dancing in and started swigging from the bottle of Liebfraumilch. Seb and Emmie's eyes met, and they laughed.

'God. It's dreadful here. You were clearly made for better things. Shall we go?' He smiled down at her. 'Would you like to come home with me?'

'Um, OK,' said Emmie.

She found her mac in the heap of coats over the banister. Anna was sitting on the stairs, talking to a boy Emmie vaguely recognised, some third year in Theatre Soc.

'I'm going now,' Emmie told her. Anna grinned and raised her eyebrows. Emmie gave a little shrug and blushed. They made a quick exit.

It was easier to talk to him walking along in the dark. It was drizzling slightly. Emmie hoped her hair wouldn't go crazy. She reached into her mac pocket for her faithful velvet scrunchy.

Soon they turned the corner into Osbourne Road, a dead end.

'Along here,' he said.

It was the last house. It was all in darkness; no working light in the hall, of course. She was just able to navigate her way around the two bikes (big racers, so boys') that almost blocked it. She skidded slightly on a free newspaper. The house smelt pretty dreadful, of damp and bacon and mud. There must be some rugby kit mouldering somewhere. Perhaps Seb didn't live a life of perfection, whatever his hair might suggest.

He led her upstairs. His room was at the front of the house, it would have been the master bedroom. He unlocked the door and pushed it open. They never locked their doors in Emmie's house. What was this, Bluebeard's castle? He didn't turn on the light. The room was illuminated in pale orange from the streetlamp outside. He walked over to his desk and switched on the lamp there. Emmie gave a tiny gasp of surprise. She had always, always wanted a lamp like that. And a desk like that. The lamp was the sort with a green glass shade, like the ones they had in old films. She walked over and ran her finger along the gold embossed border of the desk's brown leather top. There was a faint whiff of polish. Did he sit here polishing his boots and his desk and his brown leather jacket? Some of the course books were in a neat stack – the Chekhov, various Norton Anthologies, *Paradise Lost*, and the Angela Carter that one lecturer had been enthusing about – *The Bloody Chamber*. Emmie had read it before the term began. It left her dizzy. They were discussing it next seminar. And the room was pristine. Instead of the compulsory horrible '70s carpet in shades of yellow, orange and brown, the floorboards had been stripped and varnished. He had a soft red rug underneath his desk.

He switched on the bedside lamp and motioned for her to sit down. Beside the bed was a sheepskin rug, it looked soft and clean, not like the manky goatish ones most people had, but it wasn't white; more yellowish, like carnivores' teeth – and she couldn't help smiling at the thought that it was a bit of sheep's clothing discarded by a wolf.

'Would you like a drink? Gin, scotch, vodka?' He smiled down at her. She could tell that he was peering down her top. She had had a bath before the party. It seemed that the ritual preparations – the strawberry face pack, the exfoliating and polishing with pineapple body scrub, the tangerine shampoo and satsuma conditioner, the raspberry ripple (or, if her grant cheque had just come, Badedas) bubble bath – were going to have been necessary. Things happen after a Badedas bath.

'Gin, please.' She quite liked gin and tonic. She'd never had vodka. She liked whisky if it had soda in it, like her dad made.

He took two glasses out of the bedside cabinet. They sparkled in the lamplight. The spirit bottles were in a bashed red metal bucket under his desk, the sort of bucket they had on the underground, full of sand for fires. He must have stolen it.

'Nice bucket,' she said. He opened the window and reached outside to retrieve a new bottle of tonic. 'Most boys keep trainers on their windowsills.'

'Most boys. But my feet don't smell.' He grinned down at her again. She glanced down at his feet. He was wearing boots, slightly pointy, with a slight Cuban heel that was completely unnecessary as he was already so tall. He would take them off in a moment.

Press the button to see Talking Heads perform
'Take Me to the River'.

# 1950s

# Cinema Tickets for *South Pacific* (April 1958)

Back in her twenties, Margaret knew how it should happen. She would be at her desk, eyes on the catalogue cards she was working on, and he would approach. She would finish the line she was writing before looking up. Readers were such a bother, always interrupting, and the long line of digits necessary for each item must, of course, be correct.

When she did look up it would be straight into his eyes. He would be older than her; Professor Bhaer to her Jo March. He would be looking for something in particular that should have been on the shelf. Something like... well, she wasn't sure what his area of research would be yet. She would laugh and say that yes, it should have been on the shelf, but in fact it was here, on her desk, because she had been reading it at lunchtime. He would smile and ask if it could be reserved for him, when she had finished with it, of course, and she would say yes, of course, and that would mean that she would have his name, which would be something beautiful like Edmund. He might be greying at the temples, but from behind his hair would curl into the nape of his neck like Rupert Brooke's in the frontispiece to *1914*. She would notice that his hands were extremely clean – she couldn't abide borrowers who had dirty hands – though they would be strong and sensible hands.

The next day he would find her sitting in the park at lunchtime. She would look up from the book, which would be *that* book, of course. She would almost have finished it. He would ask if he could join her. Luckily, she would have already eaten her lunch, so she wouldn't have to do that in front of him. He would ask her about the book and she would have something very clever to say. The next day she would be sitting on the same bench reading when suddenly it would start to rain. He would appear with an umbrella that was big enough (just) for the two of them and he would walk her back to the library, though they would walk around Russell Square first where the raindrops would be splashing onto the paths like rain in a film.

Much later on she would ask him, in the style of Lizzy Bennet, when it was that he had first fallen in love with her and he would say that it had been when she first looked up at him on the day he came to enquire about the book, and that she had looked exactly like Tenniel's Alice, with her hair behind that band, and her look of determination and surprise and curiosity all at once, but that she was much more like the Arthur Rackham Alice who was prettier than the Tenniel one. And she would be pleased about that too, as the Tenniel Alice had such a huge forehead.

Some months later an umbrella would feature in his proposal to her. It would be as simple and beautiful as in *Persuasion* (without the seven years' misunderstanding, of course, and no annoying Louisa Musgrove having got in the way). 'Margaret, I have loved no one but you,' he might say. Or else it would be like Jo March's proposal from Professor Bhaer. Yes, he would definitely be a professor, though she had no plans whatsoever for them to open an orphanage or a boarding school. She quickly blinked away the thoughts of the orphans who really ought to be living with her. Thank goodness for Lucinda.

Now Margaret was almost fifty and, rather surprisingly, The Man Who Thought She Looked Like Tenniel's Alice had yet to appear. Her lunchtimes tended to be spent reading in the staffroom or doing the very small amounts of shopping that she required. The only reader who had taken more than a passing interest in her was Professor Gordon Roper. Professor Roper lurked behind pillars. He was often waiting before the library opened and would still be there when it closed. Sometimes she enjoyed chatting to him, but at other times she avoided Military History as that was his area and she didn't want to be waylaid. He had a particular interest in the battle sites of the English Civil War. Margaret had noticed how each historical researcher tended towards the haircut and dress style of their period, even if it were centuries ago. Professor Roper was no exception and his haircut was clearly on the Roundheads' side. The whole of the seventeenth century made her shudder. As did most of the sixteenth, fifteenth and fourteenth. The architecture had been very good, of course, but there really wasn't much point in any of the rest of it, with a few exceptions among the poets, painters and playwrights, until one hit the eighteenth century and the novel really took off.

When Margaret was engaged in any menial task at work, she liked to think of the private library that she would found. Readers would have to pass a strict interview and provide references. There would be compulsory handwashing on the way in and lockers where shoes and coats would be left. The readers would have to wear black velvet slippers. They would each have to buy their own pair and would not be allowed to take them out of the library. Her own pair would be embroidered with anemones. Lucinda would be happy to do that for her. The compulsory slippers would ensure that all footsteps were quiet and that no mud or dirt from the pavements was brought inside. Anybody who damaged a book (and that included dog-earing pages), returned one late or who attempted to eat or drink inside the building, would be arrested and jailed for life without trial. She got so lost in her daydream that when Gordon Roper came up to the desk, she found herself agreeing to go to the cinema to see *South Pacific* with him. Professor Roper had smiled, made a slight adjustment to a pile of books on her desk, and walked away. She returned her books to their original position. Later she thought she heard someone humming 'Magic Moments' in the stacks. That, surely, couldn't be him.

April had started cold and foggy. There had been snow in the first weeks but suddenly it was very warm.

They met outside the cinema and he was gentlemanly, insisting on paying for the tickets and offering to buy her sweets. She declined and was relieved that he didn't buy any for himself either. How awful to sit next to a rustler or an audible chewer. They settled into their chairs and folded their macs neatly on their knees. Smoke from many hundreds of cigarettes was already drifting around the auditorium. She was pleased that Gordon (as he insisted she call him) didn't seem to smoke cigarettes, though up close she could smell that he smoked a pipe – a smell that she loved because it reminded her of her father. She settled back and enjoyed the overture.

The colouring of the film was rather strange, lurching between what she supposed must be different filters for different moods. She wondered if the cinema might have a set of faulty reels, but nobody else seemed to be noticing. She tried not to let it distract her from the story. Gordon's left knee seemed to be slowly moving towards her right leg. He clearly had the male habit of taking up more than the fair allocation of space.

She wondered where they had made the film. Had they really all gone to the South Pacific? The plants in the film were impressive, putting her in mind of Marianne North's work. Could one make a film like this in Kew Gardens? Oh no, the sea was required. How exciting to have been Marianne North – to travel like that and have that talent. But Margaret knew that she herself wasn't that sort of person, she just wasn't adventurous enough. Nor was she, she realised, as the film began, anything like a dame. Why did so many of the men have their shirts off? Would they really have gone around like that? And Margaret didn't like the way that Bloody Mary had her hair. It would look so much nicer if it wasn't scraped back so severely. It seemed unfair, when everybody else had been made to look so nice. She was a very fine singer.

The film was starting to seem desperately sad. Emile, the planter, put her in mind of James, of course. Nellie's perkiness was annoying, but oh, to be a cockeyed optimist, how nice life would be! But when they sang 'Some Enchanted Evening' Margaret found that she had tears running down her cheeks. She hoped that they would remain invisible. What would Gordon think? She fumbled in her bag for her handkerchief. She couldn't find it. Gordon silently passed her his own clean, folded square. Not invisible, then. She dabbed at her face. The tears stopped after a while. She balled up the handkerchief and held on tight to it. Gordon reached over and gently patted her fist and she found herself smiling, as corny as Kansas in August. He left his hand on top of hers for a little while.

The plot was becoming hard to follow. There was a deeply embarrassing scene with drumming and dancing and something to do with a pig with very long and curly tusks. Margaret had to look away. And then Bloody Mary's pretty daughter was in a situation where she wanted to kiss a complete stranger. Well, there might be love at first sight, but wouldn't a young girl like that have found the whole situation rather scary? Margaret supposed that the Tonkinese wouldn't have seen *Madame Butterfly*. It was all taking rather a long time. Margaret tried to see her watch, but it was too dark. It must, surely, be nearly time for the interval. She tried to stop thinking about time and just enjoy the songs.

Now Nellie Forbush was horrified that the two dark children were Emile de Becque's. Margaret remembered how she'd felt when she'd heard about James's children; that had been a proper shock. Lucinda, good kind Lucinda, had taken it all in her stride of course, and become a long-distance mother to the pair. They would be coming to live with her soon. Poor Lucinda; a Nellie Forbush without the Emile de Becque. But Lucinda had always wanted children, always liked being busy with other people.

*Intermission*. Oh, at last.

Press the button to watch the 'Happy Talk'
scene from *South Pacific*.

'Enjoying it?' Gordon asked as the lights went up.

'Oh, very much,' she said.

'Let me get us some ices.'

'Thank you.' What a relief. She wanted to go to the cloakroom without having to say that she was going to the cloakroom.

The plot became more complicated in the second half with more military action. She suspected that Gordon would be enjoying this. She remembered him saying he'd been a radio operator during the war.

Margaret found the ending quite satisfactory. Nellie was right to stay there with Emile, the many interesting plants and the two children. Would they all, she wondered, ever go back home to meet Nellie's family in Little Rock? She wondered what reception they'd get. Nellie's parents would be pleased, no doubt, that her daughter had married so well. But the whole film left her feeling desperately sad. Very tired and very sad. The line for the exit moved slowly. Someone behind them was humming 'Happy Talk'.

When they came out of the cinema it was raining, but

neither of them had umbrellas. Gordon walked her to her bus stop.

'Margaret,' he said, 'we do have so few days in our lives.' She didn't know what to say, so she said nothing. 'I'm moving to Lyme Regis. I have a cottage there.'

'Oh,' she said. 'Won't you miss your university work?'

'That will continue, but I shall spend more time writing and less teaching. There are plenty of younger fellows who can pick that up for me.'

'Lyme Regis,' she said, 'how interesting.' She imagined him in a house near the sea, doing some wood turning and mending a net like Captain Harville in *Persuasion*. 'And all those fossils. I loved collecting things like that when I was younger.' She still had the little cabinet that had housed her finds.

'And do you have any plans for the future? Are you very tied to London? I know you're much younger than me, of course.'

'I hadn't thought about it much yet. My brother's children, orphans, are coming to London soon, though they'll be living with my friend. It's rather like *South Pacific*. James was a planter.'

'Good Lord, are they Tonkinese?' He stopped and stared at her. She couldn't see much of his expression, what with the rain and his hat, but he seemed aghast.

'Oh, no, Anglo-Indian. He was a tea planter. He married an Indian woman but they both died, he in the war, she soon afterwards.'

They were at her bus stop now. They stood in a shop doorway to get out of the rain. She could feel the water seeping through the soles of her shoes. She waited, expecting him to offer his condolences.

'Is that really wise? Wouldn't they be better off being left in India? Surely something could be done for them there – the Indian civil service or something?'

Her bus arrived.

'Well, thank you,' she said. 'That was a very nice evening. Goodbye.' Disenchanted evening, she thought, as she found her seat.

The next time she saw him it was lunchtime. He walked her back to the library. She let him take her arm.

'I'll be going down to Lyme Regis again this weekend. I'll be moving permanently soon,' he said.

'How lovely, but we will miss you at the library, and moving is always such a bother. One wants to do it as infrequently as possible.'

'But you must be a very organised person, Margaret,' he said. 'I'm sure you would be very good at anything like that.' She smiled and looked up at him and found that he was staring intently at her. Then he said, 'Can you type?' And the penny dropped. He wanted someone to be his housekeeper and secretary in retirement, to dust and organise his books and papers.

'Oh no,' she lied, 'I'm quite hopeless, terribly slow. And I hate dusting.'

'Dusting? You hate dusting?' He looked stunned.

'I'm far too busy to think about things like that. And I have so many books of my own, enough to fill two houses.'

Copy of *The Radiation Cookery Book:
A Selection of Proved Recipes for Use
with Regulo New World Gas Cookers,*
19th Edition (1936)

The house was ready. Edward had left her the half of his estate
that he'd said would have gone to James. Lucinda had moved
out of her little flat a few doors down from Margaret in The
Paragon and had bought a house nearby in Blackheath. She
had known it was right even before she'd gone inside. The
name on the panel over the stained-glass door told her that it
was exactly what she needed for Jay and Molly: The Haven.
She wished that Edward and Emmeline could have seen it
or could have been there to welcome the children with her.
Margaret hadn't been pleased about the move.

'Couldn't you all have fitted in here? Much more convenient.'

'For you, dear, but young people need space. And it will
be so nice for them to have their own rooms and a garden.'

'Hmm.' Lucinda knew Margaret could see her friend's life
being taken over by things to do with schools and appointments
at the doctor. The evenings listening to the wireless together
and reading in companionable silence would be gone, at least
until James's children could embark on their own careers.

The plan had been for Jay to come first, alone, when he
finished school in India, but Molly had written pleading to
come too and Lucinda couldn't think of a good reason for her
to be left behind. Molly could finish school in London. She

said that she wanted to be a nurse – that was easily arranged in London too.

'Why not a doctor?' Margaret had asked, when she read that letter.

What Jay was going to do was a different matter. When he was only ten, he'd written to Edward that he wanted to be a farmer or run a tea plantation. Edward had written back saying that farming was extremely difficult, and that when he'd tried it himself in Canada it had been quite a relief to give up and come home to England and be on the importing side of things instead. And the world of tea had changed so much since independence, it would probably be better to come to England and find what he wanted to do here. Later Jay had said that he'd like to be an importer like his grandfather, but Edward was by then retired and had sold his share in the firm, so that wasn't a possibility either.

'Couldn't he go to university?' Margaret suggested. 'What about Hertford College and Geology, like James?'

'Hmm,' said Lucinda. She didn't want to get his hopes up. One of the gentlemen at the centre for the blind that she ran suggested Jay join the army. Many of them were former soldiers who had lost eyes and limbs. Lucinda wanted to say that joining the army would seem rather an odd thing to suggest. Why rescue the boy from poverty in India and educate him just to push him towards the same fate as his poor father and his great-uncles? But of course, she didn't say that. Another suggested an apprenticeship, and that seemed like a good idea. Jay would be enrolled at the local technical college first. His school reports always mentioned his flair for drawing and facility with numbers. He could train to be a draftsman or some such thing. Jay and Molly must be able to support themselves.

Lucinda had her own furniture as well as plenty from Edward and Emmeline's last home, so the children would be surrounded by things that had belonged to their father and grandparents. Margaret had taken the few things she wanted, mostly books and a few pictures.

Food wasn't something that Lucinda had ever given that much thought to. It had always been plain and simple at home. Her mother had been in charge of the menus and her own contribution had been little more than showing up appropriately dressed. Food had always been a Needs Must sort of thing. Rationing hadn't made that much difference to her, if anything it had been a useful sort of guide; with such a limited palette she hadn't had to make so many decisions about what to eat.

Now, suddenly, she would have young people to cook for. Young people who would be extremely hungry, who were used to school food cooked by proper cooks. She wished she could afford a cook, but even with the money from Edward added to her own that just wasn't a possibility. And people nowadays didn't really have cooks, did they? But she did have one cookery book. It wasn't actually hers, it had been left in the house along with the stove. Perhaps the previous owners had thought that as they were leaving their once new cooker, the book should stay too. It was *The Radiation Cookery Book: A Selection of Proved Recipes for Use with Regulo New World Gas Cookers*, and it seemed to be just the thing.

*The 'Regulo' eliminates uncertainty from cooking*, the introduction told her. Elimination of uncertainty was what she needed. There were whole dinner menus that she could follow. She wondered if the children would require those every night. Perhaps some of the vegetarian ones would be particularly suitable for them, coming as they did from a predominantly Hindu country. Menu 50 looked rather good and said that it only required forty minutes. Savoury Rice, Creamed Potatoes and Meringue Pudding. She would try that one first.

Lucinda met the children at Liverpool. Molly would have run down the gangplank and into her arms if it hadn't been so busy. Lucinda put her arms out and Molly fell into them.

'Molly, my little girl!' Lucinda said and held her tight, wanting at once to cling onto her and for the child to step back so she could look at her properly. Jay came behind, more cautious, bony and awkward-looking. He extended a polite hand and Lucinda shook it.

'Jay. You look exactly like your father!'

And he did. The same curls, but darker. The same set chin. The same serious expression. The same half-smile.

'Hullo, Aunty.'

Lucinda knew the ground must be pitching and falling under the children's feet. They hadn't been on land for weeks.

'Did you come in a car?' Jay asked, hopefully, eyeing Lucinda's fox-fur scarf.

'I'm afraid not. We'll be taking a train, but we'll be home in time for supper.'

# 1990s

### Invitation to a University Reunion on
### Cream-coloured Cardboard, with Envelope
### Bearing a Second Class Postage Stamp (1998)

Who in their right mind would go to any sort of class reunion? It was ten years since graduation. The people that she had really liked – Eleanor Taylor, Anna Alton, Jo Turtle (who was now married and had become Jo King to everybody's amusement) and Ian McCloud – she was still in touch with. There was no good reason to go. She had nothing to boast about, no impressive job, no husband, no baby to show off and use to avoid making conversation; she wasn't any thinner than in her university days, though some of the clothes in her wardrobe were *from* those days. Emmie couldn't wear anything anyone might remember, and she also knew to beware of any enterprise that required new clothes – a maxim that seemed to apply to her whole life. But she figured that as she did live so close to the university and the others were all going, she might as well go. And she could always run away.

But what to wear, what to wear? Should she go dressed up or dressed down? There was to be an afternoon milling about with tea and some speeches by the current Head of the Faculty of Arts. Emmie had no recollection who the Head of the Faculty of Arts had been in her day. Then there was to be a tour of the department. Could it have changed that much in ten years? And then a wine reception with buffet and disco. My God, she thought, disco! She hadn't been to a disco in years. The only times she'd danced in the last decade had been at other people's weddings and when the city libraries' Christmas do had been somewhere that had a pathetic little dance floor for post-tiramisu shuffling about. But she had once loved dancing.

So, what to wear? She eventually settled on a slightly sticky-out skirt which had a '50s pattern that looked like grey-and-yellow linoleum, a black T-shirt, a little black cardigan, and flat black shoes. Somehow looking slightly '50s-ish seemed like a good idea in a *Peggy Sue Got Married*, high-school-reunions kind of way. She'd just seen *Grosse Point Blank*; maybe the evening would end like that. But she knew how it would end. It would end the way her evenings out always ended, with other people being a bit drunker than her, with her being nice to people, and with a trip home alone. The university had sent a list of hotels and B&Bs, but Emmie would be home in fifteen minutes.

She was almost ready. She couldn't find her other shoe. She knelt down on the floor and looked under the bed. There were some dreadful balls of dust under there, and she didn't want to get stuff on her black cardigan. She would deal with the dust tomorrow morning. She'd have nothing else to do. The shoe wasn't there. She began pulling the shoes out of her wardrobe; she had four pairs of almost identical flat black shoes, but the missing one wasn't there. She had two pairs of boots – one brown, one black – real library-lady footwear. She had some desert boots like the ones she'd worn when she was a teenager. She shoved them all aside. She tossed her one pair of trainers, her espadrilles, the slippers her dad had given her (wasn't it meant to be the other way round?), the towelling mules from the day she'd spent at a spa before Jo Turtle became Jo King (she had a feeling that other people would have treated them as disposable) and the jazz dance shoes that she'd worn to the graduation ball because she hated high heels. Perhaps she should wear those, or go in one shoe, like a sad Cinderella already on her way home.

Then she remembered. The shoe would be on the windowsill. She'd been sitting watching *Newsnight*, her bare feet tucked underneath her on the sofa. A giant spider had run into her shoe, and she'd carried it to the window and tipped it out. A spider in her shoe seemed like some sort of omen; but was it a good one or a bad one? A money spider would have been lucky. She remembered how they'd twirled the tiny creatures around their heads three times at school to guarantee future riches. There must have been a colony of them in the English room. There had been many covert twirlings while they were reading *Macbeth*. There had been ladybirds in the windowsills too. She had spent so much time looking out of windows, it was amazing that she'd ever passed any exams at all. She remembered being told off for it in a tutorial – well, kind of told off. A tutorial on the top floor of the Arts building.

'If Miss Ash didn't find the wind in the trees so interesting, perhaps she'd tell us what she thought about…' She had really liked that tutor. She supposed he would have forgotten her inattention. She had been a diligent, though, she suspected, slightly dull student – too quiet. If only she hadn't spent so much time trying to either go unnoticed or to be good. She could recognise other grown-up good girls at fifty paces now.

She found the shoe on the windowsill, hidden behind the curtains that she hadn't opened properly that morning. She loved those curtains. They were, she estimated, around seventy years old. Aunt Margaret had given them to her. ('Take them if you like, my dear, though I can't imagine why you'd want some that old and faded. I thought you people all liked bright new things.') She had wondered what Aunt Margaret's 'you people' had meant. No matter, she took the curtains and she loved them. The once creamy lining fabric had aged to a dark ivory, the same yellowish hue as piano keys and as the paperknife Aunt Margaret always used, even for junk mail. Emmie had to close the curtains carefully to avoid further rips. The design was of tumbling wisteria, the purple faded just as the real flowers did. Only a ghostly suggestion of the chintzy sheen remained. She decided on slightly redder than usual lipstick; she usually wore pinky browns. She smiled at herself in the mirror.

But when she got to the pub where they'd all agreed to meet, she saw how she was, as usual, dressed up as somebody who was nice. *Look at me, I'm Sandra Dee…* Ian was looking just as he always did in a soft blue shirt and jeans, the other girls (girls? they were all over thirty now!) looked like Robert Palmer's backing singers in little black dresses, slashes of really red lipstick and high heels. Why had she come in a dirndl skirt and flats? Might as well face it, you're addicted to being frumpy. She found herself smiling desperately, wondering if she should go home and change into a sleek black dress that she didn't possess. But it was too late.

The faculty tour showed them that the university had invested in some azure paint and that the chairs in the lecture theatres (which had been horribly squeaky with green vinyl backs and escaping foam stuffing) had been replaced with blonde pine ones. They all sat down for a minute, just to get that back-in-a-lecture feeling.

As they were led around the campus, Emmie tried to spot people she'd known, people who had once interested her. There was Sarah Miles who'd got a First. Hardly anybody got Firsts in those days. Emmie had missed one by two marks. She spotted the professor who'd supervised her dissertation on *The Figure of the Orphan in Golden Age Children's Fiction*, but he didn't look twice at her and she didn't want to be in the embarrassing situation of not being remembered. There was Angus James. He'd always had plenty to say and made jokes in tutorials. Emmie had secretly fancied him a little, but so did everybody else, even the tutors. Her maxims when it came to dating – or even having a mild interest in a person of the opposite sex – had always been Never Let Them Know You Are Interested, because nobody could possibly be interested in her, and Never Let Yourself Appear Ridiculous.

There was Debbie Baines. Emmie smiled and waved.

The address by the new Head was obviously intended to elicit donations from alumni who'd hit the big time. The penny dropped that this was why universities organised alumni reunions. People managed to titter politely at the jokes. Emmie couldn't imagine a time when she might earn enough to even consider giving some back to the university. If she were rich, wouldn't she be giving it to the Red Cross or something? And there was still the buffet and the so-called disco to get through. She could hardly remember an occasion when she'd gone out in the evening and then not wished that she'd stayed at home. Unless it was the theatre or cinema (she never regretted going to those), it only ever took minutes for her to start longing to be home again. She was going to turn into Aunt Margaret, at home listening to the radio and going to bed with the shipping forecast, but she didn't care. She wished she was at home, safe behind her lovely wisteria curtains.

It seemed that the address was over. There was polite applause and then the next (final, she hoped) shuffle into the bar. And that's when she saw him. He was waiting at the bar with that guy he'd often hung around with, Christopher Something. But she wasn't bothered about Christopher Something, only about him. Seb Soviet Worker.

**Fragment of Playlist for Alumni
Reunion Meeting (Summer 1998)**

'I Wanna Dance with Somebody'
'Girls Just Wanna Have Fun'
'Walking on Sunshine'
'The Whole of the Moon'
'Tainted Love'
'Psycho Killer'
'Love Cats'
'This Charming Man'
'Road to Nowhere'
'Ashes to Ashes'
'End of the World as We Know It'
'Dancing in the Dark'
'Should I Stay or Should I Go?'
'There Is a Light that Never Goes Out'

This time, Emmie asked if *he'd* like to go home with *her*.

## *Atlas of the World* (c. 1920)

There were two blue lines on the stick. Emmie's first feeling was one of astonishment that something like this – so biological, and so exactly like what they warned about at school – could happen to her as a supposed grown-up.

The next thing she felt was joy.

She went to lie down on her bed still holding the stick, wondering if the second line might fade away, meaning that it was a mistake. But the line stayed.

The pack had come with two tests. She decided to do the other one the next morning, just to be sure, and then if that one was also positive she would buy another test of a different brand from a different shop, just in case she'd had one from a bad batch, or from a shelf that had had too much sunlight or something.

After a while she put the stick down and rested her hands on her flat stomach and smiled. It was one of her alternate Saturdays and she didn't need to go to work. She decided not to tell anybody at all for a few days – or perhaps weeks. Her dad would be surprised, and, she expected, eventually pleased. She thought about work. Working for the local authority was a good thing. She had seen many other people go off on maternity leave and come back again months later – it seemed that they didn't starve to death. She lived pretty frugally anyway. It must be possible. She hoped people, particularly her great-aunts, wouldn't be too disapproving of her. Not such a good girl now.

And then she thought about Seb. Oh God! She hadn't even thought about him. This would be the child of Seb Soviet – she wasn't going to use that nickname even to herself anymore. She had been thinking of this baby as completely her own but it had a father. Did she have to tell him? She had no way of contacting him. He knew where she was now (if he had bothered to notice the address) but she had nothing about him. She knew that he taught English in Japan. He had told her the name of the city, but she had no recollection of what it had been. She could remember that it wasn't Tokyo. It had been somewhere that began with 'K'.

The only atlas she had was an ancient one that Aunt Lucinda had given her. She remembered thinking that an atlas was called an 'at last' because you would open it and at last you would know where a place was. She turned the pages. Japan was one of what seemed to be very few countries that weren't pink. Lots of places in Japan began with a 'K'. Knowing he lived somewhere beginning with 'K' didn't really narrow it down, and lots of places probably had different names now.

She'd never been to Japan. It might be fun to go. But one fine day, Emmie thought, he will return. *Madame Butterfly* was her favourite opera. She had a box set of cassettes of it sung by Maria Callas. It seemed quite likely that Seb would have a girlfriend, or possibly a whole string of girlfriends, in Japan. Or perhaps boyfriends. She could imagine him seducing his students too. They would be perfect and beautiful and more than ten years younger than her.

She decided that she didn't need to hurry to tell him. She was thirty-two. It was up to her what she did. She could try contacting him through the Alumni Office. They must have his address as he'd come to the reunion, or at least his parents' address as he'd said he had happened to be visiting them when he heard about the reunion. She realised that she didn't really mind, for her own sake anyway, if he came back or not.

## Woman's Hair in a Plait, Romsey Abbey, Hampshire (c. 10th Century)

Lucinda never missed a meeting of the St Cross WI. Margaret only went if the speaker was someone worth listening to. This month's meeting was a trip to Romsey Abbey. Margaret had voted for Bath. It had been ages since she'd been to Bath. She wanted to see the Royal Crescent and the Assembly Rooms again. She wanted to walk in the Parade Gardens, and gaze at the weir. *Persuasion* or *Northanger Abbey*? *Persuasion*, of course. And she wanted to visit Bath Abbey just one more time. But the votes for Romsey Abbey (nearer and consequently less expensive) had won out. A coach had been booked and left from outside The Bell at 2pm. The steps up were rather awkward, but one by one the ladies managed them.

The coach dropped them off near the Abbey – the wrong Abbey, Margaret couldn't help but think, though on balance Romsey Abbey was probably more interesting than Bath's, if one were to place them in some sort of hierarchy, though of course she wouldn't, comparisons being odious. They walked past a busker singing 'Happy Talk'. How strange, thought Margaret, that what was quite a mournful song was now considered an uplifting ditty. The busker was wearing a pink Hawaiian shirt. Lucinda, of course, dropped a pound coin into his hat where a cardboard sign asked for *Spare Change Pleaz*. They were having tea at the King John's

House Museum afterwards and were all looking forward to that. Margaret thought she would save her money for the tea. How could one know if one's change was actually spare? The busker was underselling himself too. If he hadn't had that sign, people might have been inclined to drop notes rather than coins into his hat. And he should have had a comma before 'please' and spelled it correctly.

They passed a shop selling nothing but teddy bears. The women in front stopped to admire them. Margaret had no choice but to stop too, though teddy bears always made her think of Auden's 'Nursery Rhyme' where woolly bears pursued spotted dogs and witches could make ogres out of mud.

They paused to look at the tiny ancient doors (alas, locked) on their way to the main entrance. But the key that opened them, Auden knew, would have turned to rust. The smallest could have been the doorway to the garden in *Alice's Adventures in Wonderland*. Margaret wished for a drink of some sort, or even just a glass of water, or a little bottle with *Drink Me* on the label.

They were shown around the Abbey by a volunteer guide. Margaret listened politely, waiting to be (as usual) the person with the most questions. A choir of girls were practising, their clear voices reaching the highest beams of the roof, just as their predecessors' had one thousand years ago. How typical, Margaret remarked to Lucinda, that men had claimed that boys' voices were purer and clearer and so the choirs of the great cathedrals had been predominantly male for centuries. What utter tosh.

In the north transept they paused for a good look at a sixteenth-century reredos. Other people moved on, but Margaret stopped and craned her neck to read a nineteenth-century memorial on pale grey marble:

Had Anne Godfrey left instructions for the wording? How awful to be memorialised as only a relic or a relict of somebody else. But at least the people responsible had known how to punctuate.

After their tour was finished, Margaret chatted to the guide for a while longer. If only, she thought, I wasn't so lame, I could do this. Being old was so tiresome. And she was so tired, tired in her bones. There was so much that she would like, theoretically, to do, but her limbs and eyes and heart were spent. She walked a little further looking for Saxon traces among the Norman stones. She had always felt rather ambivalent towards the Normans.

At the west end of the nave was a display cabinet she remembered from previous visits. Here lay the hair (but no scalp or skull) of a Saxon woman, one of the nuns or abbesses, still holding the shape of the head and still in its ancient plait. The label told her that the fragments of white visible were likely traces of bone. It was displayed on the original rounded pillow of wood that had supported the woman's head in her coffin. Who had invented bolsters, Margaret wondered. Perhaps the Normans had got the idea for them, from the

Saxons. It looked horribly like a chopping block, as though the hair and its invisible owner were awaiting execution, even in death. The hair had faded but you could see that it had been auburn. Margaret's hand went to her own hair, now so thin and grey, in its coiled plait at the nape of her neck. This Saxon hair had been found in a lead coffin by gravediggers in (she had to peer at the writing) 1839, and then been slung as rubbish into the abbey's coalhole before someone thought to keep it. And now here it was, under glass in the abbey. How awful, thought Margaret, to end up as this. The idea of some Victorian gravediggers throwing her hair into a coalhole was bad, but at least that had some *Hamlet* gravedigger overtones, though the owner would have wanted her mortal remains to stay with her nunnery sisters', safe under the abbey stones. Auden's blinded bears had rooted up the groves, the graves. And ending up as this, here in a case, was somehow worse. Couldn't they have reburied her in the lead coffin or given her a new one? She picked up a leaflet about it all: *The Story of the Head of Plaited Hair*. It said that the lead coffin had been preserved for a while and then melted down so that the lead could be reused. And how strange that the bones had dissolved but the hair remained, preserved by the tannin from the oak pillow. When they had opened the coffin there had just been a stain where the body had been; the only remaining bone had been from a finger, and that had dissolved to dust when it was exposed to the nineteenth century air. Dust to dust. The key that opened was ruined by rust.

Margaret began to feel slightly faint, as though her legs were starting to crumble. Perhaps the air from that lead coffin was still here. She could feel the coldness of the flagstones beneath her feet. She could smell the beeswax polish of the pews, the white chrysanthemums in the display behind her, Lucinda's Yardley Lily of the Valley soap and scent. Lucinda must be nearby, but now Margaret's vision was narrowing and she could see nothing but the hair, the plait on its wooden pillow and the glass and wood of the case.

She clutched at nothing. Her head hit the glass, there was a crack, and then she was lying on the flagstones. The girls were still singing. The organ still played. She tried to call for help but no sound came. Above her the vaulting beams were moving. The roof broke apart and everything was lily-of-the-valley sky, nothing but lily sky. She turned her head. And the girls were still singing. White chrysanthemums. Purple Michaelmas daisies. St Ethelflaeda. St Mary. If only they had gone to Bath. She tried to get up but her arms were pinned beneath her. She closed her eyes. Lucinda was holding her hand – so her arms weren't beneath her. The girls sang.

Two giant bears in fluorescent plastic coats and army pullovers loomed above her.

'Hello, Mrs. Ashes, can you hear me?' She felt a huge paw on her shoulder and then beneath her head. They were taking her hair, her plait. She tried to say no.

'It's *Miss Ash*, Miss Margaret Ash.' Lucinda's voice.

'Don't worry, Margaret, we're looking after you now. Does she like Maggie?'

Lucinda wouldn't let them call her Maggie or take her hair.

She was in the air. They were taking her away. Away from the nave and past the book stall and the holy bookmarks and the postcards and the collection box.

'Don't worry, Mrs. Ashes.'

She knew these bears had polished off the dogs.

'Do you want to come with us?'

Margaret tried to say no, she didn't want to come.

'Of course.' Lucinda's voice again. Lily of the valley. Lucinda was there.

They carried her out through the porch. She saw the sky. Lavender sky. Past the little door. Through that door might be the loveliest garden you ever saw. How she longed to wander about among those beds of bright flowers and those cool fountains, but she could not even get her head through the doorway.

Golden leaves waved above her. More yellowness bent

over her. Bears wearing green jumpers and yellow jackets decorated with rectangles each with long lines of letters and numbers. What numbers were those? Oh, call numbers of course! They were just catalogue cards, bright yellow library catalogue cards. That was all, just catalogue cards.

'Who cares for you?' thought Margaret. 'You're nothing but a pack of catalogue cards!'

At this the whole pack rose up into the air, and came flying down upon her: she gave a little scream, half of fright and half of anger, and tried to beat them off, and found herself lying in some vehicle with Lucinda sitting beside her, Lucinda holding her hand and brushing away some leaves that had fluttered down from the trees onto her face.

'Wake up, Margaret, dear,' said Lucinda.

They should have gone to Bath. In Bath, Captain Wentworth and Anne Elliot were sharing an umbrella. But the white glare and the sounds of the carriage wheels on the cobbles. And the closing of doors. But Lucinda was here. Lucinda was holding her hand. She didn't want the bears in the yellow coats. She wanted only Lucinda.

'Lucinda,' she tried to say, 'none but you. None but you.'

# 2000s

## Collection of Lost Bookmarks (Pre-2008)

Emmie always felt herself relaxing as she went through the library doors. Even on days when the heating wasn't working properly or the computers went down or all the readers seemed bad-tempered, she felt at home. She loved the *Welcome* sign in twenty-six languages, and the activities that offered sanctuary to so many people: Jigsaw Library; Toy Library; Chess Club; Spanish Conversation Club; Punjabi Women's Sewing Circle (even though when she'd joined in, one woman's seven-year-old daughter had asked her why she was pretending to be an Indian lady); Lego Club; Knit and Natter; Storytime; Teenager's Book Group; Comics Club.

It was an Inset day, a Tuesday in April; a silly day for a school to be closed. Jasmine had been going to spend the day with Monika, her best friend, but Monika's mum had rung at the crack of dawn to say that Monika had an upset stomach. There was nothing for Emmie to do but take Jassie in to work. It was unorthodox, but the shift was only from 10am until 2pm when Joanna would be in.

Jasmine was to stay in the children's section, reading and colouring in sheets that were intended for much younger children, and doing anything at all as long as it wasn't too noisy or disruptive. By 11am she was asking for her lunch, by

11.30am she was eating it in the staffroom while Emmie had her break (an hour early). Nicola, one of Emmie's favourite colleagues, was in there too. Jasmine had always liked Nicola. Nicola had been the librarian in charge of Storytime. She often opened or closed her sessions with *The Owl and the Pussycat*, and because she often wore brown patterned clothes (patterned like feathers) and had ginger hair (ginger like the pussycat) she seemed like both of them at the same time. Now, quite a few years on from her Storytime days, Jasmine still thought of honey and quince and runcible spoons whenever she saw her. Nicola still liked brown clothes though her ginger hair had faded a little.

'Hi, Jasmine, not very well?'

'I'm fine,' said Jasmine.

'Inset day,' said Emmie. 'She was meant to be at a friend's, but the friend has an upset stomach...'

'Would you like a Cheerio?' Jasmine offered Nicola the little plastic box. 'They're really nice without milk.'

'No, thanks. I'm just going to sort through the lost property.'

'Oh, I forgot library ladies aren't allowed to eat.'

'It's more that you wouldn't *want* to eat while you were touching things the readers have left behind. We find some pretty strange stuff.'

'Can I look?' There was a big cardboard crate on the table. Maybe there would be treasures that nobody had claimed.

'Of course. Jasmine can help me, Emmie.'

'I'd better get back out there,' said Emmie. 'Be good, Jassie.'

Jasmine watched as Nicola tipped the contents of the box out onto the table.

'This is all stuff that's been here for more than two years. I have a feeling that some of it has been here longer than I have. Recent stuff we keep behind the counter.'

'Can I help?'

'Sure.' Nicola pushed a strand of her hair back out of her eyes. She told Jasmine that the library issued them with white cotton gloves for tasks like this. She could bring her own in, but people might think she was bonkers or had OCD. Jasmine knew that her mum felt the same.

'It's constantly handling the plastic covers of books that have been clutched by people with colds or who might put packets of fresh meat on top of their books in their shopping trolleys, or who take their books into their bathrooms, or handle their books after putting things in their grimy bins without washing their hands afterwards,' Emmie had said, surreptitiously wiping her hands with a Wet One out of sight of the readers.

The stuff covered the table. There was a ball of wool with a knitting needle stuck in it, somebody's Maths book, a mauve wooden hairbrush with *Annabella* painted on its back, a paperback copy of *The Da Vinci Code* (why, Jassie wondered, would anybody bother bringing books *to* the library?), several umbrellas, hats, scarves, gloves, an assortment of scrunchies and hairclips. Some of them were things that Jasmine would have liked when she was little. One clip was adorned by an orange kangaroo made from painted wood; she had a feeling that it was hers. There were lots of things that babies and toddlers must have lost: beakers and little blankets, and the sorts of toys that are meant to be attached to the sides of buggies, and babies' hats and socks and little boots. There was an unopened packet of dummies; Nicola said that they put any used ones straight in the bin. There was a hard, plastic Dora the Explorer and a dinosaur, and a hideous Transformer thing. There was a Barbie in a wedding dress. Jasmine picked her up and peered at her smile.

'Just think of her, smiling away in the lost property box forever,' said Nicola. 'You can have her if you like.'

'No, thanks,' said Jasmine, and put her straight back down again. 'I don't like Barbies.'

'Me neither,' said Nicola.

Jasmine picked the Barbie up again. She put her hair in a plait and secured it with a tiny light blue towelling band, the smallest of the lost hair ties, and made her walk across the rocky terrain of lost things.

'Most toys get claimed,' said Nicola. 'We put the bears and so on up on the shelf behind the counter so that people will see them next time they come in.'

'It's like *Bagpuss*,' said Jasmine. 'I always wanted a shop like that, a shop for lost things.'

'And some mice to help run it…'

Jasmine smiled.

'I don't want this Barbie, but I could make her some other clothes with the stuff here, if that's ok.'

'Course it is,' said Nicola. 'She must be pretty sick of wearing that wedding dress by now. I wonder if the wedding happened before she got lost, or if she changed her mind about Ken and ran away. Whatever, you can use paper and any of the bits in here, nobody's going to claim them now.'

Jasmine began to sort through the things. What she hadn't noticed at first were the bookmarks. There were loads of them, all slithering between the other objects, as though it was a snakes' nest they had tipped onto the table. She abandoned the Barbie and began to pull out the bookmarks.

'We find all sorts of bookmarks. Once it was an old pound note – those were from before you were born – they were lovely, big and green. Sometimes photos and postcards. Cardboard bookmarks, like the ones we give away here, we just throw away. Nobody would ask for those back.'

'Oh.' That was sad. Jassie thought about all the bookmarks that just got chucked away.

She went back to the heap and picked through it again, looking for others. There was no money, but she added a couple of postcards to her pile. Nicola was putting other stuff into a giant carrier bag.

'I'm going to take this lot to Help the Aged,' she said.

'Can I keep the bookmarks?'

'Course you can.'

Jasmine began to line them up. But how to order them?

Some looked really old. Their owners must have been sad to lose them. Maybe, she thought, some of these had belonged to people who were now dead. The oldest one was silky like a man's tie. It said *The Bodleian Library, Oxford*, and a lovely building like a palace was embroidered on it. Lots of them were made of leather, or stuff that looked like leather; this would be a whole category. There was one from Bath Abbey and three from Jane Austen's House Museum, two red and one blue. Jasmine had been there. It had smelt lovely and she had made some lavender water with a woman in Jane Austen's kitchen. The woman had been wearing a green skirt with little boats on; Jasmine remembered that better than anything else there. There was a horrid brown leather one from Arundel Castle, and a green leather one from Fishbourne Roman Palace. Jasmine had been there too with the school. It wasn't a palace at all, more of a big shed with models and bits of mosaic. Some of the boys in her class had been told off for picking grapes in the Roman Garden. One of them, Adam, had got in double trouble for arguing that it wasn't stealing as they hadn't eaten the grapes – they'd been too sour, so they'd just thrown them down on the earth where new grape vines could grow. Was that stealing, he'd asked, or helping do gardening? Jasmine and Monika had eaten a few of the grapes and picked some rosemary to rub to make their hands smell nice. (Jasmine knew herbs, her mum grew them.) But nobody had seen so they hadn't been told off.

There was a silver leather London Eye bookmark. She'd been on the London Eye but she didn't remember going. There were photos of her when she was a baby with Mum and her dad when he'd been visiting from Japan. There were leather ones for the RNLI (which she knew was Save the Lifeboats) and some museums that Jasmine had never heard of and that sounded boring. Museum of Agricultural Implements – who would want to go there? She decided to have another section for beautiful bookmarks. Some had gold tassels and beads and looked like royal things but not as old. And then there were the ones with initials. Jasmine hunted for a 'J'. Some initials were so curly and decorated that it was impossible to tell which letter they were meant to be. Was that a 'J'? Perhaps it was an 'I' or even an 'L'. There seemed to be lots of 'M's. Maybe people with 'M' names were the sort of people who read lots of library books or had lots of bookmarks or were always losing their bookmarks. Maybe it was just one very forgetful person who bought and lost a bookmark every time they got a book out of the library. Jasmine thought of the 'M's she knew. There was Mum of course, but if she had a bookmark it would be for 'E' or would say Mum. There were lots at school – Monika as well as Marthas and Mayas and Maias and Millies and Maisies. She had Aunty Molly, who lived in New Zealand and she hadn't seen for years, but she always sent her birthday cards and little presents.

Jasmine had the bookmarks laid out on the table now. She arranged each set the way she loved arranging pencils and pens in their boxes and packets: in rainbow order, with black and white at each end (although white should perhaps go in next to yellow, it never looked right stuck up at the end of the reds by itself). There were thirty-three bookmarks. There were pressed flower ones and ones made by children out of that material with holes in that you had to stitch patterns on, there was one with a photo of otter cubs, one with fox cubs. Some didn't really belong in any sort of set, so they made a set by themselves.

'I wish you'd kept all of them,' she said. 'All the lost ones.' She looked up but Nicola had disappeared. Jasmine saw the clock. Half past 12. She sat and looked at the display she'd made. It was beautiful, even with the ones that were quite dirty. It looked like the picture of all the flags in the world at the front of the atlas, or like the cards for choosing paint colours. But most of all it looked like something in a museum, a tray of birds' eggs, or a display of feathers. She hoped the library ladies would still let her keep them, they might not, now that they could see what a valuable collection they had. She put them into a few little piles so that they wouldn't look so impressive. Nicola came back and said she could keep them.

Jasmine put the bookmarks into the front pocket of her school rucksack, where they would be safe if her water bottle leaked. She zipped it up and carried it back out into the library. Her mum was talking to an old man at the desk. He sounded kind and very polite. They were talking about a museum. He was wearing a hat made from some sort of woolly checked material and when he said goodbye, he took it off slightly. She heard her mum say 'Goodbye, Mr. Tilney' and he replied 'Goodbye, Miss Ash.' Another man went behind the counter. He kept taking steps closer to her mum as he talked, and her mum kept backing away. He had a shiny bald head. Jassie couldn't remember his name, but she knew he was the one who always wore Disney ties and was in charge of all the libraries. Her mum dodged around the counter and went off with a trolley of books that needed putting away. The man started looking at the computer screen. Jassie sat down in the children's section where the chapter books were and put the bag safely under her chair.

At home, she would take everything off her noticeboard and use it for the museum. It would go above her little chest of drawers, her cabinet of treasures, that had belonged to her old aunt who had died. She would use pins with nice coloured heads to make the display. There were some in the Everything Drawer in the kitchen. You could make pins hold things without even putting the pin through the thing, not like the way she had seen butterflies stabbed into displays. It made her feel sick just thinking about pins going through butterflies' wings and bodies. She wouldn't think about that. She took a book off the shelf next to her. It was called *Thimble Summer* (she liked books with 'summer' in the title). She began to read.

## Pair of 19th-Century Dutch Glass Vases
### – Exact Provenance Unknown

Another day, another shift that started at 10am. After dropping Jassie at school, Emmie had time to go home and hang out the washing and think about dinner before she started. She changed out of the Lands' End trousers that she thought of as her dog-walking ones, even though they didn't have a dog. She often couldn't face putting tights on first thing. Emmie knew she was extremely old-fashioned in feeling that she had to wear a skirt to work. She had fantasies about finding the Perfect Work Trousers, but she couldn't stand man-made fibres or afford the sort of beautifully cut wool trousers that she would have liked for winter. In summer she often wore linen ones; these promised so much but by the end of a day at work turned into crumpled paper bags or gave her the legs of a baggy old elephant. The words of Aunt Lucinda rang in her head when she was getting dressed:

'I was brought up to believe that nobody with a big bottom (and I count myself among that number) should ever wear trousers.'

So Emmie worried about every single pair of trousers she bought. Aunt Lucinda certainly didn't have a big bottom by today's standards. She'd had a jolly-hockey-sticks sort of figure, particularly in the photos of when she was young, but this had diminished with age so that her tweed skirts had become looser over time, and now she was over ninety and the smallest she'd been for seventy-five years. Emmie also felt compelled to wear skirts that were well below the knee – what Jassie and her friends called 'witch-length'. She and Jassie liked sitting on the sofa together and looking at clothes in catalogues.

'Mum, you'd look great in that!' Jassie would say, showing her a fitted dress or something far brighter or shorter than Emmie would ever wear. Or 'Why don't you ever wear high heels?' while pointing out a pair that were extremely high and extremely brightly coloured. But even summer wedges would be too much for Emmie. She still wasn't the sort of person who wore heels.

'Flat shoes were in when I was young,' she told Jassie. 'We were wearing shoes like Princess Diana.'

'Was she the one who died?'

'Yes. Everybody was very sad.'

'Was I sad?'

'You weren't born then, but babies aren't ever meant to be sad.' Jassie turned another page in the catalogue. They had reached beachwear.

'What about any of those, then, for next summer?'

'Oh, Jassie, I couldn't!' She didn't add that people might look at her and think her ridiculous if she wore a T-shirt with two thin lines of sequins on each shoulder or a parrot on the front, or anything with a caption. Or anything fitted.

Emmie found the Latin costumes on *Strictly Come Dancing* astonishing, almost distressing. Imagine letting the whole world see your belly button! Imagine wearing a dress that was more of a swimsuit, even if you did have a dancer's body! She could never in a million years have worn a spangly turquoise number held together by gold hoops. Emmie didn't even like wearing white nowadays – it would make her stand out and look too bright. She had developed a uniform of a black three-quarter sleeve scoop-necked T-shirt (no décolletage to be on display), a man's M&S cardigan (which would have been perfect for a male librarian) and a rather plain skirt for work (denim, subtle pattern or floral acceptable) or very plain trousers for home. 'Nothing Containing Lycra' seemed to be a good rule for workwear. Her employers and colleagues were unaware of the dress code.

'I like plain clothes,' she told Jassie, 'but that doesn't mean that you have to. You can have things as sparkly or fluorescent as you like. You can be a woman who wears high heels and does the tango.'

Jassie didn't say anything. She took another handful of popcorn and snuggled up closer to her mother.

'The popcorn duck is the best thing we ever bought,' she said.

At least, thought Emmie, my conservatism and lack of confidence doesn't extend to kitchen paraphernalia and home-decorating. She loved their candy pink kitchen. She loved choosing things like knickerbocker glory glasses with Jassie. They had a parmesan grater in the form of a green armadillo that looked as though it had been cut from one fabulous gem, a pizza cutter that was decorated to be a CND sign in rainbow colours, and most of their wooden spoons were also drumsticks or people.

Her favourite find was a Wedgwood milk jug with a pattern of green oak leaves around the rim. She suspected that it was very old. She used it occasionally and very carefully. Aunt Lucinda and Aunt Margaret had given her lots of pieces too. She had three whole tea sets in the cupboard. Perhaps she would open a café one day, just so she could use them. Margaret had given her a pair of heavy glass vases with paintings of boats on them, barges with big sails. She said that they were Dutch, and nineteenth century. Emmie was glad she had been told that – she would never have known otherwise.

'Where did they come from?' Emmie had asked.

'I just told you. Dutch. Nineteenth century,' Margaret had barked back.

'Sorry,' Emmie said. 'I meant who did they belong to?'

'Humph. My Uncle Jack. He was Governor of Orissa.'

'Oh, that's interesting,' said Emmie. 'I don't know much about him.' (Or where Orissa is, she might have added.)

'No,' said Aunt Margaret.

'But…' Emmie started.

'You're very welcome to them. He was my mother's cousin. I don't know why Lucinda always takes so long when she's making tea.'

Why hadn't Aunt Margaret wanted to tell her anything else about Uncle Jack or Orissa? She would have loved to know. Her dad still never wanted to talk about his past either. Emmie willed Aunt Lucinda to hurry up, but she still didn't appear. She was probably looking for a third choice of jam – raspberry and gooseberry were on the table but the cupboard held many more.

'Perhaps I should go and help her,' said Emmie, pushing her chair back slightly.

'Lucinda knows how to make tea. And don't sell them.'

'I'd never sell them. They're beautiful.'

'Well, I don't know about beautiful,' said Margaret, softening slightly at the sight of Lucinda coming in with a plate of scones. 'But they are jolly nice things and have been in the family for a long time.'

Margaret had supervised the wrapping of the vases in sheets of *The Times* and then in Emmie's cardigan for the journey to their new home. She must like me, Emmie had thought, or else why would she have given me these precious things? The vases stood on the little windowsill on the landing. Emmie was always meaning to see if she could find out more about them but, somehow, she never got round to it. Whenever *Antiques Roadshow* came somewhere nearby she thought of taking them along to find out more, but she never would have dared. Aunt Margaret would be up in heaven now, watching Sunday night TV and bemoaning that *One Man and His Dog* was no longer on, and she would suspect her of planning to sell them. The vases' painted barges would keep sailing by the windmills for another hundred years or more.

Emmie walked to work behind a group of Japanese students. The girls' legs were so impossibly smooth and white that it was impossible to tell if they were wearing pale tights or not. They all (boys and girls) had witty shoes; some Minnie-Mouse-style with dots and bows, some chunky trainers that would be brands that she wouldn't have heard of, some brothel creepers, some brightly coloured DMs, lace-ups and Mary Janes. She would have liked a pair of the Mary Janes but they would look frumpy on her now, or she would look like one of those middle-aged women who wore little girl sandals. They would be good library shoes, though. Her own Clarks Freckle Face ballet pumps looked dull and scuffed. She suspected that doctors would have a spiteful acronym for women who had nothing wrong with them and who wore those. She had read an article about doctors' language in a magazine while she'd been waiting for one of her antenatal appointments and lots had stuck in her head. She knew about PIA (pain in the arse), FLK (funny-looking kid), D&D (divorced and desperate, used, of course, by male doctors of female patients), NFP (normal for Portsmouth), and one she feared might be used for her: GROLIES (*Guardian* reader of low intelligence in ethnic skirt).

The Japanese students stopped suddenly and Emmie nearly barrelled into them like one of the elephants on patrol in *The Jungle Book*. Two French boys (boys they were to someone as old as her) came up short behind her in the start of a wave that might reach all the way around the city.

'So sorry,' one said. It sounded like 'zo zorry'. She turned and gave a half-smile. The Japanese girls were moving again. She overtook them on a bend, conscious that she might be late for work. How she envied these young people, growing up surrounded by other young people from all over the world. Nobody would say that anybody else was 'exotic'. Foreign students, as they'd been known, had been treated as Other when she'd been at university. There had only been a couple in her circle of friends and she hadn't stayed in touch with them. Now she thought of all the friends she could have made and kept if she hadn't been so stupidly shy and introverted. She had been aware, even at the time, that other students didn't spend as much time alone in their rooms listening to Woman's Hour on their clock radios. She thought about all the boys she might have kissed. She had never kissed anyone with a French accent – or a Spanish accent, or an Indian accent – she almost added 'or any accent at all' to herself but made the silent correction – as if Home Counties wasn't an accent! Why had her group of friends been so predominantly English and so white? Why had she been trying so hard to blend into that background? She found it astonishing now that she had thought that blond and Aryan-looking was best-looking, that she'd dwelt in a world where so many people considered Hutch better-looking than Starsky.

She should rent out the house, get a camper van and travel the world with Jassie. Go to India, at last. She'd pick out some books at lunchtime and start planning.

When she got to work, Richard, the area manager, was there already doing something on the computer.

'Emmeline,' he said, 'always a pleasure!' He had called her Emmeline since the day of her interview even though everyone else called her Emmie. Today's tie had Mr. Tickle on it – a change from his usual Disney or Winnie the Pooh ones. Joanna had arrived now, her beautiful braids, that Emmie envied, piled on top of her head today. Joanna and Nicola gave exaggerated winks behind Richard's back and nudged each other. He always manoeuvred to sit next to Emmie in meetings and at work dos. Emmie thought of the line from *Northanger Abbey* about Catherine Morland's father being *a clergyman, without being neglected, or poor, and a very respectable man, though his name was Richard.*

'And how's Jasmine?'

'Oh, fine, thanks.'

'I've brought the new summer reading scheme with things in – I'm sure she'll like it – fairground theme.' The tip of his tongue darted out; perhaps he felt a crumb of something on his top lip.

Emmie looked away. 'Well, I'd better get the doors open,' she said. She took the big bunch of keys.

He followed her, unnecessarily, ignoring Lyndsey, who had just arrived too. There would be four of them on today – luxury – plus Richard lurking about. Behind them the phone started ringing – the first people wanting to renew their books. Richard hooked back the doors while Emmie greeted the first readers of the day. Their presence was registered by an almost inaudible clicker as they crossed the threshold. Emmie returned to the counter. The phone rang again.

'Hello, may I speak to Emmie Ash?' a posh voice said.

'Speaking.'

'I'm sorry to call you at work. This is Marjorie Darling, your aunt's neighbour. I'm afraid your aunt has had a fall. She's been taken to the Royal County Hospital.'

'Oh no!' said Emmie. 'I'll be there as soon as I can.'

'She didn't want to bother anyone, but I thought I should call you. I'm afraid she may have broken something.'

After Emmie put the phone down, she saw that Richard was right next to her, looking kind and concerned. To save time, she agreed to a lift home from him so that she could collect her own car and drive to the hospital.

## Multi-coloured Patchwork Leather Bag
## – Country of Origin Unknown
## (Early 21st Century)

Emmie and Jasmine spotted Molly coming through Arrivals. There she was: 5-foot-nothing in black leggings and a big red tunic-shaped jumper. She had a round tummy and her once black hair was now mostly grey, but her face was the same as the one belonging to the little girl in plaits and a hand-knitted cardigan on top of Aunt Lucinda's hospital locker.

Molly had just one small bag on wheels and a shoulder bag made from patches of different coloured leather. Emmie hoped it wouldn't put Jasmine (who had recently found out that leather was made from cows and horses) off her great-aunt. Emmie had tricked her into her most recent pair of school shoes.

'Emmie! And little Jasmine!' Molly opened her arms wide and tried to hug them both at once.

'Aunty Molly! It's so lovely to see you! I'm so pleased you could come!'

'How is she?' The words 'I'm not too late, am I?' hung in the air.

'Oh, about the same. She knows you're coming. She's so looking forward to seeing you.'

'And I can't wait to see her! And how's your dad?'

'Fine,' said Emmie. 'He's going to meet us at the hospital later.'

'Great.'

'I forgot you had an Australian voice,' said Jasmine.

'I haven't,' said Molly, laughing, 'it's New Zealand. New Zealand is colder and nicer and has more mountains.'

They spoke every so often on the phone, but Emmie still found Molly's accent slightly surprising. How long did you have to live somewhere before you got the accent, or was there a crucial age after which you could settle anywhere without picking one up? Her dad's accent was slightly Indian English, so surely Molly's should be more or less the same? What would Professor Higgins have made of them all?

'How long have you lived in New Zealand?' Jasmine asked. 'I thought you and Grandpa were from India.'

They were walking against the flow of people. There seemed to be more people leaving England than arriving.

'We were, once. Now people in New Zealand think I'm from England. But I've lived in New Zealand longer than anywhere else, so perhaps I'm from New Zealand now, or just from lots of places. *You* must come and visit *me* sometime.' They reached the car park.

'It's such a pity that this is the first thing people see of England,' said Emmie. She swung her aunt's case up and into the boot of the car. Molly peered in at the crumpled carrier bags and an ancient Ikea catalogue. 'I mean the airport, the car park...'

'Mmm,' said Molly, blinking.

The case wasn't very heavy.

'You have travelled light.'

'Well, I thought about it and I thought, they have chemists and shops and so on in England... I've never really been one for carrying lots of stuff about.'

Soon they were on the motorway.

'Shall we go straight to the hospital? I'm longing to see Aunty and Jay,' said Molly.

'I thought you might want to go home first, have something to eat...'

'Mum's been cleaning and cleaning, and she made soup

before I even got up,' said Jasmine from the back seat. 'You're having my room and I'm going in with Mum, but I don't mind because I like going in her bed anyway. And I'm not going to play the saxophone early in the morning. Oscar, our cat, likes sleeping on my bed, but you can shut him out if you want to, but he might meow at the door.'

'Thank you, Jasmine,' said Molly, turning around to talk to her. 'It's nice of you to give me your room, and you can play your saxophone whenever you like. I like cats. And I know how important rooms are to girls. I remember when I had my own room for the first time.'

'Did you share a room with Grandpa when you were little?'

'Oh, no. I hardly saw him. The boys lived in a completely separate place. We were in dormitories in different houses.'

'Jasmine's been reading the *St. Clare's* books and *Malory Towers*,' said Emmie, who had been rereading them at the same time.

'I liked those too. But of course, we were nowhere near the sea, and nobody came riding up with lots of brothers on horseback.'

Emmie pictured the little girl in the yellow cardigan wishing that she could go home for the hols.

'Mum, your phone's buzzing,' said Jasmine.

'Try to answer it,' said Emmie. Jasmine dug around in her mum's bag.

'I can't find it! It's buried.' The buzzing stopped.

'Never mind, we'll soon be home.'

But when they got home there was a message on the answering machine, as well as one on Emmie's mobile, from the hospital saying that they should come straight away.

# Blue Cashmere Bed Socks (Early 21st Century)

Emmie reached for Jassie's hand and Molly for Emmie's, and they hurried down the corridors like dancers late for some long-finished performance. A nurse stepped out from behind the desk and stopped them before they could go onto the ward.

'Mrs. Ash…' Emmie was used to not looking around for her mum when someone said this. 'Your aunt took a turn for the worse…'

'No!' cried Molly.

The nurse extended a reassuring hand. 'She's sleeping, very peacefully…'

But Lucinda wasn't sleeping peacefully; her breathing was ragged and too loud. Molly went one side of the bed, Emmie and Jassie the other.

'She can still hear you,' the nurse said. 'Hearing is always the last thing to go.'

Lucinda lay in the bed. Her white hair was loose across the pillow.

'Aunty, it's me. I'm here to see you. It's Molly.' Molly was managing to keep her voice steady. Lucinda's eyelids flickered and she smiled. Molly kissed her cheek.

'I've never seen her with her hair down,' Jassie whispered. 'And her breathing sounds horrible.'

'You can wait outside if you want, sweetheart,' said Emmie.

'I want to stay with you.'

Molly and Emmie took Lucinda's hands. They were

cool and papery dry. Emmie hoped that they weren't feeling uncomfortably so. Lucinda had always used the most sensible products, like Atrixo and Boots Cold Cream. Emmie saw that Lucinda's toes, her poor old toes, were sticking out from under the thin hospital blanket. How could anyone be comfortable with cold feet? She moved to tuck them in. The soft blue bed socks she had brought Lucinda were still on top of the hospital cabinet with their stupid plastic tag still holding them together. How could she have been so stupid as to not get them ready for instant wear? She should have known that no member of staff would put them on Lucinda's feet unless they were de-tagged and ready. She passed them to Jassie with her free hand.

'Pull those apart, sweetheart.'

Emmie let go of Lucinda's hand to gently ease the socks on. Bad enough to be dying in hospital without having cold feet and people looking at your toenails.

She glanced at Molly – she must be exhausted. A twenty-four-hour flight and now this.

But Molly said, 'Let me take Jassie outside for a bit, you have a moment. And then I can stay here with Aunty if you need to get Jassie home.'

'I'm OK here…' said Jassie, but Molly led her outside.

Lucinda's hand was limp in Emmie's. Emmie began to stroke it.

'Aunt Lucinda, it's Emmie. Molly's come to see you and… and my dad is coming too, Jay's coming. We all love you. And thank you. Everything you have done for all of us, thank you. We're all so lucky to have had you as an aunty. Thank you. For all those times you had me to tea, and then Jassie, and we loved visiting and going to the theatre with you and on walks with you, especially the one where we saw the donkeys. You've always been so kind to us. I wouldn't be here – Jassie wouldn't be here – if you hadn't been so kind and been a mother to my dad and Molly.' Lucinda didn't seem to react, but her breathing slowed a little, as though she was falling asleep.

Smells of the patients' impending dinners and the sound of trollies and the clanking of cutlery, glasses and trays, grew closer. Words were so inadequate. Emmie wished that she had brought music, not just 'The Lark Ascending' and stuff like that, but songs that Lucinda loved, and sounds of outdoors, sounds of summer. Lucinda shouldn't be here, with the smell of mince and floor cleaner. She should be in a deckchair in her own garden surrounded by lavender and larkspur with her yellow tree peony in bloom.

Emmie reached into her bag and pulled out her cocoa butter hand cream. She put too much on her own hands and then gently stroked her aunt's in circles. She had an unused chapstick too and gently applied it to Lucinda's cracked lips. Her aunt's breathing quietened again. She blinked her eyes open.

'Raspberries... and chocolate,' she said. Her voice was creaky. Emmie gave her a sip of water. 'I had a dog, a little black dog, but he ran over a cliff. Brambles. Blackberries and raspberries.'

'It's ok, Aunty,' Emmie said. 'Everything's OK. Jay found the dog and looked after him and you got him back. My dad told me about it. Bramble was OK.'

Lucinda closed her eyes again.

'I love you,' Emmie said. 'Molly's come to see you, so I'm going to fetch her. And my dad will be here soon. I love you, I'll be back later.' She knew she should say goodbye. 'And Jassie loves you.' Emmie bent down and kissed her aunt's hand, though Lucinda had never really been one for big displays of physical affection. She stood up, trying to stop the chair from squeaking across the vinyl floor.

'Goodbye,' Emmie whispered.

There were silhouettes at the end of the ward. Jay was there too now. Lucinda's children had arrived again.

# Black-and-White Photograph of Four Young People on a Mountain Walk (1930)

'I don't want to take much back,' said Molly. 'But I don't want to have to leave you and Jay with everything to sort out.'

'I know Dad won't want much,' said Emmie. 'He never wants anything. But if we could look at it all together before you go. He offered to pay for house clearance people because he didn't want to do this. Sorry.'

'I know what he's like,' said Molly. 'I used to quiz him about what he remembered about our parents, but he always said that he had already told me everything. I know he hadn't. He must remember much more than me.'

'Sorry, Aunty,' said Emmie.

'Why are you sorry? It's not your fault. He's always been like this. Where shall we start?'

'What about the pictures?' Emmie sneakily crossed her fingers in her pocket. For her whole life she'd longed to possess the portrait of her great-grandmother, Emmeline, in a red dress. It had hung over the fireplace since Margaret and Lucinda had retired to Winchester together. It badly needed cleaning, one hundred years of hanging above fireplaces had taken their toll.

'You're the Emmeline. You should have it,' said Molly, nodding towards the picture. 'And imagine me trying to take it on the plane.'

'There are people who transport paintings…' Emmie said faintly, crossing the fingers of her other hand too.

'You have it, then Jasmine can have it. My boys aren't that bothered about paintings, or family history.'

'Thank you,' said Emmie. 'I love it. I've always loved it. But we'll get you an extra bag so you can take things that you want. And don't worry about sorting everything out. I'm a librarian. I'm good at putting things in order.'

They gazed around Aunt Lucinda's sitting room in silence. There were so many piles of books, probably not moved since Margaret had put them there. A patch of carpet had been turned into a rainbow sea of trodden-in thread around Lucinda's little table with her workbox and embroidery hoops, her scissors and silver-handled magnifying glass. There were so many vases, and ornaments, and souvenirs, and photographs of Margaret's parents and her and James as children, and Lucinda's relatives, and Emmie's father and Molly as teenagers, wedding photos, and then Emmie herself at every stage, and now Jasmine was there too. And there were so many plants that would need homes. Emmie rubbed a leaf of a scented geranium.

'This might take more than alphabetical order or the Dewey decimal system,' said Molly. 'I'll make us a cup of tea and we'll get started.'

In the hall was Aunt Lucinda's blue husky jacket, and a beige mac that had been Margaret's. There were a few dog hairs clinging to the cuffs of the jacket. Could they be Amy's – Lucinda's last dog – after so many years, or was it just that Lucinda had carried on the walks once she was dogless, still stopping to greet Amy's old acquaintances? As Lucinda and Margaret hadn't believed in hoovering, it could have been either.

Molly came back in with the cups on a tray. There was the silver sugar bowl with its little shovel, even though neither of them took sugar.

'You could take some china,' said Emmie. 'It's so pretty. Or the sugar bowl.'

'Who uses a silver coffee pot nowadays?'

A photo of her New Zealand cousins in Hawkwind T-shirts appeared behind Emmie's eyes like a PowerPoint slide. 'Are Will and Edward still into Hawkwind?'

Molly laughed. 'Hawkwind? I have no idea.'

'I think the trouble is, you learn one thing, one trivial little thing about a relative who you don't see that often, and it sticks in your mind for years. I remember you sent the aunts a photo of them chopping wood in Hawkwind T-shirts. They were posing by a big log pile with axes. Since then I've thought of them as being these big metal fans – but it must have been more than twenty years ago.'

And did her cousins know or think anything about her? She doubted it. Her mother had probably once sent photos to Molly, most likely hideous school ones. To her New Zealand cousins, Emmie was probably (if she was anything at all) a dull girl in England who ended up being a librarian and permanent spinster, but with one cute little kid. Well, that was about the size of it. She was the Platonic ideal of a library lady, though she didn't know if her cousins would think in terms of Platonic ideals.

Molly took a few books; guides to walking and climbing in Snowdonia. They had her father, James's, name in the front. Somebody, presumably him, had ticked off climbs as they had been completed and written notes in soft pencil in the margin.

'The boys will be interested in these,' she said.

A photograph fell out of one of them. There were two young women and a man smiling beside a cairn on some summit. Molly turned it over. Written in the same soft pencil was *Cadair Idris. Lucinda, Margaret, Harry and self. April 13th 1930*. Margaret's hair was arranged in a sort of 1930s style that prefigured Princess Leia. She had two plaits coiled into earphones on the sides of her head. She looked rather sulky; perhaps the hairpins had been digging into her scalp.

Emmie was impressed that the hairdo had made it to the top of the mountain intact. Aunt Margaret's hair had remained long and silky for her whole life, but the two coiled plaits had been replaced at some point by one plait formed into a neat bun at the nape of her neck. Jasmine's hair was silky like that, Emmie's curls and tendency to frizz having been obliterated or cancelled out. The Lucinda in the picture was laughing and looking sideways at James, glowing, either from the climb or because she was in love, while Harry, whoever he was, was smiling broadly, obviously in on the joke, or just happy to have made it to the top of the mountain. Molly and Emmie stared at the photo for a few moments, and then Emmie slipped it back inside the book.

'I think it belongs in there,' she said.

## Homemade Kite (Early 21ˢᵗ Century)

Molly and Emmie planned to continue their sad sorting the next Sunday while Jay looked after Jasmine. He and Jasmine were to join them at Lucinda's at the end of the day so that he could help move boxes and pieces of furniture.

Jasmine was still in her pyjamas eating cereal in front of CBBC when he arrived.

'Dad, she has to do her homework, it's making something out of things that would be thrown away,' said Emmie, pecking him on the cheek as she and Molly headed for the door.

After her second bowl of Rice Krispies, Jasmine disappeared. Jay switched off the TV and wished he'd thought to buy a newspaper. There was a strong draught coming through one of the front room windows. He would bring some excluder tape next time he came over. Outside, the trees were swaying and bucking, showing the undersides of their leaves as though there was a storm coming. Jasmine reappeared in an outfit that wasn't materially much different from her pyjamas.

'If we get this homework done,' said Jay, 'we could go to a café for lunch.'

'I don't know what to make,' said Jasmine, 'but I want it to be really good. Mum left some stuff out in the kitchen.'

There were scissors, parcel tape, sellotape and string on the kitchen table along with the recycling bucket which contained a week's worth of paper, cardboard, plastic bottles and cans.

'I want it to be something cool, not just a model of a robot,

268

or something a toddler would make,' said Jassie, staring at the junk dejectedly.

'Hmm.'

'Are you too sad to do things, Grandpa?'

'Of course not,' he said, trying to look enthusiastic, and sitting down at the kitchen table.

'Mum said Aunt Lucinda was sort of like your mum.'

'She was,' said Jay. 'Just like a mum. But let's get this done.' He picked up a kitchen roll tube and stared at it.

'I suppose I could make a holder for something,' said Jasmine, pulling a face. 'Or something out of papier maché, but we might not have enough glue.'

'Or enough time,' said Jay. Papier maché. That would take ages and be messy. 'When I was a boy, we used to make kites, I used to make them with your mum too. We'd go and fly them on the big field in the village.'

'A kite would be cool,' Jasmine said, brightening. 'What do we need?'

'Some sticks, nice straight ones, or bamboo canes, light ones, a bin bag, or just paper.'

'A bin bag would be thrown away,' said Jassie, 'but only after it's used.'

'Some strong, light string and something to make a winder, you know, to keep the string neat, and something to make the tail. And you can decorate it if you use paper, draw a face on it if you like.'

'Mum has lots of chopsticks. Would those be OK?' said Jasmine.

'Ideal for small kites.'

Jassie fetched them. 'Let's make two kites, one each,' said Jassie. 'And then it won't matter if one gets eaten by a tree, like in *Snoopy*.'

'OK. Make a cross, like one in a church, then we bind them together. Figure of eight with the string. We need it to be strong, but not heavy.'

'Did Aunt Lucinda teach you to make them?'

'In India, everyone can make kites. My sister and I still made them in England, on holiday to Cornwall. Aunt Lucinda bought us a red box kite, but these ones go really well. What do you want to use for the body?'

'Not a bin bag. A black kite would be too sad.'

'Agreed.' Jay was impressed at how fast Jasmine's fingers worked, deftly binding the chopsticks together. 'You're a natural.'

'Mum's got a box of ribbons, lots of colours, we can use those for the tails.'

'We need to make the body first, the kite bit.' They used brown paper. Jasmine drew a tiger's face on one and decorated the other with swirls and spirals of different colours.

'Which one is better?'

'I don't know,' said Jay, not wanting to say the wrong one.

'I think I'll take the patterned one to school, then we can test the other one this afternoon.'


They had lunch in a café and arrived an hour early at Lucinda's. When they knocked on the door Emmie answered looking hot, dusty and surprised.

'I'm glad you're early. We're feeling a bit defeated.'

They walked the two minutes to the water meadows. Molly and Emmie sat on a bench while Jay and Jasmine launched the tiger into the sky.

'Think of the view it has up there,' said Jay, passing the kite string to Jasmine.

# Fur Coat – Probably Wolf (Late Edwardian)

After Molly had left for New Zealand, the clearing continued. Jay had taken some books and bookcases and Margaret's now empty bureau, but nothing else.

'You and Jassie have it all,' he said. 'I don't need any more things.'

Emmie sighed, gritted her teeth and carried on by herself.

In Aunt Margaret's bedroom was a trunk. Not wanted on voyage, Emmie couldn't help thinking. Her arms itched from the dust. She went into the kitchen where she'd left her bag and swallowed an antihistamine tablet with a china cupful of water. Even the water tasted of dust. She went back upstairs.

She paused with her fingers on the lid of the trunk, hoping for something that would be easy to sort out or dispose of. Or perhaps some of the 1930s dresses that Lucinda and Margaret wore in so many of the photos. It would be so nice, she thought, to wear dresses like that all the time. Print frocks in summer and good tweeds in winter (or spring, autumn and winter). Their clothes had hardly changed since the 1940s, though Margaret had occasionally worn trousers, often as part of a suit. She'd had a dark green trouser suit that Emmie suspected was from the '70s. She had probably worn it for evening committee meetings. She had been on a lot of committees. Emmie lifted the lid. There was a plasticy garment bag inside. She unzipped it.

'Eugh.' There was nobody to hear her disgust. Inside was

something animal. She dared to touch it and found it very soft – the fur dense with an upper layer of longer white strands overlying dark grey beneath. She gingerly lifted it, bag and all, out of the trunk. Underneath it was an old box file. She would look at that later. But this coat – what creature had had a pelt like this? She had never seen Lucinda or Margaret wear a fur coat, although she could imagine they might have once, and Lucinda was wearing a fox fur in the pictures of her parents' wedding. She walked the coat over to the window and held it up to the light, half-expecting clouds of moths to fly out of it or for it to disintegrate like some ancient artefact in an *Indiana Jones* film. She held it up against herself in the mirror. It looked as though it would fit, though she certainly didn't want to put it on. Was there a way of getting fur identified? Perhaps she could send a sample to the Natural History Museum, but did she even want to know what, or should one say *who*, it was from? She dropped the coat, allowing it to fall onto the bed where it seemed to relax and recline. How would Jasmine react if she took the coat home? Probably with horror. How would Oscar react? With terror? Maybe he would love it. And how many animals had it taken to make it? Perhaps it was musquash, whatever that was. It didn't seem like any sort of cat, thank God, but then why was killing a big cat for its fur worse than killing anything else? It was probably better not to know. Wolf. It had probably once been a wolf or some wolves. She sat down on the bed and stroked the fur. It was cool, and seemed to glide underneath her fingertips, as though the movement came from the pelt, from the creature's memories. Was there some organisation that offered decent burial or disposal of fur coats? Perhaps a theatre company might want it, or a museum. She could take it to the New Forest and bury it there, return it to its element, but she might be spotted and accused of trying to hide a body. She was tempted to bundle it back into the trunk, but then she'd have to take it out again.

She lifted out the box file. It contained manila envelopes.

She opened one – newspaper cuttings. And another – letters. And another – tiny diaries – 1911 and other years. Perhaps she would just take the whole lot home and shove it in her own attic for somebody (Jasmine, she supposed) to deal with after her death. No, that would be too mean. She carried the coat downstairs and out to the boot of her car. Now she would *have* to deal with it. She went back upstairs for the box file. She had to start hurrying or she would be sorting and archiving forever.

## Selection of Letters Written by Children (1950s)

There was an envelope labelled *School Documents* in Aunt Margaret's hand. It seemed that Lucinda had been the one to write and receive the letters, but Margaret had been the one to keep them, or at least some of them. There were big time gaps and some letters from the school in India too. Emmie went through them quickly, ascertaining that they were more or less in date order. They were. Definitely Aunt Margaret's work. They were all airmail letters, written on sheets of blue or white paper that felt like the brown casings of daffodils. There were some forms and bills and school reports too. The documents ran from 1944 until 1958, but the letters were all from the latter part of this period. There must have been other letters too.

She turned the pile upside down so that the earliest letter was face down on the top and she couldn't see what was coming next and began to read.

*March 11<sup>th</sup> 1951*

*Dear Aunty,*
*I hope you are well. I am well. I hope Aunt Margaret is well too. I should be very happy to write to her if she would like to receive letters from me. It is nice to get letters from you and Grandfather. I was very sad to hear that my grandmother died before I was old enough to write letters to her. I thought I might have a grandmother who just didn't write letters.*

*I have some more sad news to tell you. A fox has got into our chicken coop and has killed them all. There were chicks too and they are all gone.*

*Jay has had another sore throat and so he may not have written to you. I was allowed to visit him in the sick bay but only on Sunday afternoon when I would have seen him if he hadn't been ill. He said that if he keeps getting sore throats, he may have his tonsils out and will miss school and swimming. He has missed swimming anyway. He says he is sad about missing swimming.*

*I am working hard just like you say and I hope you are well. I will stop now as it is almost time for tea.*

*Lots of love from*
*Molly xxxxxx*

Molly would be back in New Zealand by now. Would she want the letters? Would she mind Emmie reading them? Feeling like an eavesdropper, but unable to resist, Emmie read on.

*September 12th 1951*

*Dear Aunty,*
*I hope you are well. I have had a fever but I am nearly better now. I wasn't allowed to go with the others when they went on the picnic and to visit the market and to see a temple so I was sad about that.*

*Thank you very much for sending me the pencils. It is very nice to have some of my own, though I share them with the other girls. I was allowed to use them when I was ill. Jay wasn't allowed to visit me when I was in the sick bay because it was not Sunday afternoon.*

*Lots of love from*
*Molly xxxxx*

*Dear Aunty,*
*Thank you very much for the book that you sent me. It is very*
*nice to see the plants that grow in England in the summer.*
*Today is rainy. I have let the other girls look at the book.*
*Jay liked looking at it when I saw him on Sunday afternoon,*
*though he said he was looking only at the plants and not at*
*the fairies.*

   *Our house won at hockey but I was not on the team. Jay's*
*house came second in the boys' competition and he was on the*
*team. I expect he will tell you that when he writes.*

   *I am well and hope you are too. I'm sorry that I must stop*
*now as I have no more news.*

   *With lots of love from*
   *Molly xxxxxxxxxxxx*

It seemed that Jay hadn't written about the hockey match
(which didn't surprise Emmie) or perhaps his letter hadn't
been kept. The next one was from him.

*Dear Aunt Lucinda,*
*I hope you are well. I am well. Please could you try to find out*
*if our mother is coming to visit us soon. We have been hoping*
*for a long time. Thank you.*

   *Love from,*
   *Jay*

*July 29th 1952*

*Dear Aunt Lucinda,*
*I hope you are well. Thank you for your letter. I already knew that my grandfather sends money to the people at the tea garden so that our mother can come and visit because he wrote and told me that. We are still hoping that she will come. We have been here for years and she still hasn't come. Molly is very sad about this.*
*Our house won the hockey tournament. I scored many goals.*
*Love from,*
*Jay*

*July 30th 1952*

*Dear Miss Theodore,*
*I hope you are well. Jay and Molly are both well and working hard at their classes. I'm afraid that you will not be pleased by this response to your request. I'm sorry to tell you that we cannot allow the children to see each other except on Sunday afternoons, or to write to their relatives and supporters in England without their housemothers checking their letters. Jay and Molly are among the happy minority to have relatives and supporters in England, and we cannot treat them differently because of that. There is a strict rule that apart from in classes and at meals, the girls and boys only meet at church, at assemblies and for special events. The supervised contact on Sunday afternoons has to suffice, even for brothers and sisters. We must maintain discipline and standards and cannot have boys and girls slipping between the houses to visit each other. With students up to the age of eighteen here, I'm sure that you can understand why I must be firm on this.*
*I am sorry not to give you the answer you hoped for.*
*Yours sincerely,*
*Jennifer Gordon (Miss)*
*Matron*

*January 2nd 1953*

*Dear Aunty Lucinda,*
*Thank you very much for the scarf that you sent me. It is very*
*soft and I like the colour too. The handkerchiefs are very nice.*
*I hope you had a nice Christmas. I expect it was cold. Most of*
*the pointsetters in the garden are dying. Here they are called*
*lalupatty but Miss Gordon told us that in England they are*
*called pointsetters and you have them at Christmas.*

*School starts tomorrow.*
*I hope you are well.*
*Your loving niece*
*Molly xxxxx*

*January 2nd 1953*

*Dear Aunt Lucinda,*
*Thank you very much for the scarf and hat and the pen. They*
*will all be very useful. I hope you had a pleasant Christmas.*
*I had a pleasant Christmas. We had a Christmas tree and*
*watched a picture.*

*Miss Gordon said that I should ask you how you sent our*
*pocket money, as it has not arrived yet. I am sorry as I think it*
*is rude to ask but it usually comes in the autumn and I wanted*
*to buy a Christmas present for Molly and one for you if I had*
*been able to post it, but when I did ask I was told to ask you*
*how you had sent it as it has not arrived. I hope you will not*
*think I am rude to ask, but I know that you usually send it in*
*October and now it is January.*

*I hope you are well. I have been well apart from another*
*sore throat as usual. I had to miss church but I didn't mind.*

*With love from,*
*Jay*

*March 11<sup>th</sup> 1953*

*Dear Aunt Lucinda,*
*Thank you very much for the £5 that you sent me and Molly. £5*
*is a lot of money to have even if you do not think so. I am very*
*sorry about the other money that you sent. Miss Gordon says that*
*it must have been lost by the post office not by the school as any*
*money that arrives at the school is handled very carefully. I know*
*you said not to say any more about it. I did want to say thank you.*

*We have now finished the half-yearly examinations. I am*
*pleased to tell you that I have come second in the class. Last*
*time I was seventh so I hope you will be pleased. I have not*
*come above fourth before so I am pleased but will keep trying*
*to improve. I know that they will send you our reports. By the*
*way, I have been paying attention in Hindi, it is just that my*
*seat is by the window and the gardener found a large snake*
*one week so I was watching what happened and did do badly*
*in the test and I also find it hard to remember words in a*
*language that I no longer speak except in a lesson.*

*Anyway, I will close now as I have no more news.*
*With love from,*
*Jay*


*13<sup>th</sup> April 1953*

*Dear Miss Theodore,*
*Thank you for your letter. I am very sorry to hear of the sad death*
*of James and Molly's mother and also that this occurred so long*
*ago without you, the children or their English family finding*
*out. I have informed the children of it myself, doing so when*
*they were together, as you requested. They are understandably*
*upset. I allowed them a break from lessons for the rest of the day.*

*Yours sincerely,*
*Jennifer Gordon (Miss)*
*Matron*

*April 20<sup>th</sup> 1953*

*Dear Aunty Lucinda,*
*Thank you very much for the book and your letter. I am still*
*sad. Miss Gordon said none of my friends have mothers or*
*fathers either but that I am lucky to have a family in England.*
*Love from Molly xxxxx*


*April 20<sup>th</sup> 1953*

*Dear Aunt Lucinda,*
*Thank you for the book. It was very kind of you to send it. I*
*am sure that it will be useful.*
*I hope you are well.*
*From,*
*Jay*


Emmie blinked and scrubbed at her eyes so that she could
see her watch. She had to pick up Jassie from orchestra soon.

## Newspaper and Magazine Cuttings - Various
## (1940s Onwards)


This was the thinnest of the envelopes. Emmie tipped the contents out onto the sofa beside her. There were many soft old pieces of paper and clippings from newspapers and magazines, and letters from somebody called Frederick McKenzie at what must have been her grandfather's tea garden in India. How typical of the colonial British to call them 'tea gardens'; they were much more like 'plantations'. Emmie had been reading about it. It was hard to know which cutting to look at first. She started with this:

Cutting from *The Times* dated 15 November 1948

# WINCHESTER COLLEGE

## WAR MEMORIAL CLOISTER REDEDICATED

FROM OUR CORRESPONDENT

WINCHESTER, Nov. 14

To-day the beautiful Winchester College War Memorial cloister—" This noblest memorial of all," as Field-Marshal Lord Wavell described it in his oration—was re-dedicated in the presence of the Warden, Fellows, the school and staff, and a large number of relatives and friends of those Wyke-hamists who fell during the war. The names of the fallen have been added to the cloister without upsetting in any way the balance of Sir Herbert Baker's original design. They are inscribed on 13 panels which have been added to the insides of the inner pillars of the cloister, so that they face, across the paving stones of the ambulatory, the panels that bear the names of their fellow Wykehamists who fell in the 1914-18 war.

A prefatory panel at the entrance of the cloister reads: " Here in equal honour facing the names of the fallen in the first world war are inscribed those of the 270 Wykehamists who died serving in the same faith 1939-1945."

The rededication was carried out by the Bishop of Winchester (Dr. Mervyn Haigh). In an address Lord Wavell referred to the ideals of faith and service to Church, King, and people of their founder William of Wykeham. " So long as we maintain these traditions," he said, " and are prepared, if needs be, to give our lives in their defence, as these our brethren have done, so long will this great country of ours endure the trials and storms such as even now gather to threaten us."

Emmie remembered that Aunt Margaret had liked going to Winchester College events; she and Lucinda had seemed to enjoy so many Winchester things in their retirement – being cathedral guides when they first moved there, on the committee to save a theatre, walking in the water meadows and knowing the name of every dog in St Cross – but now Emmie understood one of the main reasons they had chosen the city. Her grandfather's name must be engraved there in the cloister. She and her dad and Jassie could visit it, though her dad probably wouldn't want to; definitely not with Jassie, anyway.

Next, a poem, 'No Ordinary Sunday' by Jon Stallworthy, cut from another old Dragon School magazine. Her grandfather had gone to that school. (She remembered Aunt Margaret saying that he had been a Dragon.) And then after that, Winchester College. Where had Aunt Margaret been to school? Emmie had no idea. She wished she had thought to ask her. Margaret had gone to Cambridge, that much she knew. Emmie hoped that the schools Margaret had gone to had been as good as the ones for her little brother. It seemed unlikely. And what about her own dad and Molly or their mother? They certainly hadn't gone to lovely schools or universities.

Next, an obituary of her grandfather from the Dragon School magazine. When she got to the end, she found a pencil and wrote at the bottom in what she hoped looked like her great-aunt's hand:

*He leaves a wife, Josmi, and two children, James and Molly.*

There was another packet of letters sent by her grandfather from India. Emmie read the first one. There wasn't anything very significant in it. He wrote about some British dignitaries visiting the tea garden. A little picture of some Indian dancers was still paperclipped to it. The next letter was briefer. The dancers, he'd written, were nobody.

It was like trying to do a jigsaw with no picture to follow and lots of the pieces missing, but now she knew more about her father's past than he had ever told her. She would give the letters and cuttings to him and hope he might tell her more, though she knew he would probably just give it all straight back to her. Perhaps he would be happy to chat about things on their next holiday, particularly after a few glasses of wine, though that was ages away.

## Leather Dog Lead Showing Signs of Wear
## (Late 20ᵗʰ Century)

Last of all, the hall. Emmie knew that she wanted the coat stand. It was tall and made from a dark wood – she guessed walnut. Amy's lead still hung from it. Emmie wondered if it was there because Aunt Lucinda couldn't bear to part with it, but she suspected that Lucinda had simply left it there and that, like so many other things, it was slowly sinking into its resting place; the layers of dust would accumulate until it became one with the coat stand, the hall, the black-and-white tiles, the earth.

She carefully lifted the lead from the hook, remembering how stiff the clasp had once been, how she had struggled to clip it onto Amy's collar, and how she'd worried in case she hadn't done it properly and Amy might go dashing off and get run over or lost. The clasp had become loose and easy over time, but Amy had become so dignified in her old age, walking slowly beside Aunt Lucinda; she would have hardly needed a lead anyway. How like Lucinda to have just one lead for Amy. It had outlived them both.

Lucinda's navy-blue quilted jacket and Aunt Margaret's mac were hanging on the other pegs. Emmie lifted the mac down first. It was a lovely one and had a brushed cotton lining of plaid, in moorland colours. She couldn't remember it ever being new or Aunt Margaret ever not having it. She slipped it on. It was a perfect fit, though shorter on her than on Margaret. The cuffs were perilously close to fraying. There was a handkerchief in the pocket, folded and clean, with some violets embroidered in one corner. It looked like the sort of thing that somebody (quite likely herself) would have given Margaret as a Christmas present. In the other pocket was the wrapper from a Keiller's butterscotch sweet. After lunch, Lucinda and Margaret would offer them to guests. They had been in a tin that had once held shortbread. Emmie had wondered whether they were the same sweets, enduring, for years and only being offered to guests who generally declined them, or whether her aunts kept a constantly replenished supply of them. There had been another box containing raisin fudge made by Lucinda. It was delicious (to children, anyway) even if it did look a bit dusty.

The butterscotch wrapper should stay in the coat too. But if she was taking Margaret's mac, she would have to take Lucinda's husky. Emmie took off the mac and folded it on top of Margaret's basket and tried on the husky. She looked at herself in the hallstand mirror. Aunt Lucinda would have said that the husky was A Nice Fit on her, but to Emmie it was too nice a fit. She buttoned it up and saw that she looked like the perfect dog walker, or perhaps a piece of luggage. In the pocket was another butterscotch wrapper (ah, not just for guests!) and a screwed-up piece of paper. Emmie flattened it and read:

Bread
Carrots
Raisins
Brown sugar
Evaporated milk
Fat balls

Was it a shopping list that included the ingredients of raisin fudge or some sort of deluxe *Blue Peter* Bird Pudding? Emmie folded the shopping list and put it into her own bag.

She would google raisin fudge and make it with Jassie. She didn't know what to do with the butterscotch wrapper. She should throw it away, obviously, but then should she throw away the one from Aunt Margaret's coat too? She screwed it up and put it into the mac pocket, thinking, 'In death they were not divided.'

## Selection of Lists (c. 2011)

Emmie still used the lists method of her childhood for getting to sleep, but now she used lyrics too. She wasn't sure if it was sadness, boredom or insomnia.

She would lie there, often with Oscar's companionship, trying to recall particular songs. 'These Foolish Things' was particularly useful because there was so much to remember but maddening because it was so easy to get the verses in the wrong order. In the end she looked up the lyrics and compiled a list of images, that she kept by the side of the bed so that she could turn the lamp on and check when necessary:

cigarette lipstick
ticket places
piano apartment
words heart
fairground swings
winds dancer
telephone answer
ghost clings
foolish things
daffodils cables
candlelights tables
heart wings
things
park evening bell

Ile-de-France gulls
spring
things
strange sweet
dear to me
near to me
trains stations
stockings invitations
ghost clings
things you
gardenia pillow
strawberries kilo
heart wings
things you
Garbo roses
waiters bar
Crosby
things you
strange sweet still
dear
near
leaves steamers
lovers dreamers
ghost clings
you.

Press the button to hear Ella Fitzgerald singing
'These Foolish Things'.

She didn't have anyone to think of as she silently sang the
words. Jassie's father was not someone she had ever been in

love with. And they had never been to Paris. And she didn't want to go to Paris with him, or with anybody she could think of. It looked as though she'd never ride to Paris, in a sports car, with the warm wind in her hair. Unless she asked Richard at the library to take her. He would probably wear his Pink Panther tie for the occasion. Narrative songs were useful and easy – so many that her parents had liked: 'The Ballad of Lucy Jordan', 'Hotel California', 'Ode to Billy Joe', 'America' by Simon and Garfunkel, 'Me and Bobby McGee', and her favourite on school nights: 'Harper Valley P.T.A.', as she liked picturing herself as the sassy single mum, even though she knew that she was really just Emmie Ash, sensible-shoed library lady and toe-er of school lines on uniform, attendance and homework completion.

Press the button to see Jeannie C. Riley singing
'Harper Valley P.T.A.'.

Her alphabetised lists had evolved:

A–Z of Jane Austen characters (first name or surname was permissible but no character could be used twice)
A–Z of characters from Shakespeare
A–Z of Anne Tyler characters (this was harder but if you couldn't rattle through them you were more likely to fall asleep)
A–Z of plants she liked in gardens / in the wild
A–Z of plants she disliked in gardens
A–Z of trees

A–Z of bands she liked / foods Jassie liked / names she might give a future cat

and

Things she remembered about her mother. There was no A–Z of these.

## Information Leaflet for a Local Museum
## (First Printed c. 2002)

The usual selection of old people was waiting outside the library. Emmie smiled and said hello and slipped in around the back. They all knew that the library wouldn't open for another fifteen minutes but still chose to be there early and wait anyhow. The sun was really warm, but they stood there in anoraks and hats, early for the winter, like everything else. Emmie was dreading her dad becoming one of these sad old people, getting up too early and wandering about by himself in old people's white trainers.

Her shift seemed to last forever, turning into a sort of perpetual tea-time but without the tea and cakes. Mr. Tilney, one of the most regular readers, approached the counter. He was wearing a mustard-coloured tweed jacket and dark green corduroy trousers and a tweed cap. Emmie recognised this as his autumn and winter uniform. He must have recently made the switch. In summer he would visit the library in a soft linen jacket. He looked like an extra from *The Wind in the Willows*. If only she had clothes like Mr. Tilney – that was how she should dress. She liked the way that he always said 'good afternoon' or 'good morning'. She hated the people who just shoved their books at her.

'Good afternoon,' he said and touched his cap.

She smiled. 'Good afternoon, Mr. Tilney.'

'Nights starting to get shorter…' he said.

'Yes, I love this time of year.' But she hated the idea of Jasmine coming home in the dark, the navy blue of her school coat so invisible. Emmie always tried to steer Jasmine's bag choices towards the brighter and more visible. If only Jasmine would carry a fluorescent rucksack or wear a high-vis jacket. But then she didn't want Jasmine to be *too* noticeable either, to be the pretty schoolgirl on her way home, caught on CCTV, waving goodbye to her friends as she got off the bus... She blinked the thoughts away and smiled at Mr. Tilney again. He looked as though he was from a world where terrible things didn't happen. Jasmine walked most of the way home with Lulu anyway.

'I wondered,' said Mr. Tilney, 'if you needed to replenish the stocks of leaflets for the museum. Do you still have plenty? I wouldn't want you to run out.'

He took a little bundle of them from his inside pocket and put them carefully down on the counter. He had two rubber bands around them. Emmie caught a waft of something like shoe polish and oil-fired central heating.

'I think we do still have a few...' said Emmie. She glanced across to the rack. The museum leaflets were there in the bottom row, almost obscured by some for the Family Conciliation Service. 'Thank you. The rack could do with a bit of a tidy. We'll move the museum ones to make them a little more visible. I'll put some out in Local History and I could send some to the other libraries if you like.'

'Thank you. That would be very good of you. We have been rather quiet lately. I do sometimes wonder if people even know that we have a local museum.'

'It's a lovely museum.'

'You should come again soon.'

'I will. I haven't been in for a while.'

She glanced down at Mr. Tilney's selection of books. All non-fiction: *Poor Jack: The 4,000-year History of the Merchant Seaman*; *Watch and Clock Making and Repairing* by W.J. Gazeley; *Maintaining Longcase Clocks: An Owner's*

*Guide to Maintenance, Restoration and Conservation*; *Lost Warships: Great Shipwrecks of Naval History*; *The Race to the White Continent: Voyages to the Antarctic*. She understood his eclectic choices – she had *A Brief History of Tea: Addiction, Exploitation and Empire, The True History of Tea,* and *Cloth Dolls from Ancient to Modern: A Collector's Guide* waiting in the staffroom.

Emmie finished stamping his books, closed them and pushed them back across the counter towards him.

Self-service was being introduced in some of the libraries. She knew that many readers would hate it and refuse to use it. They would be flummoxed by whatever 'Easy to Use' system was brought in. Of course, readers came to the library for what they could borrow, but weren't they also coming for the human contact, for the friendly words exchanged over the counter? Why else would so many of them make a point of coming on the Saturdays of bank holiday weekends? ('Thought I'd better come in today and get plenty, what with you being closed on Monday…') She supposed that a bank holiday would mean that many of them would have even less to do.

She used to love her own bank holidays with Jasmine. They would go to the beach or the New Forest or the fair, if it had come. But now Jasmine so often seemed to be invited to do things with other people. ('Can I go to the cinema with Amber and her mum?' 'Can I go skating with Lulu?' 'Mrs. Kowalski says can I go with *them* to the fair…') Empty days stretched ahead. Maybe she'd be the one queuing outside libraries soon. She looked back down at Mr. Tilney's pile of books. She imagined him in a circle of lamplight reading about grandfather clocks and icy misadventures. Perhaps reading about mending watches was her future.

'We're open on Wednesday afternoons and at weekends,' he said. 'I'd be very happy to show you around myself. And if you were interested in joining us as a volunteer…'

'Oh, I might be. I don't usually work on Wednesdays,' said Emmie. She didn't add that she had mostly been to the museum on cold or rainy afternoons when Jasmine had been a pre-schooler and the thought of the freezing metal of the swings, of having to take great wads of kitchen roll to wipe the wet slide, and of the sopping benches, had just been too horrible, and the idea of spending yet another afternoon at home making biscuits (Jasmine making biscuits, herself clearing up the inevitable drifts of flour) was also too much to contemplate.

'It's not really a museum, Mum,' Jasmine said later that evening. 'It's more of a house full of old stuff. I hate it that there are butterflies in drawers.' She shuddered, remembering how the pins pierced the butterflies' bodies and wings.

'You used to really like going there when you were little. We sometimes went if it was too rainy for the swings or if Grandpa was visiting.'

'Yeah, when I was little…' Jasmine's toast popped. She made it on the feeblest of settings, so that it was really just warm and slightly crunchy bread. She liked it thickly spread with butter and marmite or jam. Sometimes Emmie bought tubs of pear and apple spread as a healthy alternative to jam. She and Jasmine would eat it by the spoonful when the other one wasn't looking. 'It's just the sort of weird place you'd take me.'

'You liked it, you thought it was interesting – and those mice! You loved those mice.'

Each time they had visited, Emmie had bought Jasmine a felt mouse. They must have been made by a volunteer. They were mice in clothes, sort of Edwardian dress, less than 3 inches tall. The first one, a girl mouse in a spotty dress, had been named Jasmine and thereafter they all had to have names that began with 'J'. John, Jane, Jimmy, Juliet, Jasper, Jenny, Jake, Jilly, Jumpy, Joey, and finally, Jay. Jay was the grandfather mouse and had tiny wire spectacles. The grandmother mouse was called Tilly for reasons that Emmie didn't understand.

Eventually the museum stopped selling the mice and Jasmine was at school full-time and they didn't go so often. Emmie wondered what had happened to the mouse creator. Had she died or moved away? Had her eyesight become so dim that sewing was no longer possible? Perhaps she had moved on to something else like knitting draft-excluding snakes.

'What mice?' said Jasmine.

'What mice? Those mice! Those mice in clothes that you loved so much and played with all the time. Those mice! You kept them in a shoe box. It's probably under your bed still, or in one of your drawers.' Jasmine gave her a placatory smile and exited to eat her toast in front of the TV.

'Anyway,' said Emmie, 'I said I'd drop in. Mr. Tilney's one of the readers. He's nice.' Jasmine didn't reply, but something about the way her shoulder blades seemed to jut through the back of her school jumper a degree more sharply indicated that she had probably heard. 'And,' Emmie added silently, 'I miss seeing my great-aunts.'

When Jasmine reappeared in the kitchen she said, 'Anyway, Mum, why would you bother to look after another family's load of old stuff? You haven't even finished the boxes from Aunty Lucinda's house. You can just dust all the old stuff *we* have. And I don't even know who some of *our* family are.'

Emmie spent the evening reading about tea. She thought of the demure, healthy-looking, elegant woman with her glamourous dangly earrings and half-smile who'd been on packets of PG Tips. No proper schools, no proper healthcare, no proper wages, no chance of leaving.

## Display of Day-Flying Moths of Britain (c. 1911)

The next Wednesday afternoon Mr. Tilney seemed surprised to see her, and Emmie felt a little foolish. She had spent the last week looking forward to it. Here she was, in her forties and pathetically excited about helping out at the world's smallest and least glamorous museum. Now she wondered if Mr. Tilney even recognised her.

'Mr. Tilney, Emmie Ash from the library. You said... about showing me round, volunteering...' Perhaps she should forget the whole idea.

'Ah yes, Emmie from the library... Miss Ash. Yes, another volunteer would be very useful. Wednesday afternoons are one of the times we're open, so it's jolly useful that you came today.'

Emmie smiled.

'Let me show you around. What would help,' Mr. Tilney said, 'is if you could do a little polishing. I just don't seem to get time for it these days.'

Emmie tried to imagine his days. He would rise at the same time each morning and have a proper breakfast, probably an egg, or kipper or porridge or some combination. He probably put his toast in a toast rack. He would shave absolutely every day and always finish the crossword. He probably shopped almost every day, but only for what he needed – cream crackers, butter, a little stilton, proper vegetables like cauliflower and purple sprouting broccoli. He would grow perpetual spinach. She imagined him washing his pullovers by hand. He was so neat that she suspected a naval background, like the museum's founder. But, glancing around, Emmie surmised that Mr. Tilney's eyesight wasn't all that it had been. He probably had no idea how dusty the museum was.

'I'm very happy to dust and polish,' said Emmie.

He showed her where the things were kept – a cupboard that might once have been a pantry, a butler's pantry, Emmie thought, whatever that was. Perhaps where the butler locked away the choicest things – Gentleman's Relish, the best tea and brandy along with the shoe polish. Now the cupboard contained a bucket with the sort of stringy mop that could never get any floor properly clean, some petrified yellow dusters and blue J-cloths, an ancient tin of Vim, and a whole shelf of different kinds of polish – for wood, for glass, for brass, for floors, for sinks. There was a blue duster, also stringy, the kind with a handle and that is waxed and meant to just get better with age. Emmie chose this, the least petrified of the yellow ones, and a J-cloth that looked relatively unscathed. Next time she would sneak in some new ones. They could, she supposed, just leave the cupboard door open and put up a sign: *Cleaning Products and Equipment from the Late 19th to the Late 20th Century*. Nothing looked anywhere near twenty-first century. There was a tub of beeswax polish and a can of Mr Sheen that looked as though it was younger than her, though definitely older than Jassie.

'Where would you like me to start?'

'At the top?'

The stairs looked badly in need of polish, but that might make them too slippery for Mr. Tilney and any possible museum visitors. The ancient hoover really could have been one of the exhibits. She thought about the electrical testing that happened every year at the library and the labels they had on everything: *Last checked on... Do not use after...* What would this one's say? *Last checked: Never. Do not use after 1953*. She was almost surprised to see that it had a square-pronged plug. Emmie thought that she remembered round-pinned plugs, or at least her aunts having them, but perhaps that was just some sort of folk memory. Imagine the fuss now if the government decreed that plugs were going to change, the adverts, the publicity campaigns, the cries for compensation – it would be impossible. Her aunts had never owned a hoover. They used a broom and a dustpan and brush, and once a year took the smaller rugs outside and raised great clouds of dust with their ancient willow carpet beater.

She went into the Natural History room. An assassin's apparatus was on display: a killing jar complete with gauze, tweezers, a box of pins and a net. The net had come with a long detachable pole that unscrewed into many more manageable sections and had its own canvas bag. Some of the moth and butterfly drawers had been left open. She quickly closed them, worrying that the hoover might suck up the dead inhabitants despite the glass. She would have to confess and then have to try to empty the ancient dust and powder of so many wings and desiccated bodies from the bag and attempt some sort of reconstruction. Perhaps she shouldn't have come.

The hoover growled to life, emitting a smell of burning dust. It probably had a fan belt that had been replaced by somebody's stocking. Emmie remembered her dad telling her that you could do that if your fan belt snapped; she hadn't needed to try it yet, but had always hoped that she would be in a car and be able to supply an elegant stocking and carry out the temporary replacement herself if necessary. She attempted to hoover under the butterfly cabinet but hit something hard. Oh dear, she hoped it wasn't some precious thing that she had now damaged. She switched off the hoover using the rubber sole of her shoe and bent down to see what it was.

It was another much smaller cabinet. She pulled it out. There were many drawers, each with a neat label – black ink had faded to brown on white paper that had aged to yellow. Not all the drawers were labelled, and not all labels were still legible. Who could resist opening them?

Peacock feathers, stoats' tails, jays' wings: fishing flies. What a profession it must have been, trapping and killing the stoats and jays so that the bait for doomed fish could be constructed. Would it have been a trade in its own right or just a side line or hobby for a gamekeeper? She pushed it back. Far better that children visiting the museum didn't know of its existence. Some aspects of history were better left to gather dust. Emmie pulled the top drawer of the butterfly cabinet open, thinking that she ought to clean the glass. It wasn't butterflies; she had been wrong about that – it was day-flying moths.

She pictured the collectors packing their equipment into canvas haversacks and taking the train or cycling out into the countryside on sunny Sundays. They would have taken thermos flasks and sandwiches along with the killing jars and little bottles of chloroform. She imagined how their hands would have smelt when they ate their lunch.

Would chloroform be a pleasant way to go? Each butterfly or moth would try to fly out of the jar at first, beating its wings against the invisible prison walls, unable to understand why the air had suddenly become solid.

Enough of this room. She would find comfort in dusting the fragments of china and pottery in the next one. Once she had done that she tackled the room that had been the study of Dr. Tilney, the museum's founder. He had been a great traveller, a ship's doctor, and his desk, instruments and diaries were all on display. Emmie liked to imagine that he was some descendant of Henry and Catherine Tilney. His main achievements seemed to have been travelling a lot, killing and collecting lots of creatures, and never throwing anything away. He had left the house to a family trust to become a museum, and here it still was.

Later, when she came downstairs, there was a woman with little twin boys. Emmie felt a brief pang of envy. Mr. Tilney had given them sheets to follow a trail around the museum, spotting something different in each room. The trail sheet looked rather familiar. They set off into the back room where there were two hundred years of hats.

'Well, I'll just put away these things, and then I'll be off, Mr. Tilney.'

She saw him blink several times and then smile. He had clearly forgotten that she was there.

'Ah… ah… Miss… um…'

'Ash, Emmie Ash.'

'Yes, of course, Emmie, Miss Ash. Thank you. Please stay and have a cup of tea.'

Emmie glanced at her watch. Jassie had jazz band after school so there was no hurry.

'That would be lovely.'

After a Jaffa cake that was as hard as a gingernut and a cup of black Earl Grey, Emmie found herself promising to come the next week.


Soon it was part of her routine. She redid the window display, replacing the selection of chisels and wrenches with an array of Dinky toys and a rocking horse sized for a one-year-old. She made fresh copies of the trail sheet at the library and brought them in. She polished and dusted inside and outside the many cabinets, apart from the fishing flies one; she couldn't bring herself to open that again. She weeded the planters outside the front door, planting layers of bulbs for the spring and some gaudy polyanthuses to see them through the winter. She wondered if she could get her dad involved, but he wasn't that keen on museums. But perhaps Jassie was right. All she was doing was dusting and endlessly rearranging random artefacts, trying to make patterns from pieces of broken china.

## Postcard of a Surrey Vineyard (c. 2010)

Jay gave himself a mission every day. He got up almost as early as when he'd been commuting and would clean or garden or do some laundry or ironing before breakfast. His mission might be going to the library or playing tennis or golf with an old colleague, but at least once a week he would – he had to – get up into the hills. His favourite train route went along the bottom of the North Downs – Reigate – Betchworth – Deepdene – Box Hill and West Humble – Gomshall – Chilworth – Shalford and through the chalk tunnel to Guildford, from where he could stay on, if he wanted, and go to his namesake station of Ash and on to Farnborough, North Camp, and so on, to Reading. But he always wanted to get off and go for one of his walks before he got that far.

Emmie kept suggesting he get a dog. It might have been nice to have the company, but he really didn't want the tie, or to think about how sad Jasmine would be if he got one and it died. Emmie and Jasmine would sometimes visit him at weekends, and that was nice. They would meet at the Devil's Punchbowl at Hindhead Common, where they could have tea in the café. At Christmas they would make a pilgrimage to Leith Hill where he and Pammy had often taken Emmie when she was small. They had loved going up the tower there until Pammy was too ill. But whatever the walk or the season, he often returned feeling slightly unsatisfied, as though he hadn't found quite the best view or vantage point or got high enough, even though he made it to the summit every time. He might have passed seventy, but he felt as fit as he'd been at forty.

Today, Emmie and Jasmine were taking him out to lunch for his birthday. He had never been that bothered about his birthday, but Pammy had made such a thing of them and Emmie likewise thought all birthdays were a big deal. It must just be a female thing. They were trying a new place – the Gallery Restaurant at the vineyard just outside Dorking. It was on the third floor. The waiter led them to their table by a huge window. They sat down and gazed out. The vineyard stretched below them with terrace upon terrace, line upon line of green, and Jay thought for a moment that he had found his view. His eyes filled with tears.

'Allergies,' he said. He reached for his napkin, but Emmie tutted and handed him a tissue. The waiter was giving them menus. Jasmine was saying something about his present.

'Excuse me,' he said, and headed for the gents'.

When he came back, it was all just Surrey again. The other tables had filled up with Surrey people out for lunch. Emmie and Jasmine were smiling and waiting for him along with glasses of the sparkling wine they made here. The view was different now. There was a little train on wheels taking people on a tour and the sun had gone behind a cloud. It wasn't his view after all.

The lunch was good. He knew to order a pudding so that Jasmine could eat most of it for him as well as her own. She chatted enough for both him and Emmie, all about her friends at school who he could never keep track of and her saxophone lessons and the school trip she was going on where they were going to go on a climbing wall.

After they'd finished their coffee they went on the little train and took the vineyard tour themselves. On the way out he bought Emmie a bottle of wine to say thank you and a postcard for himself. Not the perfect view, but close. At home he stood it on the mantelpiece. He couldn't remember buying himself a postcard before. He must be getting soft in his old age.

## Brown Leather Music Case (c. 1978)

There was no point in Jasmine going into school before the exam. Emmie thought she would let her sleep in and left it until 8.45am to tap on Jasmine's bedroom door.

'Jassie, are you awake?'

'Yeah, Mum.'

'You'd better get up. We have to leave in an hour and I want you to have a proper breakfast.'

The bedroom door opened. Jasmine stood there in her navy school uniform, looking as neat as a metronome. She had her saxophone around her neck and sheets of music were strewn across the bed.

'Jassie, you're up!'

'Course I'm up. Silent practice, Mum.'

Emmie tried not to let her eye movements indicate that she was noticing the slick of spilt nail varnish (hers, a nice coral) on the quilt cover and the many bowls on Jassie's desk that had contained yoghurt that now looked as though they were smeared with pink cement. Jassie decanted yoghurts from their cartons because plastic smelt bad.

'Well, you can come and play downstairs if you like.'

'I thought you'd say it was too early to play.'

'Play as early as you like today.'

Jassie carefully placed the saxophone back in its case. Emmie couldn't help but reach out to touch the blue velvet lining.

'I'd love to have a dress made from that, or a scarf...' she said.

'You always say that.'

'Sorry.'

Jassie ate a minute bowl of Rice Krispies. She asked for a mug of hot chocolate. Emmie silently worried that a milky drink might dull her playing.

'You know it doesn't matter how you do, don't you? My love for you doesn't depend on you getting Grade 4 Saxophone.'

'Yeah, yeah, Mum. I know. But Mr. C. thinks I can get a Distinction, so I am going to try.'

The exam was to take place in a church hall. They often passed it and Emmie sometimes looked longingly at the posters for fêtes and bazaars, but Jasmine was resolutely beyond the age of enjoying things where there were tombolas.

A startling orange ABRSM Exam Centre poster confirmed that they were in the right place. Emmie pushed the heavy wooden door open. Jasmine was struggling slightly with her saxophone case but pretending not to be.

'It'll be nice to meet your teacher at last,' said Emmie. How strange it was; when Jasmine had been little, Emmie had known every person in her daughter's life. Now there were legions of people who she couldn't even picture, and whose names she had to try not to muddle up. Jasmine's lessons took place at school, and this Mr. C., the saxophone teacher, was one such person. She didn't even know what the 'C' stood for.

There was one other girl in a St Saviour's uniform waiting, attended by a mother who Emmie could see was trying to exude calmness. Jassie said hi to the girl. A lone woman (clearly another worried mother) in a cyclamen pink dress and red FitFlops was clutching an orange straw bag and staring at the door to the examination room. Behind a huge wooden desk, a copy of the *Hampshire Chronicle* open in front of her, a woman was asleep and snoring (not gently). Her head hung down, and the many white hairpins that had been used to restrain her iron and nickel curls stood out. She wore a baby-blue blouse. Emmie could imagine her buying it in the 'Classics' section of M&S, or perhaps from an ad in the *Telegraph* magazine. It was made of the sort of fabric that wouldn't need ironing. Somebody was playing one of Jassie's exam pieces.

'Doesn't sound as good as you,' Emmie whispered.

'Sshh, Mum,' Jassie hissed, but she did smile. The iron-haired woman stirred. She looked like an elderly elfin creature, some sort of guardian of the portal, like the citizen of Emerald City charged with guarding the Wizard's door, or a Norse troll, guarding gold, Emmie thought. She was wearing a tweedy skirt, the sort of skirt that, in theory, Emmie always meant to buy. It ended somewhere around her knees and Emmie tried not to notice that the woman's feet were planted so far apart that her thigh-length flesh-coloured undergarments were all too visible. Flesh-coloured? Not flesh-coloured, even though they had probably been described as such in a catalogue, Emmie corrected herself. Nobody had flesh that was that colour, apart from David Cameron, and that was probably only since his advisors had realised how unattractive his natural pallor was. She hoped nobody would really say flesh-coloured now and mean that disgusting fish paste shade. She glanced down at Jassie's pretty fingers. She had taken her saxophone out of its case so that it could acclimatise. Jassie's fingers looked so slim and delicate that Emmie wondered how they had the strength to play the saxophone and do so many clever things.

The invisible saxophonist stopped playing.

'Now the tests,' Jassie whispered.

The door to the examination room opened gently and a tall raven-haired man in a sandy-coloured linen jacket emerged. The iron-haired woman woke, startled, but soon regained her composure.

'Ah, Jasmine!' said the man.

'Hello, Mr. C.,' said Jasmine, with a nervous smile.

'Don't worry, you'll be fine.'

'You are Jasmine Ash?' barked the woman. Now that she was sitting up, her badge was visible. It said *Examination Supervisor*. 'You are taking Grade 4.'

'Yes,' said Jassie. Emmie wondered what would have happened if Jassie had denied it. Would she have been cursed and turned into a bear? It was usually princes who were turned into frogs and bears. Princesses just got locked in towers or sent to sleep or given enchanted shoes.

Jassie's teacher was now standing in front of them.

'Hi,' said Emmie, 'I'm Jassie's mum, Emmeline. It's really nice to meet you at last.'

'Hi,' said the teacher. 'Arun Choudhury.' He extended a hand and they shook. His was strong and warm and brown. Those were saxophonist's fingers, Emmie thought. He wore a soft white shirt and a forget-me-not-blue silk tie. His chinos were slightly crumpled around the knees, but his shoes were polished. They were brown brogues and looked as though they had been polished every Sunday night for about thirty years, and had their soles restored many times too. He was carrying a battered leather music case.

'Jasmine, we can go and warm up through here.' They disappeared into a side room and soon Emmie heard Jasmine's scales and then the pieces. Mr. C., thought Emmie. Mr. Choudhury with a battered old music case. Could it really be him? Arun and Choudhury were such common names, but–

A girl emerged from the exam room and the woman in the FitFlops smiled. Emmie looked away and tried not to hear their conversation, but it seemed that it had all gone OK.

'You'll get the results within ten days from your teacher,' said Iron Hair. 'You can go in now,' she told the next girl. 'Straight in.'

After a little while Jassie and Mr. C. emerged from the side room and sat down either side of her.

'She'll be fine,' he told Emmie.

Best not to say anything now, Emmie thought. There must be thousands of Arun Choudhurys. And she would seem so stupid if it wasn't him, but some other saxophone playing good-looking Arun Choudhury. Plus, she mustn't say anything that might embarrass or distract Jassie. She passed Jassie a bottle of water. Not long to go.

'You're at 10.43,' Iron Hair reminded them. Emmie patted her daughter's leg. Jassie stood up again. It amazed Emmie that anyone could look so nice in that school uniform, the navy-blue pleated skirt that would put inches on most people's hips, the boxy acrylic jumper with its St Saviour's crest, and the blue-and-white-striped blouse that had been designed to look frumpy or to prepare a girl for a life working as customer service assistant in a building society.

At last it was her turn. Mr. C. went in with her. Emmie watched them disappear through the door. There were a few threads of grey in his hair. She crossed her fingers tightly. A small boy came in. His father was carrying what Emmie guessed was an oboe case. She remembered how at school people had said that the oboe was a wussy sort of instrument, but better for a boy than playing the cello, but still, somehow wussy. How could they possibly have thought that? The oboe was forests and darkness. And the Arun C. at school had played the oboe. The Arun C. whom people had bullied. She remembered that belted mac, him fleeing from the bus clutching his music case, and how she had always wanted to talk to him but been too shy. Then them dancing to 'Romeo and Juliet' in the twilight of the empty playground before he disappeared to some special music college in Guildford.

She heard Jassie finish her first piece and embark

confidently on the next one. Soon he was back. The pieces must be done.

'She played beautifully,' he said, smiling. He turned to the little boy with the oboe.

'Alex! OK? Want to come and get warmed up?'

Emmie was left, still crossing her fingers. Iron Hair was asleep again, Emmie wondered if she should tell her; imagined herself saying, very quietly of course, 'When you sit like that everybody can see your knickers, though as they are so long perhaps it doesn't matter and I'm quite aware that many people go around wearing shorts of that length without a tweed skirt on top.' But maybe the exam supervisor wielded some sort of power and could deduct marks from a candidate's score if a parent acted inappropriately. She could picture the exam report Jassie would bring home. At the bottom it would say 'Marks deducted for mother's impertinence: 10'. The difference between a Distinction and a Merit or a Pass and a Fail. She thought about Jassie hoping for a Distinction. She had always got Merits before. Emmie just wanted it all to be over.

And at last Jassie was back. She gave a little half-smile.

'OK?'

'I missed a rest in the third bar of the first one.'

'Oh, that won't matter,' Emmie said airily. 'The examiner probably wouldn't even notice. Mr. C. said you played beautifully.'

'He said he'd bring the results round if they haven't come by the end of term.'

'Oh, good,' said Emmie. 'Let's go and have a doughnut on the way to school.'

'One more thing,' stage-whispered Iron Hair, as they were about to leave. 'You look like animal people. Would you like one of these?' She had a pile of leaflets secreted under her clipboard.

PAWS AND CLAWS ANIMAL RESCUE SUMMER FÊTE

TOMBOLA! LUCKY DIP!

DANCING WITH DOGS DISPLAY! GRAND RAFFLE!

STALLS GALORE!

COCONUT SHY! PET THE LLAMA!

SATURDAY JUNE 25TH

PAWS AND CLAWS SHELTER

PLAITFORD ROAD

(TURN BY THE SHOE INN!)

ENTRANCE £1 OR BY DONATION OF CAT OR DOG FOOD


PET FOOD AND OLD FUR COATS FOR ANIMAL
COMFORTERS ALWAYS WANTED!

'There,' said Emmie when she read it later. 'We can take Aunt Margaret's fur coat at last!' It had been in the cupboard under their stairs for far too long.

The Paws and Claws fête turned out to be on the same day as a pizza and cinema party miles away that Jassie needed a lift to. Emmie decided to take the coat to the animal sanctuary on her day off. It seemed wrong to bundle it into a bin bag. She folded it into an IKEA bag, though, that also wasn't dignified enough for the wolf or wolves it had once been. She took a box of Oscar's food as an extra donation.

It was best not to bring Jassie anyway; it would be impossible not to return with a hamster in need of a home or an abandoned kitten. Oscar would spend his time plotting to kill a hamster and would deeply resent a kitten entering their lives. Emmie had calculated that you would have to live to be very old to have more than four or five cats in a lifetime if they all lived long and healthy lives. Perhaps one day they could become kitten fosterers instead, not that she wanted to anticipate Oscar's old age or demise. She had passed the Shoe Inn many times; the name always made her smile. Perhaps she should go in later and have a *Hot Lunch Cooked Every Day*. There was a roundabout just before the turning where she could have chosen to go to Nomansland or Canada. Were these really places in the New Forest? Had Canada been named after this Canada? She guessed that the coat had originally come from Canada, from when Aunt Margaret's parents had lived there. She loved their bookplates which said *Et In Arcadia Ego* and *Saskatchewan*. It was a pity that the Paws and Claws shelter wasn't in Canada, New Forest.

There was an ancient mud-spattered Volvo estate in the car park with both *Black Labs On Board* and *I Heart Llamas* stickers. Emmie hearted llamas too and hoped that she might get to meet one, having missed the opportunity to pet a llama at the fête. She had always imagined that they'd be quite bad-tempered, like camels, but then wouldn't anybody be bad-tempered if they had to plod endlessly through the desert with a human on their back?

She rang the bell and waited and waited. Perhaps there was so much barking and meowing inside that nobody would hear. Perhaps she should just leave the coat and go, but it might get rained on and ruined, plus, anyone seeing it might think that someone had dumped a dead dog. She could imagine the *Echo* headline:

*Heart of Gold Volunteer Dies of Heart Attack Outside Animal Shelter.*

And if they had CCTV she would end up on the local news or *Crimewatch* as the coat-that-looked-like-a-dead-dog-dumping villain. Eventually she heard someone coming. It was a woman in a purple fleece, covered, of course, in cat and dog fur. The thing to do, Emmie thought, would be to wear mohair so that the fur didn't show, or to dress in some sort of PVC jumpsuit or dungarees. Emmie looked down at her own black jumper and saw that it was embellished with some of Oscar's fur.

'I've brought you a donation,' Emmie said.

'Bless you! Bit late opening up after the fête. Everyone still has to be fed and watered so I've been here since six, just hadn't got the front door open. What've you got there then?' Emmie followed the woman into a reception area where bin bags spilling what must be leftover soft toys donated to the fête were piled high. 'I hope it's not any more teddies. Do you want a teddy?'

'Um, no thanks,' said Emmie. 'It's a fur coat. And some cat food.'

'Bless you,' said the woman again. A whiteboard behind the desk announced that *Today's Volunteers* were *Mavis and Gilbert*. Emmie wondered where Gilbert might be. Perhaps the smell of burnt toast coming from behind the office door was a clue. There were two ancient mugs on the desk, one a red Bovril one and the other a chipped white one with *Southampton City Council – Working For You* in a faux fancy font. Would that font have a name? Municipal Filigree? Municipal Jaunty, perhaps?

Emmie lifted the box of cat food pouches out of the IKEA bag and placed it on the desk.

'Bless you. Whiskas is nice. They often have it in Lidl, though my Gilbert thinks Aldi's is better.'

Emmie smiled and brought out the coat. 'It's very old. It was my great-grandmother's, I think.'

The presumed Mavis reached out and stroked it.

'Poor thing. How can people wear fur?'

The smell of bacon being fried now swirled around them.

'What do you use them for?'

'They're just right for orphans, puppies or kittens, or the sick elderly. Really warm and comforting. We had one in like this before. The gentleman said it was wolf.'

'I thought it might be. Wouldn't it scare domestic animals?'

'I don't know if they can tell. Besides, you get those amazing animal friendships, don't you? A lioness adopting a Bambi, a tortoise with an elephant. Happens all the time.'

'Well, I hope it's useful,' said Emmie, turning to go.

'Thanks, love. Pity you missed our fête. You can come to our autumn one though. We've got Karen and her dancing dogs coming to that too.'

'Dancing dogs? That sounds brilliant.'

As Emmie drove home, she wondered if it could possibly be *her* Karen from school with the dancing dogs. She could picture Karen with a troupe of them. No career could have suited her friend better, but of course there must be many dog-obsessed Karens.

At home, Emmie googled 'Karen and her Dancing Dogs'. She found an amateurish website with photos of a rosy-cheeked woman holding various trophies, hugging her dogs, and leapfrogging and do-si-do-ing with her companions. And just as she'd fantasised, it was Karen Martin from Otterham – her Karen – Karen who drove a rusty old Mini when she was only eight and defended her against Sue Namey. But now Karen didn't just have a snappy Jack Russell and two sheepdogs, she had won rosettes for Heelwork to Music with her team of five Border Collies. Emmie put the date of the autumn fête in her diary. She would insist that Jassie came with her.

## Museum Closed Sign (20<sup>th</sup> Century)

She knew straight away that something was wrong. Where was the museum's swinging sign on the pavement? Why wasn't the door open? Instead the 'closed' sign hung in the window, but Emmie could see the lights on inside and sensed that someone was there.

Perhaps Mr. Tilney had just forgotten that it was Wednesday afternoon.

A woman in dark blue jeans tucked into knee-high leather boots answered the door. She was wearing a cropped red jacket and white shirt with a ruffle; the whole ensemble gave her the look of someone about to ride to hounds.

'Hello, I'm Emmie. I volunteer on Wednesdays.'

'My uncle mentioned you might come. Great-uncle, actually.' Mr. Tilney had never mentioned a niece before.

'Is Mr. Tilney OK?'

'He's fine, he's upstairs. We had the trustees' annual meeting last week. None of us have been here for ages, apart from Uncle Harry, of course, so I thought I'd look in.'

Emmie hung her coat on its usual peg.

'Would you like me to open up, it is nearly 2pm? You and Mr. Tilney can just—'

'We're stocktaking,' the woman interrupted her. 'Making an inventory. Feel free to open up. I don't suppose you'll be rushed off your feet.'

The woman, whose name Emmie didn't yet know, clicked

314

upstairs in her boots. Who on earth wore a shirt with a ruffle and a cropped red jacket? Perhaps the woman was on her way to an '80s theme party. It went quiet for a while. Emmie began to worry. Perhaps Mr. Tilney was being held prisoner up there and she should intervene, but then if this huntswoman was a relative... The *Can You Spot Elder Abuse?* leaflets at the library flashed into her mind. But there were plenty of weapons to hand upstairs if Mr. Tilney needed one – the original Dr. Tilney's umbrella which had seen service on five continents, the insect killing kit, a Zulu spear (though the supposed niece might grab the shield), a fireman's axe, a boomerang and a didgeridoo. But Mr. Tilney would be much too gentle to fight back. She could hear them walking about upstairs – the floorboards were so creaky.

Emmie dusted around the counter. She turned the closed sign to open and put the swing sign out on the pavement. She unlocked the back door so that visitors could go out into the garden. A light rain began to fall. Nobody came.

Emmie tidied out the drawer under the till, putting the rubber bands in their box, sharpening the pencils, sorting envelopes into sizes. She used one of the Simple wipes that she always carried to get the dust and crumbs from the corners. The compliments slips looked slightly yellow. Mr. Tilney probably only used a few each year. There was an old tobacco tin containing stamps of all denominations, including 1p and 2p. Perhaps she should slip those into a display case somewhere. The next drawer down held books of unused raffle tickets and a bag of Foxes Glacier Mints.

After a while a woman with two boys who looked about seven and five came in.

'Here we are again! They just love this place,' she said as she approached the counter and paid for their entry. The boys headed straight for the stairs. 'They love looking at all the dead bugs.'

'Rather them than me,' Emmie said, and then wondered if that sounded anti-museum, but they had all disappeared upstairs. She glanced at her watch; it was only 2.20pm. They were probably a home-educating family. They got lots at the library.

She could soon hear the children, who were wearing wellies, clomping about upstairs. Perhaps their mother would take the chance to sit down for a while in one of the uncomfortable ladder-back chairs provided in each room for visitors who might suddenly feel faint. There was a little cut-glass flask of smelling salts in one of the cabinets that could be whipped out too. Emmie had once taken off the stopper when she'd been dusting. The bottle was empty but still had the power to revive – or knock someone out – with its ghostly ammonia stench. Surely, she'd thought, it was bad enough passing out because your corset was too tight, without being revived by the stink of wet nappies?

The drizzle was turning into a downpour. A man and a woman almost fell through the door, laughing. The man had slicked-back grey hair. Emmie wondered if that made him what people called a silver fox. The woman was younger and had a perfect smooth brown bob of the kind Emmie had longed for until she'd given up longing for different hair. She wondered what products the woman used to keep it like that when it was raining.

They stopped laughing and came up to the counter, wafting restaurant-lunch garlic. Emmie noticed that the man was wearing a wedding ring, the woman was not. Oh, what a cliché.

'Two, please,' said the man.

'Is that one senior and one adult?' Emmie was tempted to ask. She took the pound coins he offered and gave them a leaflet. 'Enjoy your visit.' Five visitors in the first half-hour was good going.

She made herself a cup of peppermint tea and sat on her stool watching the rain through the window.

After a while Mr. Tilney and his niece descended, the niece holding a clipboard.

'Thank you for holding the fort,' said Mr. Tilney.

'How are you getting on?' Emmie asked.

Mr. Tilney looked at his feet. 'It's a little complicated,' he said.

'Things really can't go on like this,' his niece snapped.

'Have you been introduced?' asked Mr. Tilney. 'Miss Ash, this is my great-niece, Stephanie. Stephanie, Miss Ash.'

'Emmie, please. How do you do?' Emmie loved saying 'how do you do' because once, what now seemed like a hundred years ago, after she'd met one of the aunts' dog-walking friends, Aunt Margaret had praised her for saying 'how do you do' rather than 'pleased to meet you'. 'Would you like a cup of tea, Mr. Tilney, Stephanie?'

'Allow me,' said Mr. Tilney and he disappeared to the kitchen.

'Perhaps you can help him to face facts,' said this Stephanie, even though he was still theoretically within earshot. 'The museum doesn't get any public funding – we just run on the trust that Dr. Tilney set up. At some point we're going to have to call it a day, but there's a covenant...'

'Oh no,' said Emmie. 'Loads of people love the museum. It's a real local... thing. I mean, treasure.'

'It's nice of you to say that, but we're hardly the British Museum. Nothing here is of any significance. It's just stuff that belonged to some Victorian person. I think that, and he's my however-many-greats grandfather. He's not going to mean anything to anyone else. And let's face it, everybody has ancestors. None of the things here are worth much or mean anything.'

'Oh no,' cried Emmie. 'It's a collection. It's interesting.'

'Well some of it might be of value. At the trustees' meeting we agreed to get some valuations. That's why I'm here.' Emmie gasped.

'Oh, you can't *sell* anything. You should keep it all together.' She clutched at the counter as though Stephanie might try to take it away.

'Some of it's a collection, the dead moths and so on,

but really it's all just random stuff. Things the family have collected over the years and stuck in here. I remember my mum putting a couple of old vases in one of the cases because she hated them, and brass things she was sick of polishing. You wonder why some things are in a museum. Those gloves,' she nodded towards the Victorian kid gloves and the glove stretcher in the window, 'if someone liked and used those, why are they here? Maybe whoever it was that owned them just didn't like them and that's why they never got worn out. They are just some dull old gloves. Uncle Harry's lovely, but he's the only family member with any time or who's bothered about what's here. I've never really seen the point of it all, I mean, it's just things – just some dead people's things.'

'It would break his heart if the museum closed,' said Emmie.

'Oh, I know. I'm just playing devil's advocate.'

No, you aren't, thought Emmie. You just want to go on *Flog It!* or *Cash in the Attic*. She could picture Stephanie on *Dickinson's Real Deal* holding out for a few more £10 notes. She hated it when people said 'I'm just playing devil's advocate'. They only said that when they knew that what they were saying and thinking was nasty but they still wanted to say it. It was from the same playbook as 'I'm not racist but…' or, as people used to say at school, 'I'm not being mean but…'

'Well, you and Uncle Harry can carry on playing *Bagpuss*. We probably won't do much while he's still alive. He's eighty-seven, you know, the last of his generation.'

'No! I thought he was only about… Well, I didn't know.'

Mr. Tilney came back, walking slowly, carrying a tray. *But Emily loved him*, thought Emmie. Though if they were in *Bagpuss*, he would be Professor Yaffle, and she would probably be an unnamed mouse aspiring to be Madeleine the ragdoll, rather than Emily herself.

'I was just telling Emma about the covenant, Uncle Harry.' Emmie didn't bother to correct her; Mr. Tilney didn't seem to have heard his niece anyway.

'I'll do anything I can to help the museum,' said Emmie. 'I could help with publicity, get some of the leaflets and stationery redone... We could apply for grants...' It all sounded a bit feeble.

'Thank you, my dear,' said Mr. Tilney, putting her mug of tea down on one of the Winchester Cathedral coasters.

'I think it's going to take a bit more than that to make it into a going concern,' said Stephanie.

'How much of a going concern do we need to be?' asked Mr. Tilney. 'We just need to tick over.'

'We went through this at the meeting. Ticking over isn't enough. Bills keep going up and the investment yields don't. We can't keep running at a loss. We need to refocus.'

'Refocus the collections?' asked Emmie. 'That could be done. It would be fun. We could rotate things more, try to bring some things into the foreground more... the hats, for instance, the hats are really nice and really popular. Make it seem more of a hat museum. People love hats. Or a different museum all the time. A rotating museum. Or a circulating museum. Maybe we could lend things out...'

The garlicy couple came back down, holding hands, and walked through to the back parlour which led out to the garden.

'We could make more of the garden too. The old statues and ornaments are lovely,' said Emmie. Stephanie's eyes lit up. Emmie gulped. She shouldn't have mentioned them. 'A Museum of Garden Ornaments,' she said quickly. 'Or,' she said, 'one museum that I'd like to go to, that doesn't exist yet, A Museum of Museums. That would be really interesting. A museum about museums, or at least about this museum... this could be the first one.'

Mr. Tilney and his niece just looked at her. Mr. Tilney smiled and looked confused. It was, she realised, like Kramer's *The Coffee Table Book of Coffee Tables*, but wasn't that the way everything was going?

'Hmm,' said Stephanie. 'Well, that's a thought. I think I'll take a look at those garden ornaments.' Emmie followed her outside wondering if she should hit her over the head with a stone squirrel and hide her body in the compost heap.

The rain had stopped and the couple were snogging on the bench that was sheltered by a yew tree.

'You see how well-loved the museum is,' said Emmie. The home-educated boys and their mother appeared from behind one of Mr. Tilney's attempts at topiary. It was meant to be a ship in honour of Dr. Tilney's travels but it looked more like a banana split. Stephanie walked around the garden taking photos of the statues, ornaments and biggest pots with her phone.

'Here, where you are standing,' Emmie told her, 'dinosaurs did a dance.'

'Really? There's some valuable stuff out here,' she said.

She began to take photos of other things – the museum house from a distance, the condition of the windows and back door, garden walls, the back gate. She climbed on one of the benches to try to get some shots of the roof tiles.

'It must be worth getting on for a million,' she told Emmie. 'What's the point of thinking of past family? You have to think of present and future family. My youngest is doing Medicine.'

'Oh, that's nice,' said Emmie, faintly. 'Following in his ancestor's footsteps.'

'But the debt they come out with is horrendous. We have to look forward. And under the covenant we could have change of use to some sort of medical practice.'


Emmie told Jassie about the sinister visit over their baked potatoes with beans and cheese that night.

'Don't worry, Mum. Why don't you make your own museum?' said Jassie.

'Hmm,' said Emmie, thinking of the boxes of her aunts' papers that she still hadn't done anything with.

'There's loads of history stuff about our ancestors. Mrs.

Kowalski's done this whole family tree thing and made this book full of photos and stuff. Monika said her mum was always on ancestry.com and Kowalski is practically like Smith in Poland.'

'Well, if Mrs. Kowalski can do it…' said Emmie.

'Yeah,' said Jassie, 'you're always poking about in other people's books and old stuff.'

'I don't "poke about". Librarians are experts in information technology.'

'Whatever.'

## Class Photo from St Saviour's School for Girls
## (Summer 2011)

Jassie came home with the class photo. She was in one of the middle rows, not being particularly tall or particularly short.

'It's lovely, Jassie!'

'They made me wear a jumper out of the lost property because I didn't have mine. It was boiling that day. It stank.'

'Well, nobody can see that. Your hair looks really nice in it.'

They sat on the sofa and Emmie got Jassie to tell her the first names and surnames of every girl in the class. She wrote them on a series of white address labels and stuck them to the back. Emmie knew that they'd never remember them all otherwise. When she'd shown Jassie her old school photos at her dad's once, she'd been sorry to find that there were many classmates whose names she now couldn't recall, even though she hadn't particularly liked them.

'I love how you have friends and girls in your class whose families are from all around the world. It wasn't like that for me. I was the only mixed-race girl in the class. There wasn't even a term for mixed race.'

'Mmm,' said Jassie. 'Can Monika stay over on Friday?'

'Sure,' said Emmie. Jassie disappeared to message Monika, leaving Emmie looking at the picture. How much more confident she would have been, how much more interesting life at school would have been, if she'd had a class like Jassie's.

Things had been slightly better at her sixth form college which had a bigger catchment area. She remembered a girl, Faiza Siddiqui, who was in her Biology A level set. They'd always worked together. They'd both been applying to medical school. Emmie was predicted four Bs – and she was taking English, History, Chemistry and Biology – she wasn't even taking Physics and Maths like Faiza, who was predicted four As. Emmie had offers from every place she'd applied to, Faiza none. All Faiza got was an offer to do Biochemistry instead at her third-choice place. Then Emmie had changed her mind and applied to do English anyway. She liked to think that she had freed up a place for Faiza, who would be a much better doctor, but she didn't know how things had worked out for her as they hadn't kept in touch. Oh God, how unfair it had been. Perhaps Faiza was making pots of money as a biochemist or was a doctor now anyway. Emmie hoped so, and that things would be completely different now. She googled 'Faiza Siddiqui' but there were thousands of them, and she might have changed her name anyway.

'Monika's staying on Saturday 'cos her two grannies are coming on Friday!' Jassie yelled down the stairs.

Emmie clicked away from the Faiza Siddiquis. Why was she wasting her time like this? She opened one of the aunts' boxes and pulled out the first letter. It was from her grandfather to his mother describing a visit from a Lady Huntsford to the tea garden. She had read it before. She had looked at everything before apart from one ancient cardboard folder which looked like it just contained miscellanea. She dropped that ancient folder on the floor beside her. She wished Jassie had two grannies. She wished she herself had even one granny. Maybe she could find out more. She typed the name of the tea estate into Google. There it was – part of a different company now – but still there. She looked through the company's gallery of pictures, magnifying each one, wondering if each person might be one of her dad's cousins. The land was flatter than she'd always imagined. She went to Google Earth, but there was no great detail, and then to pages about the Brahmaputra River. Had her grandmother's ashes been scattered there? She could go there, with her dad and Jassie, or see if Molly would join them on a trip to India. They could go to the Kaziranga National Park and see one-horned rhinos and tigers and elephants. She had been such a dolt – a passive dolt. They could visit the tea garden. She went back to the website. Did 'producer owned' mean 'worker owned'? She hoped so. It said 'fair employment practices' and 'environmental standards'. And it had tours. She would just have to persuade her father. She started to print out things to show him – the most picturesque images and information about different tours of the region. She would have to pick her moment.

Emmie made herself a cup of strong black tea; she didn't have Assam, but she did have English breakfast which contained it. It would be nice if Jassie started liking tea before they went. Emmie opened the miscellanea folder. There was a reference from Margaret's first job, her life membership of the Jane Austen Society, some lawyers' letters about financial matters, and then a letter on airmail paper.

*Tea Garden 3*
*Sonajuli*
*Assam*
*April 30th 1944*

*Dear Mr. and Mrs. Ash,*
*I know that you will have by now received the dreadful news about James. Please accept my deepest sympathies and condolences. James was held in the highest esteem by all who knew him. I have lost a colleague and a friend but know that*

324

*your loss is beyond words. Please also extend my deepest sympathies to James's sister.*

*As James's friend, I feel it is my duty to inform you of something which will add to your burdens at this difficult time. Like many men far from home, James had a child, a son, with an Indian woman, here at the garden. The child's name is James Edward Ash. I believe it was James's intention to raise and support him. The child and his mother are still living in the manager's bungalow, though I'm afraid that situation cannot continue. The boy is seven years old. The mother's name is Josmi Tantiani. I recall James telling me he first noticed her when she took part in a dancing display. She was a tea picker, a very pretty girl and sweet-natured.*

*Many such children are left with their mothers, but if you wish to take him on there is a Christian home in the foothills of the Himalayas, said to be good and with a much better climate than here, where he could be raised and educated for a suitable profession. I am happy to assist in making arrangements. Please let me know your wishes at your earliest convenience. In the meantime, I will make enquiries without committing you to a course of action.*

*My best wishes to you all at this difficult time,*
*Freddie McKenzie*


Emmie set the letter aside and closed her eyes. She let her head fall back against the sofa. Oh, the horrors, the cruelty and assumptions in those few lines. That the English grandparents, thousands of miles away, could decide the fate of a child without even consulting his mother. That Josmi must have been turfed out of the home she'd shared with her husband and children, had her children taken away, and had never seen them again. And Molly wasn't even mentioned.

'I'm sorry, Josmi – Grandmother,' Emmie whispered. 'I'm so sorry they treated you like that.'

After a while Emmie opened her eyes. She had read about

those dancers and seen the little picture still paperclipped to the letter. It was black and white and faded and only about two inches square. A ring of women had been captured forever in the circle of their dance. She found the letter with the photo and the one that came after it. He had written *those dancers are nobody*. Had he ever intended to tell his English family about his Indian family? Emmie put the second letter back in the folder. Her father didn't need to read that now, after all these years. But she wanted to show him the picture, she had to show him the picture. Here, after all these years, was the photograph he'd never had of his mother.


Emmie carried the precious photograph in her wallet to work, worrying with every step that she might be mugged. She wasn't. At the library, she made two photocopies of it and then a few of it enlarged. Did one of them look like Aunty Molly? Perhaps. At lunchtime, she bought three little frames – one for the copy for Molly, one for her copy, and one for the original for her dad. When she was home again, she and Jassie studied the photograph through Aunt Lucinda's silver-handled magnifying glass.

'I think that one looks most like you and me, Mum,' said Jassie.

'Maybe,' said Emmie. 'Maybe my grandmother, maybe your great-grandmother. Let's put them in the frames so they'll be safe.'

'Have you told Grandpa yet?'

'I don't want to tell him on the phone, it's quite a thing. We'll see him soon when we go to France, if not before.'

'What was her name?' asked Jasmine.

'Josmi,' said Emmie. 'Surely I've told you that.'

'Did you kind of name me after her?'

'Well, maybe I did,' said Emmie.

## Photograph of a Group of Indian Dancers
## (c. 1930s)

They were sitting on the sofa together watching *Waterloo Road* with its heady, hypnotic mix of romance, bullying, Ofsted, and mental health and cancer storylines, when the doorbell rang.

Emmie groaned. 'Press pause,' she said over her shoulder. 'It can't be anybody.' It couldn't be anybody because hardly anybody rang their doorbell in the evening. But it was somebody.

'Oh,' said Emmie, when she opened the door.

'Mr. C.!' cried Jassie, who had followed her to see who was there.

He was wearing the same sandy-coloured linen jacket, the same shiny but ancient brogues, the same slightly crumpled trousers, this time with an ivory linen shirt, which, Emmie noticed, was (unlike her own linen shirtwaister library lady dress) not creased. He was holding a brown envelope.

'Hello, Ms. Ash, I've got Jassie's results here.' He was smiling, a very broad, confident smile. His eyes were a dark brown as soft as velvet.

'Oh, do come in – and it's Emmie.'

'Arun,' he said.

Emmie smiled and nearly said 'I know'. She led him inside.

She saw Arun glance around at the cosy little room and take in its squishy terracotta sofa, the shelves and shelves of books, the portrait over the fireplace of a beautiful Edwardian lady in a red dress, the strange collections of objects – origami birds, china jugs – and the photos of Jassie as a baby, then a toddler wearing pale blue leather reins over pink cord dungarees and standing with the man who must be her grandfather in front of a white camellia bush, school and class pictures, more with her mother, grandfather and a very old lady on days out.

'Hello, Jassie,' he said. 'Here's the result. Shall I tell you?' But he didn't tell her, he carried on smiling and handed her the envelope.

Jassie carefully opened it and pulled out the sheet of thin blue paper. It crackled in her hands like an airmail letter. She gasped.

'I got 87%! I got a Distinction! Thanks!'

'The hard work and talent are yours.'

'Darling, that's brilliant! A Distinction!' Emmie hugged her. 'Mr. C. – Arun – would you like a cup of coffee, a glass of wine? We should be celebrating.'

'Champagne?' said Jassie.

'Hmmm,' said Emmie.

'A glass of wine, just one, would be very nice,' he said, smiling.

In the kitchen, Emmie took the bottle of English wine from her dad's birthday trip from the fridge. Her aunts would have offered sherry. Sherry would be perfect. A person could sip it, but not be detained too long if they didn't want to be. She should turn into a person who offered sherry. Plus, it probably took a very long time to go off. She poured a glass of pineapple juice for Jassie and added ice cubes to make it more celebratory.

She found Jassie explaining who the people in the photos were.

'That's Great-great-aunt Lucinda, but she's not my real great-great-aunt, but she was sort of like a granny because she adopted my dad, and that's him, and that's my other granny and grandpa and my dad, but we don't see them very often.

They live in Spain and Japan. And that's Mum and Grandpa on holiday in France. I took the picture.'

'And who are these?' he asked, indicating the tiny photo of the dancers.

'We think that one of them's my grandmother,' said Emmie, 'but we aren't quite sure. I've only just found it and I haven't shown it to my dad yet.'

'May I?' he said, picking up the photo and peering at it. He walked over to the window with it, the sun was setting, but the extra light helped. 'That one,' he said, pointing to the dancer that they'd also picked out. 'Look at her arms and her fingers, they are just like yours and Jasmine's. And her cheekbones.'

'Her name was Josmi,' said Emmie, handing him a glass of wine. He put the photo in its little green wooden frame back next to the Indian girl ragdoll that sat on top of the bookcase. They raised their glasses in a toast to Jassie's Distinction, but to Emmie it felt a little as though they were toasting her grandmother too.

'I hope it's her. Everything in our family history has been people going away,' said Emmie.

'Ah,' said Arun, 'but sometimes people come back.'

Emmie smiled and wondered what to say next. Jasmine was engrossed in the exam marks sheet and wouldn't be much help.

'She did very well in all elements,' said Arun. 'I think Grade 5 around Easter.'

'Does that sound OK, Jassie?' Emmie asked, not wanting to be or seem like a Pushy Parent.

'Yeah, have we got any flapjacks left?'

'Blue tin.' Emmie had made them at the weekend. She'd hoped Jassie would want to help, but Jassie had just said 'Mum, I think I've made enough flapjacks in my life,' and wandered off. She still liked eating them, though.

'Have you always lived around here?' Emmie asked, wanting to make sure it was definitely him.

'For the last few years. And you?'

'For ages. I grew up in Surrey, near Dorking, and came to university here and just sort of stayed. My dad still lives near there.'

'Oh, Dorking. Yes, I was at school in Dorking.' He looked down into his wine glass.

'I thought it must be you. We used to be on the same bus and we…' But she trailed off, too bashful to say any more.

'Those bus rides – the worst times of my life. How happy I was when I started cycling instead.' He looked up at her and smiled. Did he remember her?

'They were awful,' said Emmie. 'That's why I wanted Jassie to go to an all girls' school, I thought it might be a bit more civilised. Boys of twelve to fifteen are mostly just horrible. All they seemed to do was spit and, and torture wasps…'

'And try to torment me,' said Arun. 'But things improved after a year, and my music college and the Guildhall were much better.'

'It was an awful place,' said Emmie.

Arun smiled at her. 'Emmeline,' he said slowly, 'I do remember you. A quiet little girl on the bus who secretly smiled at me and then who danced with me.' He raised his glass. Emmie raised hers too.

There was a crash from the kitchen, the sound of breaking china.

'Mum!'

'Oh dear,' said Emmie, hurrying away.

'Just a plate,' said Emmie, when she and Jassie returned. 'Nobody cut. And not a precious one.'

'Mum secretly likes it when plates and mugs get broken. She's got a flowerbed that is just bits of seaglass, shells and broken china.' Emmie smiled and didn't know what to say. She moved a pile of library books – *DK Eyewitness Travel Guide: India*, *Blue Guide India*, a tourist's map of Northeast India and Bangladesh, *Lonely Planet Northeast India*, *Footprint Northeast India Handbook* – so that there was room for the plate of flapjacks.

'Are you off to India?' Arun asked, looking at the books.

'Just dreaming and planning so far.'

And then the phone rang.

'Leave it, honey,' Emmie said, but the answering machine picked it up and her father's voice was amplified around the room.

'Hello, Emmeline. Hello, Jasmine. This is Dad, Grandpa. I need to talk to you. Please call me back.'

Emmie frowned, wondering what was so urgent.

'I hope nothing's wrong,' said Arun. 'I must go. I have other pupils waiting for results too. Thank you very much for the wine, and well done, Jasmine.' He finished his flapjack and picked up his music case. They both followed him to the door.

'Bye, Mr. C.! Thanks!' said Jasmine.

And he was gone.

Emmie sat back down on the sofa and took a few gulps of wine. She sometimes wished that she smoked. A few minutes later, she dialled her father's number and he picked up straight away.

'Dad? Are you OK?'

'Of course, I'm OK. Just need to check something for France.'

Emmie took another gulp of her wine. 'We're really looking forward to it, Dad.'

## Email Exchange Between a Woman in England and a Tea Company Employee in Assam (Summer 2011)

*From: EmmelineAsh@gmail.com*
*To: enquiries@finestleaftea.com*

*18.7.2011*

*Dear Sir or Madam,*
*Hello. I would be very grateful if you could help me. My grandmother Josmi Tantiani was originally a worker in the 1930s at a tea estate (Sonajuli) that I think is now owned by your company. My grandfather James Ash was a manager there too before being killed at Kohima in 1944. I wondered if you might have any records from that time, particularly things that pertain to my grandmother, about whom we know very little. She had two children (James and Margaret Ash) who were both adopted by family in England. All we know is that she died at the estate in the late 1940s.*

*I would be very grateful for any information or photographs you might have from that time. I am a librarian who grew up in England and am currently researching my family history and hope to visit India soon.*

*With many thanks,*
*Emmeline Ash*

*To: EmmelineAsh@gmail.com*
*From: enquiries@finestleaftea.com*

*19.7.2011*

*Dear Mrs. Ash,*
*Thank you for contacting Finest Leaf Tea. I am very sorry for the loss of your grandmother and grandfather. It is a very sad loss to your family.*

*I am sorry to have to inform you that we do not hold records from the previous owners of the Sonajuli Tea Estate. Ownership of the estate has changed several times since the time of your grandparents, so we are unable to give you any more information about your grandparents. I am also told that records of the garden's early times were lost during a great flood in the 1950s.*

*We would be very happy to welcome you to Finest Leaf Tea and give you a tour of the garden if you are able to visit at any time in the future or to try to answer any questions you might have about the estate as it now is.*

*With kind regards,*
*Mr. V.K. Sen*


*From: EmmelineAsh@gmail.com*
*To: enquiries@finestleaftea.com*

*19.7.2011*

*Dear Mr. Sen,*
*Thank you very much for replying to me so quickly. I will certainly visit the tea garden as soon as I am able to. I hadn't expected you to have records from so long ago, but just wanted to check. Thank you for your time. I do have one other question, which I hope you will not find strange. Please would you be able to tell me what might have happened when*

a worker on the estate died – I mean funeral arrangements and where their ashes might have been scattered? If you do not know what would have happened to workers in the 1940s, what is the practice for local people now? If I am able to visit, I would dearly love to pay my respects to my grandmother and visit the river where her ashes might have been scattered, if that is what would have been done. My grandfather is buried at Kohima War Cemetery which I would also like to visit, but I would dearly love to visit the places important in my grandmother's life and passing.

   With many thanks,
   Emmeline Ash


To: EmmelineAsh@gmail.com
From: enquiries@finestleaftea.com

20.7.2011

Dear Mrs. Ash,
Your question is not strange at all. The practice now, which I think will not have changed, is that the ashes of a Hindu are immersed in the river nearby. We are close to Brahmaputra River and tributaries which flow into the Ganges and then to the ocean. Ashes of a loved one are contained in a clay vessel which will not damage the river or its creatures. I inform you of this as we also pride ourselves on good environmental practice at Finest Leaf Tea. Ceremony with prayers and flowers which can also be observed in your country will be little changed. If you visit Finest Leaf Tea, we will be pleased to direct you to the places most familiar to our workers.

   With kind regards,
   Mr. V.K. Sen

*From: EmmelineAsh@gmail.com*
*To: enquiries@finestleaftea.com*

*20.7.2011*

*Dear Mr. Sen,*
*Thank you very much for your swift and most helpful reply. I do appreciate the time you have taken answering my questions. I hope very much to visit the tea garden and these special places in the future.*
 *With very many thanks,*
 *Emmeline Ash*

## Mason Cash Blue-and-White Cornishware Utensils Jar Containing Over 100 Single-use Wooden Chopsticks (c. Late 20ᵗʰ Century)

Jassie came home from the last saxophone lesson of the term with her report from Mr. C. in a big brown envelope.

'Mr. C. says that you have to open it straight away – he says that there's a note for you inside it.'

'I hope he's not leaving,' said Emmie, also silently hoping that the fees weren't going up. But inside was a leaflet – *Jazz on a Summer's Night* – a concert with fireworks. And on a sheet of A4, thicker and creamier than the sort that Emmie usually bought, he had written:

*Dear Emmeline,*
*A friend is conducting this, and I thought it might be useful for Jassie. I have tickets for us all if you would like to come with me. I'll bring the picnic. Jassie told me that you are vegetarians.*
*With all good wishes,*
*Arun Choudhury*

He'd included his phone number.

* * *

The concert was the Friday before they left for France. Emmie smiled. She had always wanted to go to a concert with fireworks, and to be somebody who went to events where you had a posh picnic.

The sun was so bright when Arun came to pick them up that he was just a silhouette at the front door, but she could see that he was carrying flowers.

She blinked at the sunlight and at him, then realised that she was still holding a yellow duster. The trouble with sun was that it made everything appear so dusty.

'Spring cleaning?' he asked, even though it was summer. Emmie hoped that she didn't smell of Mr Sheen, or worse, Mr Muscle. 'For you.' He handed her the flowers which were wrapped in proper florist's paper.

'Thank you.' Emmie pictured him going into a florist to choose them, or perhaps to a flower stall. How lovely to be given flowers that weren't from a supermarket.

'Oh, cornflowers – my favourites. This blue – it's the best blue in the world – and you can only get them for a few weeks each year.' She breathed in the intensity of the blue. 'It's the bluest blue.' She smiled at him across the flowers, wishing that she was wearing a dress the same blue or had eyes that blue. Then her own brown eyes met his. She heard Jassie clattering down the stairs, and suddenly she was there in the room with them, her cinnamon hair pulled back from her face, pipe-cleaner legs emerging from denim shorts, pipe-cleaner arms emerging from the sleeves of the rosy pink University of Melbourne T-shirt Molly had sent.

'I'll put them in water for you, Mum,' said Jassie, taking the flowers. She held them against her T-shirt and buried her nose in them. 'They don't smell of much, just damp paper.'

'That probably is the damp paper,' said Emmie. 'Their

smell is really subtle.' And for a moment she was back in her aunts' garden with her dad on a Sunday afternoon, eating bread and butter and the peculiar combination of things that constituted high tea, and Aunt Margaret was saying that some flowers were all very well, but they smelt of nothing but dust.

Jassie reappeared with the flowers in a cut-glass vase, a vase that Emmie had always disliked. It seemed too heavy and portentous for most flowers – a vase that took itself too seriously – and the many facets of its intricate pattern meant that it somehow never looked clean. Aunt Margaret had given it to her, though, so she would always keep it. She realised that Jassie must think it was their poshest vase and had chosen it to honour Mr. C.'s flowers.

'We're more ready than we look,' said Emmie. 'This is so kind of you. Are you sure you don't want us to bring anything?

'Nothing. The picnic's in the car.'

'What have you got?' asked Jassie.

'Jassie!'

'I'm only wondering…'

'That's OK,' said Arun, smiling. 'It's a very sensible question. I've got daktyla bread, olives, Compté cheese, chocolate muffins, strawberries, blueberries…'

'Like the Water Rat in *The Wind in The Willows…*' said Emmie. 'Actually, I have made some biscuits. I'll just get them.'

Arun followed her into the kitchen. The cookies Emmie had made were still on the rack, but they were cool now. She put them into the Cath Kidston box (her smartest plastic container) she'd put ready beside them. There was a mess of crumbs left behind. She swept them up with a wipe.

Her kitchen bin was probably the most hygienic bin in the world. Emmie knew this, being the person who cleaned it every day with either antibacterial or environmentally unfriendly bleach spray. But, even with Arun watching, she was still compelled to take one of the chopsticks she bought for the purpose and kept in a Cornishware utensils pot and use it to open the bin. The used chopstick was tossed into the bin along with the wipe and crumbs in one deft movement.

'Bin lids,' she said, as though that explained everything. 'It is my only neurosis. And I don't make Jassie do it.' Arun smiled. Oh dear, now she'd blown it. 'Anyway, I'm ready.' At least she could be someone who was ready on time, even if she was coming across as completely bonkers.

Arun looked around the kitchen. It was the prettiest kitchen he had ever seen. The walls were a warm pink and all the china was blue-and-white striped. It looked like they ate a lot of fruit – there was a bowl of nectarines and one of cherries as well as bananas and apples. It smelt lovely – of the cookies and clean laundry and something lemony, though that might have been cleaning products.


A few hours later, the three of them were sitting side by side in the canvas director's chairs Arun had brought, eating strawberries and cookies while dandelion clocks of gold, pink and green exploded over their heads to big band numbers and songs from the movies.

When Arun dropped them back at home he didn't come in, but he did take Emmie's hand and kiss her fingers.

She thought about this as she fell asleep. It seemed that she had become a teenager again.

## 4 Metres of Blue Silk Ribbon – Used (c. 2011)

'Mr. C. was at Assembly. He said he wanted to come round this evening,' said Jassie. 'He said he had a Grade 5 book for me for next term. I told him we were pretty much always in.'

'I expect he wants to talk about your next exam or something,' said Emmie, hurrying to the mirror. She had splashed pasta sauce on her black T-shirt when she was cooking and mopped it off with the green sponge scratchy; not very well, it seemed. She hurried upstairs, flinging the T-shirt into the washing basket on the landing and replacing it with an identical clean one. She cleaned her teeth for the fifth or sixth time that day and put on some lipstick. The shade of pinkish-brown that she wore was barely perceptible. Perhaps she should go back to the dark berry colours of her student days.

Back downstairs she lit her Clean Cotton candle to cover any cooking smells. She turned down the volume on the TV in case he heard it from outside the front door. Here she was, in on Friday night as usual.

She gave the surfaces a quick, unnecessary wipe (boring! boring!) and sat back down on the sofa, feeling silly, like a mistress putting on a negligee and arranging herself on top of a sateen bedspread for a married man who would fail to show up.

She wondered if he would arrive before *Gardeners' World* (if he arrived at all) and hoped that he wouldn't arrive *during* it. Then she thought of that Hardy poem –

*You did not come,*

*And marching Time drew on, and wore me numb,–*

She was being ridiculous. He was her daughter's saxophone teacher, a friend, that was all. She hadn't seen him since the concert. He had just been being nice. Nothing more. Might as well turn the TV back up and enjoy *Gardeners' World*.

Monty Don was wearing a nice blue shirt like one Arun had. Emmie hoped Carol Klein would be wearing one of her pink and green ensembles, ones she wore when she was talking about blossom or roses. Ah well, at least she could be cheered up by Carol Klein's clothes. She was just starting to drift off (it was Joe Swift on something dull to do with hostas) when Arun knocked. Emmie could hear Jassie listening to something loud in her bedroom, there was no point in yelling for her to get the door. When Emmie stood up, she found that her right foot had gone to sleep and she had to hop-shuffle into the hall. She could see Arun silhouetted through the glass. There was something big, a blur of silvery-grey and blue on the ground beside him, perhaps a big dog wearing a turquoise collar.

She opened the door. He was there, holding his music case. The thing beside him wasn't a dog, but a gleaming new kitchen bin.

'Hello. I hope you don't mind me calling round like this, Jasmine said you would be in. I have some music and information for her, and a present for you.' Emmie could only smile and manage a jumble of 'come in' and 'thank you' and 'really kind'. He balanced his music case on top of the bin and carried it all in, deftly closing the front door behind him with a gentle little back kick. Emmie led him into the sitting room and quickly switched off the TV. Why, oh why, hadn't she thought of having music on, some Ella Fitzgerald or Miles Davis or something classical to demonstrate her intelligence, taste and laid-back nature?

'*Gardeners' World*,' he said. 'The refuge of Friday night.'

'Please do sit down,' said Emmie, trying to look as though

she wasn't eyeing the bin. Could it possibly be for her, or was he on his way to a housewarming party? 'Would you like some tea or coffee, a glass of wine, something cold?' She hoped he wouldn't ask for beer. She had no beer. She should have had little bottles of French lager in the fridge. She would buy some next time she went shopping. She pictured the bottles, studded with diamonds of condensation, artistically placed next to some elegant lager glasses she had picked up on holiday in France (or would pick up this year) and a dish of olives stuffed with lemon, and perhaps some macadamia nuts (too expensive for her and Jassie to have very often) and a bowl of wild strawberries, only 7 francs a kilo. The whole ensemble would be arranged on a white wrought-iron table in a larger and more fabulous version of her garden, under the shade of the wisteria or grape vine that had magically sprouted and reached maturity in the time it took for the kettle to boil.

'Tea, please. I'm driving.'

She took a tray with the teapot, two blue-and-white mugs, a blue-and-white jug of milk and some *langues de chat*. She put it down on the coffee table, still avoiding looking at the gleaming silver bin. Jassie's music had stopped upstairs. Perhaps her biscuit detector had kicked in. But then it started again, Taylor Swift this time. They could hear Jassie singing, though not every word carried: young… saw you… close my eyes… flashback starts… standing there… summer air… the ball gowns… little did I know… throwing pebbles… baby just say yes…

'So exactly like being fifteen,' said Emmie. 'Except Jassie isn't fifteen yet. We love Taylor Swift – all those perfect lines about sneakers and bleachers. Tea?'

'Thank you.' They both watched as it streamed from the pot. Emmie was pleased that for once her teapot didn't drip.

'This is for you,' said Arun.

Emmie didn't know what to say.

'It's a bin. A Brabantia touch-free bin with battery

operated lid.' He stood and picked it up and moved it a few inches towards her.

'I don't know what to say, it's lovely, and the bow is lovely.' She carefully undid the extravagant bow and looped the ribbon into a silky coil.

'Jassie told me that your favourite colour is blue. I have put the battery in already, but it isn't switched on yet. It would have tried to escape from the ribbon. There's a switch at the back, here.'

Their hands touched as they both reached for the switch. They laughed. The bin opened with an electronic beep. 'I hope you can get used to that.'

'I'm sure I can.' The bin shut automatically after a few seconds.

'Wow!' said Emmie. 'It's wonderful.'

'I hope you aren't offended. A bin is a rather unusual present. I noticed your chopsticks, and then I happened to see this. I have the receipt if you don't want it.'

'I love it. Thank you. It's so kind of you.' She wondered if she should kiss him on the cheek but reached out and touched his hand again. 'Thank you.' The bin smiled too, making its little noise.

Taylor Swift had finished and Jassie appeared.

'Mum, can I have some ice cream? Oh! Hi, Mr. C. New bin! Cool! I've always wanted one of these. The Kowalskis have got one.'

'Mrs. Kowalski is Mrs. Perfect,' said Emmie. 'Now we can match them bin for bin.'

Jassie danced her hand over the top.

'Cool!' she said. She did it again and then sat down on the arm of Emmie's chair and helped herself to a biscuit. Arun drank his tea.

'Do you want some ice cream, Mr. C.?' asked Jassie.

'I had better go, I was just passing…'

Emmie picked up the blue ribbon but let it uncoil on the floor in front of her and stream from her feet towards Arun's.

'Please stay,' said Emmie.

'Well…'

'All Mum ever does is watch *Gardeners' World* on Fridays, unless she's taking me somewhere or going out with the library ladies or going to see my grandpa. We have cookie dough. You should stay,' said Jassie.

'Thanks, Jassie. I do go out sometimes. But it is true we have cookie dough. We also have mango sorbet. And mint choc chip,' said Emmie.

'How can I resist? I'll stay if you want me to.'

'I do,' said Emmie.

**Press the button to see Taylor Swift singing 'Love Story'.**

## Green Canvas Espadrilles (Size 38)

As they rolled along the sandy drive towards the Camping Les Pins Reception, Emmie worried, yet again, that coming this year might have been a mistake.

They had sweltered in the lines for the ferry. On the boat, Jassie had announced that she didn't really like French bread because it was so chewy. Then, as they had pulled up at a *péage* Emmie had managed to miss the bucket with her tossed euros so that they'd held up the whole queue while she got out of the car and scrabbled around on the hot concrete looking for the lost coins. She still had a headache from the thrumming of the ferry and the sun bouncing off the roads. Her new sunglasses (M&S, £5 with a 'free' case) kept slipping down her too-small nose. She had spent the whole journey shoving them back up or else holding her head at a stupid angle to try to keep them on. She was hoping the campsite shop would still be open when they arrived as she'd forgotten to pack the paracetamol, but she knew what to expect – it would be like every other campsite shop; its shelves empty but for some overpriced tins of *haricot vert* and some inflatable toys. She felt like Anne Elliot being carried into Bath against her wishes. Already she was longing for the soft sweet sadness of autumn in the countryside. Her navigational skills had taken them through too many *centre villes*.

Her father, however, seemed serene. He had always liked driving. And he just looked more and more distinguished as he aged. He was wearing a soft pale blue shirt that they'd given him for Christmas (Jassie had chosen it, saying that it was the sort of shirt that David Attenborough wore) and a Panama hat, which had also been a present from them.

Emmie had the folder she'd made Jay and the framed photo in her bag. She'd planned to tell him about it on the journey, but then it seemed better to save it until they arrived. He might be cross or distracted and go the wrong way around a roundabout. After following many more *Autres Directions* signs than seemed reasonable, they found the campsite. Her dad had chosen it because it had promised the shelter of pine trees and much larger than usual emplacements. He parked in front of the campsite shop. Jassie spotted the ice-cream sign immediately.

'Can I have one?'

'Probably,' said Emmie. 'If there's anybody there. There often isn't anybody there at campsite shops.'

But there was somebody there. A woman came out to greet them. Emmie estimated her age as mid-sixties. She had shiny silver hair cut in a short bob. She was wearing a neat white blouse, sleeveless, and with a Peter Pan collar, like something from the '50s, and an A-line cotton skirt which had an all-over pattern of leaves in a washed-out seagrass green. Emmie immediately coveted that skirt. The woman's skin was tanned to a deep walnut. Oh, to age like that, thought Emmie, to have skinny ankles and limbs like sticks of polished wood, to wear such neat clothes, clothes that are so perfect for the weather and the location.

The woman came forward smiling and reached out to shake first Emmie's, then Jay's, and then Jassie's hands. A gold bangle and two turquoise ones flashed on her wrist.

'*Bonjour*. My name is Anna. I am the patron of the campsite and very pleased to welcome you. You have come a long way?'

'It seems like a very long way,' said Emmie.

'Jay Ash,' said Jay. 'And this is my daughter, Emmeline, and my granddaughter, Jasmine.'

'How nice,' said Anna, 'three generations of a family on holiday together.'

Emmie thought that it must seem slightly sad or odd as well as nice – there were obviously people missing from their party. 'I will show you to your home for your holiday, but first, some ice creams, I think.'

Jassie grinned.

'Oh, thank you!' said Emmie. Jay reached for his wallet, but Anna gave a neat little smile and shook her head.

The campsite shop was unlike any Emmie had ever seen. The shelves were stocked with fresh fruit and salad vegetables, first-aid things and toiletries, buckets and spades, biscuits and snacks, bags of brioche, boxes of beach shoes and espadrilles.

'Choose quickly, Jassie,' said Emmie. 'And nothing too big…'

'Mum! They have Calippo Shots! What is this one?'

They had strawberry and lemonade and cola and lemon flavours (both kinds previously unknown to Jassie) as well as the lemon and lime flavour, her previous favourite, that had all but disappeared from English shops. Jassie chose strawberry and lemonade and was soon tipping the little balls of coloured ice onto her tongue. Emmie saw that the shop had paracetamol, but her headache had miraculously gone.

'This is the best place in the world!' said Jassie.

'Maybe,' said Jay, smiling at everybody.

Anna took a set of keys from a board of numbered hooks behind her desk. Emmie was pleased to see that they were cabin number 21 – it seemed auspicious.

'This way, please.'

They followed her along a sandy path which wound upwards between the shrubs and pine trees. Emmie could see that Anna's dark green espadrilles were the perfect shoes for the terrain. They were the sort with wedges and ribbons that were tied neatly around her girlishly slim ankles.

Their cabin (Emmie didn't want to call it a mobile home) looked like a shipping container on legs.

'Yay, a parasol!' said Jassie. Emmie was pleased that her dad had paid extra for the optional decking.

'I will show you everything and then you can fetch your car,' said Anna.

It was all very neat and extremely clean. It was going to be like living in a Playmobil house or perhaps in a little house on the prairie. Her dad seemed more animated than usual. Emmie noticed herself thinking that she was glad they had come.


The next morning, with her dad sitting out on the decking doing a crossword and Jassie still asleep, Emmie unpacked the folder.

'Dad, I've got something for you. I found some things that Lucinda and Margaret had – photos – and I've been doing a bit of research about the tea garden. Do you want to look at it?'

'Hmm, what?' He looked at her across the top of his glasses.

'I found a little photo that your father sent of some dancers, and in some letters, it says, I think, it says one of them is your mother, my grandmother, but it's so small…'

'What?'

'You don't have to look at it now. And it's a bit hard to see, but I've brought Lucinda's magnifying glass, and enlargement.'

'Show me.'

Emmie passed him the photo and then the magnifying glass. The sun glinted off the silver.

'It is very small,' said Jay, the corners of his mouth turning down. He peered at it, first without and then with the glass. He looked at it for a very long time. Emmie sat very still and said nothing.

'I don't know,' he said, after a while. He put the photo on the table, weighing it down with the magnifying glass. He rubbed his eyes. 'This sun is so bright. It's making my eyes water.'

'I know, Dad,' said Emmie. She put her hand on his. 'Would you like some more coffee?'

'Coffee, um, yes.'

'The enlargement's in the folder. I wanted you to see the real one first. I made copies for me and Jassie and Molly too. I posted Molly's but she probably hasn't got it yet.'

'Molly won't remember,' he said without looking up. 'She was just a baby.'

From inside the cabin Emmie saw him pick the photo up again and study it through the glass. She took her time making the coffee.

Jassie emerged from her room, her face marked by the sheets, her hair tousled.

'I just gave Grandpa the photo,' Emmie whispered. 'I'm giving him some time by himself to look at it.'

'Does he think it's her?'

'He hasn't said yet. I just hope it makes him happy.'


Jay peered at the picture. It was so small that he couldn't make out much, even with the magnifying glass, but there she was at the centre of the dance. He could hardly remember her face – but there she was – like Molly and a bit like Emmie and Jassie – or they were like her – that much he knew. Could he remember his mother? Now, it seemed that he could – the curve of her arms around him, carrying him up to bed, her hand on his forehead when he'd been ill; they'd all been ill, now he remembered, after his father had died. And he felt again a terrible pain in his stomach, and her holding him tight for the last time before he'd been taken away to school. But here she still was, not much more than a girl, but there forever in the dance.

He took the enlarged copy out of the folder. It was grainy and grey, but you could make out a little more – the shadows of some trees behind the dancers, two men with drums standing to the side, and the shape of her face, so familiar once again, his mother. He had to set it aside, worried that his tears would make it wet. He must pull himself together before Emmie came back. She mustn't see him cry. He wiped his eyes with the back of his hand and picked up his crossword again, but he couldn't see the squares. He closed his eyes and raised his face to the sun.

After a while, Emmie came out with the coffee.

'Do you think it's her, Dad?'

'Yes,' he said, 'she's there.'

# Poor-quality Photograph of a Vagrant Pelican Flying Over a Beach in Western France Taken with a Mobile Phone Camera (2011)

Emmeline and Jasmine walked to the end of the jetty. The sea was very calm. They went slowly, peering through the wooden slats to see the green water below.

'When I was little, we used to go to Brighton Pier and there were signs up telling people not to wear stilettos. I always hoped we would see somebody who had disobeyed it and got stuck. I suppose the heels might have got wedged in the gaps and they might have fallen over. Your granny always wore lovely shoes, but never pointy heels to the beach.'

'They might have got stuck there forever,' said Jassie. 'They would have had to live on seaside food. Chips and candy floss.'

'And sticks of rock and doughnuts. You'd have to hope they had an umbrella. But English people usually take anoraks to the beach,' said Emmie.

They stood at the end of the jetty and gazed out across the ocean.

'There is nothing between us and America,' said Emmie.

'Apart from whales and dolphins and ships and submarines and fish,' said Jasmine.

They stood and gazed for a little while and then turned and started the long walk back to the shore.

'Liminal,' said Emmie. 'That's one of my favourite words.' Jasmine said nothing so she carried on. 'It means on the edge between two things, that lovely vague place that isn't really one thing or another, a ragged edge, sort of blurry. I love thinking about where the land meets the ocean, or where a river meets the sea and the water must go from fresh to salty.'

'Foxes and hedgehogs sometimes go to the beach at night. I remember seeing it in a film in school. They eat shellfish and things left behind from picnics,' said Jassie.

There was an elderly couple coming towards them from the other end, wearing neat little windcheaters and slacks. They might have been brother and sister, but Emmie guessed they were married and retired locals. They all smiled and nodded as they passed.

Everybody would smile at Jassie, thought Emmie, with her gorgeous tawny hair and her tanned legs in pink shorts and her T-shirt with a big daisy on it and her tanned little feet in their turquoise crocs.

'I wish Grandpa was married to someone,' said Jasmine, and she glanced back to where the couple now stood, holding hands.

'Mmm, I guess he just never met anyone nice enough after my mum died.' Most men married again, though, didn't they? Wasn't there some statistic that 90% of widowers married within two years of their wives' deaths, something like that? It was over thirty years now, she thought, doing the sum in her head, but having to think hard about how old she herself was.

'He could marry Anna from the campsite,' said Jassie.

'It isn't always that easy. Plus, she wears a wedding ring.'

'Her husband died two years ago,' said Jassie. 'I asked her when I got the bread.'

'Jassie!'

'She didn't mind. I told her my granny died a long time ago.' They jumped down onto the beach. Emmie saw Jassie's eyes drifting towards the bar that overlooked the beach. It had an ice-cream stand with two freezers outside.

'Let's get an ice cream,' Emmie said. 'Something really French like pistachio.' Was that French? It wasn't very English anyway.

'Calippo Shots are French,' said Jassie.

'Of course, they are made by Wall's, that ancient French company,' said Emmie, pronouncing it with a terrible French accent.

Emmie hoped that they wouldn't have to go into the bar. It seemed to be full of young people laughing *and* old French men watching sport. They stood in front of the ice-cream freezers – Emmie knew that Jasmine would take ages to decide, even if there were Calippo Shots. If I were in England, mint choc chip, thought Emmie. She was glad that this once rare and rather niche flavour had had such a renaissance. But in France she would have pistachio. Green was the most magical.

Jasmine spent what seemed like ages gazing into one freezer and then the other. 'Calippo Shot,' she said at last, 'strawberry and lemonade.'

As if my magic, the bar owner appeared.

They took their ices and walked back across the road to the beach.

'I think we should go back down the jetty, then we can be the closest people to America in all of Europe,' said Jassie.

'The closest ice-cream eaters, the ones on the very edge.'

'The lemonal ones,' said Jasmine.

'Yes! Lemonal.'

The neat French couple had disappeared, they would have the jetty to themselves again. The sun was very low now and would soon disappear into the sea.

'We might see the green ray,' said Emmie.

'Huh?'

'It's a magical, scientific thing, a flash of green light just after the sun goes down, but you have to be really lucky to see it.'

They walked towards America, this time not looking through the slats but watching the sun as it sank into the sea. They sat down at the edge of the jetty and dangled their legs over the water.

'Don't fall in,' Emmie cautioned.

'Fall in?' said Jasmine, using her new and unanswerable response to any safety instructions. 'I hope we see it. Keep looking, Mum.'

They sat and watched as the sun melted away. A pathway of gold stretched ahead of them.

The sun disappeared. Emmie could feel ice cream dripping down her hand, but she didn't dare look down.

Then the sun was gone. No green ray.

'Well, we couldn't really expect to see it the first time we watched,' said Emmie, licking ice cream from her wrist and wondering if she had wipes in her bag.

'Look, Mum, look! What is it?'

A strange bird was silhouetted against the pink clouds. It had a huge bill and a heavy keel.

'A pelican! A pelican in France?'

Jasmine grabbed her mother's phone, held it up. Click.

'Well done. I hope you got it.'

Jasmine kept clicking. She was much faster than Emmie would have been, effortlessly zooming in.

'Grandpa will not believe this!'

'*I* don't believe this! A pelican!'

They watched as the bird flew north, following the line of the coast. The sky was turning mauve.


Back at the cabin, Grandpa had fallen asleep with a *Maigret* novel on his chest. They tiptoed in but he woke up anyway, making the sort of noises that only men make when they wake up. Jasmine laughed – he was like a bear in a cartoon.

'We saw a pelican, Grandpa!'

They looked up pelicans and France. The Wi-Fi was slow, but they soon found out enough for a positive identification. *Pelecanus onocrotalus*.

'They aren't native to France,' said Emmie, 'but you can get them here, just odd ones. They're called vagrants. It was a vagrant pelican.'

'What's a vagrant?' asked Jasmine.

'It means a tramp, sort of a traveller...' said Emmie. She had been going to say 'homeless' but that sounded too sad.

They sat out on their optional decking. The folder with the pictures and the printouts from the tea garden website and about different tours of Kaziranga National Park was open on the table. She saw that her father had drawn rings around a few things and added asterisks here and there. That might be a yes; they could go next year, perhaps at Easter. She must start saving.

Emmie lit citronella candles, though there didn't seem to be any mosquitos around – they agreed, yet again, that it was because they were so close to the coast. Emmie let Jasmine stay up, partly because it was a lovely evening, but also because she wanted her company, it just made things jollier.

They lay back in the white plastic loungers and looked at the stars. Emmie had a glass of rosé with ice. She'd been drinking the same bottle for three days. Jay drank red, and Jassie Orangina, which tasted so much better from the glass bottles in France. They ate strange puffy things that looked like Wotsits but were made from peanuts.

'Dad, you remember when you used to roast peanuts in their shells? We had that huge pan with a yellow handle and a bent lid. You used to make curry in it too.'

'Mr. C. brought Indian sweets to the last week of orchestra,' said Jassie.

'Remember when you used to bring them home on Fridays, Dad? And that rum and raisin chocolate for Mum, and whatever I wanted each week?'

'I remember.'

After a while Emmie noticed her father was dropping off again.

'You should go to bed, Dad. All that swimming and sea air.' He took a few moments to get up off the lounger.

'These chairs...'

Emmie watched as he walked slowly, slowly across the decking towards the door. He reminded her of something.

'You too, Jassie. I'll be in in a minute.'

After they were gone, she realised what her dad had reminded her of, and earlier too, walking alone along the beach while she and Jassie had been lounging on their towels: the penguin in *Encounters at the End of the World*, heading determinedly alone in the wrong direction towards the centre of Antarctica. Werner Herzog explained that people mustn't try to divert or stop the penguin, and that there was nothing anybody could do anyway. Unless the penguin was put in a cage, he would set off again and all anybody could do was watch as he plodded onwards, away from his fellow creatures to certain death alone in the icy interior.

She found that she had tears on her cheeks. It must be the rosé. And now she had to worry about that pelican, a vagrant, all alone in the wrong country. What could a vagrant pelican do? Where would it live? Was it always on a hopeless quest for another of its kind?

Press the button to see the depressed penguin in
Werner Herzog's *Encounters at the End of the World.*

A few days later, they were halfway through the holiday. Jasmine and Emmie were heading slowly back up the beach after another evening walk, and along the path to the campsite. Behind them, unseen, as the sun sank into the sea, the green ray shot up into the sky, and a pair of vagrant pelicans flew south together.

Emmie thought about when Jasmine had been little and

how important it had been to ensure that everything was ready for the school year; that Jassie had shiny new shoes and perfect socks, long white ones or short ones with a gingham trim to go with the green of the uniform. Later, Emmie had realised that the superior families were the ones whose children came back in sandals that were still dusty from walks back from the beach, whose brown legs spoke of long holidays in *gîtes*, the ones whose parents yawned and said that they'd just got back from Sardinia or Brittany or wherever the night before. Then she had wanted to be those families. Before the holiday, Jasmine had tried on the Rocket Dog brogues that she'd been wearing for most of the last year. They still seemed to fit – her narrow little feet seemed to have stopped growing at a 5.

Why was Emmie thinking about school shoes? They were on holiday! She realised that she was looking forward to going home because she wanted to see Arun again. And that she needed to have more adventures.

Back at the cabin they expected to find Jay in a chair on the decking, most likely asleep with his book on his chest. The book was on the table beside two used mugs, but he was nowhere to be found.

'He must have gone for a walk.' By himself, Emmie added silently, like a crazy, sad penguin.

'Perhaps we should go and look for him,' said Jassie. 'Maybe he got lost or something.'

He wasn't by the pool, which was closed now, but glittering invitingly. They walked along the sandy path towards the shop and games room. They spotted him from a distance. He was sitting outside Anna's little cottage at the top of the site. They were drinking wine and laughing. Emmie and Jassie looked at each other with big eyes and open mouths of astonishment and crept back to their own cabin.


The next day, Anna cooked them all dinner. The day after that, Jay started what became a daily routine of helping her fix things and change gas canisters for other holidaymakers, followed by lunch and sometimes dinner, sometimes just him and sometimes with Emmie and Jasmine too. On the last afternoon he and Anna sat outside together as usual, watching the lines of people moving up and down the site in their bright clothes.

'Please stay,' Anna said.

'I have to drive back with Emmeline and Jasmine, but I will come back. I can stay through September and help you get everything ready for winter.'

In the distance, a church bell rang. Bees hummed in Anna's marigolds, geraniums and lavender and her pots of marjoram, thyme and oregano.

'I think I might have found my view,' he told her.

She smiled.

He didn't try to explain.

## Postcard of a French Campsite (c. 2011)

'Mum! Postcard from Grandpa!' Jasmine read it and smiled and dropped it onto the kitchen table. It was a view of Camping Les Pins. It showed what was now one of Jay's favourite views – the clearing and the shop where they had first met Anna with a backdrop of trees and greenery and the cabins and neat lines of bushes and paths.

Emmie turned it over and read:

*We walk and swim every day. I am helping Anna to prepare the site for winter. Met her children and grandchildren – all v. nice. The last campers leave on Saturday. Much to do, but everything is lovely here on the hillside.*

*Love,*

*Grandpa x*

'Can I have it?' Jasmine asked. 'We haven't got a picture of it all like this.'

'Of course.' Emmie knew it would go into Jasmine's cabinet with the shells and the fragments of things, and the lost bookmarks. She smiled and passed it to her daughter.

## Family Ticket to Leith Hill Tower, Surrey (Spring 2012)

From the Rhododendron Wood car park, they made the short, steep climb up towards the tower. The rhododendrons and azaleas were out in a mass of purples, pinks and oranges, with occasional white ones dotted around, like brides or women in mourning dressed in the colour of purity and rebirth. The flowers seemed at home and part of the English forest though their ancestors had come from the Himalayas.

Jay carried his rucksack. It was the little one he took on walks, but it seemed much heavier than usual today with the flask of tea and lunch made by Anna for them all.

Jasmine had been moody at first at the thought of a walk but slipped into a younger incarnation of herself as the magic of the woods took effect.

'Grandpa, you really should get a dog. Dogs can have passports now. You could teach it English and Anna could teach it French. The Kowalskis are getting a chocolate Labradoodle puppy.'

The steps of the tower were steeper than he remembered and he was embarrassingly out of breath at the top, though Anna didn't seem to notice. After a while he pointed things out to her – the haze of London, the Shard, new to the skyline, and the arches of Wembley, all discernible in different directions, and the bluish line of the sea visible to the south.

'And so I can see to home,' said Anna.

'Everybody can see home from here,' said Emmie, smiling.

'They built the tower high enough so at the top it counts as a mountain,' Jay said, just as he had on every trip before with Pammy and Emmie. He had never been quite sure if it was true.

Now they were home. Anna was in the kitchen, halfway through cooking supper, and he could hear her chatting on the phone to her own daughter and grandchildren, talking so fast that he couldn't make out what any of it meant.

His back was uncomfortable. It felt as though he was still wearing the rucksack, but he was sitting on the sofa, he couldn't be. Invisible straps were digging into his shoulders, making his arms go numb, and then the weight was on his chest, too heavy to move. He tried to call for help but had no words.

He closed his eyes and saw the blue line of the sea coming closer and closer. Pammy was there beside him, Pammy with her honey-coloured hair falling across his cheek, her cool hand on his forehead, whispering his name, 'Jay, Jay, Jay,' with the pounding of their hearts, Emmie was there saying 'Daddy, everything is alright. Don't worry, Daddy, we're here.'

The moon was coming through the window, brighter and brighter, the sea was coming closer, and soft arms were around him again.

## Pottery Urn of Simple Design. Wreath of
## Assamese Flowers (2014)

Molly, her son, Edward, Emmie, Arun and Jasmine waited for
the boat with the priest and the guide arranged by the hotel.
Emmie had been disconcerted to see that her cousin Edward
wasn't the teenager in a Hawkwind T-shirt she remembered
from photos, but a middle-aged New Zealander with curly
dark grey hair. He was a mountaineer and ranger in one of
his country's national parks. He was impressively tall for
a member of her family. And Molly seemed so intrepid –
Emmie imagined the journeys she had made crisscrossing a
hand-drawn map of the world with a trail of little footprints.

'Come and visit us,' Edward said. 'You and Arun and
Jasmine.'

'I should take a leaf out of your mum's book,' she told
Edward. 'It's the first time I've been outside Europe.'

'Take two leafs and a bud, two leafs and a bud,' Jasmine
said, echoing the words of the guide at the tea garden.

'I just wish my dad could have come,' Emmie said. 'We
were planning to come together, but then…'

She had what was left of his ashes ready in the urn.
They had already scattered most of them at Prussia Cove in
Cornwall where they had taken her mum's ashes years before.
She had wondered if she should put them in two places, but it
had seemed right, and in the waters of the ocean they would
be united. On another trip, they would visit Kohima.

They had been given little cards decorated with flowers and had written their messages and wishes on them the night before.

We cannot know what it said on the cards because they were made to dissolve harmlessly in the water, but we can speculate:

*Mummy, I love you. I know you loved me. I'm so sorry I didn't get to say goodbye. With all my love forever, your Molly xxx*

*Dear Grandmother and Great-grandmother Josmi, we wish that we had met you and had lots of time together. We are returning your son to you. You would be so proud of him. With all our love, your granddaughter, Emmeline, and great-granddaughter, Jasmine xxxxx*

*Daddy, I have arrived where you started. I love you forever. Mummy loved you. Anna loved you too. Emmie xxx*

*Goodbye, my kind big brother, Jay. Rest in Peace. Molly x*

*Goodbye, Grandpa. I love you and thank you, from Jassie xxx P.S. Mum is getting married.*

There were monkeys and parrots in the trees. The boat was ready. They were taken upstream and out into the middle of the river. The waters flowed so fast, anybody and anything would soon be swept away. The prayers swirled away on the wind and combined with those from boats where other people were doing the same thing for their own loved ones.

How strange it was, Emmie thought, that this had been happening here for hundreds of years and that tomorrow, when they were gone, it would all carry on, people and time being endlessly swept away by the waters. So many people, so many lives, so many stories.

Molly and Emmie lowered the urn into the water. Jasmine let go of the flowers.

'Goodbye, Jay.'

'Goodbye, Daddy.'

'Goodbye, Grandpa. We love you.'

The prayers continued. There was music coming from the other side, drums and pipes and singing.

*And so we beat on*, thought Emmie, *boats against the current, borne back ceaselessly into the past.* But they were going with the current now, carried by the river back to where they had set out from and on towards the sea.

The End

# Please Exit Through
the Gift Shop

# ACKNOWLEDGEMENTS

I am very grateful to Lauren Parsons, Vicky Blunden, Sarah Whittaker, Emma Grundy Haigh, Eleanor Smith, Lucy Chamberlain, Ditte Loekkegaard and their colleagues at Legend Press for their invaluable help and advice. I would also like to thank Stephen, my beloved family and friends, and my dear colleagues at the University of Southampton for their help and encouragement. Special thanks go to people who shared stories with me. *The Ash Museum* is a work of fiction, but those stories were my inspiration.

I would like to thank the trustees of the real Ash Museum in Ash, Surrey for kindly allowing me to use their museum's name as the title of my novel. My fictional Ash Museum is in no way related to or inspired by the real Ash Museum which can be found at Ash Cemetery Chapel, Ash Cemetery, Ash Church Road, Ash, Surrey, GU12 6LX, UK. Please do visit their website which is www.ashmuseum.org.uk.

I am also grateful to Arts Council England for supporting the writing of this novel with a Grants for the Arts award.

LOTTERY FUNDED

Supported using public funding by

**ARTS COUNCIL
ENGLAND**